For Marianne
Hoping you "enjoy" this.

NO
SAFEGUARDS

H. Nigel Thomas

23/01/2016

GUERNICA
EDITIONS
TORONTO • BUFFALO • LANCASTER (U.K.)
2015

Michael Mirolla, editor
David Moratto, cover and interior book design
Guernica Editions Inc.
1569 Heritage Way, Oakville, (ON), Canada L6M 2Z7
2250 Military Road, Tonawanda, N.Y. 14150-6000 U.S.A.
www.GuernicaEditions.com

Distributors:
University of Toronto Press Distribution,
5201 Dufferin Street, Toronto (ON), Canada M3H 5T8
Gazelle Book Services, White Cross Mills, High Town, Lancaster LA1 4XS U.K.

First edition.
Printed in Canada.

Legal Deposit—Third Quarter
Library of Congress Catalog Card Number: 2015936503
Library and Archives Canada Cataloguing in Publication
Thomas, H. Nigel, 1947-, author
No safeguards / H. Nigel Thomas. -- 1st edition.

(Essential prose series ; 113)
Issued in print and electronic formats.
ISBN 978-1-55071-984-0 (pbk.).--ISBN 978-1-55071-985-7 (epub).--
ISBN 978-1-55071-986-4 (mobi)

I. Title. II. Series: Essential prose series ; 113

PS8589.H4578N67 2015   C813'.54   C2015-902311-4   C2015-902312-2

For all the world's oppressed children.

... And thus
Was founded a sure safeguard and defence
Against the weight of meanness, selfish care,
Coarse manners, vulgar passions that beat
On all sides from the ordinary world
In which we traffic.

——Wordsworth: *The Prelude, Book Eighth*

BOOK ONE
ROCKY FOUNDATIONS

PAUL, WHERE ARE you? You said you'd be home by October. It's May. I'm standing at the head of Anna's bed, listening to her rattling breath. A nurse with a flashlight beamed on Anna's IV is on the other side of the bed. She leaves. I glance at my watch. 9:17. I sit in the chair beside the bed and begin tonight's watch.

Departures. In the note Anna left me 19 years ago, she'd asked me not to cry and had promised to come and get Paul and me soon. If things didn't work out, she would return to St. Vincent to be with us. And, after Grama took us to live with her, Anna told me I must show that I loved her by being a good boy and by taking care of Paul. And I did; felt I owed it to her. A week after that phone conversation, she told me in a dream that I'd caused the breakup of her marriage. *Soon:* nine years later. Paul was nearly 12 and I almost 18.

Paul, where are you? Your last letter was in August. How did you end up hating Ma? *"One of these days you all will drive me so mad, I'll show up here with a Uzi and blow your asses to smithereens."* I'm still surprised that you would think let alone say that.

I glance at Ma's form in the dim light, and for a moment hold my breath as she raucously expels hers. She'd fled St. Vincent; fled from Caleb's fists; ended her marriage.

My thoughts go back to the night before my seventh birthday: the night the breakup began.

I'm tossing in bed. It's October 6. Tomorrow I'll be seven. Last year I got nothing for my birthday except the clothes that Grama sent me. I cried and tried to forget about it. I'll get nothing this year. I won't remind Ma.

Talk about such things vexes Daddy. He asks me questions I can't answer, usually before beating me. Last year I asked Ma if she'd forgotten my birthday. She said no. Her belly was big with Paul. (Now I know that Ma has always had trouble remembering birthdays.)

I didn't know that Daddy was nearby until I heard him say in his beating voice: "Jay, you hungry?"

"No, Daddy."

"Come here."

I went into the room where he was and stood facing him.

"You got a full belly. That's the best gift in the world, birthday or no birthday. Not another word about your birthday. Too much simmidimmy spoil pickney. Millions o' children the world over go to bed hungry and wake up hungry. You know that?"

I do. In the booklets the Americans send Daddy, there are pictures of naked black children with swollen bellies. "Worms and wind," Daddy says. "Sometimes they're so hungry they eat dirt." Why do their parents let them go hungry and naked, and let them eat dirt? I'm afraid to ask Daddy, so I ask Ma, and she says their parents are poor because they serve the wrong God, and God is angry with them, but God loves everyone and can do anything he wants. I remember that Christ multiplied five loaves and two fishes to feed thousands; Daddy says often that with God all things are possible. It's wrong for children to eat dirt but I'm afraid to tell her so.

Grama—everyone calls her Ma Kirton—sucked her teeth at Daddy one time and told him: "This religion o' yours—it's all foolishness and lies—lies, nothing but lies—to make poor people think injustice comes from God. Heaven is in my heart." She tapped her chest. "Hell too. When I die I done." She sucked her teeth again, grinned, and stared at Daddy.

"Get to hell out!" Daddy said, his voice trembling. "BEELZEBUB, be gone!" He balled his fists and began moving toward Grama.

Grama grabbed her handbag and scuttled. I didn't even get to kiss her.

"Zelzebub," I asked Ma as soon as Daddy left. "Ma, who is Zelzebub?"

"Who?" she said, frowning. I sidled up to her. She folded both arms around me, pressed my back against her thighs, and rocked me gently. She can't do this when Daddy is around.

"The name that Daddy called Grama."

"That's an evil angel that God threw out of heaven. He came with plenty others. And they go into people's souls and make them evil."

"One is in Grama!"

"Stop looking so frightened. No. Your father said so because he hates it when anyone badtalks his religion. Grama is a good person, Jay."

"But one time Daddy said she hates him."

"She doesn't hate anybody, Jay."

Tonight, I toss in bed and hear the Atlantic pounding away at the shore. In the distance dogs are barking. In the lulls, I hear the wind whistling through the fronds of the coconut palms that line the shore. Through the drawn curtains I see the land outside, silvery in the moonlight. The glare from the street lamp outside my window falls onto my bed.

Percy and Samuel—their fathers are elders in Daddy's church. Our parents and teachers tell us that we are hell-bound. We'll burn forever; will never turn to ash; we'll be like the stones campers and poor people use to build their cook fires. No, not like the stones: stones can't feel pain; all our feelings will remain.

The Holy Spirit tells Daddy to beat me. Every few days he flogs me "to curb the evil" in me—evil that everyone is born with but must control, because long ago Adam and Eve disobeyed God and ate an apple; evil that only the blood of God's son can remove. They killed him long ago to get his blood. Once every month they take a tiny sip of it. They don't give me any. Every night I beg God to make me good. But I can't resist stealing candy, and I want bad things to happen to Daddy and my teachers when they scream at me or beat me. I know I'll get real bad if Daddy stops beating me, bad like Joseph who steals goats and chickens and is in prison now. He used to come with his mother to Daddy's church. And Daddy said in one of his sermons that Joseph put down praying and took up thieving, and that evil grows bigger than breadfruit trees in the hearts of those who don't obey God. I don't want a breadfruit tree to grow in my heart. Why don't they give me any of Christ's blood? God, why is it so hard to be good? Why don't you make me good? You can do anything. And you know everything.

Daddy says: "We must not question God; God's ways are past finding out." In church we sing: "God moves in a mysterious way, his wonders to perform; he plants his footsteps in the sea and rides upon the storm"; and I imagine God as this huge giant, bigger than the one in "Jack and the Beanstalk" (which I sinned and read in school; Daddy says such stories are lies, and prevents Ma from reading them to me: "The bible is the only book to be read in my house;" and Grama told Ma: "Ignore the two-legged jackass and read to your child") — God with legs longer than the trunks of the tallest coconut trees, legs planted in the deepest part of the Atlantic, and long arms reaching all the way up into heaven. What would it be like to see God hurtling across Georgetown in the strong winds that come off the Atlantic? I'm glad God is invisible. My heart is drumming. I catch myself suddenly. I questioned God. I blasphemed. Something bad will happen to me.

God made everything and everyone and makes everything happen. Daddy says so. A month ago Eva-Marie drowned. She was standing alone on the seashore and, all of a sudden, a huge wave came and knocked her down and dragged her out to sea. We walked behind her coffin; and Daddy said, as they put Eva-Marie's coffin into the hole: "The Lord giveth and the Lord taketh. Blessed be the name of the Lord." And afterward, when everybody was leaving the graveside, Eva-Marie's mother threw herself on the ground, and pounded it with her head, and dirtied her clean white frock, and bawled that she wanted to be buried too. Daddy lifted her to her feet, and said: "Sister Gertrude, God do everything for the better. In his wisdom he decide heaven is the best place for Eva-Marie."

Eva-Marie won't go to heaven. It's 32 days since she died; and Frederick, whose parents are Spiritual Baptists, says Eva-Marie's spirit must wander on earth for 40 days before it goes to heaven or hell. Eva-Marie was two years older than me. A week before she died, she pulled me into a clump of fat pork bushes on the beach, pulled down my pants, hoisted her dress, lay down on her back, and told me to lie on her and wind. She said it was what adults did, and it was how women got big bellies that babies come out from. In Daddy's church, women who get big bellies and don't have husbands leave. It's why Sister Celestine left. She used to sit on the front bench. Her voice was loud when we sang, and when the holy ghost filled her she cried out and jumped up and down. Then she stopped coming to church. And one Saturday I was out front watching Ma pulling up the weeds and Sister Celestine came by with a big belly. When she saw Ma she began to sing: "Christ is getting us ready for that great day. Who will be able to stand?" When she was gone I asked Ma, why she didn't tell us hello, and Ma said Daddy didn't want her to.

Eva-Marie, why did I let her tempt me? I wasn't her husband. After I'd pulled up my pants, I became afraid and wondered what we would say when Eva-Marie's belly got big. When she died a week later, I knew God had sent that wave to punish her for what we'd done. My punishment is waiting; I will die too. I don't want to burn in hell forever. One time and turn to ashes, that would be fair. Now I keep far from the beach. I want to be a good boy. Would I become better if Daddy flogged me more to remove the evil in me? Should I tell him what Eva-Marie and I did?

Today just before suppertime I was thinking how God had ordered a man called Abraham to kill his son. What would happen if God told Daddy to sacrifice me? Would God send a ram at the right moment? I don't think so: I'm bad. Daddy would have to cut off my head and burn my body on a pile of wood to please God. And after that, I'll live on in hell. God, please, if Daddy gets such a call from you, please send an angel to stop him from killing me. For my friends Samuel and Percy too. Please. I wanted to ask Ma this evening if she thought God would send an angel to stop Daddy. She was in the kitchen and had on her green plastic apron over her loose black dress that's covered with pink flowers. She was hunched over the stove stirring a pot. The clock on the wall said 4:35. Paul—he's 11 months old—was in his pram just inside the kitchen door. He banged a plastic duck on the side of the pram and kept throwing it onto the floor so I would have to pick it up and give it to him. I pulled at Ma's apron. "Stop pulling at my apron. Act your age, Jacob!" She gave me a stern stare. She only calls me Jacob when she's mad with me, and she adds Jackson when she's lost her temper. "Ma …" It was all I said, because I began to stutter. I could feel my beige face—people say I got it from Ma and Grama—turning maroon; my heart went: harrumph, harrumph, harrumph. I became afraid that something bad would happen to me: lightning striking me dead, for one thing. At the entrance to Georgetown, there's a mango tree that's burned black. Lightning struck it. The morning after it happened, Daddy said: "See? It's a tiny sign of God's wrath. Worse will happen to you, Jay, if you end up in hell." But the tree didn't go to hell, because only people have souls.

Tonight I want to stop doing things that anger God. He could strike me dead with lightning, and I would go to hell because I have a soul. Why do I have to have a soul? Without a soul I wouldn't go to hell. I'll just die and rot. One time God set a whole town on fire and burned the people alive because of the bominations they were doing. Bad things. Otherwise God wouldn't burn them alive. A whole town on fire. I saw a cane field on fire once; Miss Bramble's house near ours had burned to the ground. Ma and I stood a long way off watching it. I held on to Ma tightly with my sweaty hands. The fire danced with the wind and crackled angrily, and we felt the heat from the towering blaze and had to move further back as long tongues of orange flames stretched towards us when the wind gusted, and sparks big as pennies fell in showers close to us. A baby died in the fire. Did God cause that? "Save her! Oh, God, save my child!" Miss Bramble bawled, and her big daughter Jenny held on to her to prevent her from falling—long after the baby would have been dead.

I'm sweating. I wipe my hands on my pyjamas and wipe my forehead on the pillowcase. I must not think. God, please, don't let me think. You're not listening to me because I did bomination with Eva-Marie. You turn your back on people who do bominations. Daddy said so in one of his sermons.

In Sunday school Brother Simmons said God had made a bet with Satan to tempt a man called Job, and God made Job suffer "diverse illnesses for more years than you children can count." And I can count up to a thousand and more if I want to. Diverse. How many is diverse? "But Job thanked God for his suffering. Job was obedient and knew that God is always right, so Satan lost the bet, and Job became a rich man afterwards." Brother Simmons said so with a big smile on his shiny, round, black face.

Daddy is not rich. He is minister of the Church of the Elect. He is Pastor Caleb Jackson; that's what the letters that come to him from America say. But the Catholics and Methodists and Anglicans and Spiritual Baptists call him Pastor Hallelujah. It's because he says hallelujah many times when he's on the pulpit and even when he's not on the pulpit. Sometimes Percy, Samuel, and Frederick call me Pickney Hallelujah; and I say: "Praise the Lord," and we all laugh before falling silent and afraid. Then we do it all over again. And sometimes I preach to them, pointing my finger at them and jumping up and down like Daddy does, and they laugh, and they say: "Amen, hallelujah, praise the Lord," and "preach to us sinners, Pickney

Hallelujah, preach." And we laugh and laugh and laugh and afterwards I feel goose bumps on my arms.

"We're poor people," Ma told me two weeks ago when she couldn't pay for me to go on a school trip. Daddy spends every day except Sunday on the beach piling up stones and shaping them. Masons and building contractors buy the stones to build houses. One time, a man—a government inspector, Ma said—came to our house. He smelled like nutmeg. He wore a beige shirtjack and green terylene trousers, and he had on shiny black shoes that went crii-ipp crii-ip crii-ip every time his feet moved. A man a lot taller than Daddy, a man with a big pointed nose and red eyes as if he'd just finished bathing in the sea; his forehead was shining; a black-black man, blacker even than Daddy, with a belly like a barrel. He stared at Ma and me as if we were pictures in Grama's photo album. He told Daddy that taking stones from the beach was breaking the law. Daddy said: "How you expect me to feed my family?" The man did not answer. He unzipped his brown briefcase that was bulging out on both sides. He took out some papers, and he looked at the papers and didn't say anything to Daddy for a while. Then he said: "Pastor Jackson, you are a man of God." He got up from the sofa where he was sitting and clapped Daddy on the shoulder and grinned. He had fat lips. There were wide spaces between his teeth. Daddy winced. The man sat back down. He said nothing for a while. Then he hit the sofa with both hands and shouted at Daddy: "Dammit, Pastor! You know as well as me you must not break the law. What is for Caesar you must give to Caesar, and what is for God you must give to God. Right, Pastor?"

"'Render therefore unto Caesar the things that are Caesar's, and unto God the things that be God's': Luke chapter 20 verse 22," Daddy said.

Ma held my hand and led me into the kitchen. While she tended her pots, I returned to the kitchen door and observed Daddy and Mr. Caesar.

"Pastor, me is no preacherman like you, so me don't know the exact words. But, Pastor Jackson, the bible say, 'come let us reason together saith the Lord'." Mr. Caesar chuckled. "And I will reason with you." He winked at Daddy. "Man of God, you sure is, Pastor. But man got to eat. Man ain't God. You, Pastor, you have a family to feed." He chuckled again. "Live off the Holy Ghost and you will become a ghost." Mr. Caesar chuckled again. "And that lad there"—he pointed to me standing at the kitchen entrance *and winked at me—"and that lovely lady who was just here ... Well, I don't have to tell you, Pastor—what will become of them? What you say: we take a short walk, Pastor?"*

"Let me pray for God's guidance first." Daddy closed his eyes and bowed his head for about a minute, then he got up, didn't say hallelujah, put on his black felt hat—he wears it for something important, like going to visit a sick member of his church—and left with Mr. Caesar.

Daddy continues to heap up and shape the stones the Atlantic throws out. Building contractors and masons come and load them onto their trucks. When I was around four, just before I started attending school, I'd sit on a stone heap and watch Daddy's arms crack open a stone with a sledge hammer, and marvel at his strength. Depending on how the stone broke, he would use smaller hammers and chisels and chip off pieces, turning the stone around several times and chipping away at it until it's just right. He keeps different piles: one for the stones that break cleanly in halves, one for those that shatter into several pieces, and one for chips. Whenever he comes upon pink stones with black spots, he brings them home. Periodically, a man comes in a truck marked Exquisite Floors, Ltd *and buys the pink stones from him.*

Then I liked being on the beach with him on sunny days when the Atlantic is a glassy blue and almost asleep. On cloudy days, it's like tossing grey smoke and seems vexed. When it's rough and roaring and chewing up the edges of the shore and trying to drown the land, I smell the ocean spray and feel it on my face and arms and legs, and taste the salt when I lick my lips; and the salt turns my arms and legs whitish after the spray has dried. Daddy likes it when it's rough; that's when it throws out the stones he needs. After my fifth birthday I stopped going to the part of the beach where Daddy works.

No matter how hungry Ma and I are, we wait until Daddy gets home, because he's the head of the household. The Apostle Paul, who my brother is named after, said so. Caleb seated at the head of the table. He's slouched forward, his eyes red, his face grey with dried sea salt, his perspiration odour strong; Anna's at his right still wearing her apron; I on his left; Paul's in his pram a little way from Anna. Caleb thanks God for the food and for the blood of Jesus that washes sinners clean, and all three of us say hallelujah and amen—even Paul gurgles. Next Caleb removes the lid off whatever Anna prepared. She passes him the plates, and he spoons the food onto them. I want a second helping, but Caleb eats the food that's left after the first serving. I stare at Anna. Sometimes she looks away silently, and sometimes she says: "Your father works hard, Jay."

We live in the upstairs of the church. People from the place called America own it. Our part has three bedrooms. The people from America have white skins, yellow hair mostly, and blue eyes, and I listen carefully when they speak. They say wahda for water, call me "a maaty faan boy," and tell Anna: "Sister, yer food's maaty good." Sometimes I don't know what they mean and ask Anna when they aren't around. They stay in one of the bedrooms when they come to visit. One time when four of them came they stayed in my bedroom too, and I slept on a piece of foam on the floor at the foot of my parents' bed. I like it when they visit. They bring chocolate and peanuts and popcorn, and the women smile at me and kiss and hug me—and Caleb never gets angry and beats me while they're visiting—and they say I'm a cute, lovely boy with "a whole heap o' good manners just lak the Lawd wants ya to." I wish Daddy would say so to me sometimes. And they question me about Bible stories, and give me a hug or candy when I answer correctly. It's only when they come that there's a lot of delicious food in the house, as much as when Anna and I, and now Paul, visit Grama Kirton. Caleb doesn't go with us when we visit Grama.

2

THE SUNDAY AFTER Anna came back from the hospital after Paul's birth, Daddy made a special collection "to ease the difficult times the Lord's been putting his servant through." Members of the congregation give us fruits and vegetables and eggs. One time Samuel's mother, Sister Simmons, arrived at the manse with a live rooster, and said: "Pastor Jackson, I giving you this fowlcock 'cause I wants you to be mighty and powerful when you goes on the pulpit to chastise sinners." I watched Anna chop off the rooster's head, then immerse the whole body in boiling water and strip the feathers. Afterwards she took out the entrails. I felt sorry for the rooster and refused to eat the meat when she served it to me.

One time I asked Anna — it was after I'd heard the story of Job — why God had made us poor. I turned around and saw Caleb standing in the doorway listening, and I began to tremble. But he did not beat me or scream at me; instead he said that one day God might make us rich. "We poor mortals don't know what plans the Almighty have in store for us. I will trade what little the Lord give me and make all the profit I can, so he will see I am a good steward and reward me. I am seeking the kingdom of heaven and all its righteous, and after that all things will be added unto me." I didn't understand. It sounded like one of those stories Brother Simmons called parboiled.

Since Paul's birth I stare at Anna and wonder if she's sick. She lies down a lot. She has headaches and says her head spins like a top. I don't see it spinning but I'm afraid to say so. Sometimes when she smiles at me it looks like she's making faces. She can't wear jewels. The Queen in the picture at school wears lots of jewels. Caleb says it's a sin to wear jewels. Grama wears jewels too: earrings that sparkle and gold bangles. Daddy says:

"Love of gold shrivels the soul." Sometimes I hear Ma mumbling to herself for as long as half an hour. One day I saw her wiping her eyes and told her not to cry, but she said that it was because dust had got into her eyes. When Daddy is home, she walks as if she's tiptoeing and deep creases appear in her forehead, and I know I must stay quiet. He hates noise, and gives Ma angry looks when Paul wails.

Before, whenever I felt grumpy, and Ma didn't pay me any mind, I'd sing: "Anna, Anna, Have you any wool? No, Sir; no Sir: I have none." And I'd get a smile or a tickle. But since Paul's birth, she ignores me or says: "You're too old to be singing such foolishness. You hear me, Jacob? You'd better not let your father hear you." So I've stopped. I tried to make up another song: "Anna, Anna! Little miss, get over here and give me a kiss ..." But Caleb would beat me if he heard me singing it, and Anna might scream at me. Sometimes when Caleb is beating me, Anna cries, and Caleb tells her that, if I end up in hell, it would be her fault. And one time he hit her and said: "You want to cry? Take that." He hit her again. "Cry! But you better don't make the neighbours know, or it will be hell to pay."

Between age four and six, before Paul's birth, I begged Anna often to tell me the story about Jacob, one of the men in the Bible that I'm named after.

Jacob was the younger son and wasn't entitled to his father's blessing, but he tricked his father into giving it to him.

"God was on Jacob's side because Jacob got rich."

"He stole the blessing, Ma. Why wasn't he punished? His mother too; she should have been punished."

"Jay, God's ways are mysterious. It was all arranged by God."

"So I am named after this same Jacob. He lied and cheated."

"Don't say that. God will be angry with you."

After Paul was born, I asked her: "When Daddy gets old and I am to get the blessing, can Paul trick Daddy into giving it to him?"

"No. It's not done like that anymore. You will get your own blessing and Paul will get his."

"That's fair. I prefer that."

But as to favourites, she doesn't have time for me since Paul came along.

My seventh birthday. "I hate my father; I hate him! I don't care if I go to hell." I begin to cry. I feel the bandage on my right foot where I cut my heel a week before. Caleb had heard me singing: "Put it in. Shove it in. Shove it in. Ram it. Ram it! Ram it!"—a calypso that's playing on all the radios. While Caleb began to unbuckle his belt, I ran out the house, across the road, into a field of bananas, then into an open field, sharp stones cutting my soles, tall weeds stinging my bare legs and sometimes my face. And then a sharp pain in my left foot. Only then did I look back and saw that Caleb wasn't following me, but there was a streak of blood on the weeds I'd trampled. I looked at my left foot and saw the gushing blood. I hopped to the base of a tree-high rock, sat there, leaned my back against the rock, and pushed together the red lips of the gash in my left heel and held them closed. I was certain I would die there and go to hell. The blood looked bright red in the yellow light of the sunset. I began to cry. What had I done wrong? All my classmates sang and danced to "Put It In! Shove It In." How was I to know it was a sin? Then I remembered: Eva-Marie, the bomination. My turn had come. God moves in mysterious ways.

The fireflies were dancing all around me when I heard Anna's frightened voice calling. "Jay, where are you?" Go away, I said silently. Go away, let me die. I want to die. I don't care if I go to hell. But she came to the base of the rock and shouted "Thank God," and sat down beside me, and pulled me to her bosom. Her chest heaved; she swallowed loud and wiped her eyes with her apron. I pointed to my cut heel. She tore a strip from her apron and bandaged my heel. By then it was dark. Holding on to her, I hopped on one leg back home. A short while later a car came to the house. She took me to the clinic, and the nurse sutured the cut and gave me an injection.

Caleb promised that I would get that beating "with compound interest" the next time I stepped out of line, and tonight I wonder when God would take my life for the bomination I committed.

Tonight I want Anna beside me, as she sat at my bedside, her belly big with Paul in it, every night until I'd fallen asleep, when I had the flu right after my birthday last year.

✳✳✳

"Jay! Jay!" I hear Anna's voice from far away. "Wake up! You're having a nightmare."

My pyjamas and the sheets are wet with pee and sweat. Anna changes the sheets and gives me a clean pair of pyjamas that I got from Grama. She turns her ears to the door to make sure Caleb is not awake. He's snoring. She closes the bedroom door and sits on the bed, and hugs me tightly for about a minute. Then she asks me to tell her about the nightmare. I don't want to. She coaxes me.

The nightmare resembles a joke one of the missionaries from The States had told Caleb. I dreamed that Percy, Samuel, and I are dead and are wandering the earth for 40 days before going to face St. Peter. We know St Peter will send us to hell. Just maybe, just maybe, I tell them, we might come to an understanding with St. Peter. "We should take gifts for St. Peter." Percy says the streets of heaven are paved with gold, so it means that in heaven they like gold. He steals his mother's wedding band to give to St. Peter. Samuel says that in heaven they like honey, so he steals a bottle of pure, amber honey for St. Peter. I remember that Peter was a fisherman, so I steal a big fried red snapper for St. Peter.

On the 40th day we find ourselves mounting up in the air and come to land on a slab of concrete against a huge gate of iron rails. "Ah yes," St Peter says as he comes to the gate. He pulls on his long silver beard. His eyes beam like two torchlights. "Three naughty thieving boys."

"St. Pe-pe-peeter," Percy stammers.

"What!"

"I brrroughht you ssssomet'ing"

"Let me see." His hand comes out from between the rails and takes the packet from Percy. "Gold! It has no value here. We walk on it. The streets are paved with it."

I hear a scream and see Percy falling down to hell.

"Lemme see what you brought," St. Peter orders Samuel.

Samuel hands him his packet. St. Peter takes out the bottle of honey and holds it up to the light. His torchlight eyes shine through it. "Good honey, this, but we have better in heaven. You fool. Here it's honey for breakfast, honey for lunch, and honey for dinner. If you're going to bribe me, give me something I will enjoy."

And with that Samuel drops down to hell.

"Your turn, Jay."

I hand my package wrapped in foil to St. Peter.

"Fish! Smells good." His eyes are like live coals now as he rips away the foil. He bites into the fish, then drops it onto the ground, and starts fanning his open mouth; his eyes tear. "Pepper! You fool! If you are going to bribe me with fish, keep the chili peppers off it!"

And on his last word I too am falling down to hell and screaming.

Anna is silent at first, then leans over and kisses me on the forehead; her arms tighten around me. She stays silent for about ten seconds. I feel her hands beginning to sweat. "Jay," she says, removing her arms and twisting her body around to face me, "Hell does not exist ... Your father must not know I told you this. This must be our secret, our own little secret."

That night. That fatal night. Next morning, I am sure that it was all a dream, part of the nightmare. As I'm leaving for school Anna says: "Remember our secret?"

I'm puzzled. "That hell does not exist?"

"Shh, not so loud." She puts a finger on her lips.

3

THE NURSE COMES to the bedside and takes a quick look at Anna. I listen to her rasping breath and for a while hold my own until she lets out hers. When the nurse leaves I stand at the head of the bed and stare at Anna's face half-hidden in the dim light. I sit down again. My fingers feel numb. I open and close them to warm them up. *Ma, you can't die. Don't do this to me.*

***

She was born in Havre de la Paix (shortened to Havre), a town of fewer than 1,200 on St. Vincent's Leeward coast. Havre is snuggled in a cove semi-hugged by two spurs of intermixed limestone and black volcanic rock jutting out into the sea like floating ribs from the mountain range that forms a spine the entire length of the island. A booklet by one of the town's residents states that Havre was built "on the floor of an extinct volcano, one of many extinct volcanoes on the leeward side of the island the force of whose eruptions had blown out their seaward rims." At Havre's northern end, the spur is less steep. At the shore, where the crater's rim had been blasted away (so that there the arms don't join), the spurs rise sheer from the sea, forming solid walls on both sides. They continue inland for a good 50 metres before rounding out in a steep slope. I surmised that, over time, soil had accumulated in the blown-out crater on whose floor the town is built. From the front porch of my grandmother's home near the seashore, I'd look inland, up at the mass of black rock intermixed with limestone that forms a 270-degree

girder, crowned at the top and contoured at the bottom with wild vege-
tation. In the rainy season, the summit is bonneted in mist, and the
rocks hold dozens of fountains that turn off when the dry season
comes. After Georgetown, on the windward side of the island, with its
numerous gentle intersecting valleys and miles of flat and rolling land,
I found Havre both suffocating and comforting. But in its calm sea
without whirlpools I became an excellent swimmer, ignoring my grandmother's fears; she'd grown up in Georgetown beside the Atlantic's
roaring, battering three-metre waves and many whirlpools with invisible hands waiting to pull you in.

To the north, over in the next valley from Havre, is all the flat land
that can be found on this part of the Leeward coast. All of it was at one
time Laird's Plantation. Beyond that there are the mountains, often
cloud-capped, and blue-grey when they're not, and a volcano, waiting
to blow out its own seaward rim. A month after Anna married Caleb
and moved to Georgetown—a Good Friday morning just before sun-
rise, it had tried, and forced the residents of Havre and all of northern
St. Vincent to move into evacuation camps. Beginning with rumbles
that sounded like thunder, followed by a loud explosion, it shook the
island and sent a succession of fireballs far up into the sky before they
fragmented and cascaded in showers of ashes and red-hot stones.

About two kilometres north of the volcano, the mountains come to
an abrupt halt at the seashore. One time when Grama, Paul, and I went
to the area by boat, to a picnic at the Falls of Baleine, I saw that there,
for almost a kilometre, black rock streaked with coral and limestone
rises perpendicular from the sea. The main road does not go beyond
Laird Plantation, now a tiny fraction of its original size. The Lairds
inherited it from other Whites to whom it had been given or sold when
the French and later the British took the island from the Kalinago. In
1795 most of those who'd survived European attacks and diseases (many
had mated with free Africans, whose means of coming to St. Vincent
is still in dispute) were banished to Honduras. The others were cor-
ralled into an area under the volcano on the windward side, where the
descendants of those not killed in earlier volcanic eruptions—over a
thousand died in the 1902 eruption—now live. When I lived in

Georgetown I sometimes saw them there, and busloads of them were always heading to and from Kingstown. When Grama, Paul, and I visited Grenada, we saw a monument at Sauteurs, at the cliff overlooking the sea where the Grenadian Kalinago had jumped to their death rather than surrender to the French. The town's name memorializes the event: *Sauteurs*—leapers. A Catholic complex—Church and school—is located on it. Grama told Paul and me to bow our heads and remain silent for a minute. A bug-eyed Paul pestered her with questions afterwards. Grama told us then that her father was Kalinago, one of the few times she ever mentioned him.

***

I catch myself biting the nail of my right thumb, a habit Grama had tried in vain to break. I check my cellphone. Nothing. No message from Paul. I stare at Anna's outline in the dim light, at her chest rising and falling and quarrelling with the air it's pulling in and pushing out.

***

I'd always sensed, even before I went to live with Grama, before I could put it into words even, that Anna was not quite the child Grama had wanted. She's certainly not the mother Paul thinks he deserves. The week our visas for Canada arrived, Grama confirmed my suspicions. "When you all reach this age, the hormones turn you all giddy, and you all think adults know nothing, like if adults weren't adolescents too; and you all want all sorts of independence that you all can't handle. That is what happened to your mother. Three years into high school she dropped out. In her second year, a group of evangelists from the States came to Havre 'to win souls for Christ'." She chuckled and slowly shook her head. "They said the Second Coming would be on August 23, 1970. They told people it was pointless to struggle to get material things when in just over a year the Rapture would happen. Your mother fell for it. She stopped swimming in the sea. 'If men look at my body and lust after it, God will hold me accountable.' She stopped wearing perfume, jewellery, and bright colours; she started hiding her hair under black scarves; she bamboozled my seamstress into sewing her three long-sleeved, ankle-length smocks, each one a different shade of grey. Then they baptized her.

"'What you intend to do with all your clothes?' I asked her.

"'Burn them. They're sinful. They imperil men's souls. And I've stopped wearing slacks. Deuteronomy forbids it.'

"She even extended her foolishness to me. One August Monday I was getting ready to go on a picnic and couldn't find the pair of Bermuda shorts I wanted to wear. I turned my dressing table inside out. In the end I wore something else. A week later I went to look for a pantsuit to wear to a social Mr. Morrison was having, and I couldn't find that either. And then it hit me. 'Anna', I called out to your mother sitting in the living room, 'you know what became of my tangerine pant suit?' She came into the bedroom with a big grin on her face. Jay, I could hear the blood beating in my temples.

"'I am only obeying God's commandment. Deuteronomy says ...'

"Jay, she didn't have time to finish. 'God's what? You damn fool!' I grabbed her by the shoulders and I shook her. 'Go, bring my clothes for me, forthwith.' I gave her such a shove she stumbled.

"'I put them in the garbage. I threw them out already. "The woman shalt not wear that which pertaineth unto a man; neither shall a man put on a woman's garment: for all that do so are abomination unto the Lord Thy God." God commands me to show you the errors in your ways.'

"Jay, I don't know how I kept from strangling Anna that day.

"The evangelists rented a small wooden house up there." Grama pointed to the northern spur, up to the hill where the church, bigger now and made of cement blocks, stands. "The converts met up there every evening to sing and pray. They called it tarrying. 'Child, see? You're trapped in a tarry ring.' I sometimes teased her. An adolescent phase. Adolescent angst. It will pass. I'd already read an article about it in *Psychology Today*. This child will come to her senses.

"The only point I fussed with her about was her frequent fasting. By the second year I was able to solve the transportation problem to school and have her come home every day. 'You're a growing child. You need your daily nourishment, plenty of it too. How can you concentrate and learn on an empty stomach?'

"'The Holy Spirit is more nourishing than anything you'll ever feed me.'

"'*The Holy Spirit*! May, a woman from Georgetown whose rotting body they found in a locked-up shack up there a few months ago, had stopped having sex with her husband *because the Holy Spirit had ordered her to.* Two years later she gave birth to a child, and people rechristened her Immaculate May. Anna, dear, stop abusing your body in the name of religion. You promise me?'

"Jay, your mother stared at the floor and said not one word. With my thumb I lifted her chin and attempted to stare into her eyes. She closed them.

"Your mother was an average student; in intelligence nowhere near you, and definitely not your brother. She failed all her third-year exams. She read the Bible when she should have been studying. Sometimes I'd overhear her trying to convert Mercy while they were doing chores. I used to listen to them and laugh.

"At the end of July 1970, your mother announced that she was not returning to school. I argued with her. 'The Second Coming might be near. The early Christians had thought so too, but, one thousand nine hundred and seventy years later, it hasn't happened. In the meantime a body, filled or unfilled with the Holy Spirit, has to eat; and everyone knows you eat better if you have a good education.' Jay, your mother refused to return to school."

A week later, Grama and I were on the back porch, the sun about an hour from setting in the Caribbean Sea; I standing, Grama sitting, Paul inside reading. I took up the conversation from where she had left off. "What happened on August 23, 1970?"

"Jay, sit."

I sat in the lounge chair beside her.

She was silent for a while, her face showing deep thought. Then she told me where I would find a bible on her bookshelves and to bring it for her. She sent me back for her glasses. She resumed the story.

"On the morning of August 23, 1970, your mother and the other converts, between 35 and 40 of them—the men in white trousers and shirts, some with shoes, some with flip-flops, and most plain bare-foot; the women in white dresses and white headscarves, some in shoes, some in flip-flops, and many barefoot—gathered in the shack up there. A huge gathering from here and all the surrounding villages came to stare at the singing and praying *saints*. Mercy and I among them. The *saints* would interrupt their praying and singing and stare out to sea every time the breeze gusted. At midnight—we were a huge crowd outside: everyone who couldn't come earlier because of work or what have you was there—we broke into loud laughter and began to heckle them. Some Rapture! 'This look more like *rupture*?' Sefus Butcher called out to them. Even so, I couldn't convince your mother to return to school.

"The Rapture didn't happen in 1970—or for that matter, since—but the Church of the Elect continued to grow. Every year the missionaries from the States would come and give out aspirins and gauze and second-hand clothes. People are cheap, you hear me. It's something priests and politicians know well. They made new converts and rented one- and two-room shacks all over the island, meeting-places for their converts. Now instead of giving a precise date, they said the Rapture was imminent.

"The next big dispute between your mother and me began one day three years later—around eleven o'clock one morning. Anna was lean-ing against the front porch railing, reading some tract or the other the church in The States sent her. I was sitting on a porch chair braiding my hair. Jay, I told your mother in dialect—she wasn't allowed to talk to me in it, just like I forbid you and Paul to—'Yo' mean to tell me, the one pickney I have is a jackass!' She was just past 17. I'm seeing her clearly like if it's happening now: in a grey-three-quarter-sleeve smock almost to her ankles, head tied in a dark brown rag. I told her: 'I can't go on feeding and clothing you. If you were still in school it would have been different. Your father left me well off: enough to educate you all the way through university. You have to find a job. Your holiness is bad for both of us.'

"'I don't have any qualifications.'

"'You should have thought about that when you left school to join that bradabangbang up there.' I'd already come close to wearing out poor Mercy's ears complaining about her. Jay, my patience had run out. Gone completely. I said to your mother: 'You bewitched or what? Their white skin and Yankee talk mesmerize you?'

"Your mother replied: 'You won't understand. Mama, you have to be born again. The natural man cannot understand the things of God.'

"'I guess that includes women too,' I told her. 'Your dear St. Paul—that misogynist and supporter of slavery—wouldn't have wanted women, natural or unnatural, to understand anything.'

"Anna said: 'I don't have to put up with your blasphemy. God will take care of you in his own way. I'm leaving this house of iniquity.'

"I thought she was joking and played along. 'How will you eat?'

"'God will take care of me,' your mother replied.

"'Child, stop your foolishness.'

"'Mama, I'm serious.'

"'What? You're going off to get knocked-up? That's what happens to know-it-all young women who leave home. I'm warning you: don't come back here with any man's bastard. Don't come back here crying to me with any inside you, in your arms, or pulling at your skirt.'

"Anna closed her eyes, stood stiffer and straighter than a coconut-trunk, and began quoting scripture." Grama put on her glasses then, flipped through the pages of the bible, until she found what she was looking for. "This is what your mother recited to me: 'Take no thought for your life, what ye shall eat, or what ye shall drink; nor yet for your body what ye shall put on.' Then your mother put down the bible, stretched out her arms as if she herself was the cross Christ was crucified on; next she clasped her hands under chin, threw back her head, gazed upwards and recited"—Grama picked up the bible and read: "Take therefore no thought for the morrow: for the morrow shall take thought for the things of itself. Sufficient unto the day is the evil thereof." Grama closed the bible and put it on the patio table. "Jay, I would have laughed if I didn't see the horror awaiting her. I was frightened.

"For a full thirty seconds your mother sneered at me, then folded her arms across her breasts and burst into song:

> *The Lord's my shepherd.*
> *I'll not want.*
> *He makes me down to lie*
> *In pastures green. he leadeth me*
> *The quiet waters by.*

"Still singing, your mother went into the house and began to pack. 'You bring pickney into this world; you don't bring their mind,' I shouted to her.

"She sang her reply:

> *My father is rich in houses and lands.*
> *He holdeth the wealth of the world in his hands.*
> *Of rubies and diamonds, of silver and gold,*
> *His coffers are full; he has riches untold.*

"'Can I borrow a suitcase?'

"I didn't answer. I still didn't believe she was serious. I put the comb next to the hairbrush and the jar of Vaseline on the patio table beside me, and if I hadn't been sitting I would have fainted. I remember that Mr. Morris came to the foot of the porch steps then. 'Look like you're having family problems, Sis,' he said.

"'You're a lucky man, Bertie. A lucky man, you hear me. You don't have any child to make you wet your pillow of a night.' Jay, the tears came then.

"'Go easy with Anna, Sis. We the older heads know the cliff. We mustn't let the young ones run carelessly and fall over it.' He went back inside his own gate and into his house.

"If your mother ever thought she was spirit, she found out soon enough that she had a body too. God fed the sparrows and clothed the lilies and dropped manna for the Israelites in the wilderness, but no such remedies awaited your mother. She moved in with Mopsy, a string-like, malnourished woman, with pop-out, iguana-like eyes—a deaconess, if you please, in the Church-of-the-Elect. She was one of a handful of field-hands who still squatted in the mud huts on Laird's plantation. Jay, imagine: your mother, who had a bathroom to herself in my house, was now bathing in the river with passers-by looking on. Fully clothed at least. Her church doctrine required it. And she began to shrink. Those workers didn't earn enough to afford proper meals.

"I gather that at the end of the first month, Mopsy said to her: 'If you going to stay here with me, you is going to have to come help me with my weeding.'

"Already inclined to be thin—even though big-boned—over that month, your mother lost 12 pounds. Mercy became alarmed when she ran into her three days after the discussion with Mopsy. Mopsy and Anna were returning from working on Laird's estate, their hoes slung over their shoulders. Mercy confronted Anna: 'Wind will blow you away. And what that hoe doing on your shoulder?' That same evening I sent Mercy in Pembroke's car to Mopsy's house, to pack Anna's things and bring her back to my house.

"A few months later Pembroke offered to sell me his store. I sold some of the shares your grandfather left me and ten of the twenty acres of land, and bought Pembroke's store and the building that housed it." (When I went to live in Havre, Pembroke was the overseer at The Laird Plantation and lived in the overseer's house. He was the oldest of around 20 children the proprietor, old man Laird, had fathered with the house servants and field-hands. Grama and Pembroke were friends. She, he, and Mr. Morris often chatted on the front porch late into the night. At 86, he came to Grama's funeral hale as ever and stood at the graveside without needing a cane.)

Grama continued: "Anna and I ran the store. For the next five years, your mother and I never had a quarrel, until she announced that she was going to marry your father, her senior by ten years. The missionaries were going to install him in the church and manse they'd built in Georgetown. It was where they'd had their greatest success. Georgetown folks needed those things they were bribing people with. The sugar factory had closed, and almost everyone out there was out of work.

"I told your mother she would regret it. That I wouldn't be surprised if religion had already twisted up the man she wanted to marry. And was I ever right. We were standing in the dining room. I held her arm and led her to the two-seater, and sat beside her. It was a Sunday, around 3 pm. She hadn't too long come in from church.

"I took your mother's hand in mine. 'Child, where did I go wrong raising you? It's clear in my head, clear as this bright, sunny Sunday afternoon, that I took a wrong turn somewhere.' Your mother did not answer me.

"'And hear me out on this: when Caleb Jackson finds the Christian cross too heavy—and he will—you know who will have to drag it? *You.* And don't you tell me "the Lord's will be done," because you don't know a damn thing about man's will, so forget about the Lord's. And please don't quote me any scripture. Six years ago, you left my house, and I got frightened that you would finish on some trash heap, so I sent Mercy to bring you back home. I don't think you ever had sex, and I know it's that more than anything else that's itching you. I was young myself. You're thinking that it's something everybody is getting except you.' Jay, I begged her to not have any children right away. 'Wait till you get to know Caleb before you conceive. Find out first if you can count on him. It's easy to leave when you don't have children. There's no load to carry; nothing to hold you back. Even when the man looks trustworthy, it's not a good idea to have more than one child, because men, after they've stripped the bloom off us—after they've turned lovely Rosy into Rosehips and pumped her soul-case dry, they drop her for firm, fresh flesh. You all fundamentalists don't believe in birth control. I'm begging you, Anna—don't let that man turn you into a brood sow and praise God for it. Rapture!'"—Grama sucked her teeth, paused and turned her head away briefly. "'You love to say that Christ's yoke easy; you better not let Caleb put bit in your mouth and saddle your back.'"

"'Mama, you're snarling.'

"'I am! Don't worry about *my* claws. Start sharpening yours.'"

Grama stared out at the dusk now covering the Caribbean Sea, and was silent for about ten seconds. "Maybe you're too young to be hearing all of this. But I'm telling you just the same. Everything has a cost.

Most times it's hidden. Soon you and Paul will be in Canada, away from me." She paused. "I'm worried. I don't want you and Paul to go there and throw away your lives." She brushed a gnat from her face.

"Back to your mother. Jay, let's face it. I knew I had one daughter; sometimes I wish I had a son too." She took a loud breath. "I married your mother in style. She was marrying a pauper. I swallowed my pride and put out the outlays for the wedding, bought furniture for the empty manse, and gave her half of all the linen, dishes, pots, and pans I had.

"I'd thought your father received a stipend from the missionaries, so I was shocked when, unannounced, I visited your mother eight months later, already pregnant with you, and found nothing worth eating in the house. In Georgetown, I knew everyone over 30. I ferreted out your parents' business. The weekly collection was dimes and quarters. Never added up to more than a few dollars. Could barely cover the electricity bill. And no stipend from the States. Nothing. Your father was following some sort of course at home, which he had to pass, and only after that would he get a stipend. I sometimes met him with the papers spread out on his desk and a pencil behind his ear. 'Mr. Jackson,' I told him—I had vowed never to get on familiar terms with him—'You haven't the means to support children.' To Anna, I said: 'Child, if you continue to starve like this, your baby will have congenital defects.' I went out and bought her vitamins and protein supplements, and I met her in town every Saturday to put $40 in her hand—'Not for you,' I insisted. 'You don't deserve it. For my unborn grandchild.' And, Jay, when you came due and she had to be hospitalized, and Caleb put her in the pauper's ward, I was livid. I had her transferred to a private ward forthwith. 'Not for you,' I told her: 'You're too hard-headed. For the sake of my grandchild.' And I paid the hospital bill.

"After your birth, I found out they'd christened you Jacob Habakkuk Zephaniah. I begged them to shorten it to Jay. Then I looked Caleb straight in the eyes and said: 'You're a father now. You need a job. God feeding the sparrows, but he's not feeding you and your family. I am. Now if you expect prayer to feed you, you better start getting results, because, beginning today, I stop.' It was then that your father took advantage of the building boom created by those people who'd gone to

England in droves decades before and were returning home to retire. The stones he collected never covered all the household expenses, but I saw he was making an effort so I didn't cut off my assistance; I only halved it.

"I warned Anna again: 'One child! One!' I grabbed her by the shoulders, right here, on this back porch where we are now, and shook her. So five years later, when she became pregnant again, I said: 'Child, this time, you're on your own.'

"Jay, I was raised mostly by my mother's mother. A broomstick of a woman. Wise and with more love in her than water in this sea." She swallowed. I heard the catch in her throat. "My unmarried mother was 17 when she had me. We were *not* a beating family. I don't beat. As you know, I can be stern and I do more helling and damning than I should—and nobody has to tell me I'm bossy—but hitting"—she shook her head—"out of the question. I told the wretch I married after the death of your grandfather: 'If you ever hit Anna, this marriage is over, and don't you ever yell at her.' One good thing I can say about your granddad Kirton is that he adored Anna. As a baby the moment Anna started wailing, he would rush to comfort her, change her diapers, wash and powder her. I never heard him say an angry thing to her, and he knew children should be hugged and encouraged to use their imagination. So, imagine the rage I was in when Anna told me Caleb often strapped you. Jay, I hope your mother forgave me for the cussing I gave her that day. 'Why didn't you grab Jay and leave?' I asked her. I told her, come hell or high water, I was going to rescue you. I would ask her in private: 'Is Caleb still hitting Jay?' And she would lower her eyes and say no. The day she showed up here dizzy and said she was leaving Caleb, she confessed that she'd lied to me, that the beatings were still happening.

"Let's go back to the beginning. I visited, to see you and Paul—for anger or not, blood is thicker than water—and I swore to my God, who, as you know, dwells nowhere else but in my own bosom, that there wouldn't be a third child. 'Your wife is tired,' I told your father. 'I would like to give her a short holiday. I don't think the Rapture will happen while she's gone, and if it does you two will meet in heaven.'

"I told Anna: 'I am taking you to Barbados to have your tubes tied.'

"Your mother replied: 'Caleb will divorce me if he finds out. He wants seven children. He already has names for the three daughters he wants: Hope, Faith, and Charity.'"

I chuckled, remembering my father's sermons on charity.

"Jay, I gave her such a stare, she lowered her head.

"'You can't blame him, Mama. He was lonely; he was an only child. Caleb was still in the womb when his father left for Panama. No one ever heard from him. His mother died from TB when he was seven. His aunt and her husband, who raised him, drowned in a fishing-boat accident when he was 15. You can't blame him for wanting a big family. Mama, I want daughters too. They care about family. Boys care only about their penises.'

"Jay, we were silent for at least a minute, then your mother said: 'Mama, I can't disobey Caleb.' Her fundamentalist foolishness.

"'You wear an IUD without his permission.'

"'That's different.'

"'So how he plans to feed these seven children?'

"Your mother did not answer. 'God will provide. Right?'" Grama said nothing for a while. "There's more to this story. You all can read it in my diary after my death ... Two weeks later your mother and I were off to Barbados."

In 2004, right after her death, I read what she'd edited out of the conversation:

> *Imagine I deprived myself of an education to raise a fool! 'Mama, I want children. Before Paul came, I was unhappy and depressed. I felt hollow and empty—like bamboo. Mama, I was born to have children, lots of children. No ifs and buts about it. I am never so happy as when I'm nursing a baby.'*
>
> *I told that fool: 'Have all the children you want, but before you do, let your husband know he'll have to break stones at night too, or become one of those preachers that can get their congregation to hand over all their wealth, because, darling, I won't feed them. In the meantime if you change your mind, let me know.'*

Maybe I should have had another child. Then again both might have turned out to be fools.

When Kirton proposed marriage I had already signed up for extramural classes to complete my secondary education. Abandoned that and married him, and spent my youth raising a child who turned out to be a fool.

The first and last sentence bothered me. I removed that notebook from the rest of Grama's journals so Anna would never have to read this entry. Now I doubt I'd ever let Paul see it. Paul too thinks that Anna is a fool. Probably heard Grama say so during the long periods he spent with her in the store. Are there parents whose children don't in some way disappoint them? Paul turned Anna's life into unrelenting pain. I too have disappointed her. If I could, I would have chosen not to.

***

"I think I know the rest of the story," I told Grama that evening nine years ago.

By then the porch light had come on, the sea looked like liquid lead, and the fireflies twinkled around us.

Anna was gone for two weeks. Sister Simmons brought breakfast and supper for Daddy and me. At lunch I went from school straight to her house.

4

GRAMA. SHE INTIMIDATED me. Not like Caleb. He inflicted pain. With her it was the feeling that no matter how hard I tried I would never meet her expectations. Bizarre feelings. Totally bizarre. Other than the duties she assigned me—mostly to look after Paul during the years we attended school in Kingstown, I never knew what her expectations were.

I wanted to know more about her origins but felt uncomfortable asking her. When we went home to bury her I began to find out. A Saturday afternoon. We'd spent the morning going over details with the undertaker. Paul was out wandering. Anna and I were sitting on the back porch, in the same spot where Grama had told me about Anna. Remembering this, I asked Anna to tell me about Grama.

She spent a couple of minutes dreamily staring out at the water, and began by talking about her father. She had only vague memories of him. He died before she was four. At age 55, he'd returned from Aruba, where he'd worked at an oil refinery, and had married Grama, then aged 19.

"Grama said it was not for love," Anna said. "She said: 'No darling, love had nothing to do with it. The young boys that made my eyes twinkle like fireflies didn't have a thing to offer me. Nothing more than a firm body and a stiff rod. My half-paralyzed mother begged me not to. She was sure I would end up horning him, but I went ahead and married the old goat. He had a three-bedroom cement house with an indoor kitchen and two bathrooms; it didn't bother me at all if his rod never did the job.

"'Mama might have been right, but fate worked it out so that I didn't have time to think about horning your father, because five years after we were married, he dropped dead on the beach. Went there to buy fish. Mama herself died eighteen months after the wedding. The only reason Kirton used to buy fish was that he was too damn afraid of the sea to go catch the fish himself. Nearly drowned when he was five. What a tightwad that man was! Raised his own chickens. Guess who cleaned the chicken shit? Kept goats and a cow, too. Said buying meat and milk and eggs was money going out of his pocket. His secret was to take in and not put out. Good thing he didn't take his own advice literally—or maybe he did. The day he dropped dead on the beach, a mason was up the hill outlining the spot where Kirton had hired him to build a pigpen. He had already worked it out that you and I would go and collect vegetable peelings from the neighbours to feed them. You know why, Anna: because he wanted us to earn our keep. What a miser that man was!

"'You know, about three months after he died—I shouldn't tell you this, Anna, I saw his death as a chance to make a life of my own choosing. Anna, his death was a blessing. He'd have robbed you of your childhood and robbed me of a life. That man had already turned me into a hag. You know that I love to read, always did. Your father ignited whenever he saw me reading. Kirton would start to twitch if the light was on after eight o'clock, would come and pull the book or magazine away from me, and order me into bed.

"'My mother used to do the laundry for the Anderson Greathouse, and I won a scholarship to Kingstown Secondary. But in my second year, barely a month after my grandmother died, my mother was walking under some coconut trees on the beach and a coconut fell and hit her on the head and brought on a stroke. She had just turned thirty. She returned from hospital half-paralysed. I, 13 years old at the time, had to take over the washing and ironing because that was what fed us. I managed to finish the second year and scraped through the third year, but I had to give up school. Mr. Bentley, a good man—he owned Bentley and Sons, a dry goods store, knew my situation and gave me a job to sell in his store. At 17 I was running it. With my pay I fed my mother and myself and had a little something for myself to buy a magazine or two and make myself look pretty.

"'I read everything in the Georgetown library, not that there was a lot to read: two bookcases. I always hoped to finish my education. I would have gone to England to study nursing—easy in those days—and gone on to university afterwards, but I stayed home to take care of my mother, and I ended up marrying your father. So when your father died, it was a relief. If I didn't have you, I would have gone to England. In those days with a year or two in high school, you could get into nursing. Instead I married Benjamin Bradley: earthly possessions: two pairs o' drawers—one on his arse and one on the clothesline, three shirts, two trousers, and a pair of sneakers. Not even a hairbrush to take the knots out of his hair. I was in love with him when your father asked for my hand. That man wanted to spend your father's money on his harlots—until I got fed-up and put his clothes in the road. By that time, child, I was ready to live without a man, and I understood why my mother used to say that sex sweet until you find out what it cost.'

"You're frowning, Jay."

"I'm wondering how come Grama talked to you like that."

"Well that was Mama alright. No use telling her her speech was vulgar. She would say: 'You understand what I'm saying?' And I would nod. And she would say: 'Good. That is what I want. I don't know anything about foul language. I don't have feathers, I don't lay eggs, and I don't cackle.'

Next Anna described Grama's break-up with Bradley. Anna was 11. She'd gone to Kingstown to sit the entrance exam to high school and returned around 4 pm. There was a crowd in front of Grama's house. A wall of women had their backs barricading the front door. Aunt Mercy broke away from them.

"Aunt Mercy told me not to come home," Anna said. "She said: 'Your stepfather almost kill your mother because she put his clothes in the road. He vex worse than a rattlesnake. Go and stay by me till I come. We getting ready to take your mother to the hospital. Somebody gone to get her friend Pembroke.' At the time Pembroke, Father Henderson, and the Methodist minister owned the only cars in Havre.

"Aunt Mercy came home a little past midnight. 'Your mother in the hospital. She been groaning and groaning. So when we feel your stepfather won't attack her again, we take her to the clinic over in Esperance. The nurse look at her left arm that swell up fatter than me leg, and red! Red and swell-up can't done. And the pain making her bawl. We carry she to Kingstown Hospital, and they keep her there.'"

Next day Anna visited Grama in the hospital.

"Grama couldn't speak," Anna said. "Couldn't chew. Her lips were swollen and blue, like 'jaw plums.' For four days she sucked liquid food through a straw. When Grama was discharged, her lower arm in a cast, her face white like chalk, she went to the police station to file a case, but the sergeant told her: 'The courts not concern with domestic comess. So you throw Bradley out. He can't satisfy you or what? And he only break your arm!'

"Grama consulted a lawyer. He said that short of killing her, Bradley could have done what he wanted to her. For $200 — Jay, that was a lot of money in 1967 — he wrote to Bradley, telling him that his wife had terminated the conjugal state as of May 11, 1967 and will soon be filing for a divorce, and he was prohibited from re-entering her premises. Something like that. Three days later Bradley broke every window in our house. Mr. Morris witnessed it and gave evidence, and Bradley spent a month in prison."

Anna grew silent for several seconds and stared thoughtfully out to sea. The wind had risen and the sea was rough and noisy. The gulls flying over it squawked loud.

"Mama was always particular about keeping documents. She kept a folder for everything and a daily journal. Peruse her papers. You will learn a lot about your grandmother. Unknown to her I used to read them over and over — until I got saved and realized it was a sin."

Two days later, I came upon the entry that I never wanted her to read and won't let Paul read.

5

ANNA'S STERTEROUS BREATHING brings me back to the present. For a moment my eyes rest on the beads of perspiration glistening on her forehead. I get up, take a tissue from the box on the night table, and dab her brow.

Paul, where the hell are you? Why have you been doing this to us? Okay, so you're punishing Ma. But me? I sit. My hands are cold but sweating, and sweat is trickling from my armpits.

Anna's breathing is now part gurgle, part whistling rattle. Each time she exhales I smell the acetone in her breath. She's stewing internally. I lean forward and enclose her right hand in both of mine. It's glacial and limp. In the dim blue light from the tiny bulb over the head of her bed, I watch her struggling body and want to comfort her, to sing her favourite hymn: "Jesus, Saviour, pilot me / O'er life's dark tempestuous sea," but know I'll sob if I start. Those hymns, singing them at home—about the only thing Paul's bullying didn't stop her from doing. Paul, where are you? Why are you doing this to us?

I let go of her hand and lean back into the chair, and my mind travels back to that trip that Ma and Grama took to Barbados. When Anna returned, she was constantly in tears and, one evening, not long after her return, Caleb struck her. Knocked her to the floor. He picked her up. Frightened. On occasion he'd hit her when he was beating me because she was interfering—and the bible instructed him never to spare the rod and spoil the child; and 'He that knoweth the will and doeth it not shall be beaten with many stripes'; and God had ordained him head of the household; the bible said so: he was to give the orders, and she was to carry them out; he was man, she was woman. A woman's role was to obey her husband and fulfill the needs of her husband and her children. It was what he instructed every couple he married: "The buck must stop somewhere"; and he laid down the law in his own home to set the example for his flock.

"I'm sorry. I'm sorry," Caleb said. "Anna, you see what you made me lose my temper and do? You had no right to do this behind my back. I'm your husband. You're under my rule. You shouldn't o' done this. Why your mother put you up to this? Why? That woman is Satan ownself. If she ever put her foot back in this house ..." He stopped.

"Go ahead, say it, Mr. Almighty! Say it!"

He lifted his arm, ready to strike again, but checked himself. "That woman! She must never come back here. Thank God, we don't depend on her anymore."

"Don't be so sure."

"You still taking money from her! You're disobeying me and taking money from that ... that ..."

"You think the pittance you get from those stones or the nickels and dimes they give you on Sundays can feed and clothe your family? Think again."

"You live too extravagantly!"

"Well I can't change how I was brought up."

"Then you married the wrong man."

She didn't answer.

"What's tied can be untied. You will have to untie them."

She didn't answer.

"I say: you will have to untie them." He held her by the neck with both hands and rocked her backward and forward.

She gasped, staggered, and let out a hoarse howl when he let her go.

"Shut up! You want to bring disgrace on me! Shut up, woman! Don't raise the devil in me!" He ran to the doors and windows, closed them, and pulled the curtains.

"*You* will go to hell. Stop choking Ma! You big brute!" I shouted. He sometimes called me a little brute.

"Go to your room," he ordered. "Go to your room before ... " I didn't move. Caleb slumped to the floor on his knees and cried out: "Lord, how did I fail you? Lord, why are you punishing me? I am not Job. I am not Job." He wiped his eyes with his hands and stared for a long time into vacant space.

In the rest of my conversation with Grama before I left for Canada, she told me that it was only after Caleb had knocked Anna down a second time that she'd found out about this first beating, and she hadn't known about the occasional slaps. The second and final beating came about three months after the first, and Anna asked Grama to keep Paul and to lend her some money to go to Canada. "'Mama, I have to leave him. God alone knows how much damage he's done to Jay. I can't let him do it to Paul too. I can't, Mama. I can't. He's already hitting Paul to stop him from crying, leaving welts on his body.' Jay, your mother was sobbing so loud and hiccupping, I had to hold her to my bosom and comfort her."

That second beating. Caleb had been in my bedroom about to beat me to "rescue my soul from the wrath to come." Anna shouted from the kitchen: "Caleb, leave Jay alone. Rescue your own soul, Caleb. Leave Jay's alone. Hell doesn't exist. I already told him so. Leave him alone! Stop terrorizing him!" I heard her fists pounding the kitchen counter. Caleb sped to her in the kitchen. I followed. Caleb let fly both hands in quick succession. "Satan! In *my* home! Not possible." His arms flew. The slaps swayed Anna left and right, right and left. When she fell, it was backwards. Her head struck the kitchen counter; she slid to the floor, lay on the tiles, and was unconscious. Caleb called her name several times, and when she didn't answer he dashed out of the house.

Years later I got the rest of the story. The Georgetown station sergeant who'd dealt with Caleb that evening was eventually posted to Havre. He bought supplies on credit from Grama, hung around the store sometimes, and took pleasure regaling the shoppers about colourful characters he'd arrested or dealt with. "Boy," he would say to me, "I remember when your father Preacherman did come to the station and beg me to lock him up." And he would enact the scene.

"Preacherman come in the police station and he say to me: 'Sarge, lock me up.'

"'What you do now, Preacherman? First you have to tell me what you do.'

"'I say lock me up. Lock me up!'

"'It ain't so we does do it. We does have to know what you do first. Yes? Sit down there.' I point he to a bench 'gainst the wall from the station counter. 'All you preacherman hot for the young girls in all you congregation. What happen: you done rape one?' (I imagined him grinning, his two upper gold-capped incisors glinting.) 'You done kill your wife or what? You catch a man on top o' she or what? Too busy with God to satisfy your wife or what? That calypso not lying at all: 'Man can't take butt.' Some men sure can't. 'Henry,' I turn to the constable what was sitting by a desk a little way from the counter listening to the conversation. 'Henry, you know where Preacherman live. Right? Go by his house and see if he done kill his wife.' To Preacherman, I say: 'Ah sending a constable to your home to see if you done kill your wife and thing.' I don't think Preacherman hear me yet.

"Boy, Henry meet your mother sprawled where Preacherman did done knock her down. She did regain consciousness and Eldica was putting ice on she cheeks. I hear is you"—he pointed to me—"that did have sense enough to run and get Eldica after your mother didn't respond. When Henry come back to the station and give me his report, I tell Preacherman to go home and take care o' his wife and to go easy on his fist. 'Your wife jaw not like them stones you does break on the seashore.' And I tell he we don't does lock up men for beating their wife; is only in Canada and them places they does do that. But careful you don't kill she, yes. 'Cause then you won't get off so easy. So tell me, nuh,'—I couldn't help teasing him little bit more—'Is what happen, Preacherman: why you knock she out? You catch another man on top o' she or what?'

"'I don't want to go home. I don't want to go home.' Sonny, that is how your father carry on. 'It go be alright, man. I tell you, it go be alright.' I tell he: 'Things don't does be bad as they look. Yes.' Now I did start to feel sorry for him. I wasn' laughing at him no more."

* * *

Until the day Grama came to get me, I don't remember much of what happened. She had to do a lot of asking around, because Daddy had left the manse and moved into a shack a few metres in from the beach about two kilometres north of Georgetown. Grama met him lying on the bare floor. He came out and sat on the middle one of three planks that formed the steps to the shack. He was unshaven and his eyes were red and haunted. At first he didn't look her in the face, and when she told him why she'd come, he said nothing. She repeated what she'd said: "Mr. Jackson, Anna left for Canada this morning. She left Paul with me. I've come for Jay. He'll be better off staying with me." For about a minute their eyes locked, then he spat, re-entered the shack, and closed the door.

She came to get me at school. I was staying with Sister Simmons. Grama didn't bother to pick up any of my things. "Whatever you need you'll get from my store. We'll make a clean start." The following Saturday Sister Simmons brought my things to Havre and Grama told her to keep them. If she were alive today, I would ask her why.

$$6$$

ANNA NEVER KEPT a journal. I'll never get to know her in the detailed sort of way I got to know Grama after her death. It's too late now to ask Anna the questions I've wanted to about Caleb. I visualize Grama writing her journal—just before supper, always at the dining table, the sun setting in the harbour tinting her golden. Paul copied her habit. But I never did in any serious sort of way, and I tend to lose whatever thoughts I write down. She kept her journals in the spare bedroom. I could have read them in secret if I wished, the way I read my mother's letters to her, but I never did until after her death. Her entries about herself, her husband, and Anna interest me most, and they are the ones I reread. The pages of the oldest journals, before she got married, are yellow and brittle. I have saved those for future reading.

AUGUST 21, 1955

I am pregnant for a man I don't love. What will this mean for me and my child when it's born? My mother agreed that Zachary Kirton offered security but not much else. It's harder to leave when you have children.

If I don't die in childbirth, I must find a way not to have any others. Kirton won't use French letters. "What I hearing here? You don't want no pickney? Well, I have a problem with French letter. When I stop to put it on, my rod fall." Must strike before his iron cools. Wish it would cool every time he climbs onto me. It takes that man a full hour and a half to come, and there's no way for me to go numb, or fall asleep. How will I stop him from turning me into a brood sow? Doc Fraser says there are creams available overseas that I can put in my vagina before I have sex. But I'll have to order them from abroad. I have no money. I have to give Kirton an accounting of every penny I spend.

Yesterday I asked Mama how she managed to have only one child. "I kept my legs closed, Cynthie. Kept my legs closed. That was all. But you can't do that. You have to satisfy your husband needs. 'Bout not having children, there's bush teas. I used to hear your grandmother talking 'bout them, but I don't know them. But, from what she used to say, is teas that prevent the man from rising. She used to talk 'bout a woman who did give her husband them kind o' teas and after that there was only six o'clock. And she used to butt him in the end. You got five, if you lucky ten, more years o' sex from Kirton, and then some long years o' drought. You better take what you can get now."

JANUARY 14, 1960

What a help Doc Fraser is! He's such an unusual, understanding, unpretentious man. You'd never know he's of plantocrat stock. He has helped me work out my fertility cycle. "Now it's up to you to fight off Kirton when he's in heat." Right after sex I douche with a vinegar mixture Elma has showed me how to prepare. It works for her. She has a man but no children. It stings the living daylights out of me. And I've just been plain lucky. Touch wood.

The older heads saw children as riches, but they keep us enslaved to men. A sensible woman would only get pregnant when she knows she can support her child herself.

JUNE 13, 1961

What sort of religious education should I give Anna? I got mine from reading. It rescued me from all that foolishness. No joke about that. That book I read on religion at 16. It disappeared from the library shortly after. No surprise there. It had come in a batch of books somebody from England had sent to the Georgetown Public Library. Diverse Religious Beliefs — I think that was the title. There were many beliefs — the book said none was superior;

"they are all intended to make us better human beings either through divine intervention or through our own effort. Many religions stress the afterlife, but their real purpose is to make our earthly life bearable." But the belief I liked best, that I copied and decided to make my own, was the one that "God isn't a being separate from human beings. Each person carries a piece of God within himself or herself. It is the total of all those pieces that comprises God. Like a plant cutting that we water and tend, so we must cultivate the divine within ourselves. That was what Christ had done, and done spectacularly. He was the son of God only in the sense that he fed, and fed off, the divine within himself. Christians on the whole are spiritually lazy. That's why they need someone to die for them.

"The miracles: turning water into wine, bringing the dead back to life, scenes of transfiguration, they were invented to impress illiterate, superstitious people—and most people, even the educated, are superstitious—that Christ was God. The death on the cross and the resurrection reflect the scapegoating which all Mediterranean peoples practised. As to the concepts of hell and heaven, they were invented to keep poor, hopeless, desperate people from committing suicide. Why else would a serf, whose life depended on the overlord whose land he lived on, and who could be beaten any time the overlord so desired; who was almost always cold, tired, and hungry; whose daughters could be—and frequently were—raped by the overlord and his male relatives, why would he want to go on living? Hell and heaven were invented for those reasons by religious leaders who depended on the overlords for their sumptuous lives. Imagine what would have happened to the landlords if the serfs had decided to find heaven on earth!"

Didn't I get the point! The barefoot and hungry, they fill the hell-fire and brimstone churches. Going to church is a Sunday fashion parade for the Methodists, Anglicans, and Catholics: their way of showing they aren't poor. When I ran Bentley's and they came to shop and ran into one another, I'd hear bits and pieces of their conversations:

"I didn't see you on Sunday."

"Couldn't come. But I have to find a way to make it up to the Lord. He gives us so much. We have to give back something."

"True, Sister, true. We don't want God to withhold his blessings."

So bribing God is part of it. When I married Kirton, he too did the fashion thing: a three-piece suit; ushering; taking up the collection. And he made me parade at his side every Sunday, his trophy all dolled up. "You wear that dress three Sundays ago; you shouldn't wear it again today." Church wear was the only thing he wasn't a skinflint about.

When Kirton died, I stopped going, and Father Henderson—I suspect he's about five years my elder, no more than thirty—came nosing around to find out why I'd stopped attending. In all that heat, he wore a choking white collar and a black soutane, probably to make his pale skin look white. Suffering for Jesus, to be an example to his flock? More like 'I'm not one of you.' "Father," I told him, mocking him, inwardly smirking—I know he has two unacknowledged children in Havre—"Have a drink first," and I served him from a bottle of Mr. Kirton's best scotch, which Kirton never drank: too expensive, no doubt. I poured myself one too and told Father Henderson what I believe. He was surprised and never expected "such sophistication from a ah ah ah—you know what I mean—country girl." The country girl *knew what he meant, and translated "ah ah ah" to mean Negro. Father Henderson could never use the word black except he was describing sin.*

"You know, Cynthia"—when Kirton was alive, Father Henderson always called me Sister Kirton—"we have two sets of beliefs, one for the priests and one for the flock."

"You don't say, Father Henderson!"

"Well, it's complicated. Ordinary people can't understand the scriptures. We have to adapt theology to the needs of humble folk. Minister to their needs. Christ himself did that. And as Paul says in one of his epistles, some people can only digest milk; it's wrong to feed them meat."

I wanted none of his milk. "Didn't I hear a British archbishop quoted on the radio saying hell is an imaginary place, and that Mary, if she existed at all, was an out-of-wedlock mother?"

Father Henderson's face looked as if it had been dunked in boiling water, his eyebrows went half-way up his forehead, his grey eyes narrowed, and his hand went to his throat as if his collar had begun to choke him.

"Are you alright, Father?" I looked at the whisky bottle on the coffee table, ready to pour him another.

He took a deep breath and a calming pause and said: "Let's just say, many of us would like to modernize theology. But, Sister Kirton, the human soul is old and needs no modernizing. Christian beliefs and rituals have been good for thousands of years; they have stood the test of millennia."

"Is that why you continue to preach about mansions in the sky for some and eternal hellfire for others? There are people inside your church ... There's an Anglican minister—can't remember his name—who doubts that Christ actually lived."

"Vincentians must not be exposed to such opinions. We're careful what books the Diocesan Bookstore stocks, and we check the libraries for subversive materials."

"Such opinions can be heard on the BBC, Father Henderson."

"Alas! We have no way to block it. The British have become a godless people." He swallowed and smoothed his hair while searching for a response. "Don't knock it, Sister Kirton, don't. The fear of hell keeps many a sinner from straying further into sin."

"That includes you too, I suppose, Father?"

He winced.

He no longer visits, but singles me out for chit-chat when he meets me at funerals, wakes, and socials.

JULY 14, 1962

I wonder what sort of life I would be leading if Kirton were alive. Kirton! I still won't use his first name. I was afraid of him. I know that now. Obsessed with wealth. At Anna's birth, he made his will and left it with his lawyer so I wouldn't get to know what was in it.

"To Cynthia Kirton nee Williams, hereinafter called my wife, I bequeath the benefit of all my immoveables for as long as she shall live, with the following conditions: I grant my wife the authority to liquidate fifty percent (50%) of all my investments, should circumstances warrant. At age 65, should my wife's economic circumstances warrant, she is authorized to dispose of another ten (10) percent of all that remains. Upon my wife's decease all my remaining property goes to my daughter Anna and her children, should she have children. I leave it up to my wife to determine the

proportions. Should Anna predecease my wife, all property remaining after my wife's death goes to her children. Should Anna be childless, it goes to the Anglican Church."

What a cold-blooded lizard! Seems I signed a pact with Lucifer himself. Kirton, bits of your lectures — boasts are more like it; that's what our "conversations" were: listening to your boasts; you were certain I had nothing to say worth listening to — come back to me.

"Let me and you get one thing straight. You going bring into this marriage more than you take out. You is supposed to be my help meet, not wait on me to give you meat. I got a simple philosophy. It got two principles. The first one is: everybody who not crippled and who over age must earn the food that go into their belly and the roof that keep rain off their head. The second one is: always save as much money as you can. But that is only the start. In Aruba, where I used to work for the Largo Oil Company, it had this beefy man name Showalter; red like stewed conch. He was the general manager. Everybody except me, afraid o' Showalter. Maybe 'cause he white. My co-workers said I was licking his arse. I find out he love West Indian food. Come from a family of five. They had a West Indian maid back in New Jersey where he grew up. Father was a boss with Standard Oil in New Jersey. Father brought him into Standard Oil straight out o' high school. Anyway I find out he love West Indian food, and if is one thing I loved to do in them days is cook. So I offer to come cook for he one Sunday as a joke. And he accept. Lived alone in this huge house in Essoville. There's where the company big shots lived. He was the number three man at Largo. I had a room in Bachelor Quarters. My neighbour was from Barbados and he used to tempt me to go to Oranjestad on a Saturday night, but I was determined to hold on to every copper I get so that if God spare my life and I go back to St. Vincent I could be somebody and command respect." (Kirton would straighten his shoulders with pride, stop talking, and stare me in the eyes, the smile playing over his papery walnut face saying, I achieved it.)

"That food I cook for Showalter sweet he till he forget I was just a two-bit black man on the janitorial staff, and we become like friends kind of. So I used to go cook for he every Sunday before I go to church and he paid me for it. From what I see, he was a lonely man. Didn't look like he was much interested in women. Of course I can't say I did know his business, because

the bosses had their private club where they use to meet, and it was for Whites only and not for Whites at the bottom neither. He really did like me, though. He make me supervisor o' the janitorial staff. I didn't have to do no cleaning after that, just give the orders and make sure they get carried out, and not be afraid to crack the whip if I had to, and it come with a nice raise in pay. His doings. One time he tell me, 'Zach.' He himself shorten my name to Zach. 'Zach, you're not like these other British West Indians here. You have ambition.' Cynthia, that statement make my head swell big with pride. I was so pleased that a White man of all people could see that. That give me the courage to ask him advice 'bout all sorts o' things. He give me a good piece o' advice about investments. He tell me if I leave my money in the bank, bankers will get rich and I will die poor. He advise me to buy shares, and he offer to do it for me. When I getting ready to leave Aruba — I went there when I was 22 and I leave when I was a month short of 55, and I never work for nobody there except Largo — and he explain what was in my portfolio, and when he tell me how much I worth, I almost shit myself. Cynthia, the trouble with Black people is they think too much about heaven and ignore their welfare on earth. He say that to me, and I think is a true statement. I pay attention to both. And another thing wrong with Black people is they hobnob with the wrong kind o' people: people like themselves who can't do nothing for them. He didn't say that. That is my saying.

"So, you see, Cynthia, I live my life according to principles that pay off. I proud o' what I accomplish in Aruba. My father, you see, was a master carpenter who couldn't think. What should o' stay up in his head sink down to his balls. Spend his whole life screwing and drinking. 110 acres — 110 acres o' good grazing and farm land that my father inherited — the Vincentian government sold for unpaid taxes, while my mother and me was living hand to mouth. I is his only child. He married my mother only because she made me. I is the only child that come from all his screwing. All my mother got from him was me, a ring, and two-three weekly beatings. He spent only enough time at home to screw my mother or beat her when she refused to let him screw her. I was already some twenty years in Aruba when he got old and shaky. People used to write and beg me to send money to look after him. My mother was long dead from all the beatings and abuse and VD that he gave her. I never answered the letters. A fellow from home who worked with me at Largo use to keep me up to date with news 'bout him. His mother used to send him news about everybody. We called him the San Nicholas Gazette. My father went to the poor home and die there and get a pauper's burial. The way I feel about it is: how a body live so it must die. What you sows, Cynthia, is what you reaps.

"Early in my life, I watch everything my father did wrong. And was the same mistakes a lot of poor people make. They get married young while they still poor and have lots of children that make them poorer. I decide I ain't getting married before I get rich, and I wasn't going to full up women all over the place with children that I would have to turn my back on, and no rum shop will ever see my face. I stick close to the church. I stayed a altar boy until I go to Aruba and would o' been one there too, but they didn't have no Anglican Church. That didn't stop me from going to church. I used to go to the Methodist."

I wanted to ask him how he satisfied his sexual needs, and did my utmost not to say: Kirton, you're sure the only thing you did for Showalter was to cook for him? Kirton, you're sure some of those shares in that portfolio didn't come from Showalter for unmentionable services rendered?

Zachary Kirton, (it should be spelt Curtain), Zachary Kirton, may you rest in peace. Earth to earth, ashes to ashes.

APRIL 14, 1966

I send Anna to the Anglican Sunday school because her father was Anglican. Yesterday, two days after her tenth birthday, she asked me why I don't go to church. I think she sees all the well-to-do women in Havre doing the fashion parade every Sunday and is wondering why I'm not among them. "God is in my heart, child," I told her. "All I have to do is look in there and I will find it."

"It, Mama? How can you call God it?"

"It, child. It. God is a force, an energy—like electricity—that makes some things work. It makes us kind, forgiving, generous; it makes us treat other people the way we want them to treat us."

Anna frowned. I saw she was puzzled, but she asked no further questions.

DECEMBER 14, 1968

For as long as I can remember I used to jot things down. Little poems. Feelings. Impressions. How a grasshopper looked crouched on the ground. An orange-and-black butterfly spread out on a flower. The weaving and unweaving of the lace-frills of the waves breaking on the seashore. At puberty, it was the changes in my body and my feelings for boys. A lot later, just before Kirton asked for my hand, they were about Benjamin—the girls he was seeing, my torn feelings at 18 when I was sure that even though my body tingled and ached for his, I couldn't marry him: nought plus nought is nought. Children and poverty don't mix—one thing Kirton got right. The lives around me were open books. Tch! Tch! Cynthia. You read them and later forgot the lessons. My years with Kirton, I sneaked out of bed when his snoring started —that man snored liked a hungry boar and slept like a corpse—and wrote my journal. I married Benjamin soon after Kirton died, and all the reasons I had for not getting too close to him at eighteen came true after I married him.

What would my life have been if instead of marrying Kirton, I'd taken those classes? Mama died 18 months after I married him. I would have been able to go to England then.

AUGUST 23, 1987

It is comforting to know Anna held on to scraps of my religious beliefs.

"You know, Mama, what you told me about God when I was little, I never forgot. You know Caleb is taking this course to become a fully qualified minister. Right?"

I nodded, afraid of what I'd say if I opened my mouth.

"After I married Caleb, they told him that seeing that I would be part of his ministry, I should follow the course too. But I wouldn't have to take the exam."

"Oh! An exam. A regular university degree. In theology?"

"No, Mama. Three men from the church headquarters in the States will come and examine Caleb, and if they're satisfied with his answers, he will move from pastor-in-training to probationary pastor."

"And get a stipend, I hope. Seems to me they'll have a good reason to fail him."

"The reason he's still on the course is he comes home tired every day. Part of the course is how to win converts from other religions, and not to let them win you over to theirs. True Believer. He's this character that's supposed to be filled with the Holy Spirit. He argues with Atheist, Agnostic, Buddhist, and Unitarian. When they tell True Believer that humans wrote the Bible, True Believer is supposed to quote the part in the Bible that says God inspired men to write it.

"And True Believer tells Buddhist that unless he gives up his beliefs in reincarnation and wash himself in Christ's blood he will go to hell; and Buddhist answers: 'I have to go to hell; each person has to, several times even, and stay there until he is ready to move on to a higher state.' But True Believer tells him, he doesn't have to, that it's as easy as accepting Christ. Unitarian asks True Believer if he would drown his disobedient children or stone them to death. And True Believer says, yes, if the Holy Ghost orders him to, just like God ordered Abraham to sacrifice Isaac. And Unitarian tells him: 'What if it's not the Holy Ghost; what if it's madness?' True Believer answers that madness is the result of possession by evil spirits and evil spirits can't live in bodies that Christ's blood has purified. And True Believer then tells him the story of Job."

"Why you all don't just use his initials? TB suits him just fine, the incurable kind."

"Mama, so that's how I came to see that what you told me when I was ten made some sense; but it was a long time before I could challenge Caleb. You see, he would have had to leave me, or leave the church if he wanted to remain with me. They are very strict about that. Believers can't be married to unbelievers."

Cur-like obedience to foolish doctrines. I'm not sure her father was much different.

7

ANNA'S RATTLING BREATH breaks into my recall. I stand, touch her forehead. It's cold and damp. I stare at her chest—heaving, rattling, battling, as it struggles to expel air and acetone. I snort and realize that I too was holding my breath until she expelled hers.

I sit, chew my thumbnail, and my mind turns again to my Vincentian past. For the nine years I lived with Grama I felt that she shouldn't be caring for me, that my place was with Anna, that she needed me. Most nights I fell asleep thinking about her, wondering if she was happy, wondering if we would ever be reunited, wondering if she was warm, especially when the BBC news gave the temperatures for Montreal or said that there was a blizzard. Night after night I dreamed we were together, and would awaken right after, usually in the middle of the night, and spend a long time thinking about her. We heard from her every two to three weeks. She sent us a parcel at Christmas and on our birthdays. Then she remembered our birthdays. Grama told us that Anna sent money to pay for our expenses, but I read all her letters (Grama caught me once and reprimanded me), and in each of them Anna apologized for not sending any money.

Paul conquered Grama's heart. She loved him unconditionally, dotingly. On Friday afternoons, when Paul and I returned from school in Kingstown, she'd be standing on the front porch waiting for us. As soon as the car door opened, Paul would break loose as if from prison and run straight into her arms, and she lifted him up, and he kissed her (the lifting was replaced by bending when Paul became too heavy, but the kissing never stopped). And while I was transporting our dirty clothes to the laundry room, Paul would be inside planting kisses on Aunt Mercy's cheeks before rushing back to Grama, by now seated on the living room sofa, waiting for him to show her his workbooks covered with stars, and regale her with all that had happened at school and at Cousin Alice's that week.

With me her physical contact was never more than a perfunctory, dutiful kiss, and an occasional hug. In the first three or so years that I lived with her—before she became tired of saying it—she would sometimes say: "You're already an old man, Jay"—her eyes narrowing, boring into me, her forehead deeply creased. "Not a hint of adventure in you. Not a playful bone in that old man's body. What are you in mourning for? Your life hasn't even started. I never see you with a cricket bat. You don't go out to the playing field to kick a soccer ball with the other children. Do like your brother. He can't play because of his asthma, but he goes out there and enjoys watching the players." Sometimes, if she thought she'd been harsh, she'd come to stand or sit beside me. "Don't think I'm blaming you for being yourself." But she would sigh and add: "Jay, I want you to be happy." One time I was standing on the front porch watching her dead-head the roses and bougainvillaea that encircled the porch; she looked up at me, and said: "Stop being so sullen." She sounded worried. It had upset me. I felt like an ingrate. Now I think she probably felt that she had failed in some way, or was guilty that Paul took up most of the space in her affection. The doubts parents have, I suppose. I have since seen it firsthand in Anna's trials with Paul.

The first few years with Grama were tough. I had to steel myself just to visit my father and deal with the shame I felt, and avoid saying anything that would hurt his feelings. When I came to Canada, away from it all, it struck me, how warm, affectionate, and harmless my father became when he was drunk, and I wondered why he wasn't that way when he was sober. One late afternoon when I'd returned from visiting Caleb, Grama asked me jokingly: "How's your father doing in his alcoholic heaven?" I was silent, and she saw that her words were hurtful, and she came out to the front porch where I was and put her arms around me and muttered: "You are too young—too young for all this. Too young." Then she sighed, left me there, and returned inside. There was an unusual silence at the supper table that evening. Even Paul was quiet.

No, it would be wrong to find fault with Grama. During the July-August holidays, she played scrabble and Chinese checkers with me, and we read together. She plied me with the books Caleb had prevented me from reading. She would come in from the store and have a short nap, write her journal, after which we'd have supper and read for two to three hours. She had all the books written by Trinidad's Prime Minister Eric Williams and the works of the earlier West Indian novelists: Lamming, Anthony, Selvon, Mais, Naipaul. Her favourite Caribbean novelist was Earl Lovelace; she loved the poems of Lorna Goodison; and she ordered many of the books of authors mentioned on BBC, especially books of poetry by poets whose works she'd heard and loved. She'd have me read their poems aloud to her: Blake's, Yeats', Auden's — I remember. Paul would pause from his own reading to listen. She had read "London" and "Sailing to Byzantium" so many times, she knew them by heart, and she would break into laughter, sometimes to the point of tears, over Auden's "As I Walked out One Evening." I remember her saying: "What a happy childhood that Mr. Yeats had. I hope it wasn't paid for with pillage." Three days before Paul and I left for Canada she received a copy of *Brave New World*. She'd ordered it after listening to a BBC programme on Aldous Huxley. At one point during the programme, she'd grown wistful, then sighed and said aloud: "Who knows what my life would have been if I had emigrated?" I wish she were alive today so I could ask her what she meant, just to hear her say it. The answers are plentiful in her journals. *Grama, we cannot conquer fate.*

When my voice changed at 13, she gave me a book that explained puberty, and read it along with me, pausing every so often to emphasize the consequences of careless sex. And I could never forget the discussion we had about *Wide Sargasso Sea*, which was on my CXC syllabus. She told me it was full of historical inaccuracies, that the sort of liberty the Black servants are shown to enjoy a few years after the abolition of slavery, was nonsense, that Rhys was flattering the white readers she knew would be buying her books. But she warned me not to raise the issue in class, for my literature teacher was the great-grandson of a plantocrat who'd resisted all British attempts to introduce universal elementary education to St. Vincent, "and even today they still own most of the wealth in St. Vincent." I didn't think the teacher would have minded, but I followed her advice. In the end I chose to write my essay on the villains and heroes in *Wide Sargasso Sea*, and she suggested I should compare Rhys' villains with Shakespeare's. What a woman! I know now that Paul and I were lucky and privileged to have her as grandmother and guardian. No wonder Paul worships her. Few Vincentians read beyond the textbooks they're forced to study. *If you want to hide something from Black people, put it in a book.* I'm sure some racist came up with that but it's only Black people who repeat it. Above all else she gave me a love for learning that Anna couldn't have given me, especially if she had remained with Caleb. Yes, I think I can forgive her for her partiality to Paul.

Before Anna left Caleb, while we lived in Georgetown, I played with Percy and Samuel, and on occasion with Frederick and a handful of schoolmates in the schoolyard. I was afraid to disobey Caleb and play with the other children on non-school days because the second time I'd done so Caleb found out and flogged me. We weren't to "mingle with the damned." The apostle Paul had advised the redeemed to shun the company of the unredeemed for they were "leagued with the devil and the Antichrist" and would "put snares in our paths." And God himself had decided before he created the world that these people should go to hell. For the same reason Caleb didn't want us to visit Grama often. I couldn't believe that Grama worshipped the devil nor could I understand why, thousands of years before Grama was born, God had decided to send her to hell. Once I heard Caleb and Brother Simmons quarrelling about this in the living room — Brother Simmons' booming voice saying: "That doctrine is rubbish; that is the stupidest thing I ever hear. So, Pastor, why you beg sinners to give their heart to the Lord? And what about: 'I came not to call the righteous, but sinners to repentance?' Is Christ himself that say that. I will take Christ word over what Paul say any day." I did not hear Caleb's answer because just then Anna grabbed my hand and pulled me through the main door so I wouldn't hear the rest of the quarrel. Brother Simmons stayed away from church for a long time after that and, when he came back, he stopped teaching Sunday school. About a month before Anna left Caleb, I asked her why God decided to send people to hell even before they were born, and she replied: "I told you already that hell does not exist. Your father gets carried away by what he reads in the Bible. God is kinder than your father thinks."

Thinking back on it now, I see that by the time Anna left for Canada, I'd lost all desire to play with anyone. I relive being on the beach with Daddy—I watch him pile and crack open stones, I hear the wind soughing in the coconut fronds, the breakers pounding the shore, the rattling of the backwash: background noise to the exploding blows of Daddy's sledgehammer—before I became afraid of him. Maybe Grama felt that the beatings had stultified me. Now I feel guilty. I haven't written Caleb since Christmas. At some level I want to know that all is well with him. I love my father—sometimes I wonder why. And I know the scriptures that "keep [my father] from falling down" have become cudgels he whips himself with. Caleb would say "flaming swords."

With Grama, I could have roamed the village if I'd wanted. During school holidays I helped her with her flower garden, or walked to her land, about a kilometre away, and brought back plumroses, oranges, mamie apples, passion fruit, mangoes—whatever fruits were in season. On occasion Millington, the only friend I had in Havre, went with me. After lunch I'd read or go swimming in the sea. Sometimes on evenings, after Grama and I had finished reading, I'd sit alone on the back porch with the light deliberately turned off, wanting to dissolve into the darkness. Sometimes, Millington, whom I met in grade three and who began at Kingstown Secondary the same time I did, would be there with me, and we'd quiz each other about things we'd studied. Sometimes we'd sit there in silence. Maybe because we didn't know what else to do.

Were we truly friends? We'd never spoken of our inner needs and fears. We'd never spoken about girls we'd "conquered" or "spoiled"—the usual talk of our classmates—for we'd done neither, and were probably anxious about our own sexuality. Perhaps that was why we were comfortable with each other. He had one other friend that I knew of: Alan, a talkative fellow from Green Hill. The same week we received our high-school-leaving results, he was spending time with Millington. Millington went to church every Sunday, belonged to the Boys' Brigade and the Methodist Youth Fellowship, but never spoke to me about religion. I felt he was straitjacketed by it. Once he shared a joke with me, and it had seemed so out of character. "Jill took Jack below the hill to taste his liquor. She did and washed out her mouth. Jill's baby came six months later, and Jack thought he was the father."

Millington lived half way up the hill on Pasture Road, in a two-bedroom wooden house perched on tree-trunk stilts, to which goats were tied on evenings. They had a pit latrine and an outdoor kitchen where his mother cooked with firewood, in cast-iron tripod pots—like most Haverites then. She looked white—a mixture of Kalinago, European, and Black probably—and was always singing hymns: one I remember well—"Dare to be a Daniel/ Dare to stand alone/ Dare to have a purpose firm/ And Dare to make it own." And I remember only because the song contrasted so vividly with her life that seemed all drudgery. Once I met her sitting on the porch grating coconuts to make coconut sugar cakes. The next day Millington brought me a couple.

Millington's father, Edward, was a short, scrawny, bowlegged man, mixed-race too. He left home at dawn to work on distant construction sites, when work was available, or on his land, when work was not. He returned at dusk in both cases. Millington's mother carried his breakfast and lunch to the land. During vacation Millington did and always wanted me to accompany him.

Millington was a year older than I. An aunt in the US paid for his school uniforms, transportation, and textbooks—the only thing personal he ever told me. Grama liked him, called him "an upright young man," and every August gave him a hundred dollars to help with his school supplies. When she found out I'd never visited Millington, she asked me what sort of friend I was to Millington. After that I'd climb the hill occasionally to visit him. My first couple of years in Canada I sent him a card at Christmas. I see the same pattern in my friendship with Jonathan. It's he who takes all the initiatives.

Yes, Paul was definitely the child Grama wished she'd had: the Paul she knew in St. Vincent. Evident in her occasional exasperations: "Your mother walks on her senses; the little intelligence she was born with she traded for foolish doctrine"; in what Anna told me; and in what I've read in Grama's journals since her death. No doubt about it, Paul was the child she'd wanted Anna to be. Surprisingly she doesn't say so in her journal. Wisdom Grama had plenty of and was probably quite aware of the traps here into which Paul and I could easily fall. I'll admit that I was jealous of Paul in the early years when she'd sit him on her lap and read to him. And she sent him to pre-school as soon as he was three. By the time he was four and a half he was reading. His favourite reading spot was on the floor in front of her. Sometimes, she'd be seated at one end of the couch, he lying on it, his head resting on her thighs. Sometimes they'd be conversing about what Paul had read or was reading. She gave him all the attention he demanded.

At six Paul had his first serious asthma attack, and from then on would wheeze heavily and have trouble breathing whenever he over-exerted himself. Wherever he went, he carried his puffer and later added an EpiPen. By the time we came to Canada he was permanently on anti-asthma drugs. He loved music and was a star player in Havre's Steelband. Anna got to see him play the summer she came back to Havre to take us to Canada. I can still hear him beating out the notes on the lead soprano pan to Abba's "I Have a Dream." Soon after we arrived in Montreal Anna enrolled him in Salah's Steelband School, so he could continue playing pan, but nothing ever came of it. Instead he spent his allowances on filthy rap—he'd despised it when he first arrived—and played it loud to offend us and the neighbours. Grama's record collection, the music we listened to in St. Vincent, was R&B, jazz, calypso and classical—everything available of Maria Callas, Leontyne Price, and Marian Anderson. During his second year here, Paul asked Grama for money to buy a state-of-the-art computer and stereo and was always adding all sorts of gadgets to them so he could download movies and songs.

8

WHEN ANNA ENTERED hospital and I understood the gravity of her illness, I pumped her for information about the years she was separated from us. I tape-recorded her answers so I could share the information with Paul.

She'd landed at Lester B. Pearson International Airport and told the immigration officer that she was here on a visit. The officer — about 25, blond hair closely cropped, bulging ears, a nub of a nose, round rosy cheeks — stared at her with "blazing blue eyes" as he questioned her. But Grama had already prepared her. She was going to stay with Daisy Bullock. Ten years earlier Grama had lent Daisy money to come to Canada. Daisy, who hadn't been keen to repay Grama, had recounted the travails of living in Canada "'without your landed.' Enough to constitute a book." Grama had kept all the letters, bundled with elastic bands. She took them out and went over them with Anna. That evening when I returned to the flat I rifled through the cartons of Grama's papers we'd brought from St. Vincent after her death — two boxes were still in St. Vincent — and found Daisy's letters. The first one read:

August 11, 1977

Dear Ma Kirton,
God name be praised. I take my pen in hand in Jesus name to tell you I done reach Canada, and only by the grace of God they didn't put me back on the plane next day. It don't sound nice to say Ma Kirton but I hope God

can help me figure out a good lie to tell so I can get my landed fast. Ma Kirton you is a good woman, I will never forget your kind favour to me. Well when I reach the airport, Oh Lord what a fright take me, is a good thing I did go to the bathroom as soon as I get off the plane, the officer send me in a room and three people one man and two woman the questions that them three ask me. Where I born, what work I does do, how many children I have, if my mother dead, how much I does work for, if I want to stay in Canada, the questions them ...

Then them went through my luggage piece by piece and search everything in my handbag. Them find I did only have a hundred and five dollars. That was when my skin get hot and sweat pop out of my forehead and flow down my arm, and other places it not polite for mention. Them ask me how I going survive three weeks on a hundred and five dollars. I think fast and I tell them Joan-Louise will house and feed me. I think is God that put that answer in my head. Them did done phone Joan-Louise and ask if I going pay she for stay by she. Is a good thing Joan-Louise did say no. Them ask she too if we is family. Joan-Louise tell them we is cousins. But I didn't know that. Them ask me the same question and I tell them Joan-Louise and me is friends. Then them say to me, only friends, and I say yes, but is possible that we is family too but I don't know. That is what save me, Ma Kirton, else all this time so I would o been back in St. Vincent hiding in my mother house too shame to show my face on the street ...

Letters about not finding work, paying lawyers to help her get her "landed," appeals, and finally paying a man to marry her so she would get her "landed." "She couldn't pay back the money right away—until Mama found out she was sending barrels to her sister regularly. So Mama wrote telling her: 'Daisy, your sister appreciates all the things you send, and begs God to shower you with blessings.' Daisy got the hint and sent back Mama's money in dribs and drabs.

"Mama told me to say I was a housewife and my husband was a church minister. She made me go to the manse and get the letters from the US missionaries that addressed Caleb as pastor of the Georgetown Church of the Elect. She removed all the letters that mentioned that he was in training. Caleb hadn't touched a single thing in the manse.

Then Mama showed me the bankbook for wages she'd secretly been paying me for the years I worked in the store alongside her. I never expected her to pay me. I was surprised. 'Take out as much money as you need.' She made me bring $6,000 in travellers' cheques to Canada. I told the immigration officer I would be in Canada for six weeks to visit the country and to shop.

"It was a different story six weeks later when I asked for refugee status, and said I was fleeing an abusive marriage and a school system in which my son was routinely flogged. The lawyer who filed my claim urged me to say that Caleb had made an attempt on my life and had vowed to kill me if I ever returned to St. Vincent, but I couldn't say that. From St. Vincent your grandmother advised me to start divorcing Caleb. I filed for a divorce.

"While my refugee claim was going through, I worked for Bertram Alexander, aka Bulljow: a Vincentian. He had a contract to clean two ten-storey office buildings at night. His wife, Mariette, a pretty, dark-skinned woman—full eyes, big smile, even white teeth—had heard of my situation through the St. Vincent and Grenadines Association of Montreal, and she got Bulljow to hire me. She died while I was in St. Vincent to bring you all here. I didn't even get to go to her funeral. Bulljow paid me minimum wage for eight hours, even when I worked ten—which was at least once a week—every Friday—and every time Manjak, the other helper, didn't show up.

"Things soured quickly between Daisy and me. Mariette and I searched through rooming house ads. We chose a room in a rooming house on Hutchinson Street: a room with sprinklers, one near to a fire escape. And I could walk to work. There was a shared kitchen and a shared bathroom on each floor.

"A late afternoon, five days after I moved in, I was in the kitchen preparing supper, and this skeleton of a man, with turkey skin, red eyes, and smelling like cat pee mixed with gin, wobbled into the kitchen. He tapped me on the shoulder, winked at me, stretched out his arms to embrace me, and began backing me into a corner. He drawled in my ear: 'How much you gonna charge me for a good time?' I screamed. A woman in a blue bathrobe came running into the kitchen.

'Bo, you scumbag, get lost!" she shouted at him, then spoke to me: 'Honey, don't take it personally. He propositions every woman here.' She turned back to Bo. 'Go to the Main, you. Pervert! Can't you see? She's a decent woman. You need a cheap whore. Pig! Go take a shower and change your clothes. Keep away from her or I'll chop off your balls.'

"Bo slinked out of the kitchen.

"'Luciana,' the woman introduced herself. She was half-Irish, half-Italian, and separated from her husband. She lived on a temporary allowance the court had awarded her while she waited for a lawsuit against her ex-husband to work its way through the courts. She'd got married at 20. Her husband had prevented her from working. They'd had no children. Her husband had insisted he didn't want her to have any. When she turned 48—she was 50 when we met, he became abusive and asked for a divorce. Luciana: a wonderful woman, Jay." Anna took a deep breath. "Jay, I could talk to her. You don't know how important it was to have somebody to talk to. Sometimes we took walks up to the mountain during the day. She drummed into my head that I should qualify for a stable job. She'd made a mistake, she said. 'Never depend on another human being, Anna. Never. Humans are fickle.' A few months later, when the case with her husband was settled, she bought a condo in Pointe-aux-Trembles and began working as a waitress. And our friendship fizzled.

"With Bulljow I worked at a break-neck pace, but other than that, things went well on the job for the first three months. Manjak—he was Barbadian, in his early twenties—came to work late or not at all. He was tall, smooth black, with bright, warm, large brown eyes, and cheeks that dimpled when he smiled. He wore dime-sized rhinestone earrings. Never hurried. Whenever Bulljow pushed him to speed up, he'd suck his teeth and say: 'You fire me and me auntie ain't gon be gi'ing you none o' her sweetness.' He said the chemicals we used were roughing up his fingers and scorching his lungs and seeping through his gloves and poisoning him. He'd heard too that they can cut his nature. 'Is half a day I does soak in a tub to get the smell off muh skin. Is four girls runnin' after me, you know, Miz Anna. Four. Once a' while I samples 'em, but I goes steady with one. She gon be muh wife. I loves her, Miz

Anna. I do. As much as I loves muhself. And I gon be faithful to her after I marry.' His face one huge grin. 'My Ma says she ain't know wha' the girls see in me.' He'd chuckle then. An overgrown, insecure kid, probably still needing to be mothered.

"Bulljow was an elder in the Pentecostal Church, but wanted it kept a secret. Manjak whispered this in my ear and winked at me. The auntie belonged to the church too. We both had a good laugh over it. Bulljow was about five-seven—an inch taller than me—his skin looked like oatmeal. He had coarse, fox-coloured hair, and pinkish eyes. They stared out at you like rats peeping out from their holes. His wide nostrils flared when he was excited and looked like a terrace above what Manjak called his trombone lips. Chest narrow like a pillow case. But you should see his gut: bulging on three sides and heading for his knees—good thing it did—a backside a foot out from the rest of his body. And oh those broomstick legs. I would hear myself thinking as I watched him waddling around: Lord, take this case. I wonder what Manjak's auntie and Mariette find in him? Guess, 'Every piece of fabric in the store got its buyer; every hoe can find a stick in the bush.'

"From the very start Bulljow dropped statements about how it pained him to see so many lost lonely Black women in Montreal, with nary a man to lean on; every which way he looked he saw Black women turning into dead wood, all their sap dried out from lack of love. He'd look at me, expecting a reply. One night when Manjak was absent, he said to me: 'You is a puzzle, you know that? One look at your hands and I know you ain't accustom to no hard work. From your speech I know you is a upper-class woman with good breeding. What you doing here?' He sounded sincere.

"'What about me that you want to know, Bulljow?'

"'Everything. But first, why you in this country?'

"'Because I left my husband and want to make a fresh start.'

"He stared at me, waiting for more. 'Why you left him? He had other women? He used to beat you?'

"Jay, he sounded like those men who expect women to jump when they say so. I said nothing.

"'Well, if any o' those is the reasons, I don't think that they is justification to leave a man. Women is the weaker vessel, and they needs a man to keep them straight and steady. Otherwise they is like a ship without a pilot drifting every-which-way on the ocean o' life. The way I sees it, a man got two duties: to screw his wife and to provide for his family. If he fall down in either department, she got a right to leave him. Now, I know there is men that fulls up women with children and don't look back. I say them kind not fit to walk the earth. How you can turn your back on your own flesh and blood? How you can do that? But a man got to keep his women satisfied and on track. A man don't got to be faithful. Solomon had six hundred wives and six hundred concubines. The Bible say that.'

"Jay, his pink eyes glowed. His figures were wrong, but I wasn't going to correct Deacon Bulljow."

"'That was one hot man, if you ask me, Anna. That Solomon was hot. And the bible say he was the wisest man that ever lived. Still and all, I think he been begging for trouble. 1,200 women to screw! 1,200! I sure he could o' use a little help, and got it unbeknownst to him. I wish I could o' been a fly on the wall to see and hear what went on in that harem. For me, ten's enough. A different one for every day o' the week and a few stand-ins for when you-all indisposed.' He stopped talking and stared hard at me, his eyes flaming. 'I hope you ain't leave your husband 'cause he hit you.' He stared at me even harder, his forehead screwed up. 'Every once in a while, a man—I mean a he-man—got to tap his wife to keep her on track and let her know he is the boss. I say it before, and I say it again: you all women is the weaker vessel and inclined to stray, and it take a slap or two once in a while to get you all back on course. The bible crystal clear 'bout that: men have to rule women. But the bible leave it up to us how to manage you all. Anyway, they "that knoweth the will and doeth it not shall be beaten with many stripes." Besides, the best cure for a nagging wife is a good slap. She will always overlook it if the follow-up is sweet, hot sex. Ask any man, the best sex is right after he beat his wife.'

"I stared into his pink eyes and at the bumps on his forehead and his lumpy skin. 'So you beat your wife!'

"He smiled and his nostrils flared. 'I ain't answering that 'cause in this country that is a dangerous question that can get me in trouble. Here the law let you all wear the pants and put us men in petticoats.'

"I laughed. *Yours will have to be made to order.*

"'You ain't tell me why you leave your husband.'

"'None of your business, Bulljow.'

"'You have children?'

"I gestured two.

"'Who caring for them?'

"'My mother.'

"'What sex they is?'

"'Boys.'

"'You is irresponsible, Anna. And cold-hearted. You go traipsing off after adventure and abandon your children!'

"'Hold it, Bulljow. What you know about me? My mother is taking excellent care of my boys. She's a better parent than me. And it's not like their father turned his back on his children.'

"'But *you* turned your back on them. I'm warning you: if your sons turn out criminals or bullers, you will be the one to blame.'

"I laughed to hide the blow. The gays I knew about had grown up in homes with mothers and fathers—church-going ones at that.

"'That woman psychiatrist: what's her name? Wesling something or the other. We were discussing her ... Never mind. She say that neglected children is the ones that turn to crime and bulling. She is a educated woman, Anna. And if she say so I have to believe her.'

"Jay, for the rest of that night I had trouble doing my work. That talk was during our four o'clock break. I couldn't find the energy to keep up after that. I was still cleaning when the office staff began entering. When I got into my room that morning, I threw myself onto the bed, pushed my face into the mattress, and bawled."

She stopped talking for a long time; resting her lungs, I at first thought, but she began to cry.

"What's the matter, Ma?"

"Nothing. Nothing."

She said nothing more about her early days in Montreal that day, nor the next.

Three days later I prompted her and she resumed.

On one of Manjak's no-show nights, they were on the sixth floor of the second building. They'd already cleaned the top four. She was wearing an old skirt, not the loose jeans she worked in, but she hadn't been able to make it to the Laundromat that week. She was bent over a desk dusting it when she suddenly felt Bulljow's body on hers. He'd sneaked up behind her, lifted her skirt and was clasping her breasts so hard, he was cutting off her breath. He pushed her body against the desk with his huge gut, and was twisting up himself to get his penis, stiff and pulsing, up against her buttocks, his breath, acid stink, hot on her neck.

"'Relax, sweetypie. Anna, honey, relax,' he said in my left ear and nibbled on it. 'I gon go gentle with you. I been saving up a whole heap o' sweet hot loving just for you. I's hungry for you, honey. Hungry! Relax, baby, relax. I's a sugar ant, Anna. And you is sweet. I can't help it. Give it to me, Anna. I don't want to steal it, Anna.' Foolishness like that, Jay.

"First I froze. Then, when he lowered one arm and fumbled with his fly, I managed to turn around and began to pull away from him. When he wouldn't let go of my skirt, I spat in his face. He let me go then. I ran behind a desk near to a window, picked up a paperweight and hurled it at him. Next a stapler. Then I pulled out a desk drawer and dumped the contents onto the desk; but, as I was about to rush him with it, I realized I could use it to break the glass and holler rape into the street below.

"Bulljow was crouched behind the desk where he'd attempted to rape me. 'All right! All Right! Calm down!' he shouted. 'You don' gotta kill me. I only trying to put a lil' sweetness in your bitter life. See? That's the thanks I get. I gives you a job; and now I offers you love, and you refuses it. You ain't even know the ABC of kindness. From now on, I gon keep me tail betwixt me legs, even if I ha' to strap it down. Don' worry; I ain't going bother you no more. You probably have a man in secret anyways. Some fellars do crazy things just for a piece o' pussy, even when it ain't sweet. Yours probably got warts growing in it, anyway.'

"I left the office and headed for the elevator.

"'Aay! Aay! What going on? You can't leave!' He followed me to the elevator. 'I alone can't clean this place before daylight.'

"Jay, I was afraid to go into the elevator, in case he came in too. The stairs were a no-no. 'I finish,' he said. 'So help me God, I won't touch you no more. I been only testing you to see if you going say yes. I swear. I won' bother you no more. As God is my witness.'

"I re-entered the office. I was trembling. I left for home an hour later. I began to sob as soon as I exited the building. The half-kilometre walk felt like 20. In my room I threw myself onto my bed and continued crying. I have never felt so vulnerable. I was too ashamed to tell Luciana.

"Bulljow phoned me around eleven. He apologized and begged me to come back. He didn't know what got into him. I didn't go the next night. But I returned. I needed the money.

"The night I returned, I told him: 'You touch me again and I'll cripple or kill you.'

"'I hear you.'

"He never bothered me after that, but a few weeks later, while we were taking a break—Manjak had cursed him out two nights earlier and left the job—he said to me: 'You's a damn lucky woman, Anna. Damn lucky. You come to Canada at the right time. There been a time when if you didn't have your papers you couldn't work. Least not legally.' He grinned, nostrils flaring, chops curling. 'If now been like then, you wouldn't o' been breaking style on me. You would o' been glad to lemme fuck you so you could keep the job. You just got to understand one thing, Anna. I is a man. I is a hot-blooded man.'

"'And I can be a killer: a cold-blooded killer.' I was sitting about a metre away from him, more afraid of his breath than his lechery.

"He shook his head slowly, with fake pity. 'Here you go, talking 'bout killing, when all I want to give you is pure first-class loving. Age don't slow me down at all. Age don't slow me down one bit. Anna, I wants you to understand this: I can't be alone with a woman without wanting to fuck her.'

"'You love your life?'

"He shook his head and pushed out his lips. 'Anna, sweety-pie, why you breaking so much style on me? Try me. Your body will trill and your soul will sing. Sweety-pie, I got the ship, and you got the port. I got the cannon and you got the fort.'

"'And I got the knife, and you got the throat.'

I laughed. Anna did too and paused to catch her breath.

"Jay, his jaw fell, his eyes widened. I had finally punctured that tyre. I knew I was safe after that.

"At the refugee board hearing, my lawyer, Maître Gupta — a beautiful South Asian woman: silk-smooth black skin, erect posture, fierce brown eyes, shoulders that said: *you can't intimidate me* — fierce, a tigress; she couldn't have been more than thirty. At the hearing she read excerpts of the Vincentian laws authorizing beatings by parents, teachers, and magistrates — Mama had got her solicitor to compile the information and send it to her. Maître Gupta asked the refugee judges, two women: 'Would you want to raise your children in such an environment?' But even she was surprised when the verdict came: 'Claim granted!' 'Honestly, I didn't think you'd get it. It's an argument that's never been successful before,' she later told me. It took two years and three months from the day I applied, and if I include the cost of the divorce, it came up to a lot more than I had. Mama made up the difference.

"I continued working for Bulljow until I got residency status. After that I worked for a cleaning agency three days a week, cleaning homes in Westmount mostly. I followed Luciana's advice and went to night school.

"Grama was excited when she read your letter about going back to school," I said. I spared her Grama's exact words: "About time. Your mother is finally learning sense. Threw her education away to follow stupid religion. You better not get it in your skull that you can get ahead in life without a decent education."

"Mama was pleased and sent me the money to come home to see you all. She was anxious for me to establish a connection with Paul. 'You left when he was two. Now he's four and always asking about you. He's nothing like Jay. Caleb would have found plenty devil to beat out of him.' And so I came home that August."

9

I **REMEMBER HER** visit. Vividly. On her second day back home—she was seated on the loveseat in the living room, I was standing by the window giving onto the street, she asked me about Caleb.

"Ma, you won't like what you hear. He's always drunk. He lives in this isolated, dreary place. Lonely, like you can't imagine. You should see the shack. No paint on it, woodlice eating through the wood, huge holes in the flooring, the galvanize rusty and leaking, sea grape, fat pork, and ping-wing all around, hemming it in, the branches and leaves even poking in the windows when they're open. Just a tiny track through the bushes down to the beach where it is. If I don't part the bushes with my hands, they hit me in the face. And when you look out the seaside window, you see these huge, loud, crashing waves rushing ashore like monsters coming to swallow up the place. When a big one breaks the shack shakes. I've never seen anybody on the beach around there. There's where Daddy lives, sleeping on a coconut-fibre mattress without any sheets. It stinks of pee. I think he wets himself when he's drunk. Know what he has in there? A green plastic lawn chair, a primus stove, two tiny pots, a cup, a peeling knife, a spoon, and a vinyl suitcase with a torn hand grip. Not a single curtain in the windows, no lock on the door.

"And when he's not breaking stones, he's drinking strong rum straight from the bottle. I go to see him every six weeks on average. It hurts to see him, Ma. Depending on when I get there, he might be sitting on the steps outside with the bottle of rum beside him or in his hand, or lying on the mattress with it beside him. First, he looks at me as if he doesn't know me. Then his eyes—they're always red—light up a little, and he grins and says to me: 'You're getting to be a big boy. Can't say your Grama not feeding you all. How's Paul?' Then he'd be silent for a spell. If we're outside, he'd just stare at the grape bushes and ping-wing; sometimes he'd pull a twig, chew on it, and talk to himself like: 'You never bring Paul. Don't want him to see the drunkard, eh? A true man takes care o' his family. I used to tell my congregation that. Your Grama taking good care o' you and Paul? I can see that,' and he'd nod. Then, Ma, his face would get hard and creased up, and he'd say: "Why did I believe God foreordained me?' And he'd laugh, a cackle: a sound to make you shiver. 'Foreordain! Crap like me! Your mother should o' follow your Grama's advice: should o' never marry me. Listen to the crap I'm telling you. Forgetting you're a child.' He'd check himself for a moment but would start again: 'How's your mother doing? You all hear from her often? Tell her I say howdy. She's not a bad woman. I know that now. God knows best.' Then his eyes would focus on me again. 'Come, give the old reprobate a hug. You ashamed of me, Jay?'

"'No, Daddy,' I shake my head and say. 'I'm not ashamed of you.'

"'You little liar! It's all in your eyes. Don't want to hurt my feelings, eh? You're a good son. I love you, Jay. Don't throw me up, son. I didn't have a father. I didn't. He got my mother pregnant and disappeared. Then she died. Then my aunt and uncle who been raising me, they upped and died too: drowned. I always said I will be there for my children. I always said so.' All this time his arm would be still around me, and the smell of the rum and his dirty clothes would be choking me. At this point, Ma, he would make every effort not to cry, but the tears would flood his eyes. The last thing he says to me every visit is: 'Leave a phone message by the shop to say when you're coming. I don't like for you to meet me drunk, and don't ever bring Paul without phoning me first.' But, Ma, I leave a message every time, and I know he gets it. But by the time I get there he forgets. Then, if he's sitting on the step, he'd stumble inside, push his hand into a hole in his mattress, and take a few bills and put forty dollars in my hand and say: 'Now, don't do like your foolish father and spend it on rum.' Ma, sitting on the bus going home, I always feel like if something sucked all the strength out of me, and I tell myself I'm not going back. When Grama asks me how he is, I say all right, and she replies: 'No, he's not alright,' and sometimes she says: 'Without women to guide them, some men lose their way in the world. Your father needs a woman with a firm hand.' Ma, don't tell Grama what I've told you. I don't want her to stop me from going to see him."

Anna patted the seat on her right. I went to sit beside her. She put her right arm around me and pulled me close to her. "We must go see him—you, Paul, and me. Give me the number at the shop. I'll ask him to meet us all in town. If that works out, you, Paul, and I will go out to Georgetown to see him. I don't want Paul to see him drunk." Then she fell silent.

***

She sounded far away when she resumed talking in her hospital bed. "I barely remember anything about my own father. I remember Mama's second marriage. I was eight. The blue dress she wore, Father Henderson in a white soutane and purple surplice, stating the marriage vows; Mama and Bradley repeating them. Afterwards all the people at the house. Mr. Morris was the emcee—twiglike in a grey herring-bone suit, gesturing wildly, with all that energy he has trouble burning off. Mama's girlhood friend Elma, who fed you and Paul lunch when you went to school in town, organized the cooking and serving. And the speeches, all that stuff that goes on at weddings. Seemed like so much fun." She clamped her lips, stared blankly ahead of her, and swallowed.

"Then Bradley moved in with us. He brought a whole set of weights that he kept in one of the cellar rooms. He almost never wore shirts. You could see the ridges of muscle on his dark brown body, especially on his arms, shoulders, and belly: hills and valleys, and his veins like termite tunnels crisscrossing his skin. He and Mama quarrelled all the time. He telling her: 'Not because you married me a pauper, I will let you crow over me. I's still a man and I have my pride.' She telling him: 'And because you're a pauper doesn't mean I have to become one too.

You're too damn lazy! Imagine I have to share-crop the land that Kirton left me! You know the value of bananas and plantain and ginger! You should be cultivating it. Instead all day you're in here lifting weights, and at nights you perfume yourself and out tomcatting—with your jackabats, your war-bins, your sluts. Lifting weights and tomcatting —that's your life. And I have to feed you with my dead husband's assets. You live a sweetman life. You're a gigolo, a parasite!'

"Sometimes Bradley would leave and not come back for two-three days. Once he was gone for a week and returned in the company of Aunt Mercy to beg Mama to take him back." She stopped talking, pouted her lips, and kept them that way for a long while.

***

Sitting on the loveseat beside her that August when she came back to see us, I told her: "Paul's been asking a lot of questions lately about his daddy, and Grama hasn't been answering him. He wants to know if his daddy is overseas like you. I told him I didn't know. He's puzzled, Ma."

I picture myself again standing at the entrance to the kitchen and observing Paul staring at her framed photograph that was on the right-hand corner table in the living room. Next Paul looked at Anna. "You're not my mother." He looked at the photograph again and asked: "You're sure you're my mother?"

"Of course, I'm sure."

"And Grama—is she *your* mother?"

"Of course, she is, and she is your grandmother. That's why you call her Grama."

"Jay, come here. Is she my mother?" He stared sceptically up into my eyes.

"Yes, Paul, she is. I remember when she was nursing you as a baby."

Paul giggled. "She nursed me?"

"Of course, I did."

"If you say so." Then shaking his head slowly, he said: "You're not my mother. Grama is my mother. You're *his* mother." He pointed to me.

"Jay, you can have her. I'll have Grama. Carry Jay back with you when you leave. He likes to boss me around."

"Come, give me a kiss and a hug," Anna told him.

Paul shook his head slowly, smiling. "I don't kiss strangers. I only kiss my Grama. Kiss Jay."

I held Paul's hand and pulled him toward Anna. He struggled to get away. "It's true, Paul. She's our mother. Come kiss her."

Paul shook his head and clamped his lips. "I'll kiss you only if Grama says it's okay."

"It's okay, Paul," Grama called from inside her bedroom.

He kissed Anna, but moved sideways when she tried to hug him. "Why didn't you bring my father?"

"Oh, he might come."

"When?"

"I don't know."

"Does he live across the sea like you? Will he come in a plane like you?"

"No, he won't. But if he comes we'll see him."

"How will he come then?"

"In a bus."

Paul frowned. "Is he going to stay with us?"

"No."

"Does he hit kids?" He stared into her eyes, hard. "William, Joseph, and Henry, their fathers beat them and leave welts on their skins. They are wicked."

"No, your father won't hit you. He will lift you up and hug you, and ask you for a kiss, and you must kiss him."

"Will he hit me if I say no?"

"No, he will not."

"I won't kiss him if I don't like him." He went into our bedroom at this point, then returned with three books. "Can you please read me *Winnie the Pooh*?"

Anna read to him.

"Have you ever seen a bear?"

"Only on television."

"I saw a whole lot of them on television. Teacher Nancy says bears live in cold places. Grama says you live in a country that's cold like the inside of a freezer."

"Bears live in the forest, Paul, and I live in a huge town with lots of houses and plenty cars, and bears are afraid to come into big towns."

"Would you like to hear me count?"

She nodded.

He counted to ten, then said: "Hold up your fingers."

She held them up. He bent two inwards.

"How many fingers do you have now?"

"Six!"

He threw himself on the floor with laughter. "Jay," he shouted, "Ma can't subtract."

"You tell me how many fingers then?"

"Eight. And they are not all called fingers. What are these called?" He closed his fingers and pointed his thumbs upward.

"I've forgotten."

"You're lying."

"Paul," Grama called out. "Watch your tongue."

"You're not telling the truth."

"Okay. Thumbs. When you add your fingers, your thumbs, and your toes, how many do you have?"

"Twenty."

He waved his hand dismissively. "That's a baby question."

***

Staring at the ceiling above her hospital bed, Anna resumed: "I was happy. That trip home made me happy. Happy to see how confident and independent Paul was." She swallowed and took a long pause. "I was surprised to see how grown and mature you were. Your behaviour, your speech, was so adult. Later, when I took psychology at CEGEP, I knew that you'd already decided it was risky to remain a child. And I knew it was because I went away and left you behind." She was silent for close to a minute.

"I see now that Paul had already rejected me.

"After Caleb didn't call I got anxious, and, Jay, you said: 'Ma, we should just go to see him.' He looked haunted. His skin oozed rum. I smelled it every time the breeze blew past him. He looked shorter. His back had slumped, and his knees were bent. Arthritis, I thought. He'd stopped shaving. His scraggly beard and moustache were grey; his hair was a matted mess."

We'd gone on a Thursday. We met him on the beach whacking away at stones; he was barefooted and shirtless, in mud-splashed green trousers rolled up to just below his knees, his face turned to the Atlantic. We were almost beside him before he saw us.

"How's the Christian soldier?" Anna greeted him.

Caleb smiled, hangdog. "You look good." He paused. "Take off your shades. Lemme see you good." He nodded slowly, three times.

"And you should be wearing goggles. I have brought you some." She went to where he stood at the stone-breaking platform and handed him the paper bag with the goggles.

"Thanks." He looked inside the bag and nodded. "Thanks. I appreciate it."

She came back to stand beside me.

Caleb turned away and faced the Atlantic. When he looked at us again, his gaze moved from her to me and back again, and the wrinkles in his forehead were deeper.

The day was cloudless, the sun already overhead. Standing on the black sand stretching down the coast for more than a mile, and with the sky and ocean, silvery and blue, behind him, Caleb looked like a pillar of iron rusting in the salt sea air. Every muscle and bone from his navel up was outlined on his bare torso, sunburnt a deep-brown. There were deep rents in his trousers where his buttocks protruded and exposed his beige drawers.

"I feel shame you meet me looking like this," he said, staring at the ground.

"Well, if you'd phoned back ..."

He walked around a half pile of broken stones and came to where we stood, a metre and a half away from the stone-breaking platform.

He faced me, put an arm on my shoulder, smiled, and said: "Jay, *my* boy." He stared out at the Atlantic and didn't speak for several seconds. "Many is the days I feel like dropping this sledgehammer and jumping in there"—he pointed to a whirlpool about ten metres out in the Atlantic—"and end it all. But I think o' the pain I would cause him." He lifted his eyes to stare at Anna, then looked at me. "So I go on living." He took a deep breath, before repeating: "For you, Jay." His arm lowered and he pulled me to him as he said it.

"I'm glad to hear it," Anna said.

He let go of me, retreated to the platform, and resumed staring out at the ocean.

We were silent for a couple of minutes. With his face turned away, Caleb said: "Jay, remember Samuel? The other evening he ask me 'bout you. It's holiday time now. He's home. Go look him up."

***

I stared hard at Anna propped up with pillows in the bed. "What did you and he talk about that you didn't want me to hear?"

"Raise the head of my bed a little higher."

I did.

She was silent. I asked her again.

"I remember sitting there on a pile of unbroken stones, trying to recall the Georgetown I knew. My eyes roved over the distant coconut palms, the manchineel, the sea almonds, the masses of green and white ping-wing leaves glistening in the sun. A strong breeze was blowing and it whistled through the leaves of the ping-wing. Further up the beach, the fronds of the coconut palms were closing and opening like fans, and the trunks were swaying. The waves crashed heavily at our backs.

"I jumped when he spoke. 'Anna, that boy suffering and is our fault. Anna, I break down after you left me.' I didn't answer. He moved to another pile of stones, almost a metre from me, and sat with his back half-turned to me.

"'When I leave home that night, Anna, I been so ashamed of myself.

I did only need to be by myself for a day or two to find out what made me hit you and how I could stop it. But you left me and I had no home to go back to.'

"Jay, I thought to myself, you hit me because you could. No law, nothing was there to stop you. You hypocrite!

"'Anna, you was my crutch. You kept me from falling down. I find that out when you left me. Without you, without the children, I became nothing.'

"I answered him in my thoughts. *I? Your crutch!* '*Head of the household.*' '*Under my subjection.*' ' *Obey my orders.*' '*Husbands control your wives*'. *I your crutch! Caleb, this must be your idea of a joke.*

"I told him to find a new crutch because I wanted him to stop drinking. I tried not to sound angry. 'If you love Jay so much to want to live, why not go a step further and stop drinking?' I told him I wanted you and Paul to be proud of him. 'Caleb, Paul doesn't know you and, at four and a half, he wants to know his father. But I won't let him meet you looking like this.'

"'*You?* You mean your *mother.*'

"'Both of us, Caleb.'

"He didn't answer. He stared out at the breakers.

"'If you weren't drunk all the time, Mama would let you visit the children.' Jay, I told him to look me in the face and promise me that he would stop drinking."

Her breath was whistling. I tried to stop her then. I felt guilty that I'd asked her to dredge all this up. I glanced at the oxygen gauge. "Raise it to five."

"Sure you want to continue, Ma?"

She nodded.

"Your throat must be dry. Let me get you some apple juice," I said to let her rest her lungs while I was gone.

"Where were we?" she asked after drinking half a glass of juice.

"You told him to promise you that he would stop drinking."

"He answered: 'Well, the rain don't stop falling because you and your mother tell it to.'

"'And if you tell yourself'?' He didn't answer and kept staring out at the Atlantic. 'Get yourself some decent clothes, Caleb. Put some teeth in your mouth. Make friends. Go back to church. Lay off the bottle. Get a wife or girlfriend. Do whatever it takes to stop you from drinking — for the sake of your health, your dignity, and the dignity of your children. Caleb?'

"For a long time we both said nothing.

"'I want Paul to meet you. I'm afraid of what he might tell you, though. He states his opinions freely. Can you clean yourself up and meet us at the bus terminal in Kingstown on Saturday morning around ten? Wear your dentures and stay away from grog beginning today. I can smell it coming through your skin. It will kill you, Caleb.'

"'Can't wear dentures. Nothing to hold them. Need new ones.'

"'Alright. Come without them.'

"'Your mother going be there?'

"'She has to be there, Caleb. Paul will be meeting you for the first time since he was two. To him you and I are strangers.'

"He said nothing. I walked over to him and stretched out my hand. He took it, held it for a moment. 'Look me fully in the eye, Caleb,' I said. 'Saturday morning, around ten?' He nodded. Jay, you won't know how happy that made me. It was the first time we'd spoken to each since I left him."

But that wasn't the end of it. The Friday night he called her. I heard them on the phone with him: Anna telling him: 'Caleb, you are drunk.' The phone ringing a second time and Grama answering it and swearing like a Bay Street whore: "Go drown your fucking self, Caleb! You call yourself a father! They should castrate men like you. I'll castrate you myself if you ever bring your drunk, stinking self onto my premises ... Fuck you too!' The phone slamming and Grama saying to Anna: "Now this jackass upset me. I won't be able to sleep. I wanted to tell you this could happen. That's why I told you not to tell Paul anything. Imagine the shit we'd be in tomorrow morning! Jay can handle it. He's been handling it since birth."

Sitting on the edge of the bed, I placed a hand on Anna's wrist and stared directly into her eyes. "Ma, what did Daddy tell you on the phone that night?"

"'I not coming to no effing town tomorrow. Eff you and eff your mother! What you want from me, eh? Ain't you already divorce me? Who effing you up in Canada? I hear they godless up there. You turn lesbian yet?' That's what your father said to me, his voice a loud slur. And then next morning, I was at the gate talking to Mr. Morris, and Mama called: 'Anna, Your drunk husband is in town, wondering where we are.'"

***

On the Tuesday following, we did meet in town. Caleb wearing new clothes, his beard shaved, his face deeply crevassed but looking less haggard. He seemed wobblier and gaunter than usual. I wondered where he found the strength to break stones. We walked a short distance from the bus terminal to a hotel restaurant—Grama holding Paul's hand, I on Anna's right, Caleb alone behind us, carrying a small black plastic bag. At the restaurant, we joined two tables in the far corner of the deserted patio dining room looking out onto a square. The waitress, a very black, attractive, young woman, her plentiful hair in a hairnet, joked with Paul as she took our orders. He'd been quiet the entire trip, and now wouldn't say what he wanted to drink. The sailor suit he wore, clothing Ma had brought him, was a size too big. He'd refused to wear the cap.

"He likes apple juice," Grama said, looking at him.

He shook his head slowly.

"Well, say what you want?"

He didn't answer.

Caleb ordered nothing. He yawned a couple of times.

The waitress went off with the orders. Paul scrutinized Caleb when he wasn't watching.

The waitress returned and gave Anna and Grama their coffee and me my orange juice.

"Have some of my juice," I told Paul, who was directly opposite me, beside Grama. I pushed the glass toward him. He drank from the straw. After drinking almost half, he pushed the glass back to me. So far we and Caleb had said nothing beyond the hellos at the bus terminal.

"A lovely day," Grama said, looking across at the sun-drenched two-storey buildings that lined the street across from Heritage Square. "How's the building business, Mr. Jackson?"

I tapped on the table in front of Daddy.

"Oh. Talking to me? What did you say?"

"How's the building business?"

"All right."

"Lots of orders?"

"Enough."

Paul got up, headed over to me, and whispered in my ear. I rose and took him to the bathroom.

When we returned, Grama said: "Paul, you've been pestering me with questions about your daddy, and now you're not even speaking to him?"

Paul smiled, turned and buried his head in her bosom.

"Come, Paul," Anna said, taking a tissue from her purse. He went to her on the other side of the table where she was sitting beside me. She wiped the corners of his mouth.

"Paul, ask Daddy the questions you were asking me in the bathroom."

He came to stand beside me and began whispering in my left ear. I pulled my head away. Paul giggled. I looked at him reprovingly. Paul sauntered off to resume his seat beside Grama. Now Paul held his stare when Daddy caught him looking. Finally he smiled at Daddy. He pulled Grama's head toward him and whispered in her ear.

"Sorry, Paul, I ask my own questions."

"Paul," Daddy said, "I bring something for you. You have to come and get it."

"Go," Ma said.

Grama pushed him gently, and waved him on with impatient hand gestures.

"What's it?" Paul asked.

"You'll have to go and see for yourself," Ma said.

He headed toward Caleb, who picked up the paper bag from the floor, and gave it to Paul. Paul removed a small square carton and began turning it over in his hands.

"Open the box," Caleb told him.

"Paul, I think I'm going deaf," Grama said.

Sheepishly Paul said: "Thanks, Daddy."

He had trouble opening the box and handed it to me. It contained a toy jeep with a remote control and the operating batteries. I put the batteries into the jeep and into the remote, and showed him how it worked. He learned quickly and soon had the jeep circling around the table.

He stayed at Caleb's side. He interrupted his game. "Do you have a cold?" He stared into Caleb's eyes.

"No. Why?"

"You smell of limacol. Grama wets my head with it when I have a cold." He picked Caleb's hand up off the table, put it against his cheeks, and opened his eyes wide. He put Caleb's hand back down, looked at his own, then frowned. "Jay, show me your hands." He came to where I was and rubbed my hands. He inspected Anna's and Grama's, then went back to Caleb and took his hands and felt them. "Your hands feel like sand and they are yellow, and feel like … like leather, like rough wood."

"That's because I work hard."

"What do you do?"

"I break stones with a hammer."

Paul stood back and tore his eyes wide. "*You* break *stones*! How?"

"With a hammer."

"You are strong!" He stared, squinting, sceptical, at Caleb's arms.

"Not really."

He picked up Caleb's left hand and sniffed it once, then a second time. "Your hand smells like … like apples when they're spoiling. Jay, come smell Daddy's hands."

Grama intervened. "Okay, Paul, it's alright. Your daddy had a headache this morning and rubbed something on his forehead for it. The smell's still on his hand."

Paul sniffed Caleb's hand again. "What did you rub?"

"Tiger Balm," Anna said.

"Ask Daddy what I told you in the bathroom," Paul said.

"You ask him," I said. "I'm not your carrier pigeon."

"Are you coming to live with us?" Paul asked Caleb.

Anna brought her hand to her forehead. "Paul, are you sure you don't want something to drink?"

He shook his head.

"To eat?"

He nodded. "A cookie."

"Would you like some milk too?" Grama asked.

"Yes, thanks. Daddy, are you coming to live with us?"

Caleb began to fidget. Anna and Grama exchanged anxious looks.

"Not right away, Paul," Grama said. "Your Daddy's work keeps him very busy in the country. Now Paul, it's your turn to offer your father something. Something to eat, maybe? Ask your father what he would like to have."

"Grama, Daddy can't chew. He has no teeth. Daddy, what happened to your teeth?"

"I lost them."

"Is that because you don't brush them? Teacher Nancy says that when we don't brush our teeth they rot, and we get toothache, and it hurts and hurts, and our teeth rot away, and we can't chew our food."

"No. That's not the reason. But I can eat cake. I'll take a cup of coffee and a piece of cake."

While Caleb ate Paul looked at his mouth furtively, then at me, and laughed.

Later, at supper Anna asked Paul if he liked his daddy.

"He's old. Is he Jay's daddy too?"

"Sure. Didn't you hear Jay call him daddy?"

"Maurice says the man he calls daddy is not his daddy."

"Who is Maurice?"

"My friend. Teacher Nancy picks on him because he's a cry-baby."

"Would you like to see your daddy again?"

"Yes, but you and he live so far away."

10

SEEMS LIKE PAUL will be always claiming my time. The year after Anna visited us, Grama sent him, two months before his sixth birthday, and reading even before he was five, to Excelsior Academy, a private school in Kingstown. I, going on twelve, started at Kingstown Secondary that same September. Responsibility for Paul took over my life. I'd wanted to join the drama club, but it would have meant remaining in school after 3 pm and returning sometimes on Saturdays. But at 3 pm, I had to walk to the northern end of Kingstown—Kingstown Secondary was at the southern end—half-way up a steep hill, and along the Leeward Highway bordering the Botanic Gardens, to meet Paul.

Grama made us stay in town. The ten or so secondary-school students from Havre who attended school in Kingstown returned home every day. Another three hundred students from Havre and the surrounding villages attended a newly built secondary school in Esperance, over the hill from Havre. But the teachers at Esperance Secondary weren't university graduates, and the curriculum didn't include foreign languages, literature, physics, and chemistry. Because of Paul's age, Grama felt that the two-way 70 km journey, up and down steep slopes and a potholed road full of hairpin curves, would overtire Paul and diminish his learning. So we boarded with Cousin Alice, Grama's cousin.

Cousin Alice lived in a two-storey house halfway down from Sion Hill. Her kitchen, living room, bathroom, and two bedrooms were on the upper floor. The entire downstairs—the back wall was built into the hill—was divided into five rooms, which she rented out. There was a narrow shed linked to the main structure by a covered walkway. Half of it was the tenants' kitchen and the other half was their bathroom. There was a tap and cement washbasin on one side of the shed where the tenants did their laundry.

Paul nicknamed her Chalice. She was in her late forties. Her father had been a British colonel who'd been posted to St. Vincent to oversee the island's constabulary. His framed photograph, in military attire, hung above the china closet. Her mother, Grama's paternal aunt, had been his housekeeper and mistress. Cousin Alice was their only child. There was no photograph of her mother. Paul asked her why. She told him he was not a magistrate and she'd committed no crime.

Her voice was piercing with a faint lisp. Her skin was off-white—like cooked tripe—and crisscrossed with veins like blue lines on a desert map. She was less than five feet; her stooped back made her chin tilt outwards and upwards and her breasts almost touch her bundle of a belly. Her face was tapered; her bulging grey eyes were at the same level as her flat nose; her lips were two thin lines that looked like a wound when they were rouged. She wore her sparse chestnut hair in a bun at the back of her head; it left her forehead bare and made her seem to be always sniffing. Paul felt she was cross-eyed. I didn't think so. She squinted and always looked at everything and everyone aslant. Her flat bottom made Paul giggle and wonder what she sat on. (His turned out to be just as flat). Once in a quarrel, Tungkance, one of the tenants, called her a mule.

"Why did she call you a mule?" Paul asked.

"She's downstairs. Go ask her yourself."

"I know why," he told me later when we were in their bedroom. "It's because she doesn't have children."

She expected us to be silent when in her house. I complied as much as I could. Paul didn't.

She got home every day around 5:30 and rose at four every morning to attend matins at the Anglican cathedral. She never gave me a key, so, at 3:30, after collecting Paul at school, he and I would go to Elma's Restaurant for a glass of milk and a slice of cake; next we'd go to the library to do our homework or read, timing it so that we'd arrive at Cousin Alice's just after she got home. For the first two years I did the trip to Excelsior at lunchtime too. Along with 20-plus school kids from the country, we ate our lunch at Elma's. Elma put us in an alcove away from the other kids, and Louise her helper always came to ask if we'd had enough to eat.

In addition to the vegetables and the dozen eggs that Grama sent each Monday, she paid Cousin Alice for our room and board, with a little extra "so she won't skimp on the meat and fish she gives you all." On Friday afternoons we travelled back to Havre in Father Henderson's car. On Monday mornings we were packed into the regular bus that carried one and one-half times the passengers it was licensed for, those Paul's age and younger sitting on the laps of adults—the journey: a constant ascent and descent of almost perpendicular hills along the edges of precipices without guardrails, some spots with just enough space for one-way traffic; the sea: sapphire, lace-fringed, lapping against the beige-and-black cliffs 100 or more metres below. That was our routine for six years, except during vacation: two weeks at Christmas, one at Easter, and the months of July and August.

At first I had trouble studying because of Paul's pestering questions. "If you don't shut up, I'll bop you. I have to study."

"And I will tell Grama. You don't have the right to hit me. I will tell her you threatened me."

"Little good it will do you. I'll just bop you again when we're in town, and give you double every time you tell."

"And you'll be sorry, because one day I'll be a king and I'll make my guards cut off your head."

"Yes. The name of your kingdom will be Wonderland, and your courtiers will be rabbits who'll constantly disappear in people's pots."

I never bopped Paul, and the pestering never stopped.

"Jay, did you know?"

"No, I don't know."

"Let me see what you're studying. Oh gases! I want to learn it too. Read it out loud."

"You are driving me crazy."

"Explain what oceanic islands are."

"I have a warning, not an explanation: leave my textbooks alone."

"When will my penis get to be big like yours?"

"Never. For troublesome boys like you it shrivels up and falls off."

"Oh, you're so funny."

Eventually I got Grama to buy us three 1,000-piece jigsaw puzzles. But it only lessened the pestering, and I had to arrange with Grama to free me from chores on weekends so I could get serious schoolwork done. She'd carry Paul to the store on Saturdays and leave him to read in the back or let him sit on a high stool at the front where he could observe the shoppers. Some Saturdays and the occasional Sunday he had practice at the Steelband Hall. On Sundays he was barred from disturbing me. He craved Grama's praise too much to disobey her when he was in Havre. In town the only way I could get him to swallow his cod liver oil pills and the Sanatogen powder mixed into his milk was to threaten to tell Grama. Cousin Alice would observe our breakfast battles, shake her head and say: "Cynthia's princes." She prepared toast, juice, hot milk, and an egg each for us; sometimes instead of toast we got oatmeal; she sat with us long enough to down her cup of cocoa and a slice of bread slathered with guava jam. The jam was a gift from Grama, from guavas that came from her land.

Cousin Alice's boyfriend, Mr. Bolo, was a security guard at the telephone company where she was a secretary. He was tall and bulky —had to bend to enter the main door—with coal-black skin, red lips, yellowish deep-set eyes, and an unsmiling face. Something was wrong with his throat: he was always clearing it. Secretly Paul called him Major Elly. He visited her without fail every Wednesday around 7 pm and stayed for two hours. The first time Paul saw him, he asked her if he was her boyfriend. Her brow wrinkled. "Yes. What else you want to know, you feisty bugger: the colour o' me drawers?"

Paul shook his head, unfazed, his face stamped with a mischievous smile. Later he asked me: "Would she have shown me her drawers for real?"

I saw Mr. Bolo on Monday mornings as well. He collected from me the foodstuff that Grama sent as well as our weekly supply of freshly laundered clothing and took them to Cousin Alice's place during his lunch break.

Cousin Alice's Wednesday supper was special. "Wednesday, dessert day!" Paul would exclaim in her presence, and wink at me. She served sponge cake, always sponge cake bought from a bakery. On Wednesdays she didn't eat supper with us. In a gold, green, or burgundy satin dress, her perfume strong, her line-like lips carmine, her grey eyes glowing, giving her usually sad but now freshly powdered face a younger, happy look—she'd wait for Mr. Bolo to come. She'd put a bottle of rum and two glasses on the sideboard and move about with a feather duster, peering here and there in the living-and-dining room for dust. Paul and I would eat supper quickly and then head to our room, where, when he was older, a giggling Paul would ask me how fast I thought Major Elly was driving into Chalice, and whether she would "get big and have a baby." Once Paul remarked that it was "useless watering her garden. Nothing grows there." I looked at him surprised and asked him what he knew about it.

"Lots. I read, you know; I see what animals do."

He certainly watched all the episodes of "Nature"—not at Cousin Alice's: she kept the TV in her bedroom—and the various programmes of animals in the wild. (Grama taped them for him and allowed him to watch them on Saturday and Sunday at home or in the backroom of the store, but restricted his TV time to two hours.) One time he said he'd want to be a cougar if he were a wild animal. I laughed, noting the obvious contradiction. "You're laughing because you're a toothless dog that can't even bark."

Mr. Bolo was married. His own home was six houses down the slope. One Wednesday his daughter, a girl of around 12, came to Cousin Alice's house to tell him that Mrs. Bolo had collapsed at her gate, and an ambulance had taken her to the hospital. We'd heard the siren and would have been able to see where the ambulance had stopped, but Mr. Bolo and Cousin Alice and Paul and I were in our respective bedrooms. The next day, Tungkance—she was pale like Cousin Alice, freckled, two metres tall, and had melon-size breasts and a "bumptious" bum that rippled when she walked; "that harlot," Cousin Alice called her—came out into the front yard, leaned her back against a white cedar tree there, and hollered up to Cousin Alice: "Adulteress, you hearing me? Adulteress, God wrath will come down on you, sure as the sun rise over Sion Hill and set in the sea. I'm warning you: leave Betsy Bolo husband alone; leave the man alone. His wife sick."

Cousin Alice had just got in from work. She rushed to the front door, closed it, shut the louvres on both sides of it, and closed the curtains. "Listen to that cow!" she said to herself. "Just listen to that harlot! Listen to *her* sermonizing *me!*"

"What does adulteress mean?" Paul asked her.

"Look, boy!" She glared at Paul and stamped the floor.

Paul went to our bedroom, spent a minute, then returned. "I checked it in the dictionary," he told her. "I know why you don't want to tell me."

"Cut it out, Paul!" I glared at him.

Paul quieted, his eyes squeezed small, his forehead wrinkled in protest, his breath raspy.

For several weeks after that Mr. Bolo's visits were never more than half an hour, and I overheard the tenants whispering among themselves that Mrs. Bolo had a brain tumour.

Marcella, Tungkance's daughter, a year older than I, lived in the room with her mother. (Two other children, darker than Marcella, visited Tungkance on occasion; they lived with their father and stepmother.) Marcella had long braids, was honey-coloured, unfreckled, sleek and pretty. She wore lipstick, short tight dresses that were then in fashion, and high heels. She attended Saint Stephens Secondary School: a ramshackle building across the street from the Grenadines Wharf. On occasion another tenant, Melvina, sometimes asked Tungkance what rich white or "mulatto" man she had lined up for Marcella. On evenings when it wasn't raining the tenants sat on plastic chairs in front of their rooms, the lights of Kingstown gleaming below them, and conversed like this. Their laughter and teasing and gossip about the people they cooked and cleaned for would drift up to Paul and me. "She got the right colour," Melvina would say. Tungkance would tell her to lay off her daughter and mind her own business. But Melvina would continue: "When you is young and you is pretty, you is lucky. You don' have to have education when you is pretty and you don' have to sweat in a hot kitchen and take abuse day in and day out, 'cause plenty rich man line up to take care o' you." (This on an evening when Tungkance was fretting with Marcella because she hadn't done her schoolwork: "You want to be servant like me for rich people? Is that you want?") Melvina was soot-black, knock-kneed, and duck-shaped—not exactly in the coterie of women who were taken care of. She had a grown daughter who lived in the country with Melvina's mother.

A Tuesday when Cousin Alice was attending a meeting of the Anglican Women's League and Tungkance and the other women hadn't yet come in from work—they got home between 7:30 and 8 pm after the families they worked for had supped, Marcella and I had arranged to have sex. I was fifteen at the time. I only had time to fondle her breasts because Paul began banging on the door, shouting: "I know what you're doing. Let me in. Let me in. I want to do it too." For days after, Paul would giggle and pester me. His brown eyes flaming, he'd say: "Kuk-Kuk, you did the nasty thing," and giggle. "What's it like? I'll tell Grama. I won't tell if you stop forcing me to drink Sanatogen and take those awful cod-liver-oil pills"—his face all screwed up. "Yuk! Tastes terrible when I burp." My answer was a firm no. He did tell and Grama responded: "Oh, Paul, when will you start writing novels?"

My second Christmas in Montreal Cousin Alice had scribbled in a Christmas card that she and Mr. Bolo were now married and that Marcella was the first runner-up in the Carnival Beauty Pageant that year. But when Cousin Alice attended Grama's funeral, she needed help to get out of the car. Her back was arched into a semi-circle, and she couldn't stand without the support of a walker. Mr. Bolo had died three months earlier from kidney failure. Caring for him, she said, had almost killed her. Marcella, beautiful: trim, svelte body, symmetrical face, seductive smile, perfect teeth, came with her to the funeral and stayed at her side. She's now a civil servant and lives with Cousin Alice: "My hand and foot, Jay. My hand and foot. A blessing, you hear me, Jay—a blessing I don't deserve."

BOOK TWO
REBELLION

PAUL AND I arrived in Montreal in the summer of 1997. For the last week of July and the first three weeks of August, we explored the city: to Parc Jean-Drapeau, where Paul wanted to go on every ride—he plagued me to take him back a second time (it was easier to give Paul what he wanted than to endure his hounding); to Parc-Mont-Royal (it was near enough for us to walk to it: a 30-minute walk at a leisurely pace); to the Botanical Gardens, the Insectarium, and the Biodôme; to the Planetarium. He picked up all the pamphlets and absorbed every scrap of information in them. Grama had given me $300. "You looked after Paul without complaining. I shouldn't have put such a huge burden on you. And you did me proud with your CXC results." By the end of August, I'd spent every cent entertaining Paul and me.

As Labour Day approached, Paul became withdrawn and admitted that he was nervous about going to school. He had to attend French school because of Bill 101, but he'd done French at Excelsior and had a French teacher from Martinique. She'd taken him and his classmates to Martinique four times, one time for six weeks. (The week after he came back he wouldn't shut up about the birds he'd seen there: the Martinique oriole, the blue-headed hummingbird, the ringed kingfisher; in his pedantic way, informing us about their plumage and habits, to the point where I offered to pay him to shut up.) And he'd peruse my French texts and brag that he'd already learned what I was studying, on occasion correcting my pronunciation. Anna had sent us conversational French and Spanish tapes.

The Sunday before school started, he told Grama on the phone that he needed her, that she should come live with us. She replied that in hot St. Vincent her joints creak like rusty hinges. Canada's cold would cripple her.

***

In St. Vincent there was no chance for me to become an amateur actor, and there was none in Montreal. At 17 going on 18, I'd already completed the first year of community college, so I entered CEGEP. Paul was five months short of 12 and had already completed secondary I—always a year ahead of his classmates. Anna didn't want Paul left alone at home. Someone had sketched for her a nightmare scenario of children left unsupervised from three until their parents got home, children who ended up being petty thieves and drug pushers. So, the first two years, I had to leave CEGEP no later than 2 pm to be home for Paul's arrival. There was no time for extra-curricular activities. I fumed quietly. It didn't help that, aside from her regular job at the Jewish General where she often accepted overtime, Anna also worked in another hospital on her days off—until one evening when she came up the stairs out of breath and dropped onto the sofa like a bag of stones. She was on two weeks' vacation then, and had chosen to work at another hospital.

"Ma," Paul asked, "when last you had a day off?"

She couldn't remember.

"Ma, I like Michael Jordan sneakers, but I don't want you like killing yourself so I can wear them."

"It's not that. It's because I want us to have our own house."

"At the rate you're going," I said, "you won't be around to live in it."

"Ma, all you do is work, work, work," Paul said. "Ma, you need a life. Do like Grama. She's cool: she gets together with friends, and they have a good time on a Saturday night. Every bank holiday she'd take us off somewhere and we'd all enjoy ourselves."

After that Anna stopped doing double shifts and worked only occasionally on her days off, but she did nothing to enrich her life. Of course, shift work didn't help.

She forgot Paul's first birthday here. She'd had a night shift. The day before he'd received a money order for $100 from Grama. The morning after, as Paul was heading off to school, he asked her if she hadn't forgotten something. She gave him a puzzled look. Tears welled up in his eyes. "Ma, yesterday was my birthday." When she attempted to hug him, he raised his arms defensively. That evening she gave him a card and $20, and ordered in pizza. But Paul, who was accustomed to having a cake baked specially for him and all the foods he liked — curried goat, oxtail, callaloo ... — on his birthday or the first day he got back to Havre from Kingstown, was not impressed. When he left for school, Anna told me that she had been counting on me to remind her. She hadn't forgotten my birthday a month earlier — a fact Paul unendingly pointed out — but, apart from giving me $30, had been too tired to do anything else.

Now, nine years later, I realize these were crucial mistakes that wounded Paul, mistakes he had no coherent language for. She and Paul didn't know each other, and she didn't know she should have spent those first couple of years forging a bond with him. I see it now: Paul's crying for Grama was his plea for help against the insecurity he'd been thrown into. I recall how Caleb prevented Anna from parenting me as she would have wanted; knocking her down when she tried to rescue me from his brutality — her flight. I should have told her that Paul felt she wasn't meeting his needs and he didn't trust her judgement. That I could have done. But I'd lived for the day when she and I would be reunited. Hurting her feelings wasn't how I wanted our reunion to begin. Yep. That's what it was. She'd left a hole in me the day she walked out on Daddy and left me behind, and I hoped to fill it when I got here. Not that I was fully conscious of this when Paul and I came here in July '97.

In Montreal, Paul fought me all the way. Here nobody knew he was Ma Kirton's Genius and wouldn't have cared. In St. Vincent, his schoolmates and the community lionized him for his brilliance. After he'd won the Vincentian Spelling Bee in the under-nine category and his photograph was splashed on the front page of *The Vincentian*, Haverites began calling him Ma Kirton's Genius. I remember the agony on Geraldine's face as pterodactyl was called. She was from Windsor Academy, Excelsior's rival. They were already into overtime, and a few minutes earlier the adjudicator had allowed the American spelling for plough, and Paul was livid. They'd already aced words like epistle, gnat, knight, knob, and cyst. When Geraldine said "t," Paul became electrified. He'd already read the couple of books on dinosaurs in the Kingstown Public Library. At ten and a half, he placed second on the island-wide high school entrance exam, and again his photograph along with the photographs of the girl who'd beaten him by a single mark and the boy he'd beaten by two marks took up the entire front page of *The Vincentian*. He was a year younger than both of them. *Future Leaders* was the banner on the front page of *The Vincentian*. SVGTV and NBC Radio sent journalists to interview the winners. Grama, Aunt Mercy, Paul and I sat in the living room and watched the TV interview. Tears rolled down Grama's cheeks as she hugged Paul fiercely and told him how proud she was of him. *"Our beginnings do not know their ends."*

In St. Vincent, Paul attended school with the children of the island's wealthiest and most accomplished people. In Montreal, his classmates were the children of tradespeople, petty clerks, janitors, housemaids, factory workers, drug pushers ... and he was shocked by their sparse knowledge and paltry (his word) vocabulary. "They can't sit still and listen for five minutes. They never read. They aren't curious about anything. They listen to vapid music and gab about the stupid TV shows they watch." They called him geek, nerd, wimp, fag. Why else would he spend so much time in the library? He was one of seven of 16 Black students in his secondary II class who did homework (the other six were girls). To the Jamaican students, he was a coconut—brown on the outside, white on the inside—because upon teasing him for the way he spoke, he replied that his vocabulary and grammar didn't come from dancehall music. (Elocution was a part of Excelsior's curriculum.) His schoolmates mocked, mimicked, humiliated, and, on occasion, assaulted him. He turned 12 that November. His Black classmates were mostly 13, 14 and one, Alfred—an unflagging persecutor—was 15. Exotic flora and fauna, ornithology, the customs of the world's peoples were Paul's interests. He loved to watch documentaries about almost anything and share the info with anyone who would listen. The films, videocassettes, and books in the Intercultural Library and the school library were the only things that pleased him about being in Montreal. And he was a news junkie. Every day he read the *Montreal Gazette*, and on weekends he added *La Presse*. Anna balked at the expense. Paul was shocked. (Current affairs was an informal part of Excelsior's curriculum. One Saturday when Grama didn't get *The Vincentian,* he'd come close to tears at the thought that he would be bested when his class teacher questioned them the following Monday about what was in the news.)

That first year in Montreal he came home from school anxious, angry, and sullen every day. The joyful, humorous Paul, who never missed an opportunity to best me, was gone. At the end of September he told me he hated being Black. "They eat, dance, talk nonsense, and harass their teachers. Klunks! Imagine, Jay, this fool telling the science teacher: 'Sah, lemme tell you a liklow secret. If you want we fi l'arn, you ha' fi' beat we.' They talk *loud*. It's hellish when it's raining, because then we stay inside. They plug their ears and yell from one end of the hallway to the other and scream to be heard over one another. Noise! Noise! Jay, it drives me crazy. Then there are these Black and Latino guys that walk around stomping the floor, ropes of gold and silver around their necks, washcloths bulging from their pockets, the crotches of their jeans down to their knees, chains dangling from their hips, like cattle that broke their tether." (Later when I started tutoring at the Côtes des Neiges Black Community Centre, I learned, usually from desperate mothers, that these were children arriving here at age 14, 15, 16, 17 and 18 who were being put in grades 9, 10 and 11 slow-learner classes in which they performed at the grade one and two level. To hide how little they knew they bullied the teachers into ignoring them. Most had long been out of school in the Caribbean and Latin America or had been attending school sporadically while their mothers were undocumented workers in Canada or waiting for their refugee claims to be heard. Most of the youngsters never returned after the initial meeting. Half of those who returned quit the tutorials after two or three weeks.) "Louts. Thorough-going louts"—Paul's voice was almost a hiss. "They eat like hyenas tearing into kill. Only the snarls are missing. Then they lick their dirty fingers and wipe them on their jeans!" He closed his eyes tight and grimaced. "And yelling with their mouths full! You cover your face and hope it doesn't land on your clothes. Half the time you don't know what they're saying because they don't have the language to say it. I can't help it, Jay. They make me feel ashamed I'm Black."

"Explain."

"Listen to this, Jay: 'Smaddy t'ief me t'ing. If I-man ketch 'im is dead him dead for true, 'cause I-man bruck him neck.'

"'Man, how yo' kayliss so! Yo' mek smaddy get in dey n tek it hout an' yo' nuh know!'

"'Ah nuh dat me a talk 'bout.'

"Jay, this at ear-splitting volume in the midst of French class!"

Excelsior Paul. "Watch it, Paul. Daddy breaks stones for a living. Grama owns a store and runs it. True, it made us live well. But there's nothing high-class about it. You'd be speaking like your Caribbean schoolmates if Grama hadn't raised you and you hadn't gone to Excelsior. There's nothing wrong with how your schoolmates speak. It's their language. When I'm with people who speak our dialect I speak it too. Grama does too. You know that. You spent a lot of time in the store with her. Aunt Mercy speaks only dialect, and she and Grama are like sisters."

"Say what you want, I still can't stand them. For your information, Grama didn't let me speak like that, not even to the people in the store."

That was true. On the couple of occasions when I had slipped and spoken to her in dialect, she told me to keep that language for my friends and to speak to her in "standard English."

Paul was no gentler on Black Canadians. Their double negatives amused him. "'That there don't mean nothing.' Why do they talk like that, Jay?"

"I hope you don't try to correct them?"

He shook his head but turned his face away and pulled at his chin, a sure sign he was lying. Now I wonder whether Grama hadn't given him too much latitude. She encouraged him to argue with her and allowed him to say whatever he wanted and to express his feelings candidly, intervening only when she thought he'd crossed the line of politeness—like when Aunt Mercy once told him to give his mouth a rest; and he replied: "My mouth isn't tired. Besides you only spent two years in school; there's a lot you can learn from me."

Grama apologized to Aunt Mercy, took Paul into her bedroom and scolded him. He was around ten at the time. She never had any such issues with me. I spoke to her only when I needed to clarify instructions about some chore she'd given me and to answer her questions—always in the fewest of words. Except for when Paul and I were in town, I found a way to let most of Paul's chatter merge with the breeze in the trees and the surf lapping the shore.

In Montreal, Paul and I shared a bedroom the first couple of years. Anna gave us the bigger bedroom. She'd fitted it with twin beds, leaving just enough space for our tiny desks and a chest of drawers each. "This is our room!" Paul said and pulled in his lips. It was less than half the size of our bedroom in St. Vincent and about a third smaller than our bedroom at Cousin Alice's.

Two months after Paul started school, I would hear him whimpering in his sleep. A mid-November morning around 3, we found him fast asleep trying to open the front door of the apartment. One morning at the beginning of December, as Paul was leaving for school, I asked him if I could borrow an eraser. Paul emptied his backpack to search for it. Something glinted among the books.

"What's under there?"

"Nothing."

"Let me see."

Paul hesitated.

I removed the books and saw a switchblade. Paul instantly put a finger on his lips, and motioned in the direction of Anna's bedroom. "I'll tell you about it later."

"Leave it with me." He gave it to me without protesting. I waited for Paul to tell me why he carried a knife, but he never did. A week later, Paul began wetting his bed. In February Anna took him to see a psychologist. We found out then that the older boys in his class were roughing him up at lunch and recess and constantly threatening to beat him up. One noon, Alfred, a lubber of a fellow, met him coming from the bathroom and slammed him into the wall outside the door three times and told him: "If yo' complain 'pon me, I-man will kick yo' ass every fucking day!"

That morning the class had laughed at Alfred. They'd heard him exclaim: "Gwan from ya! Yo' stink!" and everyone had turned to stare at him sitting in the back.

Alfred told Mme Loubier, their teacher: "*Nick a fait la chose qui fait boum.*" The laughter exploded for real then.

"Man, just tell her I farted," Nick said, causing laughter to resound a third time.

Some of it Paul had brought upon himself. In the first few weeks, he'd laughed at the stupid answers his classmates gave to their teachers' questions (as he'd have done at Excelsior and as I and my classmates would have done at Kingstown Secondary), and he hadn't understood that he shouldn't raise his hand to answer every question. (The secondary II Black girls who did homework and performed diligently spent their recess and a good part of their lunch hour in the library—far from the playground and the corridors—and answered questions in class only when the teachers called upon them to do so. This Paul would aver later, when he came to understand the stratification and socialization process.)

And it wasn't just the Black students who ridiculed him. At the beginning, he'd tried to join an Asian-White group, but they made fun of his teeth. "Man, your fangs are falling out." He had slightly crooked teeth from sucking his thumb until he was three. And they taunted him. First boy: "How many Blacks it takes to screw in a light bulb?" Second boy: "None. It's too damn complicated." Third Boy: "Naw, Paul's the exception. He got it after the hundredth try."

By the end of the fifth week they'd subjected him to one joke too many. "There was this White dude, see. Truck driver. Away on a trip for a couple o' days. Comes back. Goes to screw his wife, and sees she like has this slack hole. So he starts to rough her up to find out which Black dude she'd been fooling around with. She confesses it's the paper boy, and him just 13. She'd been to get the paper, and he saw her in her bathrobe and got this erection like a baseball bat. She fainted, and he fucked her, and now her thing can't close."

"Awesome!" Pi Chang shouted. "Paul, how's *your* baseball bat?"

"Why? You'd like it up your arse?"

"Slug him, Pi! Don't let the bastard get away with it!" Willy, the runt of the group, urged, leaping up and down, his thick spectacles glinting.

Pi grinned, his mouth grey with dental braces.

"Loosen up, man," Richard Hazan ("a two-metre bean pole") said. "You're like so fucking uptight. Be cool, man. Chill! Learn to like take a joke like a man. After that, who knows, we might accept you."

I listened to him and remembered how much Paul admired cougars. The killing instinct was there alright, but none of the discretion.

Thereafter Paul never strayed far from the everything-goes group of Blacks, Greeks, and Hispanics. With his journal open in front of him, he revealed all this to Anna and me in the intervals between the sessions.

After twelve sessions—the last six included Anna and me, the psychologist told Anna that Paul's esteem needs weren't being met. Beyond letting us find out the cause of Paul's distress, the sessions seemed useless. About the only remedy Anna could bring was to take him to a dentist and have him fitted with braces to straighten his teeth.

***

So began Paul's ambivalence for Canada and, indirectly, his hatred for Anna because she had brought him here. "Fathom that," he told her on the anniversary of our arrival. "Just fathom that!"—sounding like Grama—"We left our comfortable home for this." He made a hand-sweep, indicating the apartment. "From our back porch we used to look out over the sea, watch the sunset, the fishing boats, the fishermen pulling in their seines, the plovers diving in and out of the water." Pointing to me. "You and I used to go through Grama's orchard raiding the fruit trees and spend long hours in the sea all year round. Now we live penned up here like prisoners, our clothes reeking of our neighbours' cooking—in a country that's frozen for half the year. Open your eyes, Ma! This is no place for us. Don't take my word for it. Look at the trees. They are grey skeletons that hiss and scream like haunted ghosts all winter long. They tell you *nothing?* Some mornings it's so cold the air is blue. And the people we live among, they're just as cold, colder than the climate. Why are we here, Ma? Can you tell me why we are here? So you can earn a living emptying bedpans? It's a dying, if you ask me." Most likely he was quoting from memory one of his journal entries.

Anna ignored his rant (or so I'd thought). I chalked it up to his flair for melodrama, problems he was having with his classmates, and the traumatic experience the ice storm had been our first winter here, although we were among the few who didn't lose electricity: something about the hi-tension wires serving our area running along the cement walls of the Décarie Expressway, preventing them from snapping under the weight of ice. Even so, it left us in awe of winter's destructive power.

About two weeks after this outburst — Paul and I were standing alone on a Barclay street corner waiting for the 160 bus, I asked him why he'd become so silent at home. He breathed deeply, looked away, and said: "Bro, Ma doesn't have the intelligence to deal with my problems."

"How can you say that, Paul?"

"You're blind when it comes to Ma, Jay. Blind. You know what I mean? Ma can't cope with her own problems. You don't see her lips moving all the time? She's lost, Jay, more lost than we are."

"Paul, you don't know Ma."

"If you say so. She's clueless about what's going down in this society. That I know. She shouldn't be here and neither should we."

The bus came then, and it wasn't a discussion I wanted to engage in, there or at home. Was that a mistake?

***

Shortly after we arrived Anna assigned our chores. Whenever I cooked, Paul was to wash the dishes. Whenever Anna cooked, we were to take turns washing the dishes. It was Paul's duty as well to empty the garbage and to help me with the vacuuming. But Paul turned it into a power game he was determined to win, and it became too exhausting to battle with him. Once, when Anna told him if he didn't do his chores he shouldn't expect to eat, he smirked, sucked his teeth, and told her: "You're responsible for me until I am 18. I don't have to work for my food. You laid this egg, Ma, and you will hatch it. And why should I do chores? Your clay-coloured son"—he stuck his tongue out at me—"will do them anyway to impress you what a wonderful son he is. You prefer him anyway—admit it, Ma—because he's clay-coloured like you. Whose birthday you forget? Not his. Know why? Because I'm dark-skinned like my father, and you dump on me because he used to beat you. See? You can't answer because you know I'm right. The day I turn 18 I'll leave this jail. I would leave now and go back to Grama if I had the money."

What could she say? Initially she argued with him, but eventually she'd grimace and turn her head away. Now I understand: Paul wasn't getting from her the attention he'd gotten from Grama, his Vincentian classmates, his teachers, and those Haverites who'd renamed him Ma Kirton's Genius. Would have been impossible for her, even if she'd understood his needs. Her and Paul's temperament made for an impossible relationship. He needed Grama's authoritative presence and spontaneous warmth. Anna had neither. And because Aunt Mercy practically lived with us, someone was always on hand to give Paul the attention he craved.

The first time Paul told Anna to fuck off, I met her sitting on the sofa, her face tear-stained, singing "There is a balm in Gilead." She recounted what had happened. Paul had ridiculed her attempt to reprimand him for using the expletive. Later Paul gave me the details with relish. "I told her: 'Ma, everybody knows what fucking is. You've certainly fucked, or I wouldn't be here. Sorry, Ma. I'll say fuck whenever it suits how I feel. Cloacal expressions are good for soul. But you won't know what I'm talking about.'" He stared at me and laughed loud. "Know what that means? I'm not afraid of her and I'm not afraid of you. Now turn that into a cigar and use it." He sneered and wiggled his head and shoulders before sauntering off.

I had hoped the incident would be a one-time affair, that when alone Paul would reflect on his behaviour and know it was unpleasant and unnecessary. I even expected him to apologize to Anna the next day. Back in St. Vincent, when he got out of line, Grama sent him into our bedroom alone to reflect on his behaviour and, afterwards, asked him to tell her why his behaviour was unacceptable. Sometimes he gave a reason, sometimes he didn't, but he always apologized. But here no apology came, and one week later, his surliness resurfaced. Anna had reprimanded him for something, and he told her she was a crab that should keep on crawling. She said that in that case, he should stay clear of her claws. He said she couldn't identify claws, never mind own them. I couldn't believe he'd speak to her like that—calm and composed, as if he were the parent and she his child. When I intervened, he told me to shut up, that I was just "a defanged adder heading straight into the jaws of a waiting mongoose."

Thereafter Paul taunted her intermittently. At school he became what he first hated. Up to the end of the second year, he did his school work, but with less diligence, and still kept a playfulness about him, continuing, for instance, the alliterative play we sometimes engaged in since St. Vincent.

Paul: Just listen to my fulminating falcon of a mother.

I: No worse than you, a bellicose, bellowing bull.

Paul: That makes you my bothersome, bestial brother.

I: And you're a tiresome, tyrannical thug.

At which point all three of us broke into laughter.

And he still backslapped me—something he'd started our last year in St. Vincent—and gave me the occasional hug, palm-slap, pound, and high-five: gestures he picked up here. And he'd genuinely inquire how I had done on some paper I'd been working on or some exam I'd been studying for, and was always pleased when the result was very good or excellent. And he'd on occasion share bits of interesting information with me. Like the time he read aloud a passage from *Peoples of Africa*, dealing with the Kpelle practice in which, if the father dies, the oldest son inherits his father's wives, except, of course, the son's mother. "And, Jay, if the father wants to, he has the right to have sex with his

sons' wives or the wives of his brothers. I wonder if they still do that."
But I could see he was conflicted, caught between wanting to strength-
en our bond and severing it.

And the bolts of inexplicable, gratuitous cruelty! "Your mind is a
cornucopia of confusion. Why do I bother talking to you?" Then leaving
Anna and focusing on me: "I would educate you too if you had the
capacity to absorb it."

"I'd like to watch you say that to your classmates, to Alfred, maybe."

"He won't understand what I'm saying."

"How're you so sure I do?"

"I know you don't, and *your* mother—I was adopted—doesn't have
a clue."

"No point arguing with you. You're smart enough to know that
cruelty won't endear you to others."

"And you're not smart at all. You're a parrot. Your sayings come
from Grama. You're like the moon. You shine with borrowed light.
Parrot! I'll get you fake parrot feathers from Dollarama."

"Buy them for yourself. You're the only one here who's flying,
straight to God knows where."

On another occasion, when he'd let fly a few expletives, and Anna
begged him not to use that kind of language around her, he got his
journal, grinned at her, and read:

> *You're thirsty, Ma:*
> *Love parched.*
> *Heaven's your mirage:*
> *The oceans of water*
> *Thirst-crazed travellers,*
> *Already delirious,*
> *See in parched deserts.*

He closed the journal and stared at her with his mouth half-open,
his extended tongue twirling. He knew it annoyed her. "Ma, I need
$10,000."

"Paul, stop your foolishness."

"I'm serious, Ma."

"What for?"

"To bury Jay and you. You're the dead, Ma. Your beliefs stink. Soon you'll be stinking too. I must bury you. $10, 000 will do."

"He's just trying out his bad poetry on us. Ignore the buffoon."

"And you're a silly loon."

"And a good cut-arse will get in tune."

"Try it and you'll be in heaven soon."

Even Anna couldn't help laughing.

12

By 13 **HE** was in full-blown puberty and brought hell to our apartment. Entropy, I suppose. "Your pot never boils over on the neighbour's stove," Aunt Mercy often said. He blasted our ears and the neighbours' with hip-hop music. At home he performed his own rap compositions. He'd read a "toast" called "Dolomite" and tried to shock us with his own takes.

> *I'm Dolomite*
> *Two hundred percent spite*
> *Always ready for a fight*
> *My food is strife*
> *I'll put out your lights*
> *Put you in orbit*
> *Don't gimme no shit*
> *Take this lightning split*
> *Now git, fore I ball my fists*
> *And make you grow tits.*

"If you continue like this you'll soon be inviting us to dine on your offal."

"Offal! Listen to yourself! Shit's the word, man. You're like so fucking corked." Laughing, he grabbed his crotch, rocked his torso from side to side, and turned the scene into a ghetto sidewalk rap session:

> *You've eaten my offal all your life*
> *To make you understand*
> *I need a drum and a fife*

You think you're clever
But you're a river
Where all and sundry
Empty their sewer.

From this point on I began to worry that we'd lost the Paul that came from St. Vincent. His vulgarity made Anna wince, and when he entered his "rap space," she covered her ears or went into her bedroom, closed the doors, and turned up the volume on her television.

The neighbours complained about the noise. Anna pleaded with him to turn it down. She even bought him a set of stereo earphones. To no avail. He'd stomp on the floors and increase the volume whenever the neighbours called. One evening during my first-year university, I found two police officers in our living room when I came home. A Jamaican woman had recently moved into the apartment on our left; she didn't return our hellos. She'd knocked on our door and told Paul to turn down his music. All six speakers of his stereo were stacked on each other right up against the wall of her bedroom. He told her: "Instead o' bitching, come let me give you some loving." She called the police. A month or so after this, Lea Abramovitch, who lived directly under us, called to complain about the noise. He slammed the phone on her. She and Anna were friends of a sort. Just before we came to Montreal Anna had cared for her at the Jewish General and had mentioned that she needed a two-bedroom apartment because her children would be coming in a month, and Ms. Abramovitch had persuaded her brother Saul to let Anna have an apartment without the surcharges he added for people with children. She and Anna exchanged recipes and gave each other gifts of food. Whenever she saw us, she told us to be good boys, to make life easier for Anna, and to study hard so that one day we would make Anna proud. Despite Ms. Abramovitch's pleas, and Paul's apology (he wrote her a letter of apology), Saul ordered us to move. We refused initially, hoping his rage would cool. It was late November, and for two weeks he cut the heat to our apartment, and didn't restore it until Anna agreed to move on January 1.

We moved to Linton, to a bigger, more expensive and, overall, superior flat. The city had just planted trees at the front of the buildings and in the divide to replace, I assumed, those destroyed by the ice storm a year earlier. Our part of Linton is on a gentle slope. At the bottom of the hill, at Victoria, where the street ends, is Coronation School, looking like an ill-placed fortress. The metro and the Van Horne Shopping Centre are a mere two blocks away. Paul could still walk to school. Then the neighbourhood population was visibly Black; some called it Côte des Nègres.

The flat—we're still living in it—is on the first floor and has lots of light. The rooms are bigger too. But the garage is under us, and we hear the cars coming and going and the creaks, bangs, and thuds of the garage door every time it opens and closes. Our turn to live with noise above and below us. From then on we've had our own bedrooms. After we moved in Anna halved Paul's weekly allowance to $10, and Paul has learned—had his head slammed into reality, was how Anna put it—that he can't abuse the neighbours and get away with it.

By then Paul hardly did any schoolwork beyond French, English, and history, but he still read voraciously and watched documentaries. His favourite television stations were PBS, Télé-Québec, TVO and National Geographic. There was always something or other he was hounding me to watch with him.

At school that year, he had a showdown with his biology teacher. A February morning, a little more than a month after we'd been forced to change apartments, I went to buy computer paper at a stationery store in the Côte des Neiges Plaza, just a short distance from where we used to live, and saw Paul—in camo jacket, ochre overalls, the crotch almost at his knees, a blue head-wrap, silver studs in both ears—talking with a group of students in the Harvey's across the street from the shopping plaza. It was 9:27. School started at 8:30.

He ducked when he saw me. His friends—a mix of Blacks, Latin Americans, and Whites, held their breaths, their gaze alternating between Paul and me.

"You're shadowing me or what?" Paul eventually said.

I said nothing.

"I'm too old to need a minder."

I didn't reply.

"Anyways, I have a free period. See"—one hand behind his head, the other kneading his chin. He glanced around at his schoolmates, and I could see he was vacillating between dissing and cooperating. "You don't trust me? Go ask the principal."

"I'm on my way." I beckoned for him to follow. He didn't move. His schoolmates looked on riveted. The joint was silent.

Paul hesitated for a few seconds and then came toward me.

His Black friends steupsed.

"All right, Jay my main man—" he moved his head this way and that, signalling he was compromising, sparing me the showdown his buddies wanted—"lemme come clean with you." He was now outside the door. "I'm skipping first class. You caught me, right. Let's shake hands on it and keep it from Ma. You're one cool dude. Right, my adorable bro?" He jerked his head backwards then faced me with his eyes shut. "Anyhow I'm going to class now. No need to get all hepped up. And you, you'll be late for your class"—one hand rubbing the back of his head, the other busy at his chin: a dead give-away.

"I'm working on a school assignment at home, Paul."

"You don't trust me or what?"

***

He was standing on the sidewalk just outside the school's main entrance when I emerged from the building with a copy of the suspension letter and a photocopy of Paul's *oeuvre* that had caused the suspension. "Jay, Bro, my main man, my cool, cool brother, let's keep this from Ma, okay." He raised his hand in anticipation of sealing the deal with a high five. "You know how she worries about me. Have a heart! You won't want to burden her any more. How can you be so heartless?"

I looked at him, squinting. It was a stinging cold, sunny, windy morning, and my eyes were tearing. "Paul, what happened to the letter the principal sent Ma?"

Paul grinned, stared at the ground, gave me a darting glance, and resumed looking at the ground. "I took it from the mailbox before you guys could get to it."

For a while neither of us spoke.

"Tell you what," Paul said, breaking the silence but continuing to stare at the ground, lifting his eyes occasionally to gauge my reactions. "You'll accompany me the day I'm to be re-admitted, and you'll tell Bégin you're like standing in for Ma. You'll tell him she starts work in a factory at seven and would lose her job if she shows up for work late. You're like my cool brother, right? It's just a little favour, a little favour, man. You know how hard it is for me to like beg anybody for anything."

"Come. Let's go home," I said. "To think how hard Ma tries. Every cent she spares she puts aside for our education. And this is how you thank her?"

"Don't be such a fink, Jay. Be cool, for once at least. Don't tell me you're a *délateur*. A snitch. A snoop. Tell Ma and I'll never forgive you. What happened to our buddy system? Spare me this one time. Jay, I won't do it again. I promise."

He'd been suspended for a week and would be readmitted only if Anna accompanied him to school when the suspension ended. Caught, he told me what had happened, facing me from the far end of the dining table. He'd recorded the entire incident in his journal.

It all began with a verse fantasy he'd composed in which he proposed having sex with Mrs. Bensemana, his biology teacher. He'd circulated it among his classmates and they dared him to send it to her. And he did, by mail, signing it, "your secret admirer." The class waited, even renamed him Meatman. Weeks passed. Mrs. Bensemana said nothing. The principal never came to find out who'd done it. His classmates were disappointed. They baited him. He took the bait and sent her an unsigned note: "Your secret admirer awaits your urgent response."

Two days later, biology being his last class that day, Mrs. Bensemana kept him back when the class ended. Her classroom overlooked the school yard. He saw her looking outside. He peeped too and saw his classmates were bunched up down there, staring up at her window. "Shit! I knew she'd like know she'd hit bullseye.

"'Have a seat, Paul,' she said to me, laughing.

"She sat down on her side of the desk. Her eyes twinkling, she said: 'Is your nickname Dr. Feelgood?'

"'I don't know what you mean.'

"She chuckled. 'Never mind.'

"'Paul Jackson!' She shook her head slowly and sighed. 'Such a bright boy! Such a bright, misguided boy.' She shook her head again slowly and stared hard at me for a few moments before continuing. 'Trying to destroy yourself, Paul? What's the matter with you?' She pulled out the top right drawer of her desk, took a sheet of paper from it, and put it on her desk. It was the poem I'd sent her. She picked it up and read:

> Mrs. Bensemana,
> In a blue mist
> From sexual starvation —
> Let me be your salvation.
> Let me release you
> From the prison of privation.
> Let me unlock your fetters
> Let me feed you meat
> That matters.

> Desire for you
> Is a whorl of briars
> Flaming in me.
> I'll be my own funeral pyre,
> Unless your love, gentle as a lyre,
> A purring river, wash over me
> And quench the flames
> Rampaging in me.

"She guffawed, paused, guffawed again. Then her face turned ugly, a mask. For a while she stared in front of her and said nothing. Then in almost a whisper, she asked: 'Paul, how did you think you could get away with this?' She smoothed the back of her head. 'I'm very happily married. I thought you had been listening to Aretha Franklin's "Dr. Feelgood."'"

"She stopped speaking and gave me another burning stare. 'Here's a bit of advice. Take it for what it's worth: The benighted, the unfortunate, and the desperate—the people your generation calls losers—look for valorization in sex. It's all they have when they have it. *You* are not benighted; *you* are bright and, I hope, not weak.' She continued to stare at me. 'All living things engage in sex. There's nothing elevating or debasing about it. It's a biological function. As a Black adolescent, you won't want to be branded as a stud. I'll speak to Monsieur Gaugin and tell him to let you do a project on the subject. You've heard of Phillip Rushton, haven't you?'

"I shook my head.

"'Find out who he is and what his views are. Now back to your *opus magnum.*'

"'You can't prove I wrote it.' By now I'd stopped trembling.

"'*I can't!*' Her eyes narrowed, a hardness came into her face; she bit her lower lip. 'Paul, I always knew it was you. Which of my other students can write like this? Mrs. Mehta and I had a good laugh over it.' She locked eyes with me. 'Just confess and get it over with. You'll get a lenient punishment.' She lifted her arms and spread her palms like an open book. She kept them like that for at least twenty seconds. 'Your choice.' She shrugged.

"'You're bluffing.'

"'I am?' She pressed the intercom on the wall behind her desk. A couple of minutes later, Bégin entered, bleating like sheep in hot weather, a manila folder in his hand.

"'How're we doing, Mrs. Bensemana?'

"'Not very well, Monsieur Bégin.'

"I visualized Bégin as Paul spoke: raw-red knuckles, which he opens and closes and sometimes cuffs while talking to you; aquamarine eyes with swollen pink-rimmed lids; flaking patches of skin around his lips.

"Bégin removed a sheet of paper, and read from it. 'Dear Mr. Bégin, I found this in my son's school bag.' He held up a copy of my poem. 'X told me that a certain Paul Jackson, a classmate of his, wrote it. His classmates have even renamed him Meatman.'

"Jay, I went cold. Man, that slimy Bégin. We think he's gay."

"'Young man, today Mrs. Bensemana said to me that if you were penitent and prepared to apologize to her in front of the class, the matter would end there—*l'affaire serait terminée là.*'

"I shook my head. Man, there's no *cred* in that. That's a losers' game." Paul grinned. "Your game, Jay. If Bégin wasn't gay I'd have given him a wink."

"'Now, I'll throw the book at you. Have it your way.'

"I cupped my hands and pushed them towards him. 'Go ahead. Throw it.'" Paul stopped talking briefly and stared at me. "Jay, my only regret is that I couldn't make a video of the whole thing."

13

THINGS DID CHANGE between us. "You betrayed me, man. From now on, it's war the whole fucking way. It's over between us. Over! Fini! *Snitch!*" He sliced the air with a hand sweep. "I'm your mortal enemy ... And listen to me carefully: stop fooling with your life. Never you make the mistake of dissing me again in front of my friends, or you'll be dead, man. Dead! You're lucky I didn't tell you to kiss my arse or go fuck yourself, or give you the finger. You snitch!"

I didn't always resent how much of my time Paul took; there were pleasurable moments, like when he shared something he'd written or read me passages from books he was reading. I missed that. About a week before the incident with Mrs. Bensemana, he'd come into my bedroom, handed me a sheet of paper and said: "What you think of this? I just finished it."

> *The Metro*
> *Blue pythons speeding, hissing*
> *Through burrows underground*
> *Blessed to have food come willingly*
> *Cursed to expel it undigested*
> *From the same mouths*
> *Eating and shitting.*
>
> *Keep far from their mating*
> *It's a cataclysmic coming.*

Nodding admiringly, I handed the sheet back to him. "How many poems do you have?"

"At least a hundred."

"You must show me some more." But he never did.

During the next year he called me every insulting epithet that I'd already heard: dolt, dingbat, clotbrain, twit, boho, bozo; a few that I hadn't: foozle, gunk-head; and many I have since forgotten.

And the putdowns! "Paul, will you please turn the music down? I have a headache."

"No, it's a herniated brain. It happens to cretins who think they're Einsteins."

Not long after this Paul began putting weekly maxims outside his bedroom door. On occasion Anna invited work colleagues to the flat. After she rejoined fundamentalism her guests included church members. She argued with Paul to put his maxims up inside his room. He refused, saying they were there to make her think, "if you still think." They left me intrigued and on occasion worried. But I complimented him for those maxims I liked (a mistake I now think):

> Obedience is warm because it lives in a barn.

> Opt for comfort and lose your sight,
> Soon followed by your rights.

> Flee compliance. It's a deadly blight.

> Cultivate your thoughts;
> They're swords of light.

> Honey and traps are never far apart.

By the time he was 14 his behaviour worsened. Luck and his teachers' interventions—Mrs. Bensemana's and Mrs. Mehta's—kept him from ending up at Batshaw. He stopped participating in his classes and had some sort of arrangement with his French, English, and history teachers to hand in his assignments and pick up the corrected work at the office. That year too he read *Walden* and "Civil Disobedience" and met with Mrs. Mehta outside of class hours to discuss Thoreau and Gandhi. At the parent-teachers' meeting that May, she exclaimed to Anna about it, told her that Paul's reading scores put him at the university level, and suggested that he be sent back to St. Vincent to finish high school there. When Anna broached the subject with Paul, he said no; she should have done so the year before.

A Friday afternoon, about ten days after the parent-teacher's meeting, Paul came home sullen. "Nobody talk to me. Say one word to me and I'll kill somebody." He remained in his bedroom all evening. It turned out that three days earlier, he'd gone to see Bégin about setting up a course of independent study. It would have involved broadcasts from the learning channel, various programmes on PBS, and material from my college texts. He told Bégin that the MRE teacher insulted his intelligence and needed a course in logic, grammar, and spelling and that most of his teachers were only slightly better. Bégin had promised to look into his request. That Friday Bégin had given him his answer: "Who do you think you are? The ministry of education sets the curriculum. The gall! You think you know more than your teachers? You will follow the curriculum set by the ministry of education and no other. Now put your tail between your legs, go back to class, and do the work your teachers set for you." Paul looked away from me and took a deep breath. He was sitting on the edge of my bed; I sat at my desk. When Paul faced me again, he said: "You know what, Jay: I'm proud of how I handled myself today. I came close to telling Bégin: 'You know something about tails. They've been going up your arse for a long time.' But I swallowed, took a deep breath, and walked out of his office."

Shortly afterwards we found out that Paul had joined a gang. Then the maxims became sporadic but more caustic:

> *Clap for fucking and flying.*
> *Boo for conformity and crawling.*

Classifications are misleading:
Wasps trump cattle in all my readings.

Try raising cain;
Guaranteed to grow your brain.

Better to carp than be a harp.

Be a knife. Wait coolly to take
Your user's life.

I appeal to the living:
Let's bury the dead
And kill the half living.

The Easter weekend that year, he had one of his periodic outbursts, and I told him: "When you get to know your inner self, it will disgust you. You want us mortals to be God? First become God and show us the way. You'd better start ignoring what's wrong with others and focus on *finding and mending* the cracks in your own psyche."

"The cracks in *my* psyche, huh! Focus on *your* own cracks? Wanna know an open secret? You're a faggot." Smirking, teeth clenched, torso rocking. "You take it up the arse, Jay Jackson. You and Jonathan are lovers."

"In this day and age, there's nothing wrong with Jonathan, me — or you — being gay."

"Leave me out of it. I knew it! I knew it!" He smiled broadly, open-mouthed. He shouted to Anna in her bedroom. "Ma, there's vermin in the house. *Call* the exterminator." He bristled with excitement.

"Paul, stop it!" Anna shouted to him from inside her bedroom.

"But, Ma, he's a vector for disease."

"Oh, my sick little brother," I said, shaking my head. By now Anna was standing at her bedroom door.

"*Little brother!* Your sense of duty's killing you, man. I'm *not* your little brother. You're duller than cardboard. Jonathan will soon ditch you, and nobody else will want you. *Little brother.* You never cared that much for me anyway. You only wanted to impress Grama, and now Ma. Fuck your sense of duty, man! Go get yourself a fat plantain."

All three of us were silent for about 30 seconds. Even Paul seemed shocked. Then he said, his tone a trifle apologetic: "Do you ever get angry? What will it take to get you angry?" He came to stand within 30 cm of me.

Anna came into the dinette. I stared at her and shook my head.

"Do I have to like punch you to get something human out of you? Know what: your face looks like a gorilla's butt." He chuckled.

"Why don't you come let me like teach you how to toke? You'll understand that life—my life, your life, Ma's life—is a huge joke, and we would laugh at all the human ants scurrying everywhere, pulled by invisible strings. Man, don't I understand what Thoreau meant. 'Most men lead lives of quiet desperation.'"

"Well, Thoreau's no longer around, so he can't say what lives know-it-all punks lead, or advise them that hurling filth at others is no way to get attention."

"Why do I like bother talking to you? Why do I like cast my pearls before swine?"

"Right. Just wear them and shut your mouth."

He balled his fists and shook them. "You drivel on and on about what you don't know. At least that dunderhead"—he indicated Anna with a toss of his chin—"keeps her drivel to herself. Talk like a man! That or go let them chop off your cock. That way you'd be my sister for real. Voice like a violin in F. Like fucking cleats on my soul."

"Your soul! Where do you hide it?"

"You're *so* pathetic! No wonder those professors have you on a leash. Breaking you in for the plough. Your classmates party night and day and get better grades than you. Education's a con game, man. Sucker! Sucker-r!" He whistled and snapped his fingers. "Hey, Rover. Rover how ya doing? Praise, Rover? Okay. No fucking sleep before 4 am." He snapped his fingers again. "Read them books, boy." He laughed, and then, his tone slightly serious: "Know what you make me think of, man? That seal on the West Coast that they like released from captivity, and no matter how far away they carried it, it kept coming back to the aquarium they'd kept it in. Rats, too, man; you and Ma. Rats that come back to their cages and re-imprison themselves for pellets." He paused to catch his now wheezing breath.

He turned to stare at Anna. "Can't live without handcuffs, eh? Look at you! Had to go back to your superstitions. Now, if you'd gone there to find a man." He laughed. "What a foolish woman" — he shook his head slowly — "you belong to a religion that believed you were born to be white people's slave!" A monstrous smirk deforming his face, his voice clanking. "Know what I call you in my journal? Felicity Foil, devotee of Serena Joy."

Grinning, he looked from Anna to me, then walked to the coat closet, put on his windbreaker, and slammed the door as he left.

A week later, around 2 pm, I was sitting at the dining table desperately trying to finish a paper I was late handing in. Anna, dressed for work, came out of her bedroom and was putting her coat on when Paul, who was stretched out on the sofa said: "Ma, I'm going to spend this summer with Grama. You can afford to pay my plane fare."

"I know what I can afford, and your plane fare is not included," she told him, then walked to the phone on a side table, dialled Grama's number, and told her, in Paul's presence, not to send Paul any money for him to travel to St. Vincent. He got up with a sprint, glared at her, then went to the kitchen counter and began hurling the dishes from the drain board at her, aiming them to miss, the pieces of crockery clattering and scattering over the wooden floor.

"For God's sake, stop! Enough! Leave! Go for a walk! Calm down!" I told him, frightened, worried that he'd gone insane.

"And if I don't leave?"

I said nothing.

"You'll throw me out, right?" He gave a feral, high-pitched laugh. "And I'll pop your faggoty ass like a dry twig." He balled his fists and gestured the popping; his eyes became small and piercing, his body odour rank. "One of these days you all will drive me so mad, I'll show up here with a Uzi and blow your asses to smithereens."

We were too shocked to respond.

Seconds later he left the apartment.

14

ANNA RETURNED TO fundamentalist religion a week after Paul turned 14. Twice I had heard her wondering out loud whether Paul's "unruliness" was God's way of chastising her for leaving the Church of the Elect. "Once you're of the elect, you must return to the fold," she later told me with conviction. Her conversion had come suddenly. One of the nurses she worked with, a half-Chinese Jamaican woman called Princessa Chung, had something to do it. Anna had taken us to a party at her house—somewhere on the West Island—Kirkland probably—during our second year here. It took us two hours to get there; to a house stuffed with dollar-store figurines, doilies, and plaster and plastic plaques with inscriptions that read: GOD IS THE HEAD OF THIS HOUSE and THE FAMILY THAT PRAYS TOGETHER STAYS TOGETHER. There were three sofas in the living room, three unmatched armchairs, cabinets, several unmatched lamps, and plastic plants and plastic flowers in vases scattered all over the living-and-dining room. "She's tired of shift work and amassing stuff to start a junk business," Paul said. Thereafter he referred to her as Madam-Junk-Ma's-Friend, eventually shortening it to Madam J. She'd set up a sound system on her quite spacious lawn at the back of her house. It blasted the neighbours' ears well past 11 pm, causing Paul to quip: "They also bray." The house was crammed with residents too: sisters with their children, nieces and nephews from Jamaica going to university—enough to constitute a town—explaining, no doubt, the three sofas in the living room.

Anna joined Madam J's church following months of tribulations with Paul. Things had begun to go seriously wrong in July. On a dare, he'd tried to steal a gold chain from a jeweller in the Côte des Neiges Plaza. By the beginning of September Anna had made four trips to get him out of police custody. His gang vandalized bus shelters, spray-painted graffiti on people's homes and fences and in the metro and on buses—*throwing up, bombing,* they called it—and gathered in Van Horne Park to smoke grass. One morning in August, around 2 am, the police caught him putting graffiti on one of the doors to the Plamondon metro station. He carried no ID, and told them his name was Don Giovanni. They took him to the police station. He suffered an asthma attack while they were administering the "workover," and had to be rushed to the emergency at St. Mary's. Two evenings later—Anna was at work—I caught him smoking pot in his bedroom. He grinned and handed me the joint. "It will unplug you."

I shook my head.

"See? You're corked, man. Corked *en hostie!* Just don't rupture; they'll have to evacuate the whole goddamn neighbourhood." He guffawed and slapped the bed with his free hand.

"Focus on who's seeing you and your boys rolling and passing around joints in Van Horne Park," I told him.

***

Of course there were times too when he was helpful. That Christmas, Ma worked, and Paul actually offered to help with the cooking. He creamed the butter, broke the eggs and threw them into the mixer followed by the various ingredients for the pound cake I was making. It would have been simpler if I had done it myself—I had to interrupt what I was doing to get each ingredient for him—but I was happy that we were doing something together, instead of fighting. And he'd vacuumed the entire apartment without my asking him. On Christmas evening he greeted Ma when she arrived at the door around 7:30 and told her to sit at the table and let him serve her. She had just completed a twelve-hour shift.

Three days into the New Year, I entered the apartment in the middle of a dispute he and Anna were having in time to hear him say: "Ma, you're too old to remember some things, and I'm too young to know some things. And some things I won't learn. Because other people are dumb and obedient doesn't mean I have to be dumb and obedient too." He grinned at her, that grin with his tongue half-extended that exasperates her, then added: "Treat me like an equal and you'll be surprised the things I'll teach you." She swallowed, looked at her fingers, which she was opening and closing, then went into her bedroom.

If that was a window, it closed, and the abusive language, one-upmanship, and swagger returned. Once after that, almost a year later, he offered to make tea for us. From the gleam in his eyes and his hands kneading his chin and caressing the back of his head, I sensed that something wasn't right. I opened the teapot and saw two stainless steel balls in it. I lowered my head and sniffed. Marijuana. Paul's fingers went to his lips. I removed the balls, gave them to Paul, rinsed the pot, and put teabags in.

***

On baring her bosom to Madam J, Anna found out that Paul was a pusher at the English secondary school some distance from where we lived. One of Madam J's nieces attended the school. She'd remembered Paul from the party and had relayed the information to her aunt. "That boy, Anna, that boy going kill you unless the Lord make 'im see the herror of him ways."

The very next day, a Saturday, someone phoned the house three times and hung up each time I picked up the receiver. When the phone rang a fourth time, I screamed at Paul to pick it up. Paul was trembling. I picked up the handset and yelled: "Answer the damn phone, Paul." The caller spoke then. "Tell Meatman I book him for heaven the minute he step outside. I warn him one time too much to keep fucking clear of my turf."

Next day Anna went to Madam J's church and announced on her return home that she had "re-entered the fold." She began praying at meal times, asking God to intervene in all sorts of ways. Grama used to say about the women in Havre who got beaten by the men in their lives—most were—"they should do like your mother: chuck the good-for-nothings, and chuck the damn religion they say authorizes them to." She never needed to say that she'd set the example for Anna.

Grama had a long journal entry about a woman called Lena, whose partner, Henry—they'd been living together for 12 years—was about to leave her to marry someone in England. Lena gave him something to drink, most likely a neurotoxin, that left him a zombie. Grama disapproved of her going to get potions from the obeah man, but wrote: "I would have burned the passport and the plane ticket and put the ashes in the envelope, and written on it: 'BON VOYAGE, HENRY.'"

When Anna announced the news of her 'conversion,' I asked her if she'd fled Caleb's fists only to go looking for them again in funda-mentalist religion.

She replied: "When your travels take you to dangerous places, you're wise to return to safe ones."

"Safe?"

"Yes, better the devil you know ... Anyway a plane can't stay up in the air forever."

"So you're only refuelling?"

"No. I'm 'safe in the arms of Jesus—safe on his gentle breast. There, by his love o'ershadowed, sweetly my soul shall rest.'"

Thereafter I knew I'd simply have to accommodate her religiosity.

Not so Paul. The threat of execution having receded, his truculence returned. When Anna confronted him about his drug involvement, he turned it into humour.

"I want a straight answer from you," she insisted.

"I can give you a gay one." He grinned and changed the subject. "So, Ma, you've 're-entered the fold.' Doesn't that make you sheep? Lemme see if I can get my head around this. *You* are saved from *sin!* Get real, Ma. You don't need to be saved from sin. You *need* to *sin.*"

"We are in the last days," she said. "The Bible predicted all this. Disobedient children. All this tribulation. We're definitely in the last days."

"Then pack in all the living you can." He scrutinized her, an ironic smile playing over his face, his tongue twirling slowly in his half-open mouth. "Come clean with us, Ma. Fess up. You joined that church hoping to find a husband. Admit it, Ma. Admit it."

"Don't talk to me like that!"

"Oh, Ma, come off it."

"You're disrespectful!"

"Disrespectful! Which planet you live on, Ma? I have a classmate my age, 14, who'll soon be a father. You know, Ma, there's this girl, buddy o' mine. Her mother, Ma, went back to Jamaica for three weeks and — holy Moses — brought back a man. You should like let her coach you, Ma."

Anna went into her bedroom and closed the door.

The next day she let out to us that God's way was the only way, that God had charged her with the responsibility of saving our souls. "Especially yours, Paul. The blood of Christ can root out all that's causing havoc in you."

"So what's your religion called?" Paul asked.

She didn't answer.

"My mother has a new incarnation." He giggled. "Anna Kirton, BDMD? Aka Felicity Foil, lifelong member, chief benefactor, of the Serena Joy Sorority."

"What are you talking about?" I asked.

"BDMD? bedevilled by delusions of mass deception."

"And the Serena Joy Sorority?"

"For that, you'll have to pay me. It will cost you. Fifty bucks, Bro. I'm tired of educating you for free."

But he was more interested in taunting Anna. "Really now, Ma. Why all this foolishness?"

"'The fool says in his heart there is no God.'"

"And the wise woman parrots all she hears and dimly understands. Which god did you have in mind?"

"There's only one: the true and living one. You better stop your blasphemy. You think God is asleep, but he isn't. If you keep this up, God himself will deal with you. It's clear in the bible: 'Honour thy father and thy mother that thy days may be long in the land which the Lord thy God giveth thee.'"

"Yes, Mrs. Cohen, or is it Mrs. Stein? You parrot! That's a Jewish statement. What sort of land God ever gave to us descendants of slaves? Africa that should be ours is controlled by Europeans. Look at your church sisters. Most of them are cleaning White people's dirt, and you're just a cut above." He said nothing for a while. Then resumed. "So you want honour. You want *me* to honour *you*. What have you done to deserve it? And you want *me* to honour the *nincompoop* in St. Vincent. Hold your breath, Ma."

He stared at me. "Boy it's a good thing this isn't 1978 or she'd have had us at Jonestown drinking Jim Jones Kool-Aid." He stopped talking and gave me a mischievous grin. "You'd have downed it without a peep." Returning to Anna, he continued: "You believe that everything in the bible is there because God put it there. Right?"

She said nothing.

"Answer me, Ma. I'm serious. You believe God is just and ethical. Right?"

"Yes. God is certainly that. You got that right."

"I *did*. Hold on a *minute*." He got up, went into her bedroom, and returned flipping the pages of her bible. He sat at the dining table. "Here it is." He began to quote: "'Ye shall not eat of anything that dieth of itself. Thou shalt give it to the stranger that is in thy gates that he may eat it, or thou mayest sell it unto an alien.' Ma, this according to your belief, this is God advising his chosen people to sell diseased meat to strangers."

"Paul! You've gone too far. You made that up."

He rolled his eyes and tossed his head and looked up at the ceiling. He tapped the floor with both feet. When he looked at her again, he said: "Ma, here's your bible. Read it for yourself: Deuteronomy 14:21." He walked to the sofa where she was sitting, his thumb marking the spot, and handed her the bible.

"It can't mean that," she said after reading it. "It can't. I know it can't. I will ask Pastor Billings about it. It can't mean that."

Paul giggled and gave a loud handclap. "You're intoxicated, Ma. You've been dining on diseased meat for a long time, since you were 13, I once heard Grama say; so long you no longer smell it. There's a lot more in Deuteronomy. I could go on and on, but what difference would it make?" He shrugged his shoulders and for a few seconds stared hard at her with the corners of his mouth pulled down. "Imagine! Of all the mothers on this earth, I have to have *this one!*" He gave a drawn-out sigh. "There are thousands of gods in this world, Ma. Thousands! A shyster named Constantine, a Roman emperor, imposed Christianity on the entire Roman Empire just as Islam is imposed in some countries today, and killed all who resisted. The Europeans who captured Africans and Native Americans forced Christianity on them, but it doesn't mean that they killed off all the other gods in the world. In any event, Ma, god is only what powerful people say god is. They create god and heaven so they can enslave and rob people here and tell them they'll be paid after death. And people are so damn stupid, they swallow that shit. Even First Nations: people stripped of their land, language, and culture and beaten and buggered in Christian residential schools they were forced to attend—even they swallow that shit. Practise your foolishness if you want to; eat all the diseased meat you want to, Ma, but don't try to feed me any. Do your dining at the Serena Joy Sorority. Don't bring it home. Consider yourself warned."

Around 4 pm, Anna went down to the laundry room, and I confronted Paul.

"So Ma is BDMD. And you are what?"

"Paul Jackson, PP."

I scowled.

"Perennially Persecuted."

You must mean pampered and paranoid. "The gall! How about Loki?"

"What?"

"Loki. L-o-k-i."

"Explain."

I shook my head. "You already know everything. And *my* name?"

"Jay Jackson, MMDD: McGill's Most Docile Donkey." He laughed and punched the air with both fists. "Man, when those professors finish with you, all you'll be good for is to sweep the fucking floor."

I took a deep breath. "Paul, why are you so cruel to Ma? People join religions for all sorts of reasons. People, even the educated and powerful, are always looking for safe spaces, places where they feel at peace. If Ma's beliefs make her happy and don't meddle with our lives, we should just let her be. It's pretty clear she finds something in her church that enriches her life."

"And what might that be?"

"Ask her. She'd be glad you asked—if you can do it without insulting her."

A flicker of remorse showed in his drawn face and bowed head. "Jay, you must know that the Islamic-Judaeo-Christian god is the deadliest piece of poetry humans ever invented. Those guys leading congregations—whatever they call themselves—are conmen or fools." He sighed. "I want to be proud of Ma, the way I'm proud of Grama ... In a way I'm proud of her—how she speaks, especially at parent-teacher meetings. Then I'm always proud of her. Most of my classmates' mothers never go to parent-teacher meetings. Just as well. The teachers won't understand what they're saying. At least Grama had some influence. And sometimes Ma says things that tell me she has a brain. I know she came here, went back to school, got a profession and all that. But sometimes I think all she did at CEGEP was memorize and regurgitate what the teachers said. Haven't you noticed that she never reads? Not even the newspapers lying around. It was the first thing that struck me about her when I came here. There wasn't a single newspaper in the house and the only books were her CEGEP textbooks. After Grama, it's hard to take her, even now. Grama wanted to know about all the new ideas shaping the world and sent away for books she heard discussed on the BBC, and she read them all, some she gave to the Havre library. I'm not telling you anything you don't know. I used to hear you both reading and discussing. Sometimes I joined in. To come to a mother who never reads, who's always parroting foolishness—Jay it's tough. Tough."

"She's ashamed of you too, ashamed of your behaviour."

Frowning, he mulled over that for a while. "Jay," he said with a serious look, his gaze averted, "I wonder if Ma knows that the bible, the so-called word of God that *can't be wrong*, advises parents to stone their disobedient children to death?"

"That can't be true, Paul."

"Oh yeah. Deuteronomy chapter 22: 18-21. Go read it for yourself. Know how I know this? I heard about this group in the US that's called Christian Reconstructionists. They want to set up a Christian theocracy in Washington based on Deuteronomy and Leviticus. Jay, they believe that poverty is a punishment from God, that governments should not help the poor, that African nations are underdeveloped because they worship demons, and that developed nations should stop giving them aid. They plan to bring back slavery and to stone adulterers, homosexuals, and disobedient children to death." He stopped talking, his face stricken. "Don't take my word for it. Go google Christian Reconstructionists. And you better start working on Ma. You better rescue her from their clutches."

I was stunned. I knew Paul wasn't making this up. Sincere Paul and posturing Paul were distinctly different creatures.

"Jay, you remember when that preacher tried to upbraid Grama for not sending us to church and Sunday school?"

"Which one?"

"Bob Bowles, the Baptist preacher. He told Grama she was raising us without a Christian foundation—"

"—and without the fear of God."

> *Mrs. Kirton, at the urging of the Holy Spirit, I have come to pull you and your grandsons back from the precipice of damnation. You are raising these boys to be godless.*
>
> *Mr. Bowles—her hands on her hips, her head wagging slowly like a boxer about to slug her opponent—on the authority of my understanding, you are a pompous jackass. I don't want my grandsons to fear your god—or you. I want them to be kind, honest, just, and charitable. Your god drowns an entire planet, burns the disobedient eternally in pits of fire, tortures people to win a wager. I am training my grandsons to have minds of their own, Mr. Bowles. I don't tell them what beliefs they can or cannot hold. And now, if you don't mind, please leave my premises.*

She didn't usually state her views so publicly. In fact she'd warned us not to tell anyone what her beliefs were. Paul had asked her why, and she'd said: "My customers will stop coming to the shop and I will become poor and won't have money to pay your school fees."

We fell into a long silence. "Jay," Paul said, breaking it, "you mustn't encourage Ma in her religious foolishness. You know better. You can influence her. I was leafing through your book *Philosophical Essays*. I read Bertrand Russell's essay on why he's not a Christian, and I agree with his reasons, and Grama would too."

"Paul, Ma's beliefs make her happy. If they're nonsense, it's harmless nonsense." But even as I said it, I remembered Nietzsche's point that it's only fools and children who can be happy. And Brother Vanderbilt. He'd come from The States to conduct a revival and was staying at the manse and had given me a chocolate bar for quoting: "Unless ye become as little children, ye cannot enter into the kingdom of heaven." *Quite the parrot! They clap on the manacles early.* "It's alright, Paul. It's alright, if Ma harms no one. But I'll talk to her about Christian Reconstructionism."

***

I never did. Yes, there's something childish, bizarre even, about plunging into fountains of blood to be "redeemed," and dropping out of high school and dressing up in white waiting for Christ to come. I listen to her rattling breath. Yet it was she who'd ended my fear of going to hell. I did read Deuteronomy and Leviticus and I checked out the information Paul mentioned about Christian Reconstructionism. It's quite possible my father's church holds some or all of these beliefs. I remember hearing Caleb say the earth was created about 6,000 years ago.

***

Hardly a week later Paul burst into my bedroom one Saturday morning. "What a fool!"

"Who?"

"Ma. Who else. What a fool!"

I leaped from my desk chair and my fingers were around his throat.

"Go on, choke me."

A triumphant smile framed his face, and I became aware of what I was doing. My hands fell. I felt ashamed. "Sorry. Sorry. It's just that I've had enough—enough of your insolence. So what are you accusing Ma of now?"

"Why should I tell you? For all I know, you won't choke me afterwards, you'll kill me."

"Get on with it or get out of my room."

"She gives her pastor $370 per month."

"Come on?"

Paul nodded and pulled a sheet of paper from his shirt pocket. "See for yourself."

The sheet listed Anna's income and expenses, and there it was: "tithe: $370."

"Can you believe this? Can you?"

I remembered my father's harangues to his congregation: "For every dollar you earn, ten cents belong to Lord."

That Saturday a new caption went up on Paul's door:

PRIESTS ARE TOOLS OF THE WEALTHY
WHO EXTORT THE POOR.

The following Thursday evening, Anna was in the living room watching television, when Paul burst out of his room, breathless, his eyes glowing with mischief. "Ma," he said, "today I almost rushed home to congratulate you."

She frowned. "Congratulate *me?* Why?" She was seated on the sofa. The news was on. He stood half a metre in front of her, blocking the TV.

"You see, Ma, this school friend o' mine, Bertrand. His mother, she drags him to church with her every Sunday like you want to do to us. A deacon in Bertrand's church caught the pastor balling away at a middle-aged, brown-skin sister in the church basement. 'Oh that must be Ma,' I said. 'Finally she's getting something for all those tithes she's paying.' Then Bertrand told me the woman was from Guyana. Oh, Ma, I was *so* disappointed."

Anna exhaled loud, turned off the TV, and went into her bedroom.

I felt uncomfortable. Paul had entered taboo territory. "Why're you so obsessed with Ma's sexuality?"

"'Cause, I'm concerned about her health." One hand pulled at his chin, the other caressed the back of his neck. "'Cause sex is important. We need it. It's why you and Ma are so uptight. You two aren't like getting any."

"So you've changed your mind about Jonathan and me?"

"Who says I have? That's not sex. That's perversion." He gave a self-congratulatory chuckle and his eyes glowed.

I wondered where he got *his* sex, remembered his letter to Mrs. Bensemana, and was tempted to say that I'd seen a lot of used tissues in his wastepaper basket. Instead I went into my bedroom and hoped Paul wouldn't follow. He didn't.

The next day I was the target. Paul was lumbering around annoyingly, his torso bare, his hairy chest puffed out, his feet stomping the floor. "A brakeless bulldozer, is that's what you are?" I said.

"You're just jealous because I'm too wide and deep for your measure."

"Inflated: yes. Deep?" I shook my head. "Stay away from sharp objects."

"That's just jealousy talking. I'd be a champion sumo wrestler if I were Japanese."

"You're missing a few ifs."

"Can't help it: I'm the alpha male in here." He grinned, his arm raised, fingers wiggling.

"Just don't stake it out with pee."

"We, the powerful"—he pounded his chest—"that's not how *we* do it. If you were a real historian you'd know that we kill the males—in some cultures we eat them too—take their lands, and put their wives and daughters in our harems."

"Yeah. After your soldiers raped them. Be careful: the only woman in this house is your mother."

He clenched his teeth and closed his eyes for a few seconds. "You sicko! I'll let that one pass. What can I say? The weak have always been food for the strong. Antelopes exist to feed lions."

"And the poor?"

"Fodder for the rich." He stretched out his hand. "Hand it over, Bro. Your money and your freedom."

"Useless. In a year or less Nine Lives will take you out. Poor Grama. All that effort only to create a Minotaur."

"Cockadoodle do! See what the British have in their coat of arms? *The lion and the spear.* See what the American emblem is? *The eagle. Predators,* man ... they rule the world. It's no contest, Bro. No contest." His head moved slowly from left to right; his eyes twinkled. "Nature's law, man." He grinned. "You're the wimp here, see? I'm the nobleman, see? You're the serf. I am strong, you are weak. Do like animals in the wild. Flee. Yield your territory and your ... You don't have any women, just pathetic Jonathan." He parted his arms, gesturing: *Are you going to?*

"Some nobleman who wants his brother to be his serf."

"What am I supposed to do? You have the character of a serf." His grin got broader. "Besides I can use a valet. And you'll look lovely in livery."

"Now *I'll* give *you* a bit of advice: start learning to forgive."

"In the jungle! *Forgive!*" He wrinkled his nose.

"Then go live in the jungle. Walk on all fours. Get a prehensile tail. Leap from tree to tree. All that hate spilling out of you, it's the price you're paying for refusing to be a decent human being."

The phone rang for Paul.

While he talked on the phone, I thought of my intro to poli-sci prof, Professor Johnson, whose Ichabod-Crane nose reached out from his face like a gar's spike, his eyes gleaming electric blue, his fist-sized Adam's apple working away as he thundered: "As you've heard me say over and over again" — and some of the students would chorus along: "Power and property are synonymous. Slice it how you can, dice it how you will, in Western democracies the rich ensure that only governments who'll protect their wealth get elected. And if that protection means hordes of homeless, starving people, so be it. And they expect government to put in place the propaganda apparatus to convince the homeless and starving that their plight is the consequence of their incompetence. Two hundred years ago, they'd have said it was ordained by God." Once he'd left out the last sentence, and Jonathan, his arm raised, said: "Sir, you left out part: *Two hundred years ago, they'd have said it was ordained by God.* The next time he declaimed it, he looked at Jonathan. "Did I leave out anything?" The class laughed.

Paul ended his call and began to rap:

> *The strong kick ass, get*
> *to the head o' the class.*
> *Good guys come last.*
> *George Bush say:*
> *'Fuck with the U.S. of A,*
> *Won't get the chance*
> *to eat hay.*
> *We drop daisy cutters*
> *on your sorry ass,*
> *every which way.'*
> *Forgive your enemies,*
> *they take you for a sop,*
> *turn you into pop;*
> *put you in a blender*
> *and drink you like soursop.*

He pushed his left hand under his braids and caressed the back of his neck; with his right he kneaded his chin. He winked at me.

> *I'd kick your ass,*
> *if I thought you'd pass;*
> *show you the ropes,*
> *but you'll hang yourself*
> *when you can't cope.*
> *Man, you get more stupid,*
> *I'll be raking leaves*
> *and be left bereaved.*

He stopped, stared at me, and laughed.

"If we were Daddy you'd be raking skin."

"You admit it! Out finally!" He snorted. "Always wanted to beat me. Know why? 'Cause I kept the spotlight off you. It's a fact and you can't say boo." He wriggled his body and bared his teeth. "One time you even wanted to drown me. Don't look so shocked. When I was little you used to say that a mermaid will come and get me because she wanted a husband for her daughter. Always wanted me out of the way. One time I dreamed that you were strangling me. My antenna picked that up."

"In that case, I would have been protecting my territory, following your logic. Do us all a favour: go sit on the toilet bowl."

"*Historian!* You wish. Poor Clio, exhausted, trying to find space in your corn-grain brain. Go vent your anger on nature, man."

> *She's got you sealed,*
> *sealed, man, in a tiny tin can.*
> *Tin-man, Tin-man.*
> *Pa pa pam pam.*
> *Slam you to the macadam.*

He slapped his thighs to create a rhythm.

"I'll tell you what's eating you, man: You ain't never gonna be bright like me. Never. That's the acid, man: the acid that's eating you from inside out. He stuck his tongue out at me.

"'*You ain't never gonna be* ...'?" I chuckled.

"*You,* correcting *my* grammar! What do we know? Smoke is oxygen. Shit is food."

"For some creatures shit *is* food."

"You're one of them: a shit-eating blat."

"You throw so much of it around, I can't help ingesting some. And, speaking of oxygen, you hog ninety percent of what's in here."

"So? Asphyxiate. The world would be a cleaner place. That or let me launch you into space." He made a forward thrust with his right fist.

I laughed.

"You hen! Go ahead. Cackle. Lay. You and your rooster were out yesterday." He gave an exaggerated wink and stayed silent for a few seconds, then smiled. "Dear Bro"—he swallowed, licked his lower lip, and half-closed his eyes—"no need upsetting yourself. It's bulling alright." He tossed his locks and continued grinning with his eyes still closed. *"Perverti en hostie.* But it cools the rocks." He winked. "I better stop ripping or you'll start bawling."

15

A SUNDAY, A few months later, a day before Anna's birthday, she came in from church around 5 pm. I had cooked—a leg of lamb; oxtail with eggplant, okra, and spinach; and red beans and rice flavoured with coconut milk, recipes I'd take from a West Indian cookbook. Because of Anna's shiftwork, it was one of the rare Sundays when all three of us sat down to have a meal together. She seemed genuinely happy and had a good appetite.

"Now if only we could have family devotions together," she said. "'The family that prays together stays together.'"

"Yeah, that's written on one of Madam J's plaques. And families that *fly* together?"

I chuckled and tried to get Anna's attention.

"What are you talking about?"

"Nothing that you'll understand, Ma."

"Cut the sarcasm. Will you?"

An eerie silence settled around the dining table. Paul broke it. "Your religion should come with a warning: guaranteed to cause brain shrinkage. You know, Ma, Jay helped me see that your life is a desert, that your soul craves all this superstition." He turned to me, grinned —food in his mouth—his knife and fork in mid-air, pointed at me. "Lasso Jay. Take him, tied and suited—tied especially—out to the Olympic Stadium and have your pastor dunk him, and drag him to church with you every Sunday. And when you find out he's gay, you and your pastor can take him to the Old Port and stone him. And if the police try to stop you, tell them you're obeying God and quote them

Deuteronomy chapter 21 verses 18-21." He winked at me, then looked at Anna. "But leave *me* out of it. I have a life—and a working brain."

"And you should thank the creator for them."

I gritted my teeth and held his breath until Paul said: "Thank the creator! You must be joking. Ma, he dozed off while mixing my formula. I don't want to *thank* him. I wish he existed. I'd sue him—for malpractice." He winked at me. I turned my head away.

"I'm sick to my soul of your blasphemy. It's everywhere. Everywhere. You even post it on the door of the apartment that *I* pay rent for." Her chest heaved. She bowed her head and kept it bowed for a few seconds.

Paul chuckled and winked at me

She got up from the table brusquely, and headed to her bedroom, leaving half of the food on her plate.

"Now the waterworks begin." Paul waved his arms over the table, then suspended his open palms above it. "See, she came back home spilling foolishness and spoiled what might have been a perfect Sunday dinner. I long for the peace of my grandmother's home." He was the only one that finished his meal that Sunday.

The next day when Anna got in from work, she called me into her bedroom. "Look at this. Jay, look at what Paul left on my bed for my birthday." She was holding a coffee-table-size book.

I peered at the title and tried not to laugh. *The Kama Sutra.*

"How will I handle this, Jay?"

I couldn't answer right away. I was holding in my laughter. "By ignoring it," I managed to say, my eyes moist from trying not laugh. "I guess if you were Grama, you'd be thanking him for expanding your education." This time the laughter came, for a moment uncontrollably. "But you won't be able to pull that off, so ignore it. Pretend, you don't care. That would rile him."

Her ears were purple. "Should I say anything to him, Jay?"

"Yes, thank him for the book. Tell him you'll read it when you find time. He'll be on tenterhooks waiting for your angry reaction. And he'll be *so* disappointed."

She nodded, but I could see her hesitation, the sort of in-my-house-you-will-do-as-I-say instinct trying to censor all that I'd said. In the end she never raised the issue with Paul.

I suspect that what happened two weeks later, a Saturday when she was off and we were all home, had something to do with the attention he didn't get from giving her the *Kama Sutra*. It was around 10 am. Anna came to sit on the sofa in the living room and called to Paul to come and sit beside her, saying there was something she wanted to discuss with him. He was at the kitchen sink rinsing a glass, his back turned to her. "I'm not deaf. Tell me what you want to tell me." His back remained turned to her. "Oh, I see." He was laughing. "It's that book you were reading earlier this week, *Bringing the Black Boy to Manhood,* or some such thing. Your pastor ordered you to read it, or what? It's too late for any of that now." Facing me and indicating Anna with an out-turned thumb, he continued: "Looks like she wants to overdose me with affection." Returning to look at Anna, he said: "Is that what it instructed you to do, Ma? Too late for that. You'll blow my emotional fuse. Might even wreck your own. Then again you probably just want to hug ..." He checked himself.

If I had been near Paul I would have slapped him.

Paul chuckled. "Get real, Ma. You can't bribe me with phoney affection. You abandoned me to Grama when I was two. But, go on. Say what you have to say. You like pay the rent and buy the food, so I have to put up with you."

Anna stayed silent.

"I am listening, Ma."

She didn't speak.

"Oh man. What a life! This life! My life! Get on with it, Ma."

Anna said nothing.

"Guess I'm incomprehensible. Unknowable. Dark matter, Ma. Dark matter." He chuckled.

A long silence followed.

"You want to like tell me I'm a pile o' shit. Right, Ma? So what? Say it. I can take it. I'll even agree with you, but with a difference: *you're* the cause. And if you weren't, nature would be. My genes are probably configured for me to become a sociopath. In that case get ready to visit me in jail or to bury me."

Stop it! I wanted to shout. This was new.

Anna's eyes bulged.

Paul taunted on, definitely enjoying himself. "Did you know, Ma, that geneticists now know that we have many of the same genes as insects, bacteria, and even plants; that without them in the first place, there'd be no humans? So, you see Ma—never mind what your bible tells you—we humans run the gamut, from hi-tech to poo. More poo than hi-tech, if you ask me. But you can't *flush* me; and, alive, I'm not compostable. Your religion hasn't taken power yet, so you can't have me stoned to death for heresy or disobedience. So, until I reach legal age, you're just going to have to put up with me. Even if you hand me over to Batshaw, you'll still have to· pay for my room and board and bring me home on weekends. This Paul is shit but that Paul will be poison. You're like trapped, Ma. Get a grip. There's no disposing of me."

A long pause followed. Paul's face became one huge smile, and one hand played with his chin while the other caressed the back of his neck. I relaxed a little, understood that he was posturing.

Paul resumed calmly. "You should have read that book a long time ago—others too—before you came here even, before you had me. That way you'd have known you weren't fit to be a mother."

"You got part of that right. I should have listened to your grandmother and never have you."

I couldn't believe she'd say that.

"*The information I needed.* Thanks." Paul snorted. "You should have. I HATE MY LIFE AND I HATE YOU." He stamped the floor, followed by a spate of noisy breathing. "Finally! The answer I've been looking for. I suspected it the moment I came here. You should have aborted me. My asthma is psychosomatic. Because you rejected me in the womb. Good thing you unloaded me onto Grama. At least I had nine years of decent parenting." He nodded slowly. "*We* should parent you." He stared at me, his face twisted by an ugly grin.

"Shut up!" I said. "Shut up! Now! I won't even ask you to apologize to Ma. Boy, how I look forward to the day you turn 18. But Batshaw will take you off our hands before then, if Nine Lives doesn't pop you off first." I went to sit beside Anna and put my arm around her. She was rigid.

Paul walked to the main door and picked up his keys. "Hey, Blowhard." He rubbed his hands gleefully and stared at me. "I finally got a sizzle out of you. Just when I was preparing to zap you, I find out you're not dead after all." He winked.

I closed my eyes. "Leave. Peace. Give us some peace." I held up my free arm, open-palm: pleading.

Paul stuck his tongue out at me then left.

An hour later he came back and came straight into my room. I was at my desk. Anna had gone back to bed.

"Not again." I swivelled around, palms open, to face him. "Cut me some slack. Please. What are you: some torturing demon?"

He came forward, got on his knees and gave me bear hug. "Do you hate me?"

"Yes. Now leave. You're haunted." I tried to undo his arms.

"First say you don't hate me."

"Paul, I don't hate you."

"Not like *that*. Say it with *meaning*. With *feeling*."

"Paul, get to hell out of my room!"

He let go of me but didn't move. "That's no way to treat your younger brother. I'll forgive you if you give me a real hug."

"Come," I said, shaking my head. I put an arm around Paul and felt a spasm go through his body. He was sobbing. "What is it, Paul? What's wrong with you?" I dropped my arm.

Paul swallowed and wiped his eyes on his sleeve. "Everything sucks. Everything." He swallowed again, trying to suppress his sobbing. "Everybody hates me." He paused. "I don't want to talk about it." He sat on the side of the bed, silent for about 15 seconds. "I wish we could be like the times at Cousin Alice ... There was no Ma, just the two of us."

I didn't respond. Paul got up, punched me affectionately in the shoulder, and left.

He returned two minutes later, holding open one of my texts — *From Columbus to Castro* — and sat on the edge of the bed.

"Tell me something, Jay."

"Tell you what?"

"Why do you keep defending Ma's religion? It teaches that you and Jonathan will roast in hell forever?"

"What will we roast for, Paul?"

"For being gay! What else?"

"And you, what will *you* roast for?"

"I'm already burnt black. And that's no hyperbole."

"How?"

"If you open your eyes you'll see for yourself." After a few seconds he added: "I don't want to talk about it."

"In that case, keep it to yourself and stop bothering me. I'm trying to recover from your cruelty. You should go and apologize to Ma."

He didn't answer. He moved further onto the bed, propped himself into a sitting position with pillows, and began reading. About 20 minutes later he called to me.

"What, Paul?"

"Will you come to my funeral?"

I swivelled around to face him. "Yes, if you give me ample notice."

"Okay. Any day now. Better off dead than be a sociopath. Right?"

"Not that again. Please."

We were silent for a long while. "Want to hear something?" His eyes stared directly into mine. "People are like houses: houses with plenty rooms." He stopped talking.

"So?"

"Some rooms they don't mind showing to everybody. Some they let a few people into. Some they let nobody into."

"So?"

"If you let me into your secret rooms, I'll let you into mine."

"I don't have any."

Paul sucked his teeth and turned his head away. "Jay, I can't stand it when you're a hypocrite. You know I'm sincere." He snorted, struck the bed with the book. "A waste of time. Why am I wasting my time? Why?" He jumped out the bed and left shaking his head.

All that afternoon and for a long time that evening, I agonized over whether Paul was serious about suicide or was just trying out a new way to get attention. That sociopathic reference bothered me. Around ten, I walked to his bedroom door, prepared to talk to him, but then changed my mind.

Next day, I was relieved when, just as Anna was about to leave for church, Paul went up to her and asked: "Have you forgiven me, Ma?"

She turned her head away and opened and closed her fingers reflexively.

"Ma, I'm your screwed up kid. Give me a hug and forgive me."

He moved toward her, and she embraced him. I heard the gulp in her throat. When she released him, she reached into her purse for tissue and began to dab her eyes.

His contrition didn't outlast the day. Anna returned from church around five. Behind her Madam J waddled in on quarter-moon legs, the floor beneath her groaning, her torso looking like a giant egg; in tow one of her bevy of nieces. Anna hadn't told us she was having company—she wouldn't have wanted Paul to know, would have hoped he'd be out. Paul's eyes brightened. I had already witnessed two confrontations between him and Madam J. One on a Saturday when she'd come to help Anna dress to attend a wedding in her church:

"So you're the woman that's filling Ma's head with foolishness," Paul said.

"Boy, how you so out-o'-place and bull-buck so? Me is a grown woman. Me is not your age-mate. If me didn't know Sister Kirton, me wouldo' think you didn't get no broughtupcy."

Paul giggled. He was leaning against the kitchen counter. He drummed it several times, each beat faster than the one before.

"You mekking fun o' me or what? You better praise God you not under my roof." She made a butting gesture. "I would o' blister your backside morning, noon, and night."

Paul clapped.

Anna came out of the bathroom and pulled her into the bedroom.

On a subsequent visit it was she who goaded Paul. "Boy, you is Lucifer ownself? What wrong with you? Why you giving Sister Kirton so much botheration? Why you make evil hollowing you out like wood-lice inna dead wood? Boy, Jesus bring the dead back to life. With him all things is possible."

I held my breath and only let it out when Paul left the dinette, went into his bedroom, and closed the door.

Today, when we were all seated at table, Anna asked me to say the grace.

"I'll say it," Paul said.

Anna's eyes narrowed and her shoulders straightened.

"We're grateful to the earth and the sun and to workers everywhere for the food we're about to eat, and to Ma who paid for it and prepared it."

"So who make the sun and the earth and give the workers health and strength?" Madam J asked.

"That's your area of expertise," Paul said, putting a scoop of potato salad onto his plate. He sniffed at the salad and said: "Ma, how's it Jay's a better cook than you?"

Anna didn't answer. She was putting food onto Madam J's plate.

Madam J's gaze bored into Paul, her flat nose weighed down by thick, egg-shaped lenses. Her nut-brown complexion and thick lips —now glossed rust to match her auburn wig—were the only African traits visible. "Say praise God, I is not your mother."

"So," Paul said, reciprocating her stare, "are you president of the Serena Joy Sorority?"

Anita (late twenties, short, herself heavyset, very African looking), sitting on her aunt's left, tried to stifle her laugh, choked, and headed off to the bathroom.

Madam J clasped her hands and shook them violently, one foot pawed the floor. She lowered her hands to her lap, picked up her napkin, and began to wring it.

Paul clicked his tongue, his lips slightly apart, his eyes opened at their widest. "Jay, look! Look, Jay. She wants to wring my neck."

"You is damn right. Left to me, boy, I would slap you into next week and back to last year."

Paul dropped his knife and fork and clapped. He winked at me.

When Anita resumed her seat, Paul turned to her. "I call Ma Felicity Foil. What do you call her?" He indicated Madam J with an out-turned thumb.

Anita smiled nervously and focused on her plate.

"I'm calling a truce, okay," he said, his arms crossed in an X, his fingers splayed. "Would be a shame if we didn't show some appreciation for all the time Ma spent cooking this food."

After we'd eaten, and Anna and Madam J had settled into the living room to listen to gospel music, Paul joined Anita and me washing the dishes. "So you like *The Handmaid's Tale*," Anita said to him. We learned that she'd interrupted a teaching career in Jamaica to pursue an MA in English at Concordia and would resume her job as soon as she finished: the following April. She and Paul talked on about *The Handmaid's Tale*. "You think Atwood's book is frightening?" she told us, after peering into the living to make sure her aunt wasn't listening. "Think again. There's a group that believes God is preparing to set up a government in Washington based on the laws of Leviticus."

"Yeah, I know," Paul said.

When Madam J and Anita were leaving, Paul, his cheeks pulled back in a big grin, opened his arms to hug Madam J. Her face registered shock and she braced herself against the sliver of wall beside the coat closet.

"What kind o' unforgiving Christian is you, Sister?" his arms still open to embrace her.

"Listen, you force-ripe man." She wagged a finger in his face. "You listen to me. Stop 'busing poor Sister Kirton and me will forgive you." She winked at Anna and Anita.

Paul's grin broadened. He nodded. They embraced. "I think we can be friends as long as I protect my neck. You're kind o' cooler than I thought. Now you're Madam Cool. Know something: I *love* to go head to head with you. It's fun. Not like him." He pointed to me. "Wimps out on me all the time. No fun in that."

On Thursday of that week, Paul rapped on my door, opened it, and stood in the doorway frowning, his body hunched forward. Anna was at work.

After a long silence, I said: "So?"

Paul turned his head sideways and asked, almost inaudibly: "Bro, if I plant you, will you grow?"

The expression was from our Vincentian childhood. It seemed out of place here. "No, I'll wither. What sort of trouble you're in now?"

"Seriously, Jay. Seriously. Like I'm trying to turn a new leaf. You understand?"

Really!

"I need your help, but you mustn't let Ma in on it." His frown lines were deep; his eyes small, piercing; his stare intense, terrifying.

"No promises. Talk. I'll make up my mind after."

"I need $200."

"What for?"

"I can't tell you right now."

"Well, then I can't lend you."

"You prefer to see me get hurt?" He glanced at me and nodded slowly.

"Paul, this isn't some prank of yours?"

He shook his head slowly, fear in his bulging eyes.

"This has to do with drugs, right?"

Paul breathed deeply. His eyes were downcast when he faced me again. "I'm trying, Jay. I'm trying. I have debts to settle before I can turn the page. Okay, here's the straight goods: Nine-Lives, my supplier, refused to pay the goons who protect me; said I didn't advise him ahead of time that I was quitting, and this was leaving a hole in his overhead, since I won't be bringing in any income. Jay, I have $250 and I need $200 more to pay them off. They're snarling and getting ready to pounce."

For a while I said nothing. I'd known it could come to this; worse even. Two months earlier the son of one of Anna's co-workers was gunned down on the corner of Plamondon and Victoria. *Known to police. A settling of accounts.* "And if they shake you down again?" I tried to look into his eyes, but Paul's head was lowered.

"They'll be too paranoid to. This is like one crazy business, you hear: *Fou en hostie!* Easy to get into; once in they do everything to keep you in. Nine-Lives is like in a knot that I won't like keep my trap shut. Worrying, I guess, that he'll like have to take me out. Of course, they'll do it if I like rat on them; their insiders will tell them and they'll have no choice. They don't like the killing part; costs them too much to get the investigations bungled. But right now the goons need their *fric*, and I don't like want a broken arm or a bullet in my shin. They've given me till noon tomorrow." He was silent for a few seconds. "I'll be alright afterwards, Jay. I'm sure I'll be. I'm sure. You know how determined I am once I set my mind to something. After that Nine-Lives will like send out feelers to get me to change my mind. I won't. I promise you, I won't. I know I won't. For Grama's sake, I won't. If I like continue as I'm going, don't you see that one day she'll read terrible things in the papers about me, or hear about it on radio or TV? I'll run away if I have to. I can't continue like this, Jay. I can't. You can't imagine the nightmares I'm having. I'm ashamed of myself, Jay. If I don't change I'll kill myself before they kill me."

For a while I said nothing, and was flooded with sadness as I remembered the little amber-eyed bundle Anna brought back from the hospital, the little boy I'd been responsible for in some way since his birth. So much promise, so much pain, so much disappointment. I wiped my eyes, got up from my desk, and went to get the money for Paul.

When I returned and handed him the money, I told him: "Don't disappoint Grama, don't disappoint Ma—whatever you think about Ma, she loves you—and don't disappoint yourself." Paul hugged me; we embraced tightly for almost a minute. "I'm counting on you. Paul, I'm counting on you."

16

PAUL, WHERE are you? You haven't relapsed ...

I get up, stand over Anna, clasp her cold, limp hand. Ma, you're dying. Leaving us for good this time. I'm only twenty-six. Paul's not yet twenty-one. You are only fifty. Why, Ma, why? I release her hand, swallow to hold back the tears, and resume my seat.

***

There were other moments when Paul reached out, but they left us more perplexed than reassured. I remember one holiday Monday in particular. I was standing in the doorway to my bedroom. Paul held a notebook and stood with his back leaning against the dining table and stared at Anna on the sofa. "I don't want to hurt your feelings, Ma." He bit his lip and hung his head. "Jay, help me make Ma understand why her beliefs are wrong."

"And how am I supposed to do that?"

He donned his mischievous grin: the one with his tongue half-extended. "By being candid."

"Candid about what?"

"Everything, Jay. *Every single thing.*" He closed his eyes tightly.

"Wow!"

Paul squinted and shook his head with sincere pity. Then he sighed and went to sit on the sofa beside Anna. She attempted to get up, but he held on to her with a pleading look. He put his arms around her. Her face got taut.

"Relax, Ma. Relax."

She took a deep breath.

"Listen to this, Ma." He opened the notebook and began to rap:

> *Don't just cower.*
> *Don't be a wallflower.*
> *Oh Ma, oh Ma,*
> *Fight the power.*
> *Fight the power, Ma.*
> *Fight the power.*
> *To hell with pablum*
> *Eat meat.*
> *Food's not only wheat.*
> *Apply the heat.*
> *Get off your bum.*
> *Down a rum.*
> *Get on your own feet.*
> *Toss minders in the street.*
> *Ma, mete and defeat*
> *The God hucksters.*
> *Let them bleat.*
> *Fight the power, Ma:*
> *With a broomstick, your mind,*
> *A lawnmower. Don't cower,*
> *Ma, fight the power.*
> *Get off your back. Get on your feet*
> *Kick, box or kill the thieves*
> *The hacks.*
> *Don't go lower. Rise up. Higher.*
> *Fly free as a plover.*
> *Rise up. Fight the power.*
> *Ma, fight the power.*
> *Fight the power.*
> *Fight the power.*

She smiled, but the lines in her forehead signalled confusion.

Paul turned, stared at her, his eyes bright. "I'm only begging, begging you, Ma, to do Jay and me a favour and accept us for what we are ..." His tone sincere, pleading.

"What do you mean? Jay and you ... what about Jay and you that you want me to accept? ... What favour are you talking about, Paul?" Her voice a siren.

He turned his head away, began flicking his fingers, and remained silent for about 15 seconds. "There's something I want to tell you, Ma. But I can't, not while you still belong to *that* church."

Her reply was to embrace him tightly, her plea, I think, for understanding why she needed her religion.

His body relaxed against hers and he began to cry.

She glanced at me questioningly, then turned her attention to Paul. "There's so much you can't understand," her voice quavering, her eyes torn wide, signalling horror. "You're not old enough. You haven't walked in my shoes." She too began to cry. (I know now that terror had to do with what Bulljow told her when she first arrived here.)

Paul unwound himself from her embrace. "Ma, human nature is vast, too vast to fit your religious envelope."

Now the horror broke and her tears came. "You are 15, Paul. What can you know about human nature?"

"Not a lot, Ma. But from your beliefs, you don't know a whole lot either."

I watched the goodwill they'd begun to build fall apart as they returned behind their barricades and into their combat spaces.

I went into my bedroom wondering what Paul wanted to be accepted for. Was he asking Anna to accept his delinquent behaviour?

***

I stand, take a couple of tissues from the box on the night table, and dab the sweat beads on Anna's forehead. The nurse—a petite, mixed race woman, in everyday clothing—comes to check the IV and meets me standing at the head of the bed.

"Why didn't you ask for a pull-out bed?" she says.

I shrug.

"Go to the visitors' lounge and take a nap."

I shake my head. "Thanks."

She leaves and I sit back down.

17

BY 17 PAUL'S vitriol lessened, and his teasing of Anna became infrequent and gentler, more along the lines of: "Ma, you know why God is spelt with one 'o' and good with two?" By then she'd learned to respond with total silence. "Hazard a guess ... Well, while God was drowning the world, he fell into the water and shrank. Here's a second reason: Noah, seeing how God had destroyed his own creation, removed the second 'o'."

Now hardly any noise came from his room, and when music did, it was likely to be jazz: Coltrane, Miles Davis, Charlie Parker, Mingus, Wynton Marsalis, Oscar Peterson ... Gone was the gangster rap. I complimented him on the change. He said that music must be more than rain on a tin roof or banging on steel pipes. "I'm off lyrics for now. I want to learn to hear what those geniuses are saying with their instruments. It's taxing, but I'm listening and learning. I wish I'd continued to play pan."

One Saturday, Beatrice, Anna's co-worker and church sister — tall, half-white, grey-eyed, tomboyish, voice tremulous like the older Katherine Hepburn's — came to the house and was helping Anna make pone. They were standing at the kitchen counter with the ingredients spread out in front of them when Paul sidled up to her.

"Are you making it from corn?" Paul asked.

"Yes," Beatrice said. "You want to learn how?"

Paul shook his head. "Then I'm having none."

Beatrice looked at him, frowning.

"Didn't you know that where a man gets his corn pone is where he gets his opinions?"

"You ain't no man."

"Want to prove it?"

Beatrice grabbed him by the collar. Paul pretended she was choking him, and began to slump toward the ground. When she let him go he almost fell. She was laughing and shaking her head.

"See, Ma? That's how you should handle me. You take your parenting too seriously." But he wouldn't be Paul if he didn't offer an encore. "Beatrice, is Pastor Braxton your minister?" By now he had gone to sit on the sofa.

She shook her head.

"This woman," Paul said. "Her name's Alma. White. A virgin In her forties. Belongs to a church called Redeemed in Christ."

Paul raised himself to sit on the armrest and put on his under-the-eyelids mesmerizing look.

"Pastor Braxton—this tar-black man, six and a half feet tall, shoulders like a bronco, voice like a thunderclap, face like a bulldog—was her pastor. Three-quarters of his sermons were on adultery. So Alma she goes to see him one day in his church office. She tells him that every night she dreams that a black man on a white horse abducts her, and she always wakes up at that point.

"Pastor Braxton passes his hand over his shining pate and fingers his jowls. He gets up, walks to an inner room. He beckons her to follow him.

"Inside the room is a couch. Braxton sits on it and hits the space beside him where he wants her to sit. She sits down.

"With one hand he caresses her lips and drops the other to her tits, then onto her thighs, then under her dress.

"She jumps and stays his hand. 'Pastor Braxton, you're a married man.'

"And he's like: 'Indeed, every inch a man.'

"She relaxes her hold and Pastor Braxton proceeds to assess the goods. And he's like: 'Take off your clothes.' She obeys.

"When it's over and he's getting tissue to clean up the blood, he says: 'Sister, you sure did the right thing. Nobody should go back to the Lord with unfinished business.'

"And she's like: 'Pastor, you're always preaching about adultery.'

"And he's like: 'It's my favourite sin.'

"And she's like: 'But, Pastor, it's still a sin. Now you must marry me and make it right.'

"And he's like: 'Sister Alma, I already have a wife. And besides, if we don't sin, Christ's death would be in vain. There you have it, Sister Alma, you fulfilled your dream: I am the black man; you are the horse. And now, you must excuse me, I've just done man's work, now let me do the Lord's.'"

Beatrice nodded and turned to stare at Anna who was frozen with embarrassment. "Sister Anna, now that's some *ministering* to the flock. At least he didn't try to empty her bank account. That one with the church on Upper Lachine Road was breeding down those undocumented Vincentians, cashing their cheques, and pocketing the money, and when they complained, he turned immigration on them.

"But listen, young man, what you meant by I should belong to Braxton's church? I ain't white and I ain't no virgin, and no doctrine ever stopped me from getting a piece of swe-e-e-e-t loving. No siree, it never did. Never will."

By then too Paul's delinquency had ended and he'd stuck to his promise to stop peddling drugs — abruptly, as if it too were part of the obscene theatre he'd forced us to perform in week after week. "After 16," he said, grinning, "you get a criminal record and risk going to jail and being deported." For about three months he called himself a Rasta *sufferah*, who would one day be liberated by "the most exalted Haile Selassie, Rastafari"; marijuana was *holy herb* that put him in communion with the divine ("You mean getting high?"); Anna and I were *downpressers*, agents of Babylon, and cancers on Africa's body, and the end of our days had been prophesied.

Then one day he came home with his locks chopped off. "Looks like the *Bredahren* caught you eating pork?" But he'd done it himself, because he'd found out that the reason Rastas didn't cut their hair was because Samson's strength was in his hair. "And that shit they like lay on you about Selassie being God. Slavery: slavery! — Jay, can you believe it? — was going on inside Ethiopia while Selassie was emperor." There was a long silence in which he stared at the floor. "You can forgive 1930s Jamaicans for not knowing this. But *today?*" He shook his head. Then said after a while: "Man, the Enlightenment gave those guys a wide berth." He gestured washing his hands of them. "Walter Rodney lured me into this. To boost Black pride he left out the ugly stuff. Shouldn't have. From now on, I will believe only in myself." He swallowed and looked as if he was about to cry. But up to the time he left for Latin America, one of the *Bredahren* supplied him with *holy herb*.

Then he was working part-time at "the plantation" — Subway — and had already repeated Secondary V. Apart from English, French, and history, his final marks were marginal; Mrs. Mehta had urged him to remain in school for one more year. Half way through the year it was clear that nothing had changed. He wasn't attending classes or doing the assignments. The second time his marks were almost as poor.

"Come on," Paul said, "you don't expect me to sit in class and listen to boring teachers or slog through stuff that dulls my soul just to keep teachers and textbook publishers in business. If it doesn't feed my soul or stir my imagination, I'm not interested. I'm on the same page with Blake. 'The School Boy.'"

"And your job at Subway?" I could think of nothing more boring.

"Let's just say, it's a tiny compromise. It keeps me from peddling drugs. Okay. You want me alive. Right? And you'll be the first to agree that I shouldn't be a parasite. It may not be evident to you, but I too have pride."

Paul didn't apply to CEGEP. Instead he turned to working fulltime at Subway and complained incessantly about being "a plantation slave." He made a big show about paying for his room and board, and actually kept it up for six weeks or so.

About six months after promising to believe only in himself, he began attending meetings of ADDA (the Army for the Defence of Diasporic Africans): "Black liberators," who claimed they were "the Black descendants of Levi ... the two percent that will return the Black race to the paths of righteousness." After weeks of dissing white people, he quietly left the group.

By then Paul's shoulders had broadened to around 1.4 m. But for all that, his height was only 1.5 m—almost as broad as he was tall—and he weighed over 98 kg.—a contrast to my 1.75 m, 70 kg frame. (He inherited grandfather Zachary's physique. In photographs with Grama, she is a head taller than he and less than half his girth.) Paul had an attractive symmetrical, squarish face, aquiline nose, moderately thick lips, and a cleft chin; his eye colour remained as it had been in childhood: a pale amber that shone like jewels in his smooth coffee-brown face; he sported bushy sideburns and a beard and still wore silver studs in both ears. After the Rasta debacle he turned to wearing braids. His gut was a tun, because of his daily cortisone intake and his appetite. He had a penchant for jeans with crotches almost to his knees, prompting me to quip: "It's a good thing you no longer shoplift; you'd have a hell of a time making your getaway in those." He was especially sensitive about his feet: 6½, and his "table-top" butt. "Like Cousin Alice's."

On the street, he affected the gangster strut: the hop-and-drop-torso-rock, heels barely touching the ground. Asthma kept him from becoming a behemoth. Not that he didn't try. He joined a Côte des Neiges gym intent on doing just that, but gave up after a month. Any exertion outside his normal range made him wheeze and sent his heart racing dangerously fast. His trainer suggested gentler, tone-up exercises. Those were "for sissies: your kind, Jay." But Anna and I no longer feared that he'd end up in detention.

***

Paul, why are you punishing us? Where are you?

On November 5, 2003, Paul's 18th birthday, I said to him: "You think anyone from Havre would recognize Ma Kirton's Genius?" I meant his size.

"Go to hell! 'Cause you've begun a PhD, you think you're cute? Well, you're not. All the degrees in the world won't make you White. That's what counts here."

"Thanks for the enlightenment."

"There's more where it came from, but you'll have to pay."

"Who pays for sour gas?"

"Man, if there was dialysis for doltishness, you'd be permanently hooked up."

"For you there's verbal detox."

"Wow! I'm impressed. If this keeps up, I'll elevate you from ovine to bovine."

***

Just over two months later, January 21, 2004, we returned to Havre to attend Grama's funeral. Anna thought it was a blessing Grama didn't live long enough to find out what a disappointment Paul had become. We'd never told her what was happening to him and the gossip around Paul didn't seem to have reached her.

My last memory of her was the final ten minutes we'd spent with her the Saturday morning, in 1997, just before we left for Canada. She'd decided not to come to the airport with us, saying that she didn't want people to see her cry. It was around 5:30 am, and the sun's glow could be seen in the sky behind the rocks encircling Havre. The sea, untouched by its light, was still grey. Grama was wearing a quilted blue housecoat. She'd recently changed her glasses. Behind the convex lenses her eyes seemed to be in deep holes, the black frames contrasting with her beige face; the half-moon curves that had emerged below her cheekbones over the years were very visible. The week before, Father Henderson had persuaded her to become a volunteer instructor in the government's alphabetization programme, and I was pleased that when we left she would have something to fill our space. She'd turned to Paul, her eyes suddenly aglow. "I hope to live long enough with a lucid mind and good eyesight to read of your brilliant success." And she continued to stare at Paul for a long time. Then with a start, as if someone had poked her in the ribs, she turned to face me, and I could hear the embarrassment in her voice. "You will do quite well too, Jay. I have no doubt you will. Just learn to loosen up a little."

Loosen up? What did she mean?

The September when Paul entered secondary III and she sent him money to buy a stereo and a computer, she and Anna had quarrelled about it, and she told Anna to mind her own business; it was her money to do with as she pleased; but she stopped giving in to Paul's requests for money.

Around 11 pm the day of her burial, just after the last of those attending the wake had left the house, Anna and I were in Grama's bedroom trying to unwind. Anna was stretched out on Grama's bed; I was sitting in an armchair.

"Jay," Anna began, then paused. "Jay, I think that Mama resented me for holding her back in life."

"What do you mean?" *Do we have to talk about this now?*

"You know how she always liked to put down my father. One of those times she said that she agreed with his argument on poverty. 'Anna, I always felt something was fishy about the Dives story in the Bible. Now I know that Christ, the Christ that Christianity invented, was a politician like his inventors and told his followers what they wanted to hear. And those blessed-be-this and blessed-be-that that he spouted, if anybody tried to get me to swallow that swill, I'd knock him cold with the first thing I got my hands on. The facts are plain ... Aletha Joseph, you know who she is?'

"'Of course, Mama. Everyone does. She's the chief surgeon at the Colonial Hospital, and you and she were in class together, and you came first and she came second and sometimes third. She finished high school and you didn't. And the day after Daddy asked for your hand, you read in *The Vincentian* that she'd got a scholarship to study medicine at St Andrews in Scotland. One day Dr. Joseph dropped in the store to say hello to you, and you told me the story. And you said that it was because her parents were schoolteachers, and you said poverty was a curse, not a blessing, and anybody who said the opposite should be shot.'

"Mama nodded. 'Your father understood that sort of poverty. He fled from it and got trapped in another.'

"'Mama,' I said, 'are you sorry you had me?'

"'Anna, why are you asking me such a question?' Jay, she turned her head away but I had already seen the guilt in her face.

"'See, Mama, you can't even look at me. One time you said that if you didn't have me, you'd have gone overseas and studied and made something of your life.'

"'That's all water under the bridge, Anna. Gone, never to return. The past is the past. Let's focus on the present and the future.' Know what happened next, Jay? She got up from the dining table where we were sitting, went into her bedroom—this same room—and closed the door. Jay, I'm certain, if I'd gone into the bedroom then, I would have met her crying."

I said nothing, because I had nothing to say. I doubted about the crying. We were silent for a long while. I knew then I'd never let her see the journal entry I'd read three days earlier—the one where Grama lamented sacrificing her education to raise a fool.

"Jay," Anna said, breaking the silence, "you think the way Mama spoiled Paul has anything to do with how he turned out?"

I knew where her thoughts were heading. The next stop would be her role in Paul's "failure." I was tired and wished she'd stop talking. "Ma, some children who've had doting parents grow up to be successful and productive; some who've had doting parents grow up to be failures; some who've had abusive parents grow up to be healthy; and some who've had loving, disciplined parents grow up to be criminals. You never know ahead of time."

"But look at you, Jay. I've never had to worry about you."

"Paul will work something out. His head is stocked with knowledge. He'll do something with it." I wasn't sure about this and I'm even less so now. (He's probably reverted to drug trafficking and cut his links with us.)

"Life's no laboratory," I told her, "in which precise amounts of chemicals fired by precise amounts of energy produce precise results for precise functions. It's why we say: 'All things being equal ... in the best case scenario.' In psychological matters, who knows what the best-case scenario is?" I might have read her Yeats' "Among School Children." It was in a collection on the bookshelf to my right. But Anna wasn't Grama. Anna functioned in the concrete—a fact Paul knew and used to humiliate her. Come to think of it, it would have been more Grama explaining the poem to me. She knew it well. We'd read it together and she'd repeat over and over some of its lines. Every August, as soon as she found out which Shakespeare play was on my literature course, she made me read it aloud to her to be sure I understood Shakespeare's language. When she found out there were videocassettes of Shake-speare's plays for sale, she ordered them from England, and all three of us would watch them. On one occasion—I think it was to watch *Othello*, I asked Millington to come watch it with us. It was a Saturday evening. Around 10:30, while we were watching the credits, we heard Millington's father calling to him from the road, telling him his moth-er was worried that he wouldn't be able to wake up for church in the morning. Grama went to the front door, invited him in, and persuaded him to stay for cake and ginger beer—fare we usually had before going to bed when we were up late on a Saturday night ...

***

I look at Anna's rasping form on the bed and recall: *"Both nuns and mothers worship images, / But those the candles light are not as those / That animate a marble or a bronze repose ... / And yet they too break hearts."* I've certainly broken your heart, Ma. And I had hoped that we would explore why and move on. Ma, you believe that your departure from St. Vincent damaged us. You believed what Bulljow told you. I stand, lean over her, hold her hand, and say in a breaking voice: "Ma, you have been a wonderful mother and a good human being. I want you to know that. I want you to understand that, and when I find Paul, I'll tell him so." For a couple of minutes I stand there silently hoping she has heard and understood me, then I sit back down.

***

The day after our return trip from St. Vincent, Paul announced that he wanted to have a talk with us.

"About what?" Anna asked.

"You'll find out soon enough."

"Can't it wait?" It was a Saturday, and there were pressing things to be done after a two-week absence.

"No."

"All right."

Anna sat on the couch, Paul on the armchair, and I brought a chair from the dinette. If I'd sat beside Anna, Paul would have seen the seating arrangement as him versus Anna and me.

Paul cleared his throat, paused for a few seconds, then said: "I want to get through this without swearing."

Anna bit her lower lip, her face taut—on tenterhooks.

Paul stayed silent for another 15 seconds before saying: "Are you happy about going back home to see Grama's corpse?"

"Paul, what are you getting at?" Anna said.

"I'm saying that *you* prevented us from seeing Grama while she was still alive. You prevented me from going to see her. You never made any effort to go home and see her. My schoolmates, their single-parent mothers, go back to the Caribbean every year. And they're domestic servants and hospital maids and factory workers. They earn less than you. Besides I know that Grama offered many times to pay our passage."

"How do you know that?"

"I called her using phone cards so you won't know. She said that, in your headstrong way, you refused every offer of a vacation to all three of us." He turned to look at me. "Did *you* have a hand in this?"

"Paul, I'm not interested in spending other people's money. But Ma never discussed any of this with me."

"Thank you, Jay," Anna replied. Staring Paul fully in the face, she said: "I want you to listen carefully. This is for your benefit. Jay already knows this. When I married your father, your grandmother paid for the wedding. Later, when she found out how small your father's income was, she gave me money to run the household. She paid the hospital bill when Jay was born. I came to Canada with money she gave me. She paid for your tickets to come to Canada. While you both lived with her, she got no money from me. She preferred for me to go to school. Every Christmas, no matter how much I protested, she sent me a money order for $1,000. At various times during the year, she would send me a couple hundred dollars. She knew I worked two days per week and that it wasn't enough to pay for all my expenses." She paused, breathed audibly. "Paul, what year did you come to Canada?"

"1997."

"How old was I then?"

"Forty ... 41."

She nodded. "Paul, do you think that a woman over 40 should still be financially dependent on her mother?"

He shrugged his shoulders and twisted his lips, treating the question as rhetorical.

"So, Paul, my decisions took into account my financial means. You and Jay are *my* children. I'm glad your grandmother supported me when I needed it, but I had to take up my responsibility. I made some unwise decisions in my youth, and I am glad Mama helped me turn my life around, but when we become adults, we are responsible for ourselves and the children we bring into the world. I couldn't live up to this all the time, but in the last few years I've tried. I couldn't let you spend your grandmother's money freely as if it was air you're breathing in and out. You work. You know how hard it is to earn money. It is even harder to save it. You have some sense of this. For a while you gave me some money from your job. By the way, I haven't spent it. It's in an account with your name.

"I am saying everything in one, but you should know this. For six years before I married your father, I helped Mama run her store. I never took any salary from her because I lived at home expense free, and when I needed money I took it from the till, always letting her know. But Mama paid me a salary—on principle. I never collected it. She put it in the bank. I came here with some of that money and I used the rest along with money she gave me to get landed immigrant status in Canada. Why am I telling you this? I want you to know that your grandmother lived a principled life. If she'd disagreed with me over sending you travel money, she would have sent it directly to you. She was no pushover when she felt she was right. She understood principles. Her life was based on principles. You'll do well to copy her example."

Paul smiled sheepishly and hung his head. When he raised it, he was smiling broadly. With his eyes half-shut, squinting (one of the ways in which he resembles Anna), he nodded, then looked away as he said: "Still, I would have liked to see Grama alive. Principles and money shouldn't stand in the way of seeing my grandmother alive."

"Money always stands in the way," I said, "between what we want and what we can pay for. We all would have liked to see Grama alive, and I wish we had."

"We better set a few other things straight while we are at this," Anna said. "Jay pays for half of the food we eat in this house. I never asked him to. But he saw that rent, electricity, cable, insurance, and other bills eat up most of what I earn, and felt he should contribute. Understand one thing: I'm not asking you for money. I just want you to know that I did not have money to pay for the three of us to go home to see your grandmother, and I felt it was time for me to stop depending on her money. Maybe I'm wrong about that, but my conscience is clear."

For the next few minutes we sat in silence. I held my breath expecting Paul to bring up her tithing. I was relieved when Paul got up, put his hands on Anna's shoulder, nodded, and pecked her on the cheek. He went into his bedroom and closed the door.

I was proud of the way she handled this.

Paul was already travelling—in Cuba, I think—when I read Grama's journal entry for January 20, 2004:

> I don't understand what's going on. Paul should have finished high school by now. Junior college too. Anna says all the time: 'Paul is doing all right.' Now he rarely calls me. 'How are you doing in school?' I ask him. 'Fine, Grama, fine.' Always the same answer: "Fine, Grama, fine." When I ask him what that means he changes the subject. Three or four times he said he couldn't hear me: the connection was bad. I had no trouble hearing him. His last call was more than six months ago. They're hiding something from me.

She is very specific about Jay: 'Jay got his BA. Jay got his MA. Jay has begun a PhD.' Nothing about Paul. Nothing. They must think I was born big. Next week, I'll book a flight to Montreal for late May or early June.

I showed the entry to Anna. She didn't comment. What would Paul have told Grama? Would she have blamed Anna for how he turned out?

I was impressed with the maturity Paul showed that Saturday and, to gauge the change, I promised to intervene the next time Paul was abusive. The opportunity came one Saturday about a month later. Anna had prepared coo-coo. Paul wrinkled his nose and sniffed at the scoop she'd put on his plate. "This stuff looks like yellow shit. You know I hate it." He got up and began walking toward the sink with the plate.

"When you speak to Ma like that, I wish she'd slap you."

He stopped, stiffened, and turned to look at me. His eyes narrowed but he said nothing. He continued to the sink, scraped the food into the bin under it, put the plate in the sink, turned and stared briefly at me, then at the floor, before walking to his bedroom, and closing the door. He ate no lunch and no supper that day.

18

I **DATE HIS** depression to this confrontation. As it stretched into months, Anna and I became alarmed. He continued to work at Subway, but it was all he did outside of his bedroom. He became affectless and went into seclusion and total silence. It lasted about five months. When we tried to talk to him, he replied with shrugs and blank stares. We'd see him heading to and from the bathroom, leaving to go to work or coming in from work, heading to the fridge for food to be reheated in the microwave (sometimes still holding open the book he was reading), or serving himself from the pots on the stove or the casseroles in the oven, always taking the food to his room, returning to the sink with the dirty utensils, which now he promptly washed and put on the drain board. Once, Anna deliberately did not refill the prescription for his drugs, to force him to speak to her. Our meds were covered by her work insurance. He went to the pharmacy and paid for them himself, and left the receipts on the dining table with a note: "Ma, thanks for withholding my meds." She never did it again.

During this phase, when he needed to watch something on VHS, he used the television in the living room, but only when Anna and I weren't around; we'd occasionally catch him at the tail end of such viewings. Mostly he watched DVDs on his laptop. And he listened to music on his mp3 or used his earphones. With a cable splitter and cable extension cord, he linked the cable to a small television in his room. The TV noise was the only sound that came from his room, and it was infrequent for he was mostly a reader.

The smell of marijuana coming from his room was a different matter.

"I can't have him smoking in here."

"Where do you want him to smoke?" The conversation took place about six weeks into Paul's reclusive phase, one evening while Paul was at work.

"I don't know, but I know I don't want him smoking marijuana here. If he doesn't stop, he'll have to leave."

"And go where?"

"I don't know and I don't care."

"Did you say you don't care?"

"You know I don't mean that."

"Well, you better say what you mean when you are dealing with Paul. He is over 18, Ma! You understand? *18!*"

"Well, he should act like it."

"How is an 18-year-old supposed to act, Ma?"

"Like you did when you were 18."

I looked up at the ceiling and swallowed.

"He'll abide by my rules or find his own place."

"When has Paul ever followed your rules? When have *you* been able to *make* Paul follow *your rules?*"

"Are you blaming me for his behaviour?"

I didn't answer.

"Answer me! Are you blaming me for his behaviour?"

"I don't know, Ma. Maybe in 20 years I will. What I know is that Paul never found in you the nurture Grama and others gave him. But I don't blame you."

She was silent for several seconds. "I can't let him turn my home into a dope den. I can't have him smoking marijuana in here. This is my home too. I have the right to feel comfortable in here."

"Ma, Paul has been smoking marijuana in his room since he was 13. You smell it now because he spends more time in his room."

"And you've let him! You've let him! Jay, you disappoint me."

"There are worse things in this world than smoking marijuana. I don't care whether or not he smokes. So long as he isn't addicted. He says it helps control his asthma."

"I don't believe that."

170   H. NIGEL THOMAS

There was a long pause during which she seemed to be staring at the table top.

"Ma put aside all this anti-marijuana propaganda—from your church, George Bush, the Reform Party, or whatever they call themselves nowadays. Ma, listen to me, please, please. Paul"—I hesitated—"Paul's depressed. His withdrawal is too sudden. It's not normal. In a way, I prefer the abusive, abrasive Paul to this shadow that slinks in and out of his room. If you confront him now about his marijuana smoking, you'll push him over the edge, never mind threatening to put him out. Don't go there, Ma. Paul is still a child, still quite immature for an 18-year-old. He loves books and ideas but he doesn't know much else. I suspect he's afraid of the future." I dismissed telling her that that was probably what his marijuana smoking was about. "Paul cannot survive on his own. Not at this point in his life. If you put him out, I'll be forced to rent an apartment and let him live with me."

"What did you say?"

"You heard me, Ma."

The conversation ended there that day.

A week later it resumed. "I'm sure the neighbours are smelling it. We'll be evicted again. I can see the end: the neighbours calling the cops, the cops at the door, Paul led out in handcuffs, television cameras recording the whole thing, then seeing it again on television. I won't be able to show my face at work. It will send me straight to the Douglas."

"Cool your imagination, Ma. Douse it. Even if it ends that way, there are worse things in life: living in a refugee camp in Darfur, in the DRC, or being a surviving Rwandan Tutsi widow. Paul's depressed. Your first concern should be why. Not what the neighbours think. You should be offering him help; you should be assuring him that, whatever happens, you'll try to help him through it and would always be there for him."

"And if he begins to abuse me or tell me I am the cause of his problems?"

"You take it like an adult should. You tell him you are ready to make amends."

"*Amends!* For what? What are you hinting at?" Her voice was shrill. "And if he threatens to kill me?"

"Tell him to stop being childish. You should try to have this conversation with him in his bedroom, in his space. I don't want to be here when it's taking place."

She sighed deeply. "What a country this Canada is! Parents taking orders from their children."

She sat on a dining chair and was silent for a long time. "How come at your age you know all this?"

"Forget that, Ma. See to Paul. He needs all the encouragement he can get to pull out of this slump."

A couple weeks later, she told me she'd spoken with him, and that it had gone well. He told her he felt bad, real bad, inside. He'd refused to say about what, and refused her offer to let her insurance pay for psychological counselling.

It was another three months before Paul resumed verbal contact with us. And I bungled the one occasion when Paul might have volunteered information about his depression.

***

Paul, where are you? Why aren't you here? How have we failed you, Paul? Do you know that Ma ended her marriage and has led a loveless life here, because she didn't want you to grow up with a violent father?

***

Four months before Paul left on his travels, he came in one afternoon while I was watching *Making Sense of the Sixties*. He sat down beside me.

"This is like heavy stuff, man. Awesome! Where'd you get this?"

"In Concordia's library."

"I should o' been an adolescent then. This looks like fun. Wow. Cool, man. Ma," he called to Anna in her bedroom, "did you 'turn on, turn off, and drop out?'" She hadn't long come in from the dayshift. "Ocean would dry up first, right. Woodstock! Far out. Look at what you missed, Ma! Ma, you missed *Jimi Hendrix*: God with a guitar!"

"Paul, Ma was only 13."

"So, Jay, you guys are like *studying this*? Cool, man! Wow!"

"It's an independent study course. The professor's interested in this sort of thing. He was part of the scene."

"Your *professor*! Really. Tell me more."

I paused the VCR. "It's an interdisciplinary course. History and literature mostly. He calls it 'The Other America.' We do the readings—three of us: Jonathan, a girl called Sarah, and myself. We meet every week at his flat, near Chomedey and Maisonneuve, and discuss the works. We've done your favourite author: Thoreau, along with Emerson. Walt Whitman too. Tomorrow we begin Allan Ginsberg and William Burroughs, and in two weeks we'll be looking at *The Electric Kool-Aid Acid Test* and the Sixties Revolution, and after that three or four more authors."

Anna came into the living room then. "Jay, what are you getting Paul into?"

"What are you talking about? I just celebrated my 19th birthday!"

"In years only."

"I'll watch what I want, when I want. Who do you think you are?"

"But not where you want?"

"Jay, aren't you going to stand up for me?"

"You're quite capable of defending yourself, Paul." I got up and went to the Media Centre to continue watching the documentary.

A week later, as soon as I got in from school, Paul began to sing:

What did you learn in school today?
What did you learn, my brother Jay?
To rob the poor, turn all earth grey—
That's what you learned today?

What did you learn in school today?
What did you learn, my brother Jay?
To starve the poor, feed them hay—
That's what you learned today?

What did you learn in school today?
What did you learn, my brother Jay?
To pillage and lie, the capitalist way—
That's what you learned today?

What didn't you learn in school today?
What didn't you learn, my brother Jay?
To be a man, choose your own way?
You didn't learn that today.

"My dear brother," he said, closing his eyes and rocking his head and shoulders—swagger meant for Anna, who was in the kitchen. "I have seen *Making Sense of the Sixties*. Momsy dear." He went to where she was peeling vegetables at the sink and put his arm around her waist. "It taught me nothing I didn't already know about drugs. I'm glad to see that 35 years ago people agreed with me that education is slavery and brain death, and they did something about it. Gave the finger to the plantation and freed their minds with grass."

He walked back to the living room and sat on the sofa beside me. "By the way, Bro, as a follow-up I read two of your books: *Do It* and *Die, Nigger, Die!* Pass me *The Electric Kool-Aid Acid Test* as soon as you're done reading it. I leafed through it yesterday. You think your prof would let me sit in on the discussion, would let me *onto the bus?*"

"I don't know." Professor William Samson (he insists that we call him Bill) is flamboyantly gay; according to Jonathan, *a queen without a crown*. On the eastern wall of his living room, there's a massive painting of three life-size naked men: a European, an African, and an Asian, their interlaced bodies filling the canvas. On top of a long glassed-in mahogany bookcase that divides his living room from the dining room, he has a half-metre high carving in ebony of a penis and testicles mounted on marble. It's in your face as soon as you enter the living room.

I was tempted to lie, to say that Bill had said no. And I didn't want a confrontation with Anna. A year earlier, a Saturday evening, Jonathan had visited, and we had become engrossed in playing Chinese checkers, and Jonathan had missed the last metro and slept over. When Anna arrived from work next morning, Jonathan was still there. As soon as he left, Anna called me into her bedroom. "Why's he sleeping here? What's going on between you two?" She tried to keep her voice low. We'd thought Paul was still asleep.

I explained what had happened.

"You're sure there's nothing more going on between you two?"

"What do you mean, Ma?"

"You know what I mean."

"No. You will have to say it."

"Oh, Ma," Paul shouted from his bedroom door, "Jay's old enough to screw with whom he wants. Don't get our lives mixed up with your religion."

"Leave! Go!" She waved me away and began to cry.

***

Jonathan is gay, gay and visibly androgynous. Our friendship began banal enough my first year in CEGEP. The first full summer I spent here Jonathan found out that I didn't have a driver's licence and decided I should have one. On evenings, when the parking lot of the Versailles Shopping Centre was empty, he taught me the basics of driving in his father's 1990 Nissan Maxima—his sky-blue eyes glowing, his manner at its most earnest. At the end of every driving session, he took me home—the same duplex, now with more recent renovations —and reheated apple, blueberry or strawberry pie and served it to me with ice cream and orange or apple juice.

Sometimes his *Tante* Jeanne, an ex-nun, who lived upstairs, was there.

"You like it, the life with electricity?" *Tante* Jeanne asked me the first time we met.

I laughed and she blushed. I told her my grandmother had a washing machine and dryer, that we did our homework on a computer, and when we walked barefoot it wasn't because we didn't have shoes. She went on to talk about sending money to some nun in Haiti and then asked me: "Why you come to Canada, *donc?*"

"Il faut poser cette question à ma mère."

Thereafter our conversation was reduced to a cool hello.

A year later, when I visited one Saturday, Cecile, Jonathan's mother, gave me a bumbleberry pie to take home. Those days Anna was too tired from working long hours to be even curious about where I went. Her eyes bulged when she saw the pie.

"What's this? From your future mother-in-law or what?"

"Maybe."

"When are we meeting her?" Paul asked.

"My mother-in-law?"

"No. The daughter, smart aleck!"

"Not very soon. You'll try to steal her."

"Does Jonathan have a girlfriend?" Anna asked when I was in second-year university.

"I don't know."

That second year at McGill, Jonathan and I spent December 27-29 at his parents' chalet in Lac Sept-Îles, some 50 km northwest of Quebec City. Jonathan brought along snowshoes for both of us. He helped me put on mine, put on his own, and showed me how to walk easily in them. We slung on our backpacks and trudged through thick snow and naked yellow birches for about 200 metres to reach the chalet. Below it, at the bottom of a steep slope, was a clearing that showed their jetty, the boathouse, and the broad field of ice that was the lake, its solid white surface glowing in the late afternoon sun. To the right two of its seven islands were visible. There were over a dozen skidoos crisscrossing it.

Downstairs of the chalet, there was a well-equipped kitchen, a living room and dining room, a bedroom and a toilet. Upstairs there were three bedrooms.

Quickly we took wood inside from off the porch and lit the stove. It was a struggle keeping the cold out. We closed the trapdoor to the floor upstairs to prevent the heat from escaping and shut the doors to all the other rooms to concentrate the heat in the living room. Even so, by the time we got the temperature to 12 degrees, the sun had gone down. All around the lake gleamed, lit by the thin line of houses of those who lived there yearlong. The rest was forest all the way up the slopes. Up to 8 pm, the skidoos were still racing along the lake, their headlamps beaming. Jonathan wanted us to go walking, but at that hour I didn't feel like tromping about. Indoors it varied between 11 and 13 degrees, depending on the strength of the wind, and outdoors –22 without factoring in the wind.

We slept on sleeping bags and blankets in front of the stove. I vaguely remember hearing him adding wood to it during the night. When I awoke next morning my nose felt frozen and I would not throw off the bedclothes until, in a tussle, Jonathan pulled them off me. Two years ago, while he and I were watching *Broke-Back Mountain*, I wondered what would have happened if Jonathan had moved his sleeping bag close to me that night and pulled me into his arms.

"*C'est ça, l'hiver québécois, l'hiver que mes ancêtres ont vécu. Goûtes-y, mon vieux!*" ("This is the Quebecois winter of my ancestors. Taste it, buddy.") In those days, he spoke to me almost exclusively in French, to improve my listening and pronunciation skills. (Paul never had such language problems; overnight he became *un petit Québécois grillé.*)

After breakfast I bundled up: double gloves, a long, thick scarf piled around my neck, a toque pulled down over my ears, four layers on my torso, two on my lower limbs; Jonathan not specially so—he wasn't even wearing a toque and certainly no long johns—and we went walking on the lake, Jonathan occasionally pushing me into snowbanks and throwing snowballs at me. We walked for a good two hours, circling three of the islands and keeping out of the skidoo paths. It was around one when we returned to the chalet—icicles hanging from my nostrils and sweat saturating my underwear, Jonathan's face wind-burnt a bright pink—to eat crackers and a pot of soup we'd left to heat on the woodstove. Next day, we drove for about a kilometre along the lake road to the entrance to Parc Jacques-Cartier, put on our snowshoes and went snowshoeing on a path that paralleled a road used to bring timber out of the park.

It was on the drive back to Montreal that Jonathan told me that he was gay. I visualize the furrows in Jonathan's forehead and the sweat dripping from the steering wheel as he awaited my response. "It's alright, Jonathan." It had taken me a long time to say so, because I hadn't known what to say, and it didn't feel right that Jonathan should tell me.

Paul was around 14 and had already figured out that Jonathan was gay. I hadn't. My mind returns to Anna's obsessive fear that we might be gay—put there by what Bulljow told her when she first came to Canada.

***

I stand, stretch, touch my toes, and walk to the visitors' lounge. I check my cellphone to see if there's a message from Jonathan or Paul. I left a message on the answering machine at home telling Paul to call me on my cell as soon as he got the message. In fact it's the only reason I have a cellphone. I'm exhausted to the point of staggering, as I walk back to Anna's room, too exhausted to even feel sleepy. I stand at the bedside and try to get a view of Anna's face before I sit down again.

***

Bill agreed to have Paul come to the remaining classes. At one point Bill said that he'd been one of the students who took over the faculty club at UBC when Jerry Rubin spoke there. Paul applauded. Paul and he became fast friends. Bill plied him with books and sometimes they met for coffee. Paul probably saw him as someone who'd rebelled and who was therefore "real." I find their friendship both a puzzle and a relief: a puzzle because of Paul's homophobic taunts, a relief because it tells me Paul was merely posturing.

Anna found out about their relationship after overhearing Paul and me speculating about Bill's sexual fantasies. She questioned me about it in Paul's absence. "Ma, first: remember that Paul is 19, so if he's sleeping with Professor Samson, which I'm pretty certain he isn't doing, it's perfectly legal. Second: Professor Samson is good for Paul. Paul looks up to him. It means that he'll be able to influence Paul in a way you and I can't. To go back to school, maybe. Don't knock it. Third: You fundamentalists are apoplectic now because you've just lost your *divine right* to persecute gays. Don't count on Paul and me to help you. Fourth: Shouldn't you be having this conversation with Paul?"

Her shoulders drooped. "I never thought you'd turn against me."

"No one has turned against you, Ma. Not even Paul. His behaviour is bluster. Let go, Ma. Let go. We have to feel our own way and make decisions for ourselves, good and bad, and discover who and what we are. Just like you did. You defied Grama and dropped out of high school when you were 13 or 14 because you thought Christ was coming on a certain date."

She winced.

"I'm not blaming you, Ma. You've made up for it. And you defied Grama when you married my father."

She winced again.

"Tell me something. Let's say, for argument sake, you discovered that Paul or I or both of us were gay, what would you do? Disown us?"

She clenched her teeth, crossed her arms, and tried to fold her shoulders.

"I hope *my mother* is intelligent enough to know that any religion that urges her to reject her children for whatever reason is not worth belonging to." But I felt guilty for hurting her feelings and added, because I didn't know what else to say: "Don't worry about Paul. I'm pretty sure he isn't gay."

"And you?"

I hadn't anticipated the question. A long pause.

"And you?" Desperation. A laser stare. "Since Tamara ..."

"I don't know."

"You *don't know*. You don't know *what*?" Her voice a shriek.

"If I'm gay."

Her eyes narrowed; she frowned, pursed her lips, took a deep breath, opened and closed her fingers several times, wordlessly left the dinette, entered her bedroom, and closed the door.

***

It was the second time in two days that Anna had asked me about Tamara, a girl I dated my second year at McGill. Tamara was doing a degree in social work at McGill. "Rass-clart!" she screamed at me the last time we were together. We were in her apartment, a studio, on Aylmer. She stormed out of bed, turned on the light, put on her bathrobe, shook her fists and growled at me. "You're worse than useless. Stay away from women. Stick to wanking off." It was the third time we'd attempted to have sex, and the third time I'd ejaculated before entering her, after which my penis went limp. A couple of months later I saw her in the arms of a muscular, African-looking Italian, a phys-ed major. She worked at the library checkout counter, and would sneer at me whenever I met her there.

Ma never questioned me about my sexuality after that nor objected to Jonathan's occasional visits to the apartment. At times she muttered: "Why is God punishing me so?" About a year before she questioned me about my sexuality, she'd spoken to me about Kirk, a gay colleague, a Mohawk. His brother's naked dead body had been found covered with cigarette burns in a downtown parking lot. Kirk told her then that both of his male siblings and one of his four sisters were also gay. I wasn't sure what astonished Ma more: the brutality of the crime or Kirk's revelation about the homosexuality in his family. And one morning, just before she got sick, she returned from work distraught. She'd got news that night that Kirk—he'd gone to work at another hospital—had just died of AIDS. I related the story to Jonathan, and he said that three of his own cousins were gay, and his parents knew families in which all or almost all the children were gay.

***

I stare at Anna's rattling body. Ma, I wish I could have poured my feelings out to you. It's not so much who I'm attracted to; it's the anxiety I feel when it comes to sex. Not something a boy feels comfortable discussing with his mother, and certainly not a mother like you, who thinks the answer to all problems is to become a born-again Christian.

***

Well before Paul left for Latin America, he understood that no one totally drops out of society. At first he berated Rubin for his contradictions, but later came to see that already, in 1969, Rubin was laughing at himself. Of course, Paul knew what eventually happened to Rap Brown; knew too that Rubin had a career on Wall Street and in advertising before he died in 1994; I filled him in on Huey Newton's fate; and Paul saw from the last episode of *Making Sense of the Sixties* the value and limits of the Sixties Rebellion. And the living proof was Samson himself who'd gone on to study and become a professor.

19

WHEN PAUL ANNOUNCED his voyage to Latin America "to test [his] independence," we didn't believe him.

"You can't be serious?" I said.

"I have to go. I'm in both of your fists, and you squeeze tighter and tighter. When Ma gets tired you take over. I can't breathe. I have to get away."

He demanded the $6,000 each of us was immediately eligible for from Grama's will. The bulk of Paul's inheritance from her — $40,000 — was to be used for post-secondary education, or, failing that, would become available when he was 30. The evening that Anna informed him of this, he called Grama a "traitor ... a control freak," and much more in a volley of expletives, until his breathing became like a broken mill and his gaze went feral. I shoved him onto the sofa and jabbed an EpiPen into his thigh. When his breathing settled, he erupted into gulping sobs. She was the only non-revolutionary he venerated; her name was sacrosanct; she was infallible. That evening she seemed fated to be tossed from his halidom. But the next day her photo was still on his dressing table.

At first Anna refused to give him the money. She explained that she would now buy a house, and Paul should use the money to furnish his room. "I won't let you give it to airlines and hotels; my mother and father worked too hard for it." Her voice a screech.

"Legally you're obliged to give it to him," I told her in Paul's absence.

"Even if I think he's going to get himself killed in Latin America?"

"Yes. It's his life. He isn't your property, you know."

"And if I still refuse? I gave life to him."

"You know Paul. He'll take you to court if he has to."

In the end she gave in. When Paul began churlishly to display his airline ticket, I told him a story, making it up as I went along:

"Seeker set out on a long journey in search of Truth. Seeker visited the eminent philosophers. They told Seeker they'd never met Truth. They'd only glimpsed him darting into the bushes from afar off, and his face was always turned from them; it was only from his silhouette that they figured out it was he. One philosopher told Seeker he should visit the pope. He was said to be infallible. But Seeker had already learned that many popes had been liars; and, as to human infallibility, Seeker had profound doubts. In China they told Seeker to follow the 'Way' but refused to tell him how to find it. In India they told Seeker that Brahma was truth. But to meet Brahma Seeker had to get rid of all desire. So Seeker began to rid himself of desire. That's the story."

"You call that a story! What's your point?"

"Whatever point you see."

"I see none."

"Then there's none."

"Want some free advice? If you're gonna talk shit, make it funny. Otherwise use your mouth for something useful—like catching flies."

"Cheap! I thought you'd moved beyond this."

"I'm entitled to a relapse or two from time to time. Remember, I don't turn the other cheek. You all get boned—in every hole." His face grew serious, reflective. "I shouldn't have said that. Sorry. I take it back."

"You'd have been able to tell your own version of this story if you'd read Thoreau carefully."

"You ain't such a crack reader yourself, or you'd know Thoreau says we shouldn't follow his example; we should come up with our own quest. Ber!" He stuck his tongue out at me.

"When I pass by the Van Horne Shopping Centre I'll get you a pacifier."

"And a tube of KY for yourself."

"And while I'm at it I'll get two or three for you and a carton of condoms. Carry a good supply with you."

"You're such an asshole." He grinned widely. "One day I'll disown you — totally. And watch how you'll go down on your knees and beg me to become your loving brother again. You piss me off all the time, but I'll forgive you this time: the last time."

"I appreciate it. Now how about acting like a *loving* brother."

He gave me a sheepish grin and hugged me.

***

The evening before his departure for Cuba, the first of several destinations, Anna worked the evening shift. She'd exchanged her Saturday dayshift for a Friday evening one so she could accompany Paul to the airport. That evening Paul was sitting on the living room sofa, feet on the coffee table, TV remote in one hand. I was at the dining table.

"Hey, Bro," Paul said, looking across at me.

I waited for him to speak.

"Maybe if I call you loser, you'll look at me when I'm talking to you."

I was in no mood for his games.

"I'll call you queer, then. Aren't you queer? Admit it."

I glowered at Paul.

Paul winked, got up, and walked over to the table. He put a hand on my shoulder.

I stiffened.

"Relax, Bro. Relax." Then he placed both arms affectionately around me, letting them fall down to my chest. "You're lousy sometimes but mostly you're my loving brother," he said into my ear, as if telling me a secret. "You wanna share a joint with me?"

I shook my head slowly.

"Please? Just once. Please? I have something important to say to you, but I'll tell you only if we share a joint together." He clasped me tightly.

I shook my head.

"Then to hell with you!" He removed his arms violently and boxed me hard in the right shoulder.

"Paul, go smoke your joint. You don't need my permission."

"Why're you such a wet blanket? Why, Jay? Why?" He was wiping his eyes with the back of his hand. He walked toward the door, opened the coat closet, put on his jacket, and left the apartment.

Instantly I knew I should have begged him to come back. It has haunted me since.

When Paul returned, he headed straight to his room. It was past midnight, and Anna was already home from work.

At the airport next morning, he hugged Anna calmly, genuinely, and said: "Ma, I've made your life miserable. I know I have. I wish I hadn't. Sorry for the sleepless nights, the trips to the police station. I'd take it all back if I could." She was crying and made no attempt to hide it. When he embraced me, he said: "I better say it now, in case we don't see each other again. Thanks, man. Thanks." He paused and I could see he was trying not to cry. "You've been a good brother. You've always been there for me. In Kingstown, and afterwards here." He swallowed. "I've been too arrogant to tell you." He pressed me closely. "But I'm not forgiving you for last night." He let go of me and wagged a finger at me. "You dissed me, man. Everyone's not as strong as you. I wanted to tell you—only you, because I know you care and you'd understand—the real reason I'm setting off on this journey."

"You'll write to me about it. Here's a copy of the *Tao Te Ching*. I've found it helpful."

"I *won't* write to you about it. I won't." He pushed the book into the outer pouch of his carry-on case.

By then we were standing outside the security zone. Paul walked to the threshold, then turned and waved to us. A second later, he disappeared behind the door's frosted glass. I have dreamt about that door twice. Once it was Paul's rapping, his shadow moving frantically on the other side of it, trying to break through to me. The other time it was like the morning Paul left, but he'd forgotten his medication, and I couldn't get beyond the door to give it to him.

What did he want to tell me? There were times when I thought that his asthma was in some way responsible for his anger; anger that was attenuated in St. Vincent because everyone fussed over him, and he did not yet know the limits asthma would put on his life. Here, he came to understand those limits and the drugs he'd have to take until he died. Ma and I had spoken about this as the possible cause for his delinquent behaviour, but, beyond inviting him to tell us what was bothering him, we'd never raised it with him; and after his 14th birthday we stopped asking him to tell us because his response was always: "You all won't leave me alone: that's what's bothering me."

After returning from the airport, Anna spent the day in bed. She came out of her room around 7 pm, her eyes red from crying. At the last minute, when Paul couldn't get an appointment with his own doctor, she'd got Dr. Ramnaran, whom she worked with, to prescribe him a large supply of anti-asthma drugs and to give him a standing prescription for more, with suggestions of alternatives in case the first choices weren't in stock. She worried that he'd have an asthma attack in some remote place and be out of medication.

Was I wrong not to share a joint with him? Why didn't I? Jonathan and I have done it with school pals to put them at ease. Couldn't I have done the same with him? What has he gone to Latin America in search of?

I feel no need for any such journey. One day I hope to go to Africa to satisfy my curiosity. Maybe even work there, but not for reasons of self-discovery. Am I already jaded? I have no illusions about people's capacity for good and evil. Studying history, I reflect on the foibles of so-called great men and women, know about that need so many have to dominate others lest they become the dominated. Eat lunch or be lunch, as they say in the corporate world. If you are not at the table, you're on the table. We keep our booted foot on others' necks so our necks won't be under their boots, and find rationalizations for not lifting the foot: like Britons who rule the waves and enslave so they never will be slaves. Yet their missionaries go around proclaiming the golden rule. Contradictions that Paul certainly understands. I hope he never embraces the so-called logic of ruthless power. Occidental ideals: freedom, justice, democracy—true only for the ruling elite. Professor Johnson, his electric-blue eyes riveted on us, once said: "There's a huge difference between tyrants and democrats," and paused for a good 15 seconds: "Tyrants do their dirty work in daylight; democrats do theirs at night." Empires eagerly succeed one another and build with the remnants of the empires they've ruined. Manifest Destiny! God's chosen peoples—authorized to enslave, pillage, steal, entire continents even. God's rain falls on the just and the unjust. Yeah right. Go ahead and kid me while you turn me into a tool. And the powerless masses, they indeed lead lives of quiet desperation, and must keep their desperation quiet to avoid being punished. 'Laugh and the whole world laughs with you; weep and you weep alone.'

Anna became convinced that Paul's going away was to punish her. On her days off, I would find her sitting on the sofa, hands supporting her chin, staring blankly at the living room wall. She stopped wearing lipstick, stopped dyeing her hair and going to the hairdresser. Instead she bought a cheap black wig that she slipped on whenever she went out. Before, she'd obsessively iron everything that wasn't knitted. Now she never bothered with an ironing board; on occasion I felt forced to tell her that her dress was crumpled. She settled on wearing brown and beige knitted tops and sweat pants, except when she went to church.

When she saw the damage Stan had inflicted on Guatemala, she thought we'd hear from Paul; at the very least he'd let us know that he was all right. One of the hardest hit areas was Atitlán, which Paul had described in a letter to me. I kept this information from her, and reminded her that from Paul's last letter it was possible that he was no longer in Guatemala. She began to worry that he might be dead, and hounded me to get in touch with Foreign Affairs to see what information they had on those Canadians in Guatemala when Stan struck. Paul's name wasn't on their list. Insomnia took over her life and she lost her appetite. Within weeks she shed 35 of her 150 pounds, the flesh on her arms jiggled, her cheekbones began to look shorn, and hanging skin replaced her double chin; her face became anaemic, hard, and creased. Occasionally I heard her sniffling and would turn to see her crying.

In February, she began to have trouble climbing Linton's slope and the four steps to our ground-floor apartment, and was given sick leave a month before her heart truly failed. Then she mentioned Paul in every conversation. I listened quietly, sometimes with my arms around her.

Two days before she became too out-of-breath and delirious to speak coherently, she said, her eyes closed: "Paul, where is Paul? Jay, don't let him go to the dogs. He listens to you. He pretends he doesn't but he does. Keep at him. You promise me?"

"I will, Ma. I promise."

She opened her eyes and angled her gaze at me sitting on the chair to her right.

"I'll try, Ma. Rest. You need to rest." I leaned forward and placed a hand on hers.

"Jay ... was I wrong ... was I wrong to leave you all and come away?"

"Rest, Ma. Rest. You're overtiring yourself. Paul is one of those children who must have their way, regardless."

"I was selfish."

"No, you weren't."

"I shouldn't have come away."

"It's okay, Ma. I don't blame you."

"Paul does. I could have worked ... in the store with Mama ... be there ... for you all."

"Rest, Ma."

"He came to a stranger. It was a stranger he came to. He needed a mother. He came to stranger, Jay."

"No, you were not." I squeezed her hand. "Stop worrying, Ma. Stop blaming yourself. If Paul were here, he'd tell you the same thing. I'm sure he knows now that you've been the best mother you could be."

"But not ... the mother ... he needed." She began to cry. "Remember when he first came, he asked me why we were here? 'So you can earn a living emptying bedpans'?" She paused. "Mrs. Mehta opened my eyes. 'Send him back to St. Vincent to finish his schooling. Here's not the right place for a child like Paul.' But it was too late. I didn't listen to what Paul was saying."

Beads of sweat popped up on her forehead. I took a tissue from the box on her night table and dabbed them. I upped the oxygen meter by half a point. She nodded. "Jay, he needed a mother who could follow him in what he was thinking and learning, somebody like Mama. Jay, he was telling us that the school he was in would destroy him, and we didn't listen." She paused. "For four years, Jay, I've wanted to beg him for forgiveness. Now I am dying and he isn't here. Say sorry to him for me, Jay. Tell him I'm sorry I didn't listen to him."

***

The room is quiet. I stand and stare at Anna's outline in the half upright bed. She has stopped breathing. I look at my watch. 5:13 am. I press her bell. The nurse comes, then Dr. Christine Lim.

Dr. Lim nods as she lifts the stethoscope from Anna's chest and reaches for the clipboard with Anna's chart. She looks up at me and asks: "Have you someone at home?"

"No."

"You should. You're the one needing attention now."

I**T'S JUNE. ANNA'S** illness became serious a month before I was to write my major comprehensive exam. I had it rescheduled for late fall. Still no word about Paul, and now I'm thinking something I was loathe to before: that Paul might be one of those swallowed up in the land-slides that buried thousands when Stan struck.

***

It's a month since my mother's death and two days since my return from St. Vincent. I delayed the funeral for two weeks and placed obitu-ary notices in the Montreal and Vincentian newspapers, hoping that Paul might be e-mailing his school friends, who'd see the notice and inform him. I don't have Paul's e-mail address.

I told those Haverites who asked for Ma Kirton's Genius that Paul was distraught and didn't want to be at the burial ceremony. Some frowned; a few snickered. Most likely Vincentians living in Montreal— at least ten belong to Anna's church—had already phoned home the information.

Caleb—looking a full decade older than 60, physique gaunt as a Bushman's, eyes sunken, skin a translucent mahogany and scrolled like antique porcelain—came to the funeral. I told him that Paul was doing research in a remote region of Guatemala, and couldn't be reached.

Caleb and I met a few days later in a café overlooking the Kings-town harbour. As grey and glossy black grackles flew onto the tables to gobble up any unattended food, and the horns of arriving and departing schooners sounded, we chitchatted—each uncomfortable with the other—about the changing weather in St. Vincent, the fear that the banana industry would be gone in a few years, the increase in tourism, a recent news item about black tourists being kept out of a hotel in the Grenadines, hotels blocking the public entrances to beaches to keep out the local population, the increased number of sex workers because of the tourist industry, etc. During the long pauses Caleb fidgeted, and I stared out at the ships in the blue-green water and at the northern tip of Bequia, a grey blur in the distance. "I was just thinking," Caleb said toward the end, breaking a long silence, "that with all that good breeding your grandmother give you, and all that education you got in Canada, that you find me doltish. Doltish." He gave an embarrassed grin, revealing his false teeth. "Is Anna who teach me that word. Before I used to say dotish." He paused again then looked at me attentively. "No use talking to you 'bout religion 'cause your grandmother already turned you and your brother into infidels."

"Ma became a Baptist—a Foot-Washing Baptist—five, no six, years before she died."

His face beamed, and he half lifted himself from his seat with excitement. "I know it! Once God done choose you, you can't get away. Can't get away."

I contemplated my father, remembered his beliefs centred on hell, his frequent citation: "The fear of the Lord is the beginning of wisdom"; my own singing along with the other youngsters: "Saviour, while my heart is tender / I will yield that heart to thee: / All my joys to thee surrender: / thine and only thine to be."

"God ways mighty mysterious, you know," Caleb said, staring out blankly over the harbour. "I sit here thinking that I put down preaching and take up drinking after Anna leave me, and I put down drinking when she come back from Canada and tell me to stop. And if you all didn't go live with your grandmother and I didn't have to come and visit you all there, I would own nothing today. As much as I hated that woman, she put me on my feet. And she didn't have to do it, because her daughter did done divorce me, and it was my fault. Your grandmother had modern ideas. I know that now." He smiled. "Imagine: I used to forbid your mother from reading books to you. I remember when Paul win that spelling bee and his picture was in the papers, I could o' hardly stay on the ground. That is how proud I was. And I know he win it 'cause your grandmother pay good money to send him to the best school. The day I see his picture on the front on the paper, I say: 'Praise God I don't drink no more 'cause I don't want to bring no more shame to my children.'"

I put my hand on his and squeezed it.

"Beulah want you to come have supper with us before you go back. Will you come?"

"Sure. With pleasure, Daddy."

Caleb smiled and seemed relieved.

Two days later I went, a Saturday afternoon.

Beulah is Kalinago; homely; somewhere in her fifties; tiny: hardly more than five feet. Her bright, brown eyes stared at me unabashedly from an almost circular shale-coloured face. She looks sexless, mannish even: narrow hips and mere hints of breasts. A scarf of grey-green stripes hid her hair. She wore a loose shift of calico print: red, yellow, and mauve flowers on a green field. Most likely she'd made it herself. The outmoded sewing machine, one with a foot pedal, was in a corner of the living room. Caleb and she belong to some sort of holiness church. She's childless. Caleb's her second husband.

I had come without a cap or raincoat during a drizzle. "You too careless with your health," she scolded me, and instantly went out the back door of the kitchen and returned with a root of ginger, which in minutes she transformed into steaming, aromatic tea. "This will sweat out any cold that taking root in you." Dinner was a large bowl of spicy, delicious goat stew—the goat was culled from her herd—with lots of meat, tannias, eddoes, breadfruit, christophene, green papaya, and pigeon peas, chased down with ginger beer. She didn't eat with us. Instead she kept moving back and forth between the table and the kitchen sink while waiting to take the empty bowls from us.

She and Caleb live in a simply furnished, modest two-bedroom bungalow, about two kilometres inland from the shack where I used to visit him. About a year after Caleb had promised Anna to stop drinking, he came to visit Paul and me at Grama's place; and in one of the two sentences he usually exchanged with Grama, he mentioned that the plantation near Georgetown had been bought by the Vincentian government and was being leased in ten-acre plots with buy-options to landless people. Grama asked if he was leasing any. He said he'd love to but didn't have the obligatory two-thousand-dollar down payment. "Go make the arrangements," she told him. She lent him the money. When he came to wish us goodbye the July we left for Canada, he informed Grama that he'd just made the final payment for the land and would soon be repaying her. In one of our infrequent letters, he told me that he'd acquired a second holding and was building a house.

He no longer breaks stones for a living. "We get enough from the land, just barely enough, to live on, but we live. By the grace of God, we live." While he and I talked, Beulah went out into the drizzle and returned with avocados, hog plums, grafted mangoes, and tangerines for me.

"You and Paul is the only blood family I have," Caleb said as he accompanied me to the main road to catch a bus to Kingstown.

"I'll write you often," I told him. On the way into town I remembered what he'd said about God making him wealthy one day if he was a good steward, and I wondered how much of Deuteronomy was colouring my father's thinking. I was happy to see his new-found confidence, but saddened by the doctrines that probably informed it. Guess I have to be grateful for small mercies. Whatever gets us through life and keeps us out of prison, the insane asylum, and in Daddy's case, away from the bottle. I know nothing about my paternal relatives. I'll have to remedy that, but one challenge at a time. First I must find Paul.

Aunt Mercy, frail but still independent, occupies Grama's house. She'd moved in with Grama after Paul and I left for Canada. She apologized that she hadn't been able to care adequately for the garden. To me, it seemed well cared for. Grama had expanded it after we left. Bougainvillea ran along the porch railing in banners of fuchsia, mauve, and splashes of white. Two poinciana trees she'd planted at the front the same year we left were now about four metres high and flowering: one pink, one yellow. The white and pink queen of flowers that had always been there was now at least three metres high. At the back, where the land bordered the beach road, she'd planted a hibiscus hedge and four royal palms. The palms were now the same height as the house. The trees on the rest of the land that stretched up the steep hillside to where the new road had been blasted out of rock were covered in bromeliads and epiphytes. The tracks that Paul and I had made to get to the mango, plumrose, guava, and golden apple trees were overgrown. My grandmother's will reserves 20 percent of her estate for Aunt Mercy's needs. Anna had been her liquidator and had transferred power of attorney to me.

***

It's 8:12 pm. I hear the stomping of Jonathan's turned-out feet even before he gets to the door. He's been sleeping at the flat since Anna's death. Night before last when he came in his father's car to pick me up at the airport, I told him I was fine now, but Jonathan's defiant. He stays in my room, plugs in his laptop there, and works quietly. I have moved into Anna's room.

Beatrice called me earlier to find out if she should bring me food. I thanked her and said no.

"You got in touch with Paul yet?"

She's definitely fond of Paul and he of her. One evening around the time Paul came out of his depression I met him writing. He said it was a story he was calling "the charcoal people, people like the members of Ma's church, and that Beatrice was the narrator." He must have noted my perplexed look for he said: "Those people turned to charcoal in kilns of conformity ... ideology. People like Ma. People like Madam J. Fuel. If you and I don't watch out, we'll become charcoal too."

21

I REMEMBER PAUL'S journals. He began keeping them quite young, probably in imitation of Grama, somewhere around six, around the time he started school at Excelsior. In the early days he pestered us about the words he couldn't spell. Would his journals tell me anything? *No, I won't read them without his permission.* I remember when Grama caught me reading one of Ma's letters to her. It was the one about her acceptance into nursing school. Grama had already read it aloud to us. But I wanted to be sure she hadn't left out anything.

The sun was setting out in the harbour, its light tinting the room golden. Grama's form was silhouetted against the window, and for a moment I couldn't see the anger in her eyes. The lower drawer of the china closet from which I'd removed the letter was still open. She pulled the letter from me, put it back in the envelope, returned it to the drawer, and pushed it back in.

I'd wanted to know everything about my mother, and I knew adults told each other things they hid from children.

"Stop staring at the floor and look me in the face. Never you read anyone's letters or diaries or personal papers without their permission. Never you do that! It's a serious violation of people's privacy."

No, I won't venture into Paul's journals. They're probably locked away in his filing cabinet anyway.

I go to my bedroom and quietly take from the night table the three letters and two postcards that Paul sent me during the early part of his travel. Jonathan is snoring away. I go to Anna's room and sit on the edge of the bed and turn on the reading lamp. I re-read the first letter, reliving the joy I'd felt when I received it. It arrived two weeks after Paul had left. In it Paul calls me Kuk-Kuk, the name lovingly stamped with guardian, adviser, brother, defender, at a time when Paul affectionately looked up to me—before he became Ma Kirton's Genius.

> *Havana, Cuba.*
> *25 March 2005*
>
> *Dear Kuk-Kuk,*
> *Surprised. Right? How's your schoolwork progressing?*
> *Cuba's great and beautiful, and people are nice and everything. I am happy to say that here there are no signs of the consumer society that's poisoning us North Americans and choking our landscape with garbage. But it's not what I expected. But, then, I'm not sure what I expected. I sort of had the fantasy that I'd see El Commandante giving one of his long speeches. I have this weird feeling that something's wrong. People look happy enough, though —happier than in Montreal, for sure.*
> *I'm in Havana at the moment. It's really fantastic to look at all the beautiful buildings and squares—plazas, they call them here—everywhere from the colonial period, even though most of them need a good repair job. They're impressive, but I can't forget they were built on the backs of slaves and the poor. (Cuba and Brazil were the last New-World states to abolish slavery.) Havana, they say, is very European. I haven't been to Europe, so I don't know. Santiago, people here say, is Africa transplanted to Cuba. I'll be taking the train there in a couple of days.*
> *Just thinking how great it would have been if you and I were making this trip together. Surprised to hear me say that, right? Remember when we went to St. Lucia? That's when I found out all your names and you became my Kuk-Kuk. Remembering what an asshole you were the night before I left, I should rename you Fucked-up. Anyhow, for now, you're a tiny bit forgiven and have become again my Kuk-Kuk.*
>
> *One Love,*
> *Paul*

Anna was excited about the letter. I didn't let her read it. "Why didn't he write to me?"

I remember the St. Lucia excursion well. I was 13, Paul seven. Havre's Methodist Church had organized it as a fundraiser. We'd spent a weekend there.

I recall the ship sailing into the Castries harbour with land on both sides all the way into downtown Castries, Paul's hounding Grama to take him to the Union Nature Trail, and Grama frantically asking the hotel staff how to get there. He had binoculars that Anna had sent him a couple months before. He'd spent a lot of time on deck looking at the birds skimming the surface of the sea and identifying them by their crests, mantles, and what not. In the end we didn't visit the Trail because the guides didn't work on Sundays, and the ship back to St. Vincent set sail Sunday at midnight. He'd wanted to see the Saint Lucia parrot in its natural habitat. In his scrapbook on Caribbean birds he had photographs of it.

(A year later, instead of a weekend excursion to Grenada, Grama made it a five-day trip. We took the plane—a 30-minute flight—and Grama called ahead to arrange an outing to the Ridge and Lake Circle Trail so Paul could observe the birds and she could see the wild orchids. But it rained four of the five days we were there, and we didn't go. We never even got a chance to bathe in Grande Anse's turquoise waters and could only stare at it from atop the fort overlooking St Georges. When we got back to St. Vincent, Paul compensated by spending an entire day at the Botanical Gardens observing and photographing the parrots breeding in captivity there. Yes, you gave Paul what he wanted. He hounded you until he got it.)

*Kuk-Kuk.*We'd needed travel documents for the St. Lucia trip, and Paul wanted to know everyone's middle names. His is Ezekiel. He paused on Habakkuk and knocked his teeth together: "Kuk-kuk!" He laughed. "It rhymes with ..." His eyes glowed.

"You better not say it."

"Can I call you Kuk-Kuk?"

"No."

"I want to call you Kuk-Kuk. I mean it in a nice way. As a friend. Can I? Please, Big Brother?"

"No."

Thereafter he called me Kuk-Kuk, and when Grama slipped and called me Kuk-Kuk too, he told her to stick to Jay. And he never used it when strangers were around. In Montreal, after Paul became full of vitriol, Kuk-Kuk died and Jay was reborn, often with a qualifying expletive; except, when in contempt, I became "Jacob Habakkuk Zephaniah," followed by explosive laughter and thigh-slapping.

I pick up the postcard Paul sent from Belize. It's a scene taken at a sixty-degree angle of Hopkins Beach. It shows a deserted beach of golden-sand and a broad expanse of blue-green water—intent on evoking serenity. The text is in tightly-packed, very fine script:

> *Dangriga, Belize*
> *April 14, 2005*
>
> *As you can see, I'm in Belize. Hoping tomorrow to meet with a Garifuna historian. They're descendants of the Black Caribs (Kalinago, Garifuna) the British banished here from our home island at the end of the 18th century—in order to occupy their land. They've kept their language and traditions. Cool. Rediscovering how much I loved to bird-watch. The tanagers here and the vast range of parrots—mostly green—and trogons are something to see. Nature's artistry. Wow! Exciting! Bro, this trip is great. I'm finding my bearings. Getting in touch with my deeper self. I can feel the ugliness oozing out of me. I know now it's what I came to do. Keep your ears in good form. You'll hear a lot when I come back.*
>
> *One love,*
> *Paul*

The card arrived on one of Anna's days off, and she'd got it from the mailbox. "He didn't even mention me. Jay, he didn't mention me."

"Ma, he's doing it deliberately because he knows you'll be hurt. Cheer up, Ma. Don't fall into his traps."

She did brighten up. Even ate supper that evening, and instead of shutting herself away in her bedroom, she stayed in the living room, and chatted about Georgetown of all places, recalling the people we knew there, mostly members of Caleb's congregation, and wondering what had become of them.

***

If the embassy doesn't locate Paul within the next two weeks I think I'll have to forgo teaching this fall, suspend my studies, and go in search of him. Not that that would bother Paul. When I began my doctorate Paul smirked and said: "If you truly had intellect you wouldn't go chasing after degrees. See, I didn't even get a high school diploma because it's all in here." He tapped his skull. "You must collect degrees otherwise people won't think you're bright. Wouldn't you love to have my intellect?"

***

The other postcard, six weeks later, came from Honduras. It features an impressive sculpture of a Neanderthal-like figure holding something. The printed explanation says it's a monkey man, the Mayan Storm God holding a sceptre or a torch.

> *Tegucigalpa*
> *April 21, 2005*
>
> *I'm in Honduras. You, a historian, should be here to see the impressive achievements of the Maya. It's they who should have conquered Europe. Just think what they might have done, if they'd only discovered the wheel.*
>
> *Getting ready to move on to Guatemala. Have to see Tikal, the great Mayan site there, to compare it to Copán, the Honduran one.*
>
> *One love,*
> *Paul*

For a while I listen to Jonathan's snoring. Of late I find myself trying to read but not seeing the words. Without realizing it, I discover I'm up and pacing the space from the bedroom door to the window. Definitely. I'll have to go and check out the newspapers of the past months. How seriously is the Canadian High Commission working to find him? The week it became clear that Anna was dying, I sent Foreign Affairs several photos of Paul and a lot of personal data. Paul hadn't registered with the Canadian High Commission, and the Guatemalan government has no record that he left the country. His visa was for three months. To continue living legally in Guatemala he should have left the country before the three-month expiry date and re-enter. "We will try contacting the language schools in Antigua in the hope of tracing his whereabouts," a Marjorie Bligh from Foreign Affairs told me in an e-mail. "We're fairly confident that he's not in prison. The Guatemalan authorities are under international obligation to contact us in such cases."

**

I look down at the two letters on the bed and pick one up.

> *Santa Elena*
> *Costa Rica*
> *May 11, 2005*

> *Dear Jay,*
> *I'm in Costa Rica. Skipped going to Guatemala and came here instead to find out if what I'd been hearing about Costa Rica is true—that it's the Switzerland of the New World and Central America's most ecologically conscious nation. Ticans definitely love nature. No ifs and buts about that. And that's all fine by me.*
> *I travelled south on the Caribbean side. Stayed five days in a village called Cahuita. Lots of Blacks—Blacks are rare in San Jose—descendants of Jamaicans, live there. Their forebears worked for United Fruit, and now they work for the companies that have replaced United Fruit: Dole, Del Monte, Chiquita, etc. I was*

struck by how friendly Cahuitans are. They live like folks back in St. Vincent: same kinds o' houses, same sort o' farming and fishing, and they're friendly. There's a national park there, and miles and miles of beach in the form of an upside-down L. Strangely, on the horizontal arm of the L the sand is black, and on the vertical—the more popular half and beachfront for the national park—the sand is golden. Much of it is unsafe for swimming. It's full of dangerous currents.

From there I took a day trip south, not far from the border with Panama, to Puerto Viejo. It's a tourist slum for rich White boys who surf in the day and get stoned and laid at night. On the bus back, we were stopped by immigration officers who began to check people's papers. I didn't have my passport on me. Guess what, they didn't check me. I mentioned this to my landlord. He said that it was because I looked exactly like one of the fellows who operate the Cahuita National Park. Now, of course, I know I have to carry my passport around with me while I'm in Costa Rica.

A few days later I went back to San Jose and caught a bus to the Pacific Coast, to Jaco of all places. It's worse than Puerto Viejo. A one hundred percent tourist town. Nothing but surfing, swilling, and pleasuring. Giant waves that surfers love are the pull there. Further south is Manuel Antonio National Park. There are a couple of good beaches there—the only ones that could compare to our Grenadines beaches. I enjoyed bathing there. I had the pleasure of seeing sloths hanging upside-down in the trees, fat agoutis running across the paths in the Park, and iguanas sunning themselves on the rocks right beside the bathers, unafraid of people.

But the best part of my trip so far has been my visit to the erupting volcano Arenal. Imagine my surprise when the bus arrived at La Fortuna on the other side of the volcano. There were scouts looking for people to fill the hotel rooms. I'm glad I didn't book ahead. I got a room with hot water for US$10 a night. In the evening, a group of us: Swedish, Dutch, New Zealander, and British, boarded a minibus to see the volcano. We saw about a dozen bursts of lava lighting up the night sky. Afterwards we went to bathe in the thermal baths nearby. When I entered the first pool a White woman touched her husband and pointed at me. They both glared at me and got out of the pool quickly. It was only then that I became conscious that I was the only Black person there, and it occurred to me then that I was often the only Black person on the buses once I left the Caribbean coast.

All the members of the tour except me spoke to the chauffeur and workers at the spas in Spanish, which they said they'd learned in Antigua, Guatemala. Bro, I'll be heading there. I plan to come back to Canada fluent in Spanish. People here are friendly but, once you leave the Caribbean coast, few speak English, so when they begin talking to me on the buses, the conversation goes nowhere. I have to remedy that.

The next morning, I was part of a tour that took five college students from Brooklyn and me across Lake Arenal. The students left on a hiking tour once we disembarked, and a vehicle took me along a gravel road to Santa Elena (where I'm writing you from now). I've come here to visit the Monteverde Cloud Forest: El Bosque nubloso. I wanted to ascend it on foot, but, considering my frail lungs, I took a cab; inexpensive by North American standards. Once on the summit, I took one of the forest trails and was lucky enough to see a toucan. There's something majestic about being in a forest like this. I've recognized the cottonwood—here called the ceiba; one grows in our orchard in St. Vincent; it's the biggest tree in it—and the naked Indian (el indio desnudo). Many, many more of them are trees that grow in St. Vincent. There are some magnificent subspecies of balisier here that I've not seen in St. Vincent. Being in nature is what I most enjoy about Costa Rica. I've bought a videocassette of the Cloud Forest especially for you, so you'll have an idea of what I'm writing about.

It's pleasant being in Costa Rica. People here are poor but dignified and except for Coca-Cola in San Jose, I feel safe in most areas. Unlike in Belize and Honduras, where the price for everything triples and quadruples once they identify you as a foreigner,

I never feel anyone here is trying to gyp me. I wonder how long Ticans would remain like this.

Tomorrow I head back to San Jose, and in two or three days I should be in Guatemala. My health is holding so far. I use my puffer a great deal at times and at times hardly at all, depending on where I am and how much dust or pollen is in the air. I've had to use my EpiPen only once.

Oh, yes. The birds here. My old passion. My Cahuita landlord was fascinated by all the time I spent watching the tanagers — in blue, red, and mixtures of yellow, grey black, etc.: four sub-species, six different plumages — feasting on the fruit he puts out for them. What a richness of species! And the plumage! But for my frail lungs, I'd become an ornithologist. I never weary of watching them. To date, across Costa Rica, I have seen 47 species or subspecies for the first time. I keep a bird chart to help me identify them.

I'm thinking more and more that, when I return, I should seriously consider writing. I wonder if I could convince Ma to release that $40,000. After all, writing fulltime is like attending university. Don't you agree? I would need that money long before I'm thirty because when I return I plan to be fully fledged.

One love,
Paul

It was some three months later that his Guatemala letter arrived.

Antigua, Guatemala
August 12, 2005

Dear Bro,
Sorry about the delay since my last letter. I've been busy learning Spanish and not much more. My money is almost all gone. I'm tempted to beg for some of yours. In fact, I'll have no choice. I've already sold my laptop. My binoculars and camera will be next.

Man, I thought Costa Rica was lovely (I mean physically lovely), but that's because I hadn't seen Guatemala. A pity they don't know better than to litter their highways and landscape with garbage. Do you know what it is to wake up every day fronting a perfectly conical volcano—Agua—in all its majesty! In the morning I go walking—up a hill from which I am able to see the steam rising from Fuego, a perpetually erupting volcano. Antigua is in a lake bed at the foot of three volcanoes. I hope none does any serious erupting while I'm here.

I've done a weekend trip to Tikal. Guess what? A monkey pissed on me there. The forest there abounds in wild turkey and quetzals whose plumes were once reserved for royal personages.

Yes, I had the chance to compare the Mayan sites at Copán and Tikal. I can't say which is better. Just that I don't know how Europeans can say that these people were primitive. At the Anthropological Museum in Guatemala City, there are tablets of their hieroglyphs along with a wealth of artefacts. Of course, there are lessons to be learnt too. What made their civilization great was also what destroyed it. One hypothesis is that they wreaked ecological havoc when they cut down the trees to feed the expanding city.

I've also visited the Western highlands—the city of Quetzaltenango—and saw some of the most stunning scenery ever. I was there a Sunday when a whole posse of people, men and women dressed in black, emerged from a church carrying what I can only call a mini island. There must have been a hundred or more people all dressed in black carrying the damn thing on their shoulders. A marching band led them. It had a life-size statue of the Virgin Mary, one of Christ, one of John-Paul II, and a huge cross. All arranged with stones and shrubbery to form a landscape kind of. Guess you could call it an island of belief on human pillars. I've since learned that it's called una anda (whatever the hell that means, something to do with walking). Here you see that religion is indeed a burden. A burden people here take seriously. As seriously as Sisyphus his boulder. And I can see why. Most possess *nothing else. Perhaps the burden is ballast. (Existential ballast. I've just finished reading Camus' Myth of Sisyphus).*

I know you know some Spanish, so I'm trying out my newly learned Spanish on you. ¿Cómo son tus cursos? Es posible que estés preparando tus exámenes. ¿Y Jonathan? Ahora que sea posible ¿Cuándo será el matrimonio? Espero que me invites. Pero, tienes que comprarme mi vestido. Porque ahora, estoy pobrísimo.

Enough of that. There's so much to tell you about Guatemala. This must be one of the most dangerous countries on the planet. I fear going to Guatemala City alone, afraid I would get robbed. Here they hold up buses constantly, rob all the passengers, and shoot dead any who resist. Here human life is cheap. I stay on because it's inexpensive to live and study here, if one follows the lead of the locals. It looks like the entire city of Antigua depends on its Spanish language schools, some 75 of them, a teacher per student. Whole families live off the room and board they receive from students; there's a travel agency on every corner offering tours to everywhere and to everything; every coffee farm expects you to visit—for a fee of course—and of course the schools are in collusion. If you don't watch it, you spend more time on dubious local tours than studying Spanish, but after a couple of weeks the serious students catch on. And you should see the large number of restaurants filled with foreign students, their prices closer to New York's than Guatemala's. Many of the ruins left over from earthquakes have been preserved. To visit them one pays of course.

The streets are of uncemented cobblestones. Much of the ancient colonial architecture is preserved here. (In fact, the city is a UNESCO World Heritage site). And the yard of every house is entered from a locked gate. There's a solid wall from one street corner to the other. You cannot see into anyone's yard or around anyone's house, giving the impression that every house is a fortress. One disadvantage of this is that the streets are like tunnels that trap vehicle exhaust—of which there's plenty. Vehicles here are poorly maintained. They emit thick, oily, black diesel smoke. It's a challenge for me to breathe in these streets. There are some areas I avoid completely, if I don't want to cough up my lungs. Like the bus terminus, which, unfortunately, is beside the market; there fruits are abundant and cheap, but because of the choking air, I'm forced to buy my fruits at the supermarket.

As you would have already surmised, I'm keeping a detailed journal. I plan to use it when I come back and try my hand at writing. How about these entries?

Observing the volcanoes sentinelling Lake Atitlán, I think of the grandiose in nature but also of its destructive forces that we flee from or surrender to, depending. To the extent that we carry parallel forces within us, my question is: How do we deal with them? Etc.

This lake, Atitlán—its grandeur and splendour—makes me think of God in the way early humanity, without the benefit of science, would. Here, people's religion isn't far removed from that. In Antigua, my landlady went to mass daily and believed that tracing the sign of the cross on her grandchildren's forehead would protect them from danger when they're outside the house. It's pathetic to see how people are too stupid or too lazy to discover God for themselves—if they need God. In any event, like Grama, I believe that God is everywhere, is inseparable from phenomena, and is eternal only in the sense that phenomena are or aren't eternal ...

Here, as elsewhere in the developing world, missionaries are busy saving souls because it's easier and cheaper than saving bodies. The conquistadors and their successors raped the indigenous populations of their land and material treasures to build their European and Euro-American empires. They laid an impregnable base that has completely deformed the psyche of Third Worlders. Now the descendants of those made wealthy through rapine are busy saving souls and protecting wealth, and further impoverishing Third-Worlders for American, Asian, European, and their own interests ...

Here, no doubt, there must be the dignified poor. I'd love to meet them. Today I met a Mayan girl selling trinkets—she looks twelve but is really sixteen or seventeen—who was fascinated by my beard, and wanted to fondle it. I gave her a quetzal. She wanted to give me a necklace, and I hope nothing else ...

The family I stay with, who live six in two rooms in their four-room rented flat (one room's for the boarder who pays the rent, the other for the boarder who pays for the family's food and other bills), has concluded that dignity's too expensive to preserve. They beg and borrow from the boarders, and hope that what's borrowed won't be repaid—and forever lie about being robbed, medical bills, and heaven knows what.

Forty-four percent of Guatemala's population is under 15. What does the future hold for them? Already, in Guatemala City, many are Pandilleros and Pandillas (adult and juvenile criminals).

Everywhere there are the inveterate sellers. They use their children strategically. If they are lucky they make enough for beans and tortillas.

And there are paradoxes. Overweight shoeshine boys with gleaming gold teeth and cell phones—which probably lead some to believe that material poverty is apparent rather than real.

Jay, you think that with a little polishing and editing, newspapers or magazines would buy such stuff?

You who are squeamishly clean will have a hard time in Guatemala. Here you wipe your arse after shitting, fold the paper and throw it into a garbage bin, often one without a cover. I'm not sure how many people wash their hands after. Sometimes there's no washbasin nearby and quite often no soap. I saw my landlady's grandson wash his hands after using the toilet in the same water that she later used to wash the dishes. At times like these I wish there was a God I could pray to for special favours—like sparing me from fecal-borne diseases. Unlike Costa Ricans, who don't gyp you, here everyone gyps you or tries to. You've got to do some serious bargaining here. Vendors here will strip you of every penny if you let them.

Living here is imposing a rigid discipline on me—not quite a straitjacket but close—that I didn't have in Montreal. I'm up at five—then the temperature's somewhere around 12—and walk for an hour. By the time I shower and breakfast, it's 7 o'clock. I read until noon, then have lunch and head off to classes. Classes end at five. There's nothing for me to do in the evenings except read. By now, you've guessed it—I who crave attention 24/7 am lonely, unbearably so at times. The foreign students in Antigua throng the bars, but, apart from their being smoke-filled (legislation is pending to make them smoke-free), my asthma medication, not to mention my poverty, prevents me from drinking, so I stay away from them. I have no access to television where I'm staying. The set is in one of the two bedrooms the family occupies, and as I've mentioned earlier, I've sold my laptop. Here you can buy in English pretty well all the books written about the Mayan and Aztec civilizations, including a couple by the Canadian Ronald Wright. At the moment I'm reading a very interesting one written in early colonial times. It's called the Popol Vuh.

Looking forward to finishing the Spanish course. I don't think I'll visit any more countries—haven't the funds for it—so you're likely to see me in a month or two. Prepare yourself for long nights of conversation.

One love,
Paul

I remain seated on the side of the bed, still holding the pages of Paul's Guatemala letter. I'm happy that there's been tangible emotional growth in Paul—and yes, I think that Paul's writing is worth something—but if he's dead none of it will matter. It's ten months since this letter was written. And Paul implied that he was tired of travelling and would be home within a month or two. Two months would have taken him into October, the month when Stan struck. Last night I dreamed that Paul had been arrested for drug possession, and I was on my way to bail him out of prison but couldn't get to the airport.

All this criminality he wrote about. If he's been killed, they'd eventually trace his identity. He wouldn't be so foolhardy to travel without identification. He implied as much in his Costa Rica letter. Of course his body could be in some shallow grave or in some forest off the beaten path. Sometimes it's where adventures end. I think of Timothy Treadwell who created a new persona and went to the wilds of Alaska to prove he could interact with grizzlies and protect them from human predators; and after 12 successful summers finished the 13th in a grizzly's maw. Sometimes it's where adventures end.

BOOK THREE
REUNION IN THE LABYRINTH

$$22$$

IT'S 5:45 PM, OCTOBER 7, my birthday. Jonathan's mother has invited me for supper at 7. I'm rushing. I have to get to the Radisson metro station. The telephone's ringing. I don't have time to answer it. The answering machine comes on. "This is a message for Mr. Jay Jackson, from Marjorie Bligh at the Canadian High Commission in Guatemala City. It's to let you know we have news of your brother Paul. The Guatemalan government informed us that at 9:15 am Guatemalan time, he boarded a flight for Miami, and from there will take one to Montreal. He knows you've been looking for him."

"Ms. Bligh, this is Jay Jackson. Thanks for letting me know. Is Paul alright?"

"I think he is. I just wanted you to know he has been located and is on his way to Montreal. If the flights were on time, he should be there already."

"Thanks." I hang up the phone and feel slightly dizzy. I sit on the sofa. My heart is racing. I try to control my breathing. The phone will be ringing any time now. It's 14 months — 14 months. *Too fast, Jay. Too fast. He hasn't told you his story yet. Wait.*

The phone rings. The caller ID screen says it's a public telephone.

"I don't know if I should speak to you," I say.

"You're expecting me. Good."

Silence.

"Shouldn't you be welcoming me back? Glad that all's well?"

"So all *is* well! And you want me to kill the fatted calf?" Silence. "I don't have all evening. I'm dressing to go out."

"Okay. Okay. You're in a position to make me crawl, so I'll crawl. I'll brown-nose if that'll make you happy." Silence. "Jay, I need to get into the apartment."

"Ma could let you in."

"Ma is dead, Jay."

"You know that, Paul! You know that and you didn't come home." I hang up the phone and the dizziness returns.

The phone rings again.

"Jay, calm down. Please. I found out yesterday. I went to Guatemala City with a friend, and I ran into my ex-Spanish teacher in front of the Cathedral tour-guiding a group of students. He told me somebody had come to the school trying to find me and had placed ads to let me know my mother had died. I booked my passage immediately—at great risk—right away and went back to Huehuetenango to collect a few things. I have been on buses and planes for the last 36 hours."

"Paul, it's my birthday and I have a supper engagement at 7."

"Happy birthday."

"I'll leave a key under the mat at the front door."

"I need money for the cab too."

Of course you do. The opposite would have been news. Guess I shouldn't knock it; cheaper than getting you out of jail.

"I have only eight US dollars, and I'm hungry and stink."

"I'll leave $60 with the key, enough for the taxi and a meal. It's a loan. Understand? A loan!"

"Not so fast, Bro. Not so fast, my Kuk-kuk! Wait until I explain myself." He hangs up the phone.

Jay, let him explain himself. My eyes overflow. The dizziness is gone and I feel calmer. *Fool, phone Mme Beaulieu. Tell her Paul has arrived and you can't come.*

"I am *soulagée.* Wait your brother and *amène-le.* One *instant. Jonathan, Paul est arrivé. Je te passe Jay.*"

"*Pas vrai! Paul est arrivé!*"

"*Oui. Il vient tout juste de me téléphoner de l'Aéroport Trudeau.*"

"We can go get him."

"He's already on his way."

"Wait for him. I'll come get you. We have to celebrate this. Whoo-hoo!"

I'm silent.

"Cheer up, man. He's alive and back home. *A tout à l'heure.*" He hangs up.

I go out to the corridor and put the money under the mat and return inside and leave the door unlocked.

Twenty minutes later Paul raps and enters the apartment. He drops the grey carry-on case, all the luggage he has, at the door and comes toward me with his arms wide open. His beige shirt and white cotton slacks are crumpled. He seems thinner. His eyes are red and his forehead glows. His head is shaved and his face is clean-shaven with some of its roundness gone. He reeks of stale sweat. I stay seated on the sofa, my arms folded. He sits beside me and puts an arm around me. We sit there for what seems to be a long time until I hear Jonathan's stomping heels followed by his rapping and the key turning the lock.

"Go have a quick shower, Paul. Jonathan's mother wants you to come for supper."

Paul leaves us, and Jonathan sits beside me. "He's lost a lot of weight, at least ten kilos. What do you think, Jay?"

"Jonathan, I'm not thinking."

Jonathan puts his arm on my shoulder. We sit in silence while Paul is getting ready.

Paul comes into the living room. He's dressed in olive green slacks and a pale grey knitted long-sleeve shirt. A teal-blue hand-knitted cardigan printed with geometric Mayan motifs is draped over his left shoulder. His eyes are riveted on Jonathan. "Congrats. Have you guys got married?"

"*Tu te trompes,*" Jonathan says. "We're not a couple, if that's what you're implying."

Paul's lips retract, one hand goes to the back of his head and the other to his chin.

"Let's go," Jonathan says.

Raymond Beaulieu, his thick white hair glossy under the foyer light, squinting in spite of his glasses, is at the door when we arrive. I introduce Paul. Raymond is 77, 15 years older than Cecile. I admire him. As a young man, barely in his twenties, Raymond worked to unionize his co-workers, and was branded a communist by Premier Duplessis. For 18 months he'd had to sleep in a different house every night to avoid being arrested and thrown in jail. In his later years he joined the administration of the CSN.

Inside, Cecile Beaulieu—coiffed with a gleaming gold pom-pom, cheeks pink and round, pendant jade earrings, an emerald-green silk dress, a beige apron—pulls me to her bosom and gives me a loud lip smack on both cheeks. "*Bonne fête, mon fils!*"

I introduce Paul and she searches our faces for resemblances.

Supper is onion soup au gratiné, stuffed tomatoes, lamb with rosemary sauce, roasted potatoes, and a mixture of roasted red, green, and yellow peppers, washed down with Beaujolais red wine.

While Cecile is in the kitchen putting together the dessert, Raymond says: "So, Monsieur le Voyageur, tell us about your trip."

"Nothing special to tell. I got malaria once, stomach trouble a few times. Got robbed once. On another occasion had to crouch behind a car until a gun battle ended."

"*Ça alors! Parle-nous ça.*"

"The robbery or the shoot-out?"

"*Le vol d'abord.*"

"*Maman,*" Jonathan calls. "*Viens écouter ça.*"

Cecile comes and stands at the entrance between the kitchen and the dining room.

"It happened a Saturday night. We'd gone clubbing, four of us, in Guatemala City. We'd arranged for an SUV to pick us up at 3:15 am to take us back to Antigua, less than an hour's drive from Guatemala City. When we left the club, we saw a black car following us. About half way between Antigua and Guatemala City, on a stretch of downhill road, the car sped past us, stopped, and blocked us. Three masked guys came out from the black car, their guns trained on the SUV. 'Get the fuck out and put your hands up,' one of them shouted in perfect English. Next they shot bullets into the tyres of the SUV. We got out of the SUV. They ordered us to face a steep bank and to empty our pockets. We did.

One frisked us to make sure we'd handed over everything, while the others trained their guns on us. They demanded our watches too. Hans—from Germany—lost his Swatch. I'm sure it all took less than three minutes but it felt longer. Then they got into their car and sped back toward Guatemala City.

"Ten minutes later a police cruiser with two officers came by. Our chauffeur explained what had happened. They squeezed us into their cruiser and took us back to Antigua.

"'*¡Estén feliz que no hayan muertos!*'" (Be glad there were no deaths) the officer who did all the talking said to us.

"Eleven days after the robbery, the police officer who'd interviewed us came to the school with our wallets. He said somebody found them in a forest somewhere outside of Guatemala City. Everything except our money and credit cards was still in them. I lost about $30. I kind o' knew this sort of thing could happen, so the only ID I had in my wallet that night was the data page from my passport. I'd left my ATM and credit cards at home too. The other guys weren't so lucky. Of course, the robbery never made the news. Too routine I guess.

"All in all, we just happened to be at the wrong place at the wrong time. I stayed in Guatemala for 13 months after that and nothing like this happened to me again. And of all the students in the school—there were over a hundred of us—we were the only ones that got robbed ... Guess because we'd had the temerity to go into the capital on a Saturday night."

"*Et pourtant tu y'es resté pour encore combien de temps?*" Raymond asks.

"Thirteen months. That's a long story that will take more than a thousand and one nights."

"Coffee's ready," Cecile says.

Long before the party is over Paul falls asleep on the living room sofa. Around 1 am, Cecile prepares the spare room for him. I share Jonathan's bed.

23

I**T'S SUNDAY. WE'RE** back at the apartment. Each of us waits for the other to make the first move. Paul's in his bedroom.

Is he hiding from me?

I'll settle the estate as soon as possible and give him his share and wash my hands of him. Here he's back after fourteen months of silence and can't even say sorry.

I'm hungry. We'd had toast, coffee, and orange juice at the Beaulieus'. *Don't cook, Jay. Don't be his servant.* I go to the kitchen, grab a handful of cookies, open the fridge, pour myself a tumbler of apple juice, and take them to my room. I pull out Marcel Trudel's *L'Esclavage noir au Canada français* from my bookshelf. It's on the list of texts for my major comprehensive exam. At least now I can reschedule the exam for January or February. I pile up the pillows, cushion them against the headboard, and nestle myself in the bed, supporting the book on my pulled-up legs. My eyes rove over the words without registering their meaning. I can't concentrate, and know I'll never be able to until I find out why Paul had been incommunicado.

Paul raps and enters. "What's there to eat? I'm hungry."

"Cookies and juice."

"That's not food."

"There are lots of restaurants on Victoria and Côte des Neiges."

"I thought you'd be glad to see me."

I ignore the opening.

"I checked the fridge. There's no food in it. Give me some money. I'll go buy groceries and cook."

Let's see where this is headed.

"See, you're smiling. Tell me you're glad to see me alive, Jay. I want to hear it."

"Only you would say something like that. Only you. I gave up teaching, rescheduled my comprehensives, because I was preparing to come to Guatemala to try to find you. You don't believe me? Phone Marjorie Bligh at the Canadian High Commission in Guatemala. She thought I would end up getting conned by crooks, or, worse, getting kidnapped. She'll tell you how many times I called and quarrelled with them because they hadn't located you.

"You're a selfish, sadistic lout! You enjoy torturing people. You want to be a writer? Use writing to explore your own sickness. It wasn't enough for you to torture Ma while you lived with us; you continued to do so after you left. *Ma! Ma* who did nothing but sacrifice her entire life for us! While you were here I hated you for it, but I forgave you. It was adolescence, I said. It was your frustrations because you no longer got the adoration you got in St. Vincent. You were lashing out at us in anger for your asthma, for the rotten deal life has given you." I try to stop, but it's no use. "But life also gave you the best intellect any human being can have. You turned that too into a whip. Deliberately. To flog us."

Paul's staring at the floor.

"Then you went away, and you made Ma feel she meant nothing to you. How has Ma ever wronged you? How? You and I received the best parenting Caribbean children without fathers can ever get. The son for whose health Ma ended her marriage rejected her. Unbelievable. She bore it in silence. She did. Her only concern was that you were in good health and not in trouble. Instead of blaming you she blamed herself. She never judged you. In the end, I was glad she had her religion. Her belief in God and the afterlife was a great solace to her. But I can tell you, before her illness came, she cried a lot, grieved a lot, ate very little, and went into a depression over the fact that you never even said hello to her in your cards and letters to me. You are a *monster*.

"You were in Guatemala for a year and a half. We got *one* letter. One! No address. No way to contact you. Not a telephone. I have e-mail. I'm sure there are ISPs in Guatemala. And you damn well could have phoned—collect. You have a sick sense of power.

"Go! Get out of my sight! Leave! My wallet's in my jacket pocket. Take what you want and go buy your food. Close the bedroom door and keep out of my sight."

Paul leaves and I begin to sob. My thoughts go back to the day that Jonathan drove me to collect Anna's ashes at the crematorium, and later to the funeral service in the church Anna belonged to. Paul wasn't there, and I'd wondered if he too might be dead.

I feel listless and exhausted and eventually sleepy. When I awaken, I smell cooking. I get out of bed and see a sheet of paper on the floor inside the door. I pick it up, put it on the dressing table, and head to the bathroom.

I return and read the note. *"In much of what you say, Jay, you are right. Ma never deserved to be treated the way I treated her. But consider this. I hated myself, and I hated her for having had me. But if I am as heartless as you make me out to be, I would prefer to be dead. And there are many times I wanted to be dead, since I was 12. At times I deliberately courted it. Not writing to Ma or mentioning her when I wrote you was just a continuation of my behaviour before I left. You're right. I wanted to make her suffer. It's childish. I know. But I didn't see the consequences you mentioned —*

The telephone rings. A male voice says: *"¿Puedo hablar con Pablo, por favor?"*

"Paul, take the phone."

—If you remember well, I was supposed to leave Guatemala two months or so after I wrote you. Well, I didn't. There was a good reason for it. For that same reason, I couldn't write and didn't want anyone contacting me. Of course, some good later came of all this, but it further complicated the issue. If you will allow me to, you'll get to know the full story in due time.

Would you at least tell me what happened to Ma, what her illness was, where she's buried, etc.? I want to know.

Twenty minutes later Paul knocks on the door. "Dinner's ready. That's if you trust a monster like me not to poison you."

There's a long silence.

"What did you cook?"

"Chicken paella."

The table's set with a green damask tablecloth, beige linen napkins, crystal wine glasses, Royal Doulton plates, and sterling flatware—all of which Anna had brought back from St. Vincent after Grama's funeral. The paella is in one of Grama's Royal Doulton serving platters, and the salad in a crystal salad bowl.

Some Christmas dinner this.

Paul's watching me intensely. "Go on. Don't hold back. Say what you're thinking."

I want to say, what sort of bribe is this? Instead I ask: "Where did you learn to do stuff like this?"

"Can't tell you right now. Do you like it?"

I don't answer.

"Sit." Paul goes to the kitchen counter and returns with a bottle of Frontera. "Inexpensive but good." He fills my glass and pours himself half a glass.

"I didn't know you were allowed to drink. I was surprised when I saw you drinking last night."

"A glass of wine a day is fine. I'm having half a glass now and will have another half a glass later." He holds up the glass for a toast. "Here's to my jewel of a brother."

I don't reciprocate. "What's all this buttering up for?"

"You have every right to be angry with me. Did you read my note?"

"Yes."

"And?"

"And what! You said you have some explaining to do. I'll wait until I hear it." I sip the wine, then taste the paella. It's delicious.

"You'll never taste chicken paella better than this. Carlos' mother was impressed with it." His brow contracts. A look of embarrassment comes over his face.

"So I guess that was Carlos on the phone just now?"

He nods.

You could give Carlos the telephone number to call you here, but you yourself didn't have the decency to call. "You and he are what? Business partners?"

"Business partners! I know what you're thinking. But if I was in the drug business I wouldn't arrive here penniless."

"Maybe you spent it all to bribe the immigration officers so you could leave. Maybe you're lucky to make it out alive. I guess that's part of the forthcoming explanation."

His face grows tense, a hand goes to his chin, he bites his lower lip, and looks down at the table.

Bullseye.

His salad contains red beans, onions, tomatoes, and avocado. It's delicious. "At least you've learnt to cook. It's no longer a sissy occupation."

"Drop it, Jay. Remember I left here on a voyage of self-discovery. What I was before doesn't count. I was just over 19 when I left. It feels like I have lived two lifetimes since. On the plane, I kept telling myself that you and I are going to get along swell because we are more alike than you know, and now here we are bickering."

"Judging from how you treated Ma, basic decency isn't something we have in common. I'll say no more. I promise." I give him facing palms.

"Where's Ma buried?"

"In Havre. I put off the funeral here for two weeks, hoping you'd find out. I had her cremated and took the ashes to Havre. I lied to cover up your absence. I fooled Daddy but I didn't fool Haverites. Members from Ma's church had already sent home the news about you."

"Excuse me. I have to check the oven."

"What's in it?"

"Yucca pone."

"You can bake too!"

His face breaks into a huge grin. "Learned it all from a cookbook, to vary the monotonous diet in Guatemala."

"Even so you've managed to lose weight."

"Nine kilos. Almost 20 pounds. I left here swaddled in fat. I vowed to take off a layer or two before I got back. The Guatemalan diet made it hard—rice, corn, beans, potatoes—but I was determined. I walked a lot, taught two days a week, and wrote and read in the evenings. Had to leave lots of blanks in my writing though because my diaries were here. Where are Grama's journals, Jay?"

"The ones we brought back are still in Ma's room. Remember? There are two cartons we left back in St. Vincent."

I offer to wash the dishes. Paul shakes his head. "I'll do it. It's good to be home again. Are you happy to see me, Jay?"

"I am happy that you are alive."

"But not to see me, right? And here I was thinking we'd be like buddies again, pick up from where we left off in St. Vincent."

"Never mind St. Vincent, we'll talk at the appropriate time. Okay?"

"Why not now?"

"Because I don't want to. Isn't that a good enough reason? And you'd better watch your tone. I'm not obliged to take it anymore."

I return to my room and phone Jonathan. Jonathan reminds me that we'd planned to see CRAZY at 6:30. I speak to Cecile, to thank her for the birthday supper and the sweater she and Raymond gave me.

While dressing I think of Paul's cooking and washing the dishes. Manipulation. He's being silky smooth because he already suspects I'm the liquidator for Ma's will. I'm surprised he hasn't asked about it yet. After brushing my teeth, I stay in the bathroom a long time thinking. Was Paul the victim of too much attention? In St. Vincent he loved —needed?—Grama so much that he never did anything to anger her. He did his schoolwork without prompting, read all his textbooks by the first month of the school year and turned to mine and all the stuff he found in the library. Reads twice as fast as me. Knowledge flows into him and stays there like water in an elastic cistern. No one could have predicted that he'd become contemptuous of academe. *It has happened to others, Jay. Remember CLR James. In secondary school he revolted against his precocity. He later went on to become a leading intellectual. Ease up on Paul.*

On my way back to the bedroom, Paul, stretched out on the sofa, asks: "You're going out?"

"That's evident. Isn't it?"

"Quit barking at me! I can't take it. If you want me to leave, I'll leave, but I have nowhere to go."

"Tomorrow I'll begin the process of settling Ma's will. Understand? You'll have your share. I'll turn every cent over to you, including the money Grama said you shouldn't have until you are 30, and cut my ties with you."

"I won't let you violate the terms of her will."

"You asked to have it when you were in Costa Rica. I have lots to do. Managing your inheritance isn't on the list."

"That's more than a year ago. In my short life, a year is a long time, especially the first one without a mother and a brother breathing down my neck."

There's a long silence. *Yes, I'm being hard on him.*

"You want to come see a movie with us? I mean Jonathan and me?"

"I don't know? Should I?"

"Suit yourself." But he gets up, goes to the bathroom, comes back, and dresses hurriedly.

"How come you've lost so much weight?" I ask while Paul is bent tying his shoe laces.

"I don't have AIDS. Okay? I eat less and walk more. I've told you so already. Are you trying to catch me out in lies?"

"On our way out I'll go to the ATM at the shopping centre and get you some money, so you don't have to remain cooped up in here. Who's Carlos?"

His face darkens. One hand goes to the back of his head, the other to his chin.

"By the way, would CSIS, Interpol, or the RCMP be knocking on our doors soon?"

"If they were after me, they'd have held me at the airport."

"Only if they have enough on you to hold you. Perhaps, they're waiting for more. I want to know if the telephone is going to be bugged or is already bugged."

"It won't be."

"Paul, it's almost 14 months that you've been incommunicado. You didn't even get in touch with us when Stan struck Guatemala."

"You'll find out why in due course." He's shaking his head slowly. "Seems like you want me to give you a blow-by-account. I'll tell you alright, but in little bits."

I feel like saying: *Who in hell do you think you are?* Instead I take a deep breath.

We're still standing inside the door of the apartment.

"Give me a hug, Jay. Tell me you're just as concerned about me as you were before we came to Canada and I went bonkers. It's important. Tell me you don't judge me."

"Did you read *The Way of Life?*"

"At least five times. Thanks. Didn't I thank you in one of my letters? I meant to."

"Well, you should know I try not to judge anybody. But I want to know if the RCMP or CSIS will be bugging—or has already bugged—our phone." I put my hands on his shoulders and stare into his eyes. "Paul, I want to know that you are safe. That nothing's hanging over you. Is that different from how I was when we were in St. Vincent?"

"Yes and no. You're punishing, you're cold."

"Sorry. Ma's death, my suspended studies, your absence, sleepless nights. I can't help it."

"Forgive me, Jay. Forgive me. I'm clean enough. If anything was going to happen to me, it would have happened at the Guatemala airport or at Trudeau. I'm fine." His eyes well up.

"Do you still smoke?"

"No. Let's go. We'll discuss all this in due time. First, let me recover."

24

WE'RE BACK HOME and I'm lying in bed. The outing didn't go well. Neither Jonathan nor I had seen *CRAZY* while it was making a splash, and so we profited from its return at the Park Cinema to see it. When Jonathan met us in the foyer and saw Paul, his face became a frown. He nodded at Paul and gave me a mechanical hug. After seeing a film together, he and I would go off to a coffee shop and discuss it. We rarely agree about movies.We'd disagreed about *Broke-Back Mountain*. I defended Ennis' reticence and caution, arguing that that was how it had to be for most men who lived in places hostile to gays, not to mention bisexual men. For Jonathan there's no such thing as bisexuality: "so-called bisexuals" are homosexuals who won't accept their sexual orientation, or sexual tourists/adventurers sampling the forbidden. Usually he has so many opinions about what he's seen, he can never get them out in a single sitting. But today when we got to the café, he ordered his usual hot apple cider and sipped it quietly.

"How did you find *CRAZY*?" I eventually asked him.

"Okay."

"I thought it was excellent."

He didn't reply. Instead he encircled his cup with both hands as if warming them, and stared at the table with his head down.

Paul looked on, his eyes a glassy intensity, the redness from yesterday gone. Jonathan made brief eye contact with Paul and resumed staring at the table. Paul got up and headed to the bathroom.

In the interim Jonathan and I said nothing. When Paul returned, he put on his jacket. "I'll leave you two to yourselves. Jay, I need the keys to get in."

Jonathan said: "Have mine." He took them off his key ring and gave them to Paul.

As soon as Paul was out the door Jonathan asked: "How long are you going to carry that load?"

The question made me uncomfortable. "Not for long."

"I hope so. Pardon me. I shouldn't be meddling in your family's business."

"Jonathan, you are family: you're my brother in everything but biology. Did you like *CRAZY*?"

"Yes, but I don't feel like discussing *that*."

"What do you *want* to discuss?"

"You *know* what I want to discuss." He looked away and took a deep breath. Still looking away he said: "Last night, while you were asleep beside me, I remained awake a long time thinking about you. I wanted to be in your arms."

I held my breath, surprised.

Jonathan swallowed hard, bit his lip, and his face began to contort. He lowered his head. I watched him trying to control his emotions. He took a deep breath, then asked: "Jay, do you have a secret life?"

Perplexed by the question, I shook my head.

A couple came to sit at a table to our immediate left. The café was almost full: students working on their laptops everywhere. Jonathan lowered his voice to a whisper. "Well, I am more puzzled."

I breathed deeply. "Jonathan, you and I saw *Kinsey* and discussed it. Right? Remember what he said about how different everyone's sexuality is?"

Jonathan groaned. "Sorry I have to be so direct. Have you ever slept with anyone, Jay? I don't mean that girl you tried fooling the public with." He grimaced.

"Yes. With you. Last night."

"*Arrête de niaiser!*"

Where was this headed? I wiped my sweating hands on my thighs.

"Why's it so hard to answer?"

"Because it is, Jonathan. It is."

"What do you mean?"

"I've never had the courage to pursue anyone that far or to fall for anyone pursuing me. Not successfully at any rate."

"Not even me!"

This was slippery terrain. I tried to find an innocuous answer. "Jonathan, I never thought you were interested in me that way. Why didn't you raise the subject before? Why only now?"

"We've just watched *CRAZY*, haven't we?" His eyes brilliantly blue, his face flushed, he looked away. "Your mother's dead, Paul's been found, and you've just celebrated your 27th birthday. I know there'll be radical changes in your life." He stopped talking, looked down at the table, then fixed me with a shy smile. "Frankly, I'm being selfish. Not to put too fine a point on it, I don't want to be left out."

"Of course, you'll be included. Unless you choose not to. You'll remain my closest friend."

Jonathan groaned. "Why are you so damn naïve?" He clenched his teeth, hissed. "Remember what Paul said when he saw us sitting on the sofa? ... For years, Jay—years—I've been hoping that you'd see I desire you as more than a friend ... and would reciprocate. The nights I've spent fantasizing about the sort of life we could have together!" He shook his head slowly. "I've been in love with you since we met in CEGEP. Remember when I told you Mama thought you were my boyfriend? That wasn't the whole story. I'd told her that I *wanted* you to be my boyfriend, but you weren't taking any of my hints. You understand, Jay? Do you? I want you—more than anything else, more than my PhD even."

I was stumped. I thought of sex with Jonathan and felt my skin constricting. "Jonathan, when I complete my doctorate I'd like to teach on the African continent, and eventually I would like to resettle in the Caribbean. It's a deep need I feel. I have to experience Africa. It's vital for my psyche. Don't ask me why because I don't know why. Apart from South Africa, there's nowhere in Africa where you and I could be together as a couple. Have you seen or read the news lately about Nigeria's antigay legislation, and about the havoc Anglican bishops from Nigeria, Rwanda, Tanzania are causing in the Anglican Church worldwide over the gay issue? In the North of Nigeria, we'd certainly face death by stoning. All African countries, except South Africa—all,

Jonathan, all—are busy expanding their anti-gay laws. Speaking about the Caribbean—and it's there that I may well have to work, do you know about the Caribbean songs advocating death for gays? When I was home for my mother's funeral, those were the songs playing on the buses and in people's homes. Even the politicians have been using them against their rivals in their campaigns, because, for Africans and West Indians, to be gay is to be subhuman. A minister in the government of St. Vincent, my birthplace, said at a conference recently that he'd like to set all gays on fire. I read in a Vincentian online newspaper that in his final rally just before voting day last year, the prime minister hurled homophobic abuse at the opposition's campaign manager, believed to be gay, and then played T.O.K.'s 'Burn Chi-Chi Man-dem,' to great applause. You know what West Indians and Africans call homosexuality? The white man's disease. Do you know how many West Indians are murdered each year just because they're gay? Do you know how many of the murderers are arrested and charged? None. The police look the other way. Sometimes they lead the assault. It's ten years in prison, Jonathan—ten years—that's the penalty for committing same-sex acts in all the countries of the English-speaking Caribbean—if the person survives it to trial. And you know what's just as awful: they think their treatment of gays makes them morally superior to Europeans and Canadians, and righteous in God's sight. Their model for dealing with gays is the Sodom and Gomorrah story."

His knuckles went white from the force with which he held onto the edge of the table.

"The summer just before I left Havre to come here, the townspeople almost killed two gay fellows. They surrounded their house, stood three-four at every window, broke down the door, entered, and boxed, kicked and stomped the fellow and his partner. You know what the police said when they came: 'Serve the bullers right. The laws must change so we can clean the vermin out.' No charges were ever laid. I heard a woman telling my grandmother that if she'd been there she'd have doused them with kerosene and set them on fire: 'Set them on fire same way God rain down fire on Sodom and Gomorrah.' A few days later someone burned their house down."

For a long time Jonathan stared through the glass into the lighted street, his worry lines deep. "And you want to return there!" He shook his head with incredulity. "How could you want to return to such a place?" He pleated his lips and pressed them together, and stared with squinting eyes into mine.

"Because it's my home, Jonathan."

"Some home."

"There's another thing, Jonathan. I want to be a father and have a home with my children and their mother."

His face turned grey. He looked away. I felt guilty lying to him.

Did I take Jonathan for granted? He had latched on to me the way I imagine parents take to their adopted children, and he'd got all the help he needed from his parents.

If I'd known about the sexual attraction, would I have befriended him with the same openness? At the time he disclosed his sexuality, our friendship was three years old. He'd already become like a brother, and his sexuality mattered only insofar as he was or wasn't comfortable with it. Our friendship would have probably ended if he'd told me the full story. I'd have felt that his kindness was motivated by his desire. Took him seven years to tell me that he's been in love with me. And why hadn't I suspected? On the trip back to Montreal that December I'd felt that he was merely sharing his pain. He talked of his classmates' cruelty in high school. They'd replaced his name with *tapette* and *fiffy*. Having seen *CRAZY*, I understand now what he'd borne. He told me he'd chosen to attend an English CEGEP to avoid meeting his high school classmates.

Two summers after that first visit to Lac Sept-Îles, I went back, this time for a week. Then we were both MA students at Concordia. That was when I told him about my own sexual ambivalence, and it was then that Jonathan said that his mother had thought he and I were lovers. He was feeling me out—I see that now—and I chose not to notice.

That week. On the Tuesday we sprayed the exposed parts of their bodies with musk oil to keep away the mosquitoes and black flies, got into the family's powerboat, meandered among the numerous Sea-Doos blasting our eardrums and churning the water, traversed the lake, headed under a bridge, and continued upstream into the smaller Lac-aux-chiens, where the only sounds were birdcalls, mostly loons and crows, and the play of the breeze in the birches, pines, and poplars. Once we left the boat Jonathan got very agitated. We were sitting on a flat stone at the water's edge. I had taken off my sneakers and my feet were dangling in the water. Jonathan kept looking at me, his cheeks a deep pink, a guilty look in his eyes, as if he'd been caught doing something he shouldn't have been doing, and I could hear his breathing. Then he got up and walked a few metres away from the water's edge and into the forest; he returned and stood with his back turned to me before walking off again along the shoreline. Eventually I asked him if he was alright. He said yes. God, I'm daft!

I liked being with his family. One New Year's Day I was there and an LP by *Les Bottines souriantes* was on the turntable. I was fascinated; I'd never heard that sort of music before. In the evening, after supper and the washing up of the dishes, Raymond got out his accordion, Cecile two spoons, and Jeanne sang. Jonathan groaned and said to me: "Every year they do this. The neighbours must think we're just a bunch of hicks." But eventually he joined in, clapping. I clapped along with him. Jeanne, her voice faraway, wistful, sang what I later learned was "*le Rossignol sauvage.*" That year, when my birthday came around, Jonathan gave me a Bottines souriantes LP. I've since replaced it with the CD.

Eventually I took them things Caribbean: Jamaican patties, coconut fudge, guava jelly (from packages Grama sent us); but what they most enjoyed was Anna's black cake.

Anna never met them. Cecile wanted to meet her, but Anna kept putting it off, and eventually the interest waned. Once too I had suggested bringing Paul to Lac-sept-Îles. Paul had complained that I never took him along. Jonathan did not answer.

***

Paul raps and enters.

"Sorry."

"It's alright."

He half-sits on the edge of the dressing table across from the bed. "Jonathan's in love with you, Jay."

"You've said so many times before."

"Now I'm saying it for real. He used to blush whenever I caught him looking at you. That's why I always teased you about him. Even Ma saw how besotted he was by you. 'I can't understand why Jay doesn't take you along with him and Jonathan. I just don't understand what those two have in common.' That was a lot of criticism for her to make of her golden boy."

"And you believed there was something between us?"

"I said it as a putdown. No more than that. I knew there couldn't be anything between you two. You'd have felt you needed Ma's approval first. Sorry. Just kidding." He claps his thighs and guffaws and then his face gets serious. "You're her firstborn. You took up all the space in Ma's heart, Jay. None left for me. What can I say?" He shrugs his shoulders.

"Paul, don't say that. Your rejection of Ma drove her into a depression."

"Her guilt you mean. You loved her too much to see her faults. I was angry with her. I had to let her know. I'm not saying she wasn't dutiful and all that, but I felt like a foster child."

"You never gave her much of a chance to be affectionate to you. I remember a caring mother, who left my father after he gave her one beating too many." I tell him about Anna before she left our father.

"Why you never told me this before."

"You never allowed me to."

"You didn't try hard enough."

I sigh in frustration.

"You and she bonded. Deep. Wow. After coming such a long way, like why did Ma like go back to those beliefs?" He becomes reflective, nods a couple of times. "I understand. I can see why she wouldn't want to see the cruelty you suffered begin all over again with me. I could never say she was a cruel woman. In my mind I see her comforting you after Daddy flogged you. That sort of thing creates strong attachments and powerful painful memories. I remember all the guys who were cruel to me in school; my skin gets cold when I think about it. I don't forgive easily. People hurt me, and I stay hurt and become their enemy."

"You have to get beyond that."

He comes to sit on the side of the bed, his back to the dressing table. He puts his hand on mine and keeps it there for a long time without saying anything.

"Know something, Jay. I forgave Ma."

"Would have been nice if she'd died knowing it." *For what?*

"During those months you didn't hear from me, I was thinking about a lot o' things. You don't understand what happened to me when I came here. You don't. You saw my acting out, that's all you saw. But Ma should have known better. There are many mothers here who should know better, but they don't think or they refuse to think. Coming here was like taking me from a boat and throwing me into the sea and telling me to swim and keep clear of the sharks. Trouble is no one had taught me how to swim or how to defy sharks."

"No one can. Life's a blind journey. Besides Grama wanted us to come."

"Yes, but if Grama had lived here and seen how this society's run, she would've felt otherwise. She'd have known you don't take someone from a secure environment and toss him into chaos without prior preparation. You came prepared. You'd already learned how to be responsible for yourself and me, from the time you were 11."

I see his point. I nod. "Well, Grama is dead so we can't ask her. But you are right up to a point. Ma did realize that bringing you here when she did was a mistake."

"I'm glad she acknowledged it. When?"

"On her deathbed ... I'll tell you about it some other time."

"Clarify something for me, Jay." He stares hard at me.

"Clarify what?"

"Are you gay?"

I reply as calmly as I can. "Do you mean if men arouse me erotically?"

Paul snorts, closes his eyes, all the while shaking his head. "Yes. You're so damn clinical!"

"Have you seen *Kinsey*?"

"No."

"Well, sexuality is a lot more complex than being gay or straight."

"Did you remain in touch with that beautiful Jamaican dougla girl who had trouble with her H's, that girl you dated three or four years after we came here. For a while you two had a serious thing going."

"Tamara. No."

25

FOR A LONG while neither of us speaks.

"Back to Jonathan, Jay."

"What about Jonathan?"

"He wants you all to himself. You *don't* know that? That's why I left and came home."

For a while I'm silent. "Life comes with constraints, Paul." I stare into his eyes before adding: "Yours is your asthma."

"And looks. Adipose challenged too." He chuckles.

Ouch. "Ma's was a fear of men after Daddy's abuse. You remember how you used to tease her about joining the Baptists to find a husband?"

"What about it?"

"She'd sometimes say: 'I have news for Paul. I had enough battles with Caleb to last two life times. Baptists believe that men should control women. These born-again men ...' She laughed. 'The other day I heard this woman comic on the radio saying that women should have keys to their vaginas that they could leave at home. That way when rapists jumped them, they could say: "Sorry, buddy: I left the key at home. Not just leave it at home: put it in a safety deposit box." Then her face got serious and she said: 'When I got here I used to work for a deacon in the Pentecostal Church. He tried to rape me. Those scandals with those televangelists, they never surprised me.'" For a moment I reflect on the full story she told me on her deathbed. "Ma had her head on, Paul—she did—more than you ever gave her credit for. One of her church members, Brother Isaac, an undocumented immigrant, almost half her age, proposed marriage to her. 'Sistah Hanna, will you join me in 'oly matrimony, and become my queen?' ... 'Some king.' Paul I never heard Ma laugh so much."

Paul looks away, uninterested in the story.We're silent for a while. Paul breaks it. "I'm older. Nineteen months older than when I left. Feels like two lifetimes." It's as if he's speaking to himself. "I've had a lot of time to think, to reflect, to learn." He gazes at me, makes sure he has my attention. "I wanted to be away from you especially, because even more than Grama, you've parented me. You're the only unbroken link I've known. One day I'll tell you what I went through."

"Paul, Stan struck Guatemala, and you didn't even contact us to let know you were safe."

"I was afraid to write or call. I'll tell you the full story. One day."

"What did you want to tell me the evening before you left?"

His face tautens and he angles his head to the right and breathes out loud. One hand goes to his chin, the other to the back of his head. "That I was disgusted by the fool I'd made of myself ... my life was in shards; I didn't know if they could be put back together ... that I wanted to commit suicide: the things that brought on my depression. You'd never imagine how envious I was of you."

I'm silent. I never believed that someone like Paul who'd thrived on academic excellence could so easily turn his back on it.

"It's why we had to share a joint. It would have been too painful otherwise. And maybe I might not have told you after all." He looks away, grins guiltily. "And there was ... never mind."

"*Never mind* what?"

"You won't understand."

Another long silence. Paul breaks it. "I need your opinion on something. You remember Brady and Jack, right?"

I nod.

"The day after the villagers burned down their house, Elka, one of those who still lived in the shanty on Laird's Estate, told Grama: 'It served them right.'

"'How what they did in the privacy o' their own home concern you all?' Grama said.

"'Is abomination, Ma Kirton. Pure abomination! They lucky we

didn't burn them up too, just like God burned them sodomites in Sodom and Gomorrah.'

"'It's not their fault, Elka. God made them that way. We should
leave it up to God. If they're to burn then let God do it.'

"'No, Ma Kirton. No!' She stamped the floor. 'If God did make
them so he wouldn't o' destroy Sodom and Gomorrah. You have it all
wrong. Is 'cause they choose to serve Satan. We is Christian soldiers,
Ma Kirton. The Holy Ghost live in us and inspire us to take action
against them.' Then she frowned and stared hard at Grama. 'I see
where you is coming from. You is in their league, Ma Kirton. You is in
their league.'

"'What you mean, Elka?'

"'You want me to be plain. Well, I will be plain. Rumour have it
that you and Mercy is lesbians. And the way you is in agreement with
abomination ... hmm. Watch it; your house going be next.'"

"Really! Paul, you heard that?"

Paul nods.

"Grama, what did she say?"

"She reached under the counter and took up a box of matches and
handed it to Elka; next she opened the till, took a five-dollar bill from
it, and put it on the counter. 'Here's the matches and take this to pay
for the kerosene.' Elka left the shop then." Paul pauses. "Jay, you've
never heard people whispering about Grama?"

"No. Remember, I was rarely in the store."

"You think there was anything to those rumours?"

"No ... Aunt Mercy and Grama were friends since Ma was a tod-
dler, before Granddad's death, before Grama remarried. She and Grama
were like sisters. You saw how they lived. Some parasite of a man that
Grama spurned after she left Bradley probably started it. Grama was
too independent for them."

"Could have been Sefus Butcher."

"Sefus who?"

"Butcher. You wouldn't know him. He used to hang around the
store saying he was courting Grama. Bantering mostly. A comic. Grama
felt that if he'd lived abroad, he would have made a good living as a

comedian or storyteller. Mostly Grama hid from him. Sometimes she'd send me out front to reconnoitre; when he was there, she'd give me her instructions to take to Lucy, or send me to call Lucy if there were no customers. But she couldn't always to do that. Sefus proposed marriage, a common-law relationship, even setting up a rumshop upstairs."

"'Who will bankroll you, Sefus?' Grama asked him. He lived in a mud hut right up under the rocks. That same year or the year after the November rains washed it half way down the hill.

"'Youself, Ma Kirton, and with the profit I make I will pay you back before you can say: "Sefus, honey boy, I love you with all my heart." But by that time, me and you going be husband and wife, blend together like cake, sweet-sweet, sweeter than cake, and what's mines going be yours and what's yours going be mine.'

"He told her one day: 'Ma Kirton, the only thing missing from your life is my sweet loving. I keeping the piston well oiled for when you ready to get the engine rolling.'

"'Lay down the tracks first, Sefus. Lucy, what I will do with this piece o' twine?' She pointed to Sefus. 'Tie up myself with it?' He was tall, almost two metres, but couldn't have weighed more than 65 kilos.

"'Ma Kirton, you is not listening—if you try me—all o' me—you will be a contented queen.'

"'Sure, Sefus: on the toilet seat with grugru branches on my head.'

"Three customers had come into the store. They laughed.

"'Sefus, I'm seeing you and hearing you, and understanding you.' She cleared her throat, looked at Lucy, and winked.

"'But, Ma Kirton, you never taste me. Don't let looks fool you.'

"'Sefus, carry your sniffing someplace else. Nobody in here is in heat.'

"'That's 'cause you and Mercy does *zamay*.'

"That day—it was during school holidays—Aunt Mercy was in the storeroom at the back listening to him. She came to the front. And you know, Jay, with that stare she has when she angles her head, screws up her forehead, tears her eyes wide, and fixes you, she said: 'Go long, Sefus, you already get enough love in Laird stables where your pappy raise you.'

"Jay, everybody laughed. Everybody.

"'Make me catch you alone one o' these nights when you going home, I will show you what I learn in Laird stables.'"

Paul takes a deep breath. "I loved listening to Sefus. One day a woman came into the shop with her arm in a sling, and when she left Sefus said: 'Is sweat rice that cause that.'

"'How you know? She tell you?' Lucy asked him.

"Sefus laughed. 'He catch she doing it. Since then he going round saying, he can't leave her, that she tie him.'

"'Sefus, that don't mean *she* can't leave him.'

"'Lucy, if she did want to leave him you think she would o' sweat the rice in the first place?'

"Grama never told me what 'sweat-rice' meant. She said she didn't know. You know what it is, Jay?"

"No."

"It's when a woman lets her menstrual blood drip into her man's food. Zora Neale Hurston writes about it. Some women believe it will make a man stay forever."

"And men who want to keep women for life, what do they do?"

"I don't know. He was a boat repairman and used to work mornings and take the afternoons off. 'How come you always here, Sefus? How come you're not at the rum shop?' Grama said to him one time.

"'Ma Kirton, I saving my liver for when you and me get married. The doctor tell me to stay off grog. I come here and admire your golden eyes, watch your sweet smile, drool over your honey lips, and don't get me started 'bout your bouncing behind.'

"I think Grama enjoyed his flirting and his thinking. One day he and Elka got into an argument about God and the Devil.

"'Elka, the Devil didn't have no mother. God is his mother and father. Everything in him come from God, so God and the Devil is one. And that means that Jesus and the Devil is brothers. Is another one o' those stories where God set one brother up against the other.'

"'Sefus!' Elka shouted. 'Stop it! You is blaspheming! Stop it!'

"'Ma Kirton, you see why I want you to married me? You and me know them stories in the bible is pure make-up thing. Elka, if God didn't want me to think he shouldn't o' put brains in my head.' Jay, you missed a lot not being in the store. I'll be using a lot of that stuff in my fiction.".

Silence.

I break it. "Give Bill a call. He's been worried about you."

"I will, tomorrow. I sent him a card from each of the countries I visited. It was he who told me I should come clean with you."

"About what?"

Paul looks at the floor, swallows loud, then breathes loud and turns his head away for a while. He takes another deep breath. "When I told him about wanting to leave home, he asked why and said that going away should be about more than just running away from family; that most people who leave home discover it's themselves they're trying to run away from ... " He sighs, stops talking, purses his lips and shakes his head. Something about this is stressing him. "I told Bill how impressed I was by Thoreau's Walden sojourn. He said to forget about Thoreau, that Thoreau was preparing himself for that since birth. 'If you must go away, go somewhere with a different culture, where no one knows you. It will help you to see with new eyes.' He'd gone to Chile, excited by Allende's election victory in the early seventies, and had to be evacuated by the Canadian High Commission when trouble broke after Allende's overthrow.

"I told him about the nasty, homophobic stuff I used to lay on you." He stares into my eyes, then looks away and pauses. "Jay, you're lucky. Damn lucky."

"Meaning?"

"You're healthy. You never faced high school bullying. You even had Ma all to yourself. You've had Jonathan, faithful as a dog, for a friend. Now you can even have him as a boyfriend, if you were so inclined. You hit six on the dice all the time. The guys I chilled with. *Un vrai calvaire*. All they did was smoke and listen to crude rap. They were afraid to think. They wanted to destroy everything they were afraid of or didn't understand ... I know that now."

Seems to me you weren't so different. "So why did you hang out with them?"

"I *had* to hang out with them. In high school you belonged to a posse or you were toast. Toast, man. Toast. Guys saw who your posse was and knew there'd be trouble if they messed with you. I needed those guys for security. It was that or get pushed around, beat up, and dissed all the time. But there were dues, membership dues. Understand what I mean?" He swallows.

"I left here to learn to be on my own, to put distance between them and me, and distance between you and Ma and me." He stares at the floor, compresses his lips. "It was the right decision. Didn't always seem so, but it was the right decision." He's nodding slowly. "Bill was right. There was a lot to learn. As long as I was learning I was distracted. I was in places where no one knew me, so no one could judge me. I didn't have to prove anything to anybody. I felt free. Afraid too. And always vulnerable. And I began to understand that in life we are alone. Those evenings by myself were what I needed. It wasn't easy. But it was good medicine." He frowns, then looks at me, and smiles nervously. "In Central America I had a lot of time to look back on what was happening, and I could see that we are like Armistead Maupin's characters. You know his books?"

I shake my head.

"You must read them. We know that we're dissatisfied with what we have. We think there's something better, but we're not sure what it is; we know there's some place we want to get to, but not much more; we set out looking for it, but what we find isn't the place we're looking for. We search in the concrete for something that's not concrete at all. And as to that thing we call happiness, we're all searching for it, and we rarely find it, and if we do, it lasts no longer than fog at daybreak. And we are angry that it doesn't last or come when we want it. And sometimes we feel we have to lash out at somebody for this."

"Like you lashed out at Ma."

"Yes. And you. And I did because I could do so safely."

Silence. A long one.

"Lashed out at myself too. I know that now." He tilts his head upwards and pulls in his lips. "We have to invent our own happiness. I mean ways to feel at peace. I, for one, mustn't be idle for long periods.

Even during periods of reflection I should keep a notebook beside me. When I'm idle desperation overwhelms me." He lowers his head and stares at me. "You've never had to learn any of this. You've never had an idle moment in your life."

"Is that a good thing, Paul?"

"For you, perhaps it isn't. For me it is."

Silence. It lasts a good two minutes.

"You know what my main weakness is?"

I shake my head.

"Being ignored. It's hard, hard to admit this. I've done a lot of things I didn't want to do to get noticed." He stops talking, twists and turns his neck, stretches his arms, and breathes out loud. "I cried when I found this out one rainy night in Antigua, Guatemala ... Things would have been better between us, a helluva lot better"—he nods slowly—"if you'd answered me more often, taken up my taunts, pushed me to do my school work, and quarrelled with me about the company I kept. Pin me to the wall. Understand what I mean?"

No kidding. So you could pop me like a dry twig.

"You thought I wanted to be left alone. I used to say so, and I fooled you all." He sighs. "Anyhow you had your own work to do. Sometimes I insulted you just to get your attention, like calling you vermin. That shit I spouted about the weak being food for the strong, that's stuff I was repeating, stuff that this Italian army cadet in our group used to say. I already knew that the powerful turn the weak into tools. I don't condone it, but I understand why poor people in Mexico, Jamaica and other places turn to drug trafficking and setting up their own protection army, knowing full well they could be killed. They know that in the scheme of things their lives ain't shit, and they refuse to be shit rags for the powerful who make the laws that protect their power and their loot. You're a historian. You know the how and why of colonialism. I know about it from your textbooks. When I learned that Britain went to war with China to keep selling opium to the Chinese, I understood how deeply depraved we human beings are ... I am sceptical about what the Capitalist media tell us. I saw how the media work in Central America, whose opinions are broadcast, whose are ignored." He looks away, bites his lower lip.

Silence.

"Yes, I wanted you to give me shit. That's what I wanted, as long as you didn't let Ma in on it. I found that out for certain while I was travelling and had nobody to dump on. Another thing: I can't live without affection." A pained look envelops his face. "It frightens me, Jay. Loneliness frightens me."

"Who is Carlos?"

There's panic in his face, and one hand rubs the back of his neck, the other kneads his chin. His eyelids flutter. "Ahm, he's Maria's brother. She's your age. A couple months older. Gilead-balm for my tired soul."

"*Gilead balm!*"

He nods and smiles and takes furtive glances at me.

"So you'll be heading back to Guatemala soon?"

"Yes. Until she can come here. I want to be with her at Christmas."

"Wow! How long have you known each other?"

"Eleven months and fifteen days. We've lived with her widowed mother at her house. She passed me off as a boarder." His left hand goes back to his neck, his eyelids flutter, his right plays with his chin.

"So you took up with Maria and forgot about us?"

"That's not quite how it happened."

"How did you meet her?"

"It began on a bus in Quetzaltenango, also called Xela, Guatemala's second city. I had fled there from Antigua. But after two days, I thought it would be better to go north, to Huehuetenango, Hue for short; partly to check it out, partly to see whether I could lie low there and find a way to sneak over into Mexico.

"I was on one of these chicken buses: imported old school buses with leg room for elementary school kids. I got to the station early, and I was the second person to board the bus. There was one other passenger, a young woman, about five rows back of me. A newspaper vendor came inside the bus, and I bought a newspaper. While I was looking for coins to pay her, she exclaimed, '*¡Qué bellísima barba! ¡Me lo permite tocarla!*' (What a beautiful beard! May I caress it?) And, without waiting for a reply, she began fondling my beard, and asked: '*Me* *quieres?'* (You desire me?) Jay, I was too surprised to say anything. And she's like, *Por favor, deme tus direcciones.'* (Give me your contact information, please.) I told her I was heading to Hue and didn't know when I would return. She reached for the newspaper she'd sold me and wrote a telephone number on it, and said I should call her when I got back to Xela.

"The young woman five seats back was Maria. As soon as the newspaper vendor left, she came to sit beside me, and we chatted all the way to Hue. She wanted to know why I was going to Hue. I lied, of course. She told me she lived there, with her mother and brother, who taught French. She was eager to know where in Hue I'd be staying. I told her I didn't know yet. She said maybe I could stay with them. She called her mother on her cell, and then said it was okay. They live in zone II, near the centre of Hue, a few blocks uphill from the central market, about 20 metres from the Temple of Minerva. Three nights later, she came into my room and said, *'¡Qué bellísima barba! ¡Me lo permite tocarla!'* I laughed because I had already shaved my head and beard. She bent down and kissed me. And so on and so forth.

"She's Ladino, a mixture of Spanish and Maya, and is as dark as most South Asians. She's a trifle taller than me and a bit on the heavy side. Guess from all that starchy food. In bright light her hair looks blue-black, like the feathers of a male grackle."

"She persuaded me to stay on in Hue to perfect my Spanish." He smiles broadly and looks away. "And I didn't object. We're as good as married. She and I quarrelled once, about why I wasn't in touch with you all. I told her you and Ma had put me out because I'd flunked school, and so I left home angry and wasn't ready to mend the break." The left hand to the back of his neck, the right to his chin.

"You told her that!"

"What else could I tell her?"

"The truth." I wonder where this bullshit is heading.

"She was puzzled about where I got the money to travel. I told her the truth: that I inherited it from my grandmother."

This is the first truthful part of your story but I won't challenge you.
"So you were in Guatemala City when you found out about Ma's death?"

"Yes. One of Maria's aunts was dying in a hospital there. She, Carlos, and Rosa went to visit her, and, since I didn't teach on Thursdays and Fridays, I went along too."

"You left out something important: What made you run away from Antigua and want to sneak across the border into Mexico?"

"I'll tell you in due course."

"Why not now?"

"I'll tell you. Don't worry. No one's coming to arrest me."

A long silence.

"So you're in love."

"I am. It's the best feeling in the world. Here's somebody who loves my ugly asthmatic body. And I love her too. It's a helluva lot more than I've come to expect. Too much rejection. From every quarter."

"Not from us and not from your teachers. Be fair! *You* rejected them."

"I have news for you. My chemistry teacher, the computer science teacher — they were bigots. I won't even go into the details about the chemistry teacher. Suffice it to say he had it in for me because of the way I'd answered a question."

"What was the question?"

"'Where are you from? You don't speak like a Black.' Imagine asking me that, and in front of the entire class! He had this thick accent that would make us laugh at times. He was hump-backed, shorter than me, and his beady eyes peered through glasses centimetres thick. I answered: '*La Terre, monsieur. Et vous?*' The class exploded with laughter and desk drumming. Jay, he turned lilac and held on to his desk. It was cruel of me. I know that now. If I ever run into him I'll apologize. After that, every day he'd ask me questions about things he knew I didn't know and sneer at me. Every day, for about two months, I wanted to kill him. I stopped going to his class. He lost control of his class shortly afterwards and was off for a long time on burn-out leave.

"And as for Illich, the computer science teacher, oh boy." He shook his head and clenched his teeth. "I wanted to *spit* in *his* face. Richard Hazan sat beside me in the computer room. One day he put a paper clip in the computer I was using and shorted it. I knew he'd done it, but you don't rat, see. Illich said it was me: 'It works with electricity, not witchcraft.' Jay, he said that to *me*. The sonofabitch said that to me. The class laughed. I brought the computer crashing to the floor and headed for the door. He tried to step in my way. When I lifted my foot to kick him, he moved aside. I never went back to his class. A monstrous eel, that's what he looked like. Blue-stone eyes. Smelled like ham. A week later, he tried to apologize to me in the corridor and begged me to return to class. I clamped my lips, afraid of what I'd say to him."

I want to tell him his reaction was excessive, but remember there are no half measures with Paul.

"Jay, I've told you before, I'm telling you again: count your blessings you didn't have to go to high school here."

Silence.

"Love can do miraculous things. I lost that anger in Guatemala."

No kidding. "I've heard all you said, but I'm still puzzled by why you chose to fail in high school."

"*Chose!* Wrong word. I won't study boring stuff." He pauses, smiles. "And let's just say my academic success would have been a big thing for Ma, something for her to brag about. She was living her life through us."

"What's wrong about her bragging?"

"How many times do I have to tell you? You didn't go to high school here. You went to Kingstown Secondary where it was cool to succeed. You studied all the time, even during vacation. That won't gain you any cred here. We went through this already when Ma had me see that psychologist."

"But some students resist and succeed."

"Yes, geeks. Guys like Alvin. This pitch-black Jamaican with a chest like a steamer trunk and the face of a bulldog. He and a girl called Gina were the only Black geeks that hung out with us. He graduated my fourth year there, won several prizes, and was valedictorian. One day when the Jamaicans were carrying on about what to do with all the 'battybwoy-them like pest all 'bout the place,' he said: 'You all sound like those lunatic Christian Reconstructionists. I bet unno twenty dollars unno don't know what Jamaica motto is.'

"'I know Barbados motto: Pride and Industry,' Doc said. He was a gigolo. A dougla fellow from Grenada moved away from the group and shouted: 'All you motto is: Woman fi get lick and battybwoy fi dead,' before bolting up the stairs, leaving thunderous laughter from the non-JAs. We 'small-islanders' loved it when the Trinnies and JAs got their comeuppance.

"Then Alvin said in disgust: 'Out of many one people. That include battybwoy too. Every day is battybwoy this and battybwoy that; chi-chi man this and chi-chi man that. That is all unno know?' He didn't stay around for their reaction.

"That's how I found out about Christian Reconstructionists. I asked Wilma if she was one. She belonged to a religion like Ma's and saw every military conflict as the beginning of Armageddon. You remember that conversation we had about them?"

I nod.

"Alvin was a born leader. No doubt about it. He insisted that we go to the protest that Reverend Gray led when the police killed that fellow from St. Vincent. His girlfriend, his father, mother, and an older brother—a law student—were all there. His father was on the executive of the Montreal Caribbean Cultural Association then. I'm sure you've seen him talking on television about police brutality and racial profiling.

"I don't know how Alvin got away with it. Guess he had the brawn to protect his brains. But some of those guys owned guns or had easy access to them. Every once in a while he and Doc would come close to blows. Tall and good looking—that was Doc—could easily be a GQ model. Alvin gave him the name Doc. One day Alvin was getting on his case about his occupation, and he told Alvin to bugger off, that Alvin's role was to solve equations and his was to heal."

"Just two academic students? There had to be others."

"Sure, in the elite classes—the Black geeks. There was one geek class per grade. Ten-ten twelve Blacks in each, mostly girls and gays. They didn't hang out with us. Probably hid from us. Probably ashamed of us. And yeah, the Black girls on the whole. They all did some homework. Even the worst slackers among them got serious at exam time. But for Black guys in the group I hung out with, a successful Cedien had to be good at sports, have a great body, and a big dick. And in gym the Black guys who did teased the ones who didn't."

Silence—a long one.

"Gay guys are just as obsessed with dick size. Some gay dating sites request it as part of the dater's profile, sites like Priapus. Carlos and I used to read them and laugh."

"Is Carlos gay?"

"I don't know." Hands to the back of his neck and his chin.

"Continue."

"I skipped gym on account of all that. When I did push-ups and my breathing got loud, this guy used to laugh and say: 'My papa did have a 'orse what sound just like you. Them did shoot it for put it out o' him misery.' Too much locker room shit, Jay—too much. I'm no athlete. An upside-down bottle: *une bouteille renversée*—a Haitian called me that in a cuss-out. *Una botella invertida,* the Hispanics took it up, laughed, high-fived." He pauses, stares at the floor. "Still you have to give me some credit. I kept up English, French, and history all the way. Bégin didn't give me the English prize—I won it fair and square. He vetoed Mrs. Mehta's decision, because I'd screwed up in most of the other subjects. Those teachers understood me. They did, and they taught what I liked, and they could teach."

"Then why didn't you do better in biology? Mrs. Bensemana got you out of police custody a couple o' times. You even had fantasies of screwing her."

"She's a good teacher and a good person. I'll grant her that. One time she was on duty when Alfred was picking on Milford and John—two Black, openly gay geek guys with lockers close to us—and the other guys were egging him on, and she told Alfred: 'You're seeing in them something that is in you. Deal with your problem and leave them alone.'" He stares at the floor, his forehead screwed up. "She shouldn't have let Bégin suspend me. Take Madame Loubier. One time we were doing this assignment on verbs that end in 'er'. One of the sentences we had to make was with the words *sucer, bébé* and *pouce.* My sentence was: '*Maintenant le bébé suce son pouce. Quoi sucera-t-il lorsqu'il sera grand?*' You know what Madame Loubier did? She ticked the first sentence correct and ignored the rest. You know why? She knew that was hormone blabber. But Mrs. Bensemana—some biology teacher—

she couldn't let it go. Had to humiliate me. Push me to the wall. And I had to get even. I just had to get even."

"Paul, get real! You told her you wanted to screw her. And you gave your classmates copies of your request. And when she first ignored you, you went after her again. If you were adult, you'd have been accused of stalking. So you failed biology to punish *her*?" I chuckle.

"I attended her classes—a lot more than I did for the courses I failed outright. I loved her class. I just didn't do the assignments. I got 88 on the provincial exam, zero for class work, and 62 after they normalized it. I didn't fail biology. Well for me—my standards—a 60 is a failure … Jay, you saw how I howled when I looked at Grama lying in the casket. Afterwards I had nightmares in which she stared at me in silent anger."

Silence. Paul opens and closes his fingers the way Anna did when she was flustered.

"*Metamorphoses*. Sometimes we escape into traps. Daphne escaped Apollo's lust and became a tree. I fell into that depression when I knew I'd trapped myself. You set fire to your enemy's house and end up burning down your own. You discover that the people you see as enemies are really friends. Our intellect and our instincts are at war. Intellect loses and later punishes us with the knowledge that we were daft. Addicts must know this … These are thoughts I explore in my journal under the heading Self-Amputation. You too could benefit from similar self-exploration."

"Maybe, Paul. But we hope that common decency trumps all else. Think back to the fairy tales Grama read to you. Witchery in them was just another name for cruelty—cruelty that turns beauty into ugliness. But kindness, love, and justice turn even frogs into princely human beings. It's why some people love Christianity. It's a lovely fairy tale for adults who need it. And all of us need a fairy tale at times."

Paul sneers, tries to hide it, and gives a yes-and-no headshake. "Then here's something I think you should know. Remember that asthma attack I had at the police station? Well, a month after the incident Mrs. Mehta pushed me to get involved in a mentoring programme the cops were trying to establish with inner-city high schools. Ma had to agree. I told her I wouldn't do it if she told you. Did she tell you?

"No, she never did." *Of course, she told me.*

"You see, that's how much I looked up to you. I didn't want you to know that I'd sunk so low. I had one outing with the cops, François and Nadine. Both French-Canadian. François looked like he was in his late forties or early fifties: youngish face, hair completely grey, kind brown eyes—not eyes you associate with cops. Nadine was young, late twenties, brown eyes too, face like a hatchet. Tall. As tall as François. Dressed in civvies, they came to the school one Thursday just before lunch hour. I was in English class. Mrs. Mehta talked with them outside the door. I got into the car, not a police cruiser, and they took me to a fast food joint outside Côte des Neiges. François told me that my teachers said I was very bright, but they were worried I might go delinquent. He showed me pictures of his three children—a boy 19 in CEGEP, a girl 16 just finishing high school, and a girl 11. He'd sent all his children to Collège Français, a private school. His wife taught in a private school on the South Shore. Nadine asked me about St. Vincent. I told them about Grama, Cousin Alice, Aunt Mercy, you, and Ma. They already knew about you. Guess Mrs. Mehta had filled them in. François did most of the talking. He gave me his phone number and arranged for me to go see a film with his children the following Saturday. I didn't go and I never called." He falls silent for a long time, swallows a few times. "My classmates would have put a price on my head. They'd have branded me a snitch, a *délateur.*" He bites his lower lip and swallows. "That's no fairy tale.

"For a while I'd see François around, and he'd wave to me and smile, or just honk the horn. One day I was on Isabella near Victoria, and he came by with a male partner, and he pulled over and motioned for me to come to the car window. He wanted to know if I was staying clean. Then he said, he understood. *'Tes paires! C'est toujours le même problème. Je comprends. C'est pas facile.'* Then he disappeared from Côte des Neiges."

Anna had predicted that nothing would come of it, that Paul had pretended to go along to please Mrs. Mehta.

Paul's breathing is loud. This is stressing him. A long silence. "I'm tired, Jay. I need to go lie down."

26

IT'S 1:12 PM June 29, 2007. Paul and I are in the sitting room. Everything that can be boxed is in cartons. The movers will be here in three hours. Seated in the armchair, I stare at the wall ahead. There used to be a blown-up print there: boisterous white waves and green swaying coconut palms in the foreground, grey mountains in the background, the sea a washed-out blue: a panoramic photo of the Georgetown Coast. Anna had bought it from a Vincentian photographer one year when she went with a colleague to the annual St. Vincent and Grenadines Thousand Islands Park Picnic. The space the picture covered is a clean rectangle in a sea of smudge.

Paul, his head thrown back on the sofa, is staring sideways at the floor.

It has come to this. We must all go off to our separate lives. In two days Jonathan begins a tenure-track appointment at the University of Moncton. In August he'll defend his dissertation.

"I'm hungry. Let's order some food," Paul says.

"I'm not hungry."

Paul gets up from the sofa, walks across to me, and taps me on the shoulder. "Cheer up, Bro. It's not a funeral. You and I are still here ... for each other."

Jonathan remained hopeful that he and I would get together. He was willing to accept a CEGEP job offer and remain here, if I would agree to become his partner: sacrifice a university tenure-track position to enter into a hopeless relationship.

"Jonathan, there's no magic formula anywhere to imbue friendship with erotic desire." I felt bad right after saying so.

We were sitting near a street window in a café near Bleury and Saint Catherine—a grey, late, Thursday April afternoon. I had turned in my grades for Introduction to History earlier that day and felt like celebrating. Saint Catherine Street was thronged with people heading home from work or to the shops.

In the tense silence, I recalled parts of the conversation we'd had the Sunday after we'd seen CRAZY.

"Jay," Jonathan said, "I've told you over and over, I'll be patient."

You'll be patient, but I'm exasperated.

"I'll make this deal with you. You don't have to have sex with me."

I wondered what fanciful planet he inhabited. "And if it doesn't work out?"

"It will be my fault, not yours."

I shook my head and tried to tamp down my frustration. "Jonathan, this horse stopped breathing a long time ago. In fact, it never breathed. Take the job in Moncton. Focus on putting the finishing touches on your dissertation." I hated my bluntness.

His face taut, his frown lines deep, Jonathan turned his head to the left in the direction of the counter so I wouldn't see how pained he was. "Why did you give up?"

"My mother's death, Paul's disappearance. For a long time I felt stunned."

"You think you might go back to it in a few years?" He turned to look at me now. "Teaching history might rekindle the urge."

"Who knows? Right now I feel like my guts have been scooped out."

We slipped into another silence, I into a reverie. Jonathan rapping his knuckles on the table broke it. "You're far away. I want you here, beside me, in my arms, if you'd let me."

People came and left. Neither of us felt like getting up.

"So," Jonathan said, his eyes glassy, "this is how it ends?"

"No, Jonathan. There's no ending. We'll remain brothers. I want you to be happy. Be adventurous until you find the right person. I'm like the brother you'll share your joys and grief with when you need to. We'll celebrate our triumphs and mourn our failures."

"You frustrate me. Why can't we do all that and be a couple too?"

"Lovely exteriors—in fairy tales they're made of candy—conceal witches. Sirens lure mariners to their deaths. Beautiful maidens in castles make knights abandon their quests."

"You're speaking in codes. I don't understand what you're saying."

"Neither do I. It's logorrhoea. Let's go. You have my new address. As soon as I know the telephone number, you'll have it. You'll have no excuse not to visit me when you're in town. When you get hitched, your boyfriend will be welcome too."

That night and the following night I dreamed the same dream: that I murdered someone through the mail with neurotoxins, that the police are investigating, that I think cameras are recording my movements, and that one of my friends knows the facts. And now last night's dream.

> It begins with Jonathan and me alone in the basement of Jonathan's house. At some point it changes to me at eight. Anna, her cheeks swollen, her head bandaged, sends me off to school. At lunch hour I come home; she isn't there, and there's no food. At some point a missionary from the States, the station sergeant, and Caleb enter the dream. Caleb staggers while the station sergeant handcuffs him, and the missionary shouts: "He's a fraud. Lock him up." Then there's an open door that gives way to the street and reveals the profile of Jonathan, pacing back and forth.

What should I make of this dream? I'd blamed myself for the second beating that Caleb gave Anna. Did I blame Grama for the first? I'd known that Grama had made her do something that Caleb thought was wrong, that the something meant she would have no more children. That much I'd understood until Grama told me the full story. Was that why I felt so distant from her? Now I see Anna's abandonment—from clumsiness or panic, not cruelty, I'm sure. I must have accepted it as a just punishment for causing the beating. Between my father's coming to Sister Simmons' place at the beginning and Grama's coming to get me at school, I remember nothing, not even how I ended up at Sister Simmons'. Now I remember Anna saying a second time that she didn't want to die before making amends—and I'd cut her off. Told her to stop it. Felt I couldn't go through another episode about how she'd wronged Paul. Maybe it wasn't about Paul after all. And what's the connection to Jonathan?

Paul's phoning for food brings me back to the present. I wonder what Paul dreams about. At least he's putting his life back together. Bill persuaded him to go back to school. To Concordia to study creative writing. They were pleased with his writing portfolio and accepted him.

***

Three months ago, two weeks after Paul's return from a visit to see "Maria," he and I went to St. Vincent to put Aunt Mercy into a nursing home. Dementia had come upon her suddenly. She couldn't understand, she'd say, why Cynthia had gone to town and stayed so long. We told her Grama was dead. She said she knew. But a few minutes later she would wonder why Cynthia had stayed so long. "I certain-sure Lucy getting worried. Nobody to relieve her for her lunch." We told her the store had been sold. We asked her if she remembered Anna. She said yes. "She in Canada with two beautiful boys, one the spitting image o' Cynthia." She'd stopped cooking, insisting that she was waiting for Cynthia to bring the groceries, and wouldn't let anyone cook for her.

It was during the March reading week, at the peak of the dry season. We were on the front porch. The air turned misty beige whenever the breeze gusted; the soil was powdery and golden, the grass and weeds were shrivelled, the rose bushes speckled with blight and many of the flowering plants dead. The bougainvillaea, blooming lusciously when I went home to bury Anna's ashes the year before, now looked scraggly and struggling. Aunt Mercy's sudden dementia made her forget to water them. Mr. Morris would have done it but now he spent most of his days in a wheelchair on his front porch. Nine months before he had come to Anna's funeral looking quite strong. Now he was a paraplegic. I stared at the houses stretching up the steep slope, many many more than when I lived in Havre, some perched precariously on the lower precipices. Looming above the town and girding it as they had always done were the sheer black and limestone cliffs, looking now like semi-bald pates because of the shrunk foliage.

"Jay." Paul broke the reverie and then paused to suck apple juice through a straw from a two-litre bottle. He was shirtless and barefoot, the fat folds in his waist and stomach prominent. He pointed to the main door at my back, to a horseshoe nailed at the top, just above where the glass ended. "Know how that got there?"

I shook my head.

"Aunt Mercy put it there. A lot of people put horseshoes on their front doors and slept with their bibles open at the 23rd psalm with a pair of scissors in the form of a cross on it. That's what Aunt Mercy told me.

"Remember Jestina? Used to crow like a cock and curse with rapping speed. Talked like a man too sometimes, with a deep-deep voice. Like an old woman too: cracks in her voice. Clucked like a baby. The works. No joke. She'd run after people and try to butt them, like a bull. And people believed the horns were there, only invisible. After she started pelting people with shit, her family began tying her up."

"You remember all that?"

"Because I saw it all."

"Did Grama know you went?"

He shook his head.

"*You* sneaked away and went!"

"Aunt Mercy took me. She told Mr. Morris that she was going up the hill to see the happenings. I begged her to carry me and promised to keep it a secret, so she took me.

"Jay, you don't remember the Sunday when everybody in Havre took sago palms and coconut fronds and surrounded Jestina's house and beat the ground and the house walls, inside and out?"

I shook my head. "I remember it caused a commotion, but not the specifics."

"Some weird shit, man. To frighten the spirits and drive them away. Afterwards they washed down the inside and outside of the house and sprinkled the yard with turpentine and Dettol. There was an account of it in the newspapers."

"Did Grama go?"

"No. In the store next day she argued with a woman called Eloise about it. Grama told her that educated people said evil spirits don't exist.

"Eloise gasped. 'Ma Kirton, shame on you! You don't know that people what educated plenty serve the devil! They belongs to the Anti-Christ Legion. I will tell Pastor Boatswain to come and enlighten you 'bout the ways of the educated.'

"'Eloise, all that light will blind me.'

"'Ma Kirton, since you doubting what everybody see with their own eyes and hear with their own ears, and now you even refusing help—you sure is not you that put the jumbie-them in Jestina?'

"'You want me to put one in you, Eloise? How about my husband's? He will give you lots of loving, make you work hard, and save your money.' Then she told Lucy to dispatch Eloise quickly, that all that jumbie talk was threatening to turn her into a jumbie too.

"Jay, wait till you hear this." Paul went inside and returned with a bound notebook from the two boxes of Grama's papers that we would be carrying back, and began to read:

August 16, 1995

Everybody is afraid to venture out after dark. Havre has gone crazy. Jumbie this and jumbie that! Jumbie! Jumbie! Jumbie! Every single newspaper has it in their headline. You mean to tell me there's nobody intelligent enough in these newspaper offices to go ask a psychiatrist to explain what this poor child is going through? That child is suffering from multiple personality disorder. Somebody she trusted probably did something terrible to her. Anna, you better send for these children quickly. They won't stay a day longer in this benighted place if I could help it.

"You know what, Jay: Grama was too hard on Haverites. I saw how Catholicism works in Guatemala. Cofradias. Maximo. San Simon. You just have to admire the naive faith of those Mayans and Ladinos. Stuff they've elaborated to help them in their dire lives. If Ma were still alive,

I'd be patient with her. You were right, Jay. I know now that she found companionship in her church. Going back to her beliefs in God was the price she paid to have it.

"Jay, I plan to use Grama's journals in my writing. You won't mind, would you?"

I shook my head.

"And I'm coming back here to comb the newspapers for stories like Jestina's. One day I'll write a novel in which the community believes that Grama sold her soul to the devil to get rich. I'll probably throw in as well the speculation that she and Aunt Mercy were lovers. That way there'll be two motives for the community's dirty work."

For a while we said nothing.

"You remember Millington?" I said.

"Millington. Millington."

"The light-skinned fellow, lighter than me, almost white; narrow face; deep set, bright eyes, a wiry body; and very straight, overly long legs. Come on, you must remember him?"

Paul frowned.

"He went to Kingstown Secondary with me. He used to come here and we'd study together. Sometimes he and I went to the land together. Come on, you must remember him."

"How could I forget?" Paul slapped his forehead. "When that teacher flogged you and you came home with your back all cut up and wouldn't tell Grama why, she walked up the hill and asked him. I went with her. Oh yes, Millington. You and he were on the back porch sometimes. A mixed-race fellow."

"I hear he's now a Methodist minister in Barbados. He was Jestina's neighbour. He said Jestina's father used to try to beat the evil spirits out of her, and her parents force-fed her pepper, corila, and mauby-bark concentrate to make her blood bitter and unpalatable to the spirits. One day Father Henderson came here to collect a donation from Grama to bury a woman who'd left no burial money, and Grama and he got to talking about Jestina. Grama begged him to intervene to get psychiatric help for Jestina. He said that God lets these things happen to test the faithful and make them better Christians."

Paul nodded. "Grama has an entry about it." He turned the pages of the notebook and read: 'Henderson. God's servant! Tell me about it. He's as hollow as bamboo and has the compassion of an ice-pick.'"

"You remember how it all ended?"

Paul nodded. "They found her body tangled up in one of the fishermen's seines. One morning she untied herself, sneaked out of the house, and threw herself into the sea. By then her eyes were like balls of tumeric. The shoppers said it was the devil's fire. Grama told them it was liver damage."

"*Benighted.* I have news for Grama. Those superstitions are everywhere. One day I was at Jonathan's house, and we heard his aunt screaming on the downstairs balcony, and ran to see what had happened. We met her frozen against the wall. When she could speak, she said a black cat had come onto the balcony and meowed at her. She was convinced that the cat was the devil who'd come to take possession of her soul."

Paul laughed.

"Jay, you're sure you want to return to live here?"

"Sure. If I'm offered a teaching job, I'd come back. It's home. Remember, you never wanted to leave, and at the beginning you wanted Ma to send you back."

"And when Mrs. Mehta told Ma to send me back I said no. You all thought it was because I belonged to a gang."

I waited for him to go on, but he said nothing more.

A gust of wind showered the porch with dust. Paul coughed and used his puffer. We moved to the back porch. Five white egrets feasting on the mealy bugs on the hibiscus hedge eyed us nervously then flew a short distance away onto the beach. To their left, up the hill to where our property bordered the new road at the top of the escarpment, the white cedars, glossy green among the fruit trees, were covered in pale lilac, bell-shaped blossoms—defiant of the drought. The lone cottonwood near the top was shedding fleece, which the breeze dislodged each time it gusted. The sun wasn't high enough yet to swamp the porch with light. The beach road behind the fence was deserted; the beach too. The fishing canoes were out, looking like whales with their humps above the water. The waves, like long rolls of white lace unwinding and rewinding, formed a feathery line at the shore, their breaking no louder than the backwash from a canoe. The sky a cloudless azure; the sea a lolite plain, out of which leaping flying fish created momentary silver flashes against the blue of the sky. A flock of plovers glided like miniature white airplanes above the water and occasionally dived into it. Except for the fronds of the royal palms flapping against each other when the breeze gusted and the gentle roll of the surf, all was silent. I adjusted a lounge chair to the reclining position and lay on it.

Paul remained standing, his stomach pressed against the porch railing. We were waiting for an appraiser to come to assess the property and put it on the market.

Staring out to sea, Paul asked: "Jay, do you sometimes feel lost?"

"Depends on what you mean by lost."

"Sort of like—you don't know where you're going and you feel disconnected from everyone." He glanced at me sideways. "Someone to keep you company as you travel ..." He waited for me to respond.

I didn't.

"The day before I left for Guatemala I sat in Simón Bolívar Park in San Jose thinking about it, and saw life as a labyrinth in which we're trapped. Trapped terribly if we're condemned to be there alone."

A crow flew onto one of the royal palms and croaked. Soon about 20 flitted about on the royal palms, some of them croaking, all of them eyeing Paul and me. They took turns flying down to the hibiscus hedge to eat the mealy bugs there. The egrets hadn't come back.

"Yes, life can be like a labyrinth," I said. "But I suspect that even when our hands are clasped in someone else's we might still be thrashing about alone. Sometimes I think imagination is our only salvation, the only place where there's freedom and choice ... What do you do when the hand you hold is pulling away? Daddy became a drunk when Ma left him. We're not sure what the relationship between Grama and Aunt Mercy was, but now Aunt Mercy is alone and demented and we had to put her in a nursing home. Look at our neighbour Mr. Morris. When you and I came to live with Grama, he and Mrs. Morris were together. You were too young to remember. He taught here in Havre, and she taught over the hill, in Esperance. One noon when I came in for lunch, I met him sitting on the sofa dabbing his eyes with a handkerchief. Mrs. Morris had left him and returned to live with her mother, and all he begged her to she wouldn't come back. She told him marriage was stifling her. Soon after she went to England to study and came back with a degree in maths and was my teacher at Kingstown Secondary. She never remarried and neither did he."

Silence.

"Now here's Mr. Morris, a paraplegic, three years after he retired. Paul, defying loneliness, avoiding hurting others, and being self-sufficient as is humanly possible—if we can do that and still have a hand to hold, it's all we can ask for. Almost all else is beyond our control ... Trouble is, that hand can bring crippling burdens. It's the story of our parents' marriage."

With a faraway look Paul nodded slowly. "There was this guy in Spanish class with me. Hans. From Munich. A philosophy student. We talked a lot and shared the odd joint. He lent me his copy of Camus' *Myth of Sisyphus*. I'd already studied *L'Etranger* in Mme Loubier's class. The senseless cruelty of his character Merseault chilled me. But Sisyphus—Camus didn't invent him, the Greeks did—threw me for a curve ... I thought about Sisyphus for weeks until I realized that I had long felt that life was meaningless; I'd even tried to put it in words. I'd have told you so that morning when I begged you to let me into your secrets so I could share mine with you too. That way if you tried to embarrass me, I could embarrass you too ... In the end I linked Sisyphus and Matthew Arnold's 'Dover Beach,' which I'd studied with Mrs. Mehta. I've gone over that poem so many times, I know it by heart." He stopped talking for a long while and resumed staring out to sea. He turned, look at me with a cynical smile. "So why don't you clasp someone's hand?"

I stared at the coconut palms lining the beach to his far right.

Paul continued: "You never answered my question about whether you're gay."

"You should talk. Your Maria saga is fiction."

"You don't know that."

"I know when you're lying. You don't have to tell me anything you're uncomfortable revealing."

"That way you won't feel obliged to reveal anything yourself."

Silence.

**

On the plane back to Montreal, I asked Paul how he felt about selling the property.

"Grama's no longer there. I don't know. Not sure I want to talk about it. How about you?"

I looked away, into the aisle, and remained silent. I felt like a tree one of whose main branches had just been chopped off.

27

SIX WEEKS AGO, on the Friday of the Victoria Day weekend, Paul said: "Let's go dancing on Sunday night."

"I have wooden legs."

"Mine are of cast iron."

"Where will we go?"

"You'll see."

We left home around 10 pm. At the Beaudry metro station, Paul said it was our stop. We exited into the Gay Village. I affected nonchalance. In July 2006, during the Out Games, Jonathan and I had wound our way through the throngs of people down there. Before that, on a couple of Thursday evenings, Jonathan's usual down time, he'd taken me to a bar in the area.

Now Paul and I walked east along Saint Catherine Street. After about a minute, Paul crossed to the south side and pointed out a sauna. "I tried to get in there once."

I said nothing.

"The desk clerk said I looked underage and asked me for ID. I was a couple months short of 18. When I got back onto the sidewalk, I saw the Jacques-Cartier Bridge on my left and thought: there's my answer, but I couldn't bring myself to do it."

"Paul, what's all this about?"

"Stop pretending to be naïve. Maria is Carlos' sister alright, but she's married and has her own home. Carlos is the real deal. Now it's your turn to come clean with me about Jonathan."

"We're not boyfriends. I'm bisexual. I'm sure I've already told you so."

"Never had sex with Jonathan?"

"No."

"That girl you used to date ..."

"Tamara."

"She was the female part. How about the guy part?"

"I tried sleeping with a Haitian guy after that but lost interest when I got to his place."

"Bisexual, 27, and never had sex with a guy! You've *a lot* of catching up to do, Bro. You must begin tonight."

In a café near Plessis, we had coffee, served by an anorexic-looking fellow. One hemisphere of his hair was dyed turquoise, the other purple. The things people do to get noticed. While sipping my coffee, I recalled the Saturday morning when Paul abused Anna and me and later cried in his bedroom and threatened to commit suicide. *'If you let me into your secret rooms I'll let you into mine.'* So that was it. And there was a joke that Paul related a few weeks before he left for Central America. He said he'd read it in a book of Black American folklore. I thought he'd told it to upset Anna.

> There were these cops on the beat in Central Park, New York, and they saw these men coming out of the bushes one by one and got suspicious, so they started questioning them. "What yall doing in there?" they asked the first one.
>
> "Blowing bubbles," he said.
>
> They asked the next one who came out. He said the same thing.
>
> "Blowing bubbles! Grown men blowing bubbles! And at this time o' night!" They were sure it was some sort o' code.
>
> "Don't tell me,' they said to the next man who came out, "that you've been blowing bubbles, too?"
>
> "I am Bubbles," he replied.

"Jay, for years I tried. Jay, I tried to tell you. Remember I even told Ma one time to mind her own business when she was poking her nose into you and Jonathan's business. If you'd said thanks, I might have told you then. Once I even wrote it in a note to give to you but I tore it up. How could you not suspect? Why do you think I asked you about Grama and Aunt Mercy? Why I brought up the story about Jack and Brady? Jay, I mentioned the word gay every day, and *you* didn't pick up that I was trying to tell you something?" He shook his head with incredulity.

"I see that now. You're right. It was probably because of *how* you mentioned it."

My mind turned to Anna, the guilt she died with, the fear she had that leaving us behind in St. Vincent might have made us gay.

Around midnight Paul suggested we go to Parking, but there was a $65 cover charge. We headed down to Extasis. It was too crowded. In the end we went to Sky. On one of the dance floors, where the majority of the dancers looked like CEGEP and high-school students, we heard a voice calling: "Well, hello, Meatman."

"Gina! Really! Meet my brother, Jay."

"Yeah. Right. Usually you all say cousin."

"Seriously. Seriously."

"There's a couple o' people over here who know you." She held on to Paul's sleeve and threaded her way through the crowd and over to the bar. I followed.

"¡Emilia! ¡Qué sorpresa! ¿Qué haces aquí? ¡Gúicho también! ¡No es posible! You guys like want to give me a heart attack or what."

"If Said had come tonight ..."

"Said!"

Emilia nodded and grinned.

"Yeah, Bégin. Man, that pedophile was a whole lot smarter than we gave him credit for," Gúicho said. "But Said isn't gettable." He rolled his eyes and smacked his lips.

"Slut!" Gina said.

Gúicho licked his lips, half turned, slapped his flat bottom, and wiggled his hips. Barely five feet. Belly already a bundle.

Gina shook her head. "I've given up trying to reform this child."

"So," Paul said, "you guys ran into one another in the Village?"

All three shook their heads slowly, exchanged glances, and guffawed.

"We came out to each other since high school," Gina said.

"Not Said," Gúicho said. "We met him here."

"He suspected you," Gina said looking at Paul and pointing to Gúicho. "We talked one time about testing you, and have you cover up for Emilia, the way Gúicho covered up for me." She stared straight into Paul's eyes and nodded. "Milford poopooed the idea. He did." She nodded slowly, looking at Paul's surprised face. "He and his boyfriend John, yeah, they knew about us. Respected our wish to stay closeted. And Doc knew. This boy" — she wagged a finger at Gúicho — "tried to make him one time. This boy's dangerous ..." Gúicho twirled his tongue at her. "Doc threatened to out him. He came close to shitting his pants, and spilled the beans about all of us. And you know what this slut said when we found out: 'He's so fucking handsome, why should I just abandon him to women?' Those times when Doc flirted with me, he'd give me this knowing wink, his signal that our secret was safe with him."

Paul said nothing.

"Remember?" Gina grinned. "'Gúicho, life ain't fair. You alone getting all the va in Gina?' That was code — Doc privately making fun of Gúicho and reassuring us, sort of, that he wouldn't out us. Cool guy, that Doc." She pulled Emilia to her and kissed her and put an arm around Gúicho.

Paul turned to face me. "See what I mean? Characters in a Maupin novel."

"So, Meatman," Gúicho said, his eyes on Jay, "Where you found this Adonis? Can I borrow him for one night?"

"Sorry. Gúicho, my brother Jay."

"*Le mon oncle!*" His hand went to his mouth.

"Gúicho!" Gina and Emilia shouted.

"Well," Gúicho said, his eyes roving up and down my body, "some uncle, this one. I can drop my drawers for him — right here, this minute." He winked at Gina. With that he pulled Paul toward the dance floor. Gina and Emilia followed them. It was Paul's hip-hop sort of music. I leaned against the bar counter and awaited their return.

When Paul came back, he whispered into my ear: "Gúicho sure wants to savour what's in your pants."

"Tell him I already have a boyfriend."

"Can't. l told him you're single. Tonight you'll give it up, Bro. Besides, let's face it: brothers who sin together bond better."

By now Gúicho was standing in front of us and staring at Paul, who nodded. Paul moved away. Emilia and Gina were still on the dance floor.

"So you want to bed me?" I said.

"I'd love to." Gúicho grinned, and his right hand came forward and began to caress my chest. "I like a man that's direct. Are you a bottom or a top?"

"I'm a vampire."

Gúicho's hand dropped, he moved backwards a step. "I'll wear the toothmarks proudly," his voice keening.

"If you live."

Gúicho lowered his head, looked nervously right, left, hesitated a second, then slinked away.

About five minutes later Paul returned. "Jay, what's wrong with you? Why'd you tell him you're a vampire? His mouth flaps like a torn sail. Tomorrow morning all of Montreal will be thinking you're into weird shit."

"And if you're his friend, tell him if he keeps offering his body to everyone like that, one day he'll meet a true vampire or worse. Ma had a co-worker whose brother's body was found covered with cigarette burns in a parking lot."

***

There were lots of blanks to fill in that Victoria Day. We'd taken a cab home around two and slept until ten. I awoke and smelled coffee brewing and heard Paul moving about in the kitchen. He always gets up early. Needs a lot less sleep than I. At 3 pm we were still sitting at the table catching up on each other's secret lives, Paul's mostly.

"My history teacher, Monsieur Gaugin. Remember him? Guadeloupéen. A fitness nut. Streamlined body, V-torso, six pack, powerful thighs, the works, and a grin that could make you come. I couldn't look at him. Gave me a hard-on. He was one sweet mother. Sweeter than sweet."

I shook my head and smiled at Paul's lingo.

"One afternoon, man—around the time I turned 14—he kept me in to punish me for an incomplete assignment. Jay, I did everything in my power not to walk up to his desk and kiss him. When he told me the detention was over, I couldn't get up right away; I was fantasizing that he and I were having sex." He laughed. "Desire, man. I came home, wrote a story in which he and I had sex, and ..."

We were silent for a few seconds.

"There's more—lot's more. Listen to this." He put his hand on his forehead, closed his eyes, and recited:

> Harriet Mole is a horny soul.
> And a horny soul is she.
> Gaugin she longs for,
> And Gaugin she grunts for
> And Gaugin it won't be.

> Ugly Marie
> Looks like a bowl:
> A full bowl is she.
> Dip in your hand.
> It will come
> Out full of candy.

"Cool. Right? You see, Bro, when reality doesn't meet your needs, there's always fantasy."

"Paul, you confuse me. That was when? The year after that showdown with Mrs. Bensemana?"

"No. The same year. Later. She was in February, and he was in November."

"At least you didn't send him your limericks." I imagined his doing so, Gaugin reporting it to the office, Paul suspended, and Anna in Bégin's office hearing that Paul had attempted to seduce a male teacher. I chuckled. In February it was a woman, in November a man. I chuckled again, until it dawned on me that she would have believed she'd caused it. "There's something in all this that I don't get. Explain yourself, Paul."

"What's there to explain?" He clasped his hands and put both thumbs under his chin, his elbows on the table. "In Mrs. Bensemana's case, I wanted to like throw those guys off my scent, and get some acclaim for it. I don't think I calculated it as precisely, not the acclaim part. But the rest: definitely."

"And with Gaugin?"

He unclasped his hands, put them on his thighs, and made a couple of ironing movements. "It was a fantasy. He wasn't into guys. In class, his eyes turned molten when the girls flirted with him. Bégin —*he* loved guys. Brown meat. Muscle. Beefcake. Those Hispanics used to tease the hell out of Said—we mentioned him last night—a Pakistani chap" —

"South Asian?"

"South Asian chap, a body-builder. Bégin loved to clap him on the shoulder, his pedophile eyes flaming blue, his cheeks pink. And you should see Said: stiff with embarrassment."

"And if you'd thought Gaugin was into guys?"

"Moot point. He wasn't."

"So you sublimated your lust for Gaugin into love for his subject?"

"He never hurt my eyes; that's for sure. But that's not why I did well in history. He cared enough to push me to do my work, and I appreciated it. Take Mrs. Loubier. She looked like a light bulb on stilts. Her looks didn't affect my performance."

I recalled his references to homosexuality: *"Call the exterminators, Ma; there's vermin in the house";* his numerous speculative crude and cruel remarks made in connection with Jonathan.

"Jay, you remember how I hung around with that gay-bashing group ADDA? Looking back now, I can say those guys like frighten me. You remember when Mrs. Mehta told Ma to send me back to St. Vincent and I said no? Well, the real reason was that I knew men turned me on, and St. Vincent was the last place I wanted to be ... because of what had happened to Jack and Brady. Seriously, Jay, how could you not have suspected? Remember that exchange we had about condoms?"

"We were trading insults, Paul."

"Oh. I thought you'd finally understood. Bill urged me to tell you. And it was one of the things I wanted to tell you the night before I left home. But you were such an asshole. Best favour you ever did me: taking me to Bill's place. That humungous cock in ebony. A dead giveaway."

We both laughed. Paul coughed.

"The things he said in those discussions you-all had impressed me: justice for the poor, trying to see things from another person's perspective, resisting materialism, penetrating to the core of our being, defining ourselves, being truthful to ourselves and others. Not sure about that one. Honestly, I was surprised that he was gay and decent."

"Be serious!"

"You didn't go to high school here. You won't know. The stuff those Black and Latino guys said about gays — in English, in French, in Spanish, in Creole. If it was just name calling alone: chi-chi man, battybwoy, faggot, bullerman, *ma sissy, ma comère, fiffy, tapette, folle, pédé, maricón,* woman-man, fruit, antipympym, *hueco, güicoy* — it wouldn't be half as bad. They'd speculate about what they'd do if a gay guy were to approach them. They were certain gays want to sleep with every man they lay eyes on. They all claimed to have had an uncle or a cousin who'd beaten up — in some cases killed — a gay pedophile. And there was the way they treated Milford and his boyfriend John, these two Black out-gay guys in school."

"Gina mentioned them last night."

"Correct. They called John *la Gallina* and Milford Millicent. Every day — every day, until Milford fought back — those two had to run the gauntlet. On good days they blew them kisses and pinched their buns. On bad days they slammed them into lockers, always with a mocking, 'Watch where you going, man'; or tripped them when they walked by, followed by: 'Jeez, man, wha' you doing down there? You after my cock or what?' Or they'd get a lecture from one of the Jamaicans: 'Millicent, where you pick up yo' nastiness? How come you 'low yourself for catch honky disease? Is cause o' all the honky blood in you, or what? If you been live in Jamaica, man, them would o' beat it out o ' your backside or else kill you — long time, man! You think is joke I joking? I serious.

Kill yo' ass long time.' Sometimes they'd sing 'Burn Chi-Chi Man-Them' and 'Boom! Bye-Bye! Inna Batty Bwoy Head,' shape their hands into a pistol and shout: 'Pow! Battybwoy fi dead. Me say, shoot the batty bwoy-them. Kill them. Them no fi live none 't all.' Jay, I felt like sputum."

"That was their objective."

"And then one day the unexpected happened. 'Millicent, is true unno kaka hole does get slack and unno does have for plug it with cotton wool like them does do dead people?' This from Alfred.

"'Didn't I see a roll of paper towels in your locker?' Milford countered. 'Know why? Guys like you are straight in the day and get fisted at night.'

"Silence. We could hear the hum of the fluorescent lights.

"Alfred lurched at him and swung at his head. Milford dodged the blow, kneed him in the groin, and delivered a quick punch. Alfred doubled over. Milford kicked him several times. 'You fucking dunce, fucking pile o' shit! What the fuck you know about me? Fucking twit! I ain't no fucking Rueben James.' His hazel eyes flamed. His whitish skin was flushed red. His broad nose flared ... Shithead Illich was on recess duty about ten metres down the corridor from us. He took them both to Bégin's office.

"You remember the day I threatened to bring home a Uzi and blow off your heads?"

I nodded.

"Well, that was a week after that fight, the day Alfred and Milford returned after their suspension. Alfred brought a shotgun to school to kill Milford. He showed us the shotgun in class and said he would off Milford at lunch. Richard Hazan went to get Bégin. Bégin came to the class and sent everyone out except Alfred. The police arrived even before we cleared the stairs.

"Milford and John." He took a deep breath. "Those guys were brave or just plain stupid. John, *la Gallina*: skinny, with a waist that couldn't have been more than 25; loose-jointed, with a hip-swishing walk, dark-skinned like me. He was in geek classes, doing advanced everything. That only made it worse. Milford was in advanced English and French. John and Milford changed schools the following September, and Alfred ended up in jail a few months later. Too old for Batshaw. He was already 18 and one of Nine Lives' *gorillas*—enforcers."

Paul grew silent, looked around the dinette, seemed a trifle shaken, was probably thinking *he* barely avoided going to Batshaw.

"So, you see, Jay, I did everything to cover up, even fooled around with girls. I'm into men, period. One girl told her friends: 'Him not cock, me dear, him is capon.' Whenever they wanted to diss me they'd say: 'Meatman, is true you're a capon?'" He swallowed loud, lowered his head, and stared mutely at the table for close to a minute.

"Thanks, man, thanks for taking me to Bill's lectures. He saved my life." He nodded slowly—several times. "I found his number in the phone book and called him. He told me to come to his Concordia office. I told him how I was back in St. Vincent, how abusive I was to you and Ma and how trapped I felt; how I hated myself, my body, my sexual desires, my pot dependence; how angry I was because of my asthma and sexuality; how unjust and unfair it all was; the depression I'd just come out of; that it was all too much for me. I put my head on his desk and howled.

"When I quieted, he said: 'Paul, it's not easy. Classmates, television, advertisers. First, they try to humiliate you by pushing false ideals. Then they try to con you into believing they can transform you. They use hypnotic ads to make you swallow the lies they peddle and want you addicted to. There's no valid reason, Paul—no valid reason at all—for people to hate their bodies or themselves. But advertisers want us feel we're Cinderella's sisters and tell us their products can turn us into Cinderella. Paul, if a body were so valuable, we wouldn't get rid of corpses ... The body is a container for consciousness—nothing more. And consciousness, awareness, is what we should cultivate. Our intellects, our compassion for others—that's what we should cultivate. Don't get me wrong. I'm not saying we shouldn't take care of our bodies, eating well and exercising to make them function properly. You don't want the container to leak or get brittle. But we don't have to think of bodies in terms of ugly and beautiful. Beauty and ugliness are in the acts we commit. First commandment: Love yourself. Second: Define yourself; that is to say, resist all those who come ready to stuff you into their moulds.'

"Jay, next, he made me look him in the eye, and he asked me: 'What is it about same-sex desire that bothers you?'

"'It's freaky. It's not natural.'

"'*Not natural.* I see. You were made in a lab, or was it a factory?'

"'I don't understand.'

"'You mean you gestated in a womb like every other human being? Who the hell are we to say that any part of what nature gives birth to isn't natural? The gall! You've fallen into the trap set by our persecutors. They hide behind religious tomes and laws they and their ancestors create to justify their dirty work. They are the perverts, not us. Ignore them, Paul, and look to your own happiness.'

"Jay, over the next two months, he and I talked about all sorts of things: about his first boyfriend; about having to tell his mother—his father died when he was 12—he would stop coming home if she didn't stop pestering him about grandchildren; about a gay uncle who'd committed suicide because his father had forced him to get married and he couldn't bring himself to tell his wife she wasn't what he wanted; about hate mail his students or colleagues—he didn't know which—sent him in the early years of his university career. 'We have to cultivate an inner strength to fight all this and make sure it doesn't poison our psyche.' He told me to phone him if I ever needed to talk." Paul quieted, relaxed, grew contemplative. "Jay, older gay men should do more of this for younger men who're struggling with their sexuality."

Paul stayed silent for a few seconds. "And it wasn't just being gay. I'd failed Grama. Not the sex thing. I'd have shared that with her. Easily. More easily than with you. Grama was an intelligent woman with a brain twice Ma's, and centuries more enlightened. She gave Brady's mother quite a lecture about a month after he and Jack fled Havre. I can still see his mother, in a blue-and-red plaid head-wrap and loose calico dress, talking to Grama. 'Thank God he run way to Trinidad. Me hope he stay there till he dead, and don't come back here to disgrace me further. Not even for my funeral. Ma Kirton, is two weeks I did not put my head outside my door. Ma Kirton, shame almost kill me. That boy disgrace me. My only child, Ma Kirton: the only one. I did everything to raise that boy to fear the Lord. What more I could o' do?'

"'Don't stop loving and supporting him. Is not his fault. Educated people say that is how they born. You can't change how nature made you. These things are beyond our understanding and our control.'

"'But Ma Kirton the bible condemn it.'

"'Plenty things the bible condemn. You buy salted pigtail from me all the time. The bible condemns that. That dress you wearing, it's made from polyester and cotton. The bible says you should be killed for wearing that. Love your son, you hear me, love your son, and give him all the support you can.'"

Paul stopped talking. He looked around the room, got up, stretched, and then sat back down. "All that stuff's been already archived. That load is on the ground now, and I won't be hoisting it again." He stared at me intensely. "Why aren't you and Jonathan together?"

I looked away and began recalling what I'd told Jonathan, and decided to skip all but the bit about wanting a wife and children.

"Sounds like a cop-out."

"You don't see my dilemma?"

"What *dilemma*?"

"Bisexuality. Sleeping with a man, desiring a woman. Sleeping with a woman, desiring a man."

"So, do both. People do combined sex all the time. In threesomes and foursomes even. I've heard stories of married men who take gays home to screw them and their wives. Get a dose of the real world. See sex as recreation, like a tennis match. One of Carlos' friends wanted us to take part in an orgy. I was tempted, but in the end I chickened out."

"Settle for pickups, right? Pleasure tools—and discard them like paper plates and cups. Right, Paul?"

"Wrong analogy. It's more like recycling. You and Jonathan are like two Victorian biddies without hats and lorgnettes. A good reason you should hitch."

"Your reasoning makes all Victorian biddies lesbians." I chuckled. "Paul, I'm *not* sexually attracted to him."

"Come on! He's not *that* bad. He's not bad-looking at all. Just kind o' intense. Wound up, that's all. Nothing there a few orgasms won't uncoil. He's tall, well proportioned. A trifle effeminate, but when his blue eyes light up and he smiles—oh boy. And his buns are cute. Seriously, Jay, there's more than enough there to turn you on. And he has a mind. Think about that. Loyal partners with good minds are hard to find. Most people are one or the other, not both."

"Sounds like you're attracted to him ... Jonathan's a brother, Paul."

"You're rationalizing. He wants you for a lover."

"Well, I didn't know that at the beginning. Gays talk about David and Jonathan being lovers ..."

"Yeah, I read Stephen Schecter's poem after I heard a review of it on CBC. I was tempted to pass it on to you, but I was afraid you'd out me to Ma."

"Jonathan used to tell me about his sexual frustrations and the kind o' guys that turned him on: dark guys, *foncé*. Mediterranean, Latin-American types, I thought. For a while he dated a Portuguese guy."

"Probably an ebonophile. Useless baggage, Jay. Drop it. Just jump into the sack with him. If you have to, take a couple of drinks before to loosen up or smoke a joint. Your hormones will do the rest. God, you're so earnest!"

For a while neither of us spoke.

"Constraints," I mumbled.

"What?"

"Constraints."

"You know, this is like *so* tiresome. Get real. Gay men meet and have sex in dark places without even seeing each other's faces, without telling each other their names. You're squirming. I'll skip the rest."

Another long silence. Paul broke it. "A little bed-hopping hurts no one. You'll lose Jonathan. You know how hard it is to find meaningful love in the gay world? Harder still after you've passed your prime."

"When's that?"

"Thirty. Look at the websites where gay guys post their profiles, you'll see. I saw one the other day by this overweight, midget of a guy, 61 years old and looking every day of 80. You know what it said? 'If you're over 30, fat, ugly, and effeminate, please don't contact me.' Jay, you have two and a half years—two and a half!" He grinned. "Afterwards it's a fire sale."

28

WITH THE MONEY I inherited from Anna's insurance and pension fund — I didn't need to spend the $46, 000 I'd got directly from Grama — I bought the condo I'm moving into today. The week before Anna took sick, she and I had gone over the details of the type of condo she should buy. She'd wanted one with three bedrooms, so there'd always be a room for Paul. It was then that I became aware of the wealth my grandmother had left. Petroleum, Coca Cola, and other shares Granddad had bought in the 1940s netted over US$300,000, and there were the shares Grama had bought in IBM, Cable and Wireless, British Telecom and other companies. They were worth almost as much. I gave Paul his share and begged him not to spend the capital. "We trivialize what we haven't worked for. I plan to repay what I've taken to buy the condo, and to give the earnings from Grama's money to charity. Just remember that you want to be a writer. Earnings from that money might well make the difference between eating and starving."

"As long as there's food in your house, Jay, I'll never starve."

"Don't assume that I'll always be around."

He didn't answer.

Two weeks earlier, Paul said he hoped cultural differences wouldn't "come between the three of us."

"*Three of us?*"

"Well, you know, when Carlos comes and we're living together ... "

"Living together!" ... "Oh no. I need my own space."

He stared at me stone-faced, shoulders slumped.

"Paul, my second bedroom will be my study. I'm not saying that ..."

—I stopped—*you couldn't stay with me in a pinch, if you needed to*. It was unwise to give Paul such an opening.

"What are you not saying?"

"Paul, let's get this straight ..." I took three loud breaths before continuing. "Paul, I came to Canada, glad that finally, finally, I could be close with my mother. While she was in St. Vincent I couldn't. She was too afraid of Daddy. It's like she didn't know if she had the right to show me affection. Whenever he was around she was afraid any af- fectionate gesture from her to me would anger him. One time he shout- ed at her: 'Stop hugging him up? You want him to grow up like a gal?' Then Ma went away and left us with Grama. Grama was good and kind to me, but I think she saw me as something already warped by my father. Maybe it was I who rejected her. Maybe I felt that if I got close to her I would be disloyal to Ma. Who knows?

"And then I came here ... And you and Ma made me grow up faster than I wanted ... I had to comfort Ma when you abused her; when your abuse got to be too much and she wanted to put you out, I had to defend you. You want to know why I'm not involved with anyone? I'll tell you. I'm weary. Exhausted. My own space—peace, rest—it's what I long for.

"If there was a time when I wasn't responsible for you, I don't re- member it. From now on, Paul, I'll be responsible for myself. No Jona- than or Janet. At least not before I've caught my breath and find out who Jay is and what he wants from life."

Paul stared at me, attentively, silently.

"I'm not blaming you for any of this. And I don't want you to blame yourself either. None of this was your choosing. Not even your cruel behaviour here."

Paul looked away, his head hung low.

"All I am saying is that I want space in which to catch my breath and grow; that now you must assume responsibility for your own life, for your decisions, for your behaviour. In retrospect, your trip away wasn't a bad thing, just that you handled it badly."

Paul nodded slowly, stared ahead of him, pressed his lips, and pulled at his chin. "Funny"—he was looking away from me—"I always took it for granted that you'd be always there—always, but I never wondered what it meant for you ... That time when you gave me the money to cut loose from Nine Lives—I never even paid you back—and you hugged me and cried and begged me not to disappoint myself and Grama—you didn't include yourself—you won't know how important it was for me. You pulled me out from a current that was about to drown me." He paused, glanced sideways at me. "Afterwards, it was like, I can't disappoint Jay; I mustn't disappoint Jay. That's when I began turning my life around. That's when, Jay." He fell silent and stared at the floor. "You are right. You must be tired. I see that now. In your place, I would be too." He walked toward me, put his hands on my shoulders and looked up into my eyes. "Just promise me that you won't ever abandon me."

"I promise."

Two days after this conversation, Paul found a studio apartment on Fort and Tupper, a few metro stops from my own place near Maisonneuve and Champlain.

****

I've known since April that this September I'll begin teaching college-level history. I shared the news with Paul the day I got the appointment letter. Paul was sitting in the armchair in the living room.

"So you're going to teach." Paul stood, walked to the living room window, and stared out on to Linton. "Going to teach history, you are. Whose? You think you'll like it?" He turned his head to make eye contact with me.

I shrugged. I was standing in the dinette with my buttocks leaning against the table, the appointment letter in my hand. "Time will tell."

"Teachers," Paul resumed staring onto the street. "The civilian corps, doing with books what armed forces like NATO do abroad with guns and bombs. Most teachers aren't bright enough to know how they're being used." He smiled cynically and a long silence followed. "It's one of the reasons I revolted in high school. Most humans, more than 90 percent, will never be more than tools, *quincaillerie*, in the hands of the powerful. In university you studied Howard Zinn. He got it down pat about the powerful, how they pay—I say bribe—the executives they hire with enough of the spoils to buy their loyalty while they screw wealth out of everyone else. You must read *Las Venas abiertas de América Latina*, Eduardo Galeano's book. And if they allow you to, teach it to your students. It's been translated into English. I read somewhere that the wealth of the world's 300 richest people exceeds that of 40 percent of the world's entire population." He walked to the sofa and sat down. "In Latin America they use troops, corrupt politicians, and assassins to insure it. Here they use teachers, politicians, and the media; of course, they own the media."

"So, are you preparing yourself for a career on Wall Street?" I asked him.

Paul put his left hand behind his neck, his right on chin, and smiled his smile of embarrassment, all the while slowly shaking his head. "I'm going to write. Books like Zinn's, Galeano's, and Rodney's. I'll be like Thoreau's rooster. I'll wake sleeping humanity up."

"And the capitalist press will help you?"

Paul crinkled his nose, bit his lower lip, and was silent for a moment. "I'll publish them myself."

"Naiveté, Paul. You're naïve. Zinn, Galeano, Rodney, their ideas are out there because they don't threaten anybody. In any case most people are already programmed to cooperate in their own oppression; some even promote it. It's why capitalism is so successful."

Paul nodded almost imperceptibly, brought his right hand to his lips, and bit the nail of his index finger. Lowering his hand, he said, still nodding: "Humanity is in deep shit, Jay. Deep shit ... But we have to find a reason to go on living. Teach your students to think, Jay. Do like Bill."

Now I look across at Paul stretched out on the sofa reading *La Presse*. That's the Paul I love, the one Grama sought to mould, the one, had she been alive, she would be proud of.

Tomorrow, Paul leaves for his second trip to see Carlos. I hope Carlos has a good sense of humour because it would be difficult not to call him Maria. I laugh. If all goes as planned, they will come back together. On Paul's trip in February, he wasn't allowed to re-enter Guatemala because he'd overstayed his time on his earlier visit. At least that's the story he gave me. He went to Mexico, to Comitán, and Carlos joined him there. The "sissy exercises" he'd spurned before, he now pursues enthusiastically. His body looks better, firmer, and he has lost another four kilos.

I recall our conversation on the back porch in St. Vincent. I hope Paul doesn't have impossible expectations of Carlos. "I am beginning to feel afraid," he told me the day after he bought his ticket for this trip. We were in the dinette wrapping dishes and putting them in cartons. "I'm worried about all the things that could go wrong."

I was too, not the least that for Carlos Paul might be no more than an immigrant visa to Canada. "You're wise to worry a little, but why paralyze yourself with fear? Just be there for him. You don't have to win all the battles. I know you on that score. You and Carlos have been apart for some time. You'll need to readjust to each other, and you'll be discovering parts of him you don't yet know. You haven't seen him outside of his family and his culture. And he'll be learning new things about you and about himself as he faces new experiences. That takes a lot of energy, creates a lot of anxiety, and can unleash a lot of ugliness. You know what I'm talking about."

"So you think it will be difficult?"

"Think back to how lost you felt when we first arrived. Try to imagine Carlos with no support community and having to accept minimum-wage work. I suspect he held your hand a lot when you were in Huehuetenango. Be prepared to hold his when he comes. As to competition from other guys, what can I say? Gays aren't famous for fidelity." I chuckled. "Your forehead's wide; has space for many horns."

"Go to hell!" He balled his free fist and waved it at me. He put down the plate that he was wrapping and fell into deep thought. Then he moved to where I was on the other side of the table and embraced me. Smiling and staring intensely into my eyes, he said: "If things go sour, you'll be there for me, right?"

I nodded.

He squeezed me tightly. "That's *my* brother."

Now, recalling all this, I would like to tell him that at times nothing fills the sort of emptiness he felt in San Jose. It's our attempts to avoid it, to erase it, to flee from it that turn some people into alcoholics, drug addicts, or religious fanatics; and, rather than face it, many people endure abusive relationships. Feelings of emptiness are a part of life and have to be understood, struggled with, and borne, even as we try to forget how easily life could wow us one minute and shred us in the next. But Paul must know this. He rides the waves of turbulence while I'm a mere step from stagnation.

29

THE FOOD DELIVERYMAN is buzzing. Paul goes to the door and pays him.

"Come eat, Jay. I ordered for you too. Our last meal together in this apartment. It seems epochs ago since we moved here. So much has happened since." He purses his lips and avoids my eyes.

We sit at the table, the Styrofoam containers spread out in front of us, paper napkins serving as trivets.

"Oh," Paul says, "this is what you've been eagerly waiting for: the last revelation." He stands, pulls a sheaf of papers from his seat pocket, and puts it on the table in front of me. "Eat first. You won't want this soup to get cold." He'd ordered cowheel soup along with jerk chicken and rice-and-red-beans from a Caribbean restaurant. I had taken him and Jonathan there for lunch one Saturday, and Paul fell in love with the food. We eat in silence.

I get up, take the sheaf of papers, go to my bedroom, and sit on the edge of the bed. Now that the drapes are down the sunlight hits me full blast. I go to the armchair, move it out of the sun, sit in it, and begin to read.

> *Okay. Here's the lowdown on what happened. You know I needed my pot. At the very least a couple joints each day. Well there was this guy—clean-cut, sort of friendly—who used to supply me in Antigua. A fellow in his early thirties, short—about my height— olive complexion, bright, brown eyes. Rarely looked me in the eye when he spoke. He didn't live in Antigua. In fact, I don't know*

where he lived, most likely in one of the upland villages surround-
ing Antigua. He'd come in on a Saturday. He had a large clientele.
A student at the school had put me on to him. He met us at dif-
ferent hours, each person in a different place. My meeting place
was the Central Park on a Saturday.

I used to wait for him around 11 am at a park bench on the
southern side. He'd come and sit beside me. We'd pretend a casual
conversation. After a while I'd pass him the payment for my week's
supply. He'd walk to a coffee shop across the street, presumably to
count it. Then he'd come back with a paper bag, take a candy out
of it and pass the candy to me; next he'd take one out for himself
and put it in his mouth, and pass the paper bag to me. He'd wait
around for a minute, then leave. I would leave a few minutes after.

But for two weeks he didn't come. I panicked because I need-
ed the pot to control my asthma, or thought I did. The third week
someone else came and sat beside me and asked me how much I
needed. I told him a gram. He handed it to me and stretched his
hand for the money. As soon as I gave it to him, he flashed me his
police badge. Seconds later an older cop, holding a camcorder,
came. They handcuffed me and took me to the police station.

I'll cut a long story short by saying that after threats, etc., we
settled for a bribe of $1,000: nothing less. They insisted. I paid
them $500 that Saturday and said I would let you send me the
money to pay them the remaining $500 on Monday. They asked
for my passport then. I said it was locked in the school's vault and
the school was closed until Monday. They stared at me sceptically
and I held my gaze.

They said that at 5 pm Monday they'd come where I lived to
collect the remaining $500, and if I reneged, they'd re-arrest me.
There was no point, the older cop said, in my trying to leave Gua-
temala before paying them because they'd already put the informa-
tion into the computer, and it would show up if I attempted to pass
through Guatemalan emigration before they erased it. Every phone
call I make would be monitored (all overseas calls have been, he
said, since 9-11). From my ID cards they already knew everything

about me in Canada "even your address and telephone number."
Letters addressed to me would be intercepted. I wouldn't be able to
hide because my picture with the caption "fugitive" would be post-
ed everywhere and printed in the newspapers. He asked me if I
understood. I nodded. He said I had two hours in which to contact
you—he lifted two fingers to emphasize it—before the system
began monitoring me. Then he made me sign a blank report, and
winked at me. If I had been thinking straight I would have left the
country in those two hours.

My passport was not in the school's vault. I went back to the
family I boarded with, packed as much as I could in a backpack,
left everything else, and boarded the next bus for Quetzaltenango.
You know the rest of the story.

For five hundred dollars! This defies logic. For five hundred dollars you put us through 14 months of hell! Angry, I go to the living room to confront him. A lot of this is poppycock. Why couldn't he write us using a false name? That canard about telephones being tapped and letters intercepted. Not credible. Paul's too intelligent not to have seen through that.

I meet him lying on his back on the sofa, both arms propping up the section of *La Presse* he's pretending to read. "Paul, assuming that what's written here is true, the police gave you two hours to contact me. We have an answering machine. Why didn't you?"

"What can I say? My brain was addled. It's as simple as that. Couldn't think clearly. The whole thing sucked. I think it was my desire to win, to beat the bastards at their own game. They thought they were in for duck soup, cauldrons of it." He breathes deeply, looks up at me guiltily, and then lowers his eyes. "And I didn't want Ma to judge me. She already saw me as some sort of criminal. What would she have thought if the report came to her that I was arrested on drug charges in Guatemala? Put yourself in my shoes—my phoning, her picking up the receiver; my saying: 'Ma, I've been busted for marijuana and I need 500 US dollars to bribe my way out of trouble and $500 more to replace what I've already paid'; her giving me an earful, her turning the guilt churn as fast as it would go, not to mention vilifying me with Madam J and all those muttonheads in her church."

I want to say, Paul, I don't know how you ever got to believe the things you do about Ma. "So you had to keep this from me until now? It's another one of your power games, isn't it?"

"No. It's not. I wanted you to see first that I'd changed, that I'm no longer the scoundrel—isn't that how you and Ma saw me?—that left here in March 2005."

"Sometimes, I wonder if you're as intelligent as your school performance made you out to be. There are areas in which you're completely daft. You left here a pothead."

"*Don't call me that!*" His eyes are squeezed tight, and his cheeks retracted in explosive anger. He snorts to relieve the tension. "See? That's what I mean." He tosses the newspaper onto the floor and sits up with a sprint.

"Let's get this straight. You had to have your pot every day: morning and evening—and I'm sure midday too—and you *object* to being called *a pothead?*"

"*Yes*. It's a putdown the way you say it. See? That's why I'd have preferred to rot in jail than have you and Ma sit in judgement over me."

"Jail? Paul, you said, '*preferred to rot in jail!*' Quite frankly, parts of your story aren't credible. Any blithering idiot could have seen through what you claim that cop said about intercepting your letters and phone calls."

"Yes!" He strikes the sofa angrily with both hands. "I've left out parts. Now, seeing your reaction, I'm glad I did. I'll never tell you."

I stare at him hard.

Paul turns his head away.

"As you wish. I hope the RCMP or CSIS never shows up at your door or mine. Does the Canadian High Commission know about your being arrested for drug possession?"

"I don't know. If those cops recorded it, the answer is yes. It's international protocol. Every time foreign nationals contravene the laws of the country they are visiting, the diplomatic services of the visitor's country must be notified. Is that all?"

I could tell you, that not knowing your whereabouts exhausted me to the point where I abandoned my studies, but what purpose would it serve? And for all I know, you might find pleasure in the anxiety and trouble you'd put us through. For a few seconds I resent him; then I recall the inquisitive 6-7 year old busybody at Cousin Alice's, and I'm flooded with the conflicting emotions of care and resentment I had back then. *Drop it, Jay. Let him be. Let the past stay in the past.* "You are right, Paul. We are as we are, and nobody should judge us because nobody can truly know who we are. But I want you to set aside your silly views of Ma. Earning a living prevented her from giving you the attention you got from Grama, Aunt Mercy, and even Lucy. It wasn't her fault. And I don't care if you think I sound like an uncle."

Paul stands and comes to where I'm leaning against the dining table. "You're angry with me. I've been waiting for you to curse me out. You've always choked back your anger." He puts both hands on my shoulders and looks up into my eyes. "I caused you to give up your doctoral studies, right?"

I look away, then turn to face him, and force a smile. "It's okay, Paul. Don't worry about it."

Paul pulls me closer and begins to cry.

"It's all right, Paul. It's all right. You've come a long way. I'm no longer worried about you."

He swallows, says nothing for a while. "Glad to hear it. I could have told you long ago not to worry so much. Greedy, ugly caterpillars become beautiful butterflies."

"I know now that you won't throw away your life. That's worth more than a PhD. Besides, I can return to it in the future."

There's a long pause. Paul ends it, speaking slowly. "I spent a night in jail. That's what I left out. I only agreed to the bribe on the Sunday morning. The younger cop came back to ask me if I'd changed my mind and I told him yes. Bedbugs, fleas, and mosquitoes bit me all night. Four of us were in a cell that's a third the size of my bedroom … The morning before I boarded the plane, they beat me up. They slammed me against the wall and slapped me several times. Three of them held me down while one held a cushion over my mouth and nose until I started choking. I hadn't planned a story for them about why I'd overstayed my time and didn't know about the ads—they knew about them, and wanted answers, and I didn't have any. I was waiting for them to tell me about the arrest. They didn't and I would have been a fool to tell them. They made me give them all the money I had on me; said they'd keep me in custody if I didn't. $90 that Carlos' mother had lent me. It pissed them off that I didn't have more. That US$8-story I gave you the evening I came back was pure fiction. Luckily, I had a toonie in a pocket of my carry-on, or I'd have had trouble calling you from the airport."

We remain silently embracing each other for several seconds.

"Thanks," Paul says, wiping his eyes with his shirt sleeve. He steps back to look me in the eyes. "You will never think of me again as Loki. You're going to be proud of me the way I'm already proud of you. That's a promise I will keep. And I will hound you until you finish your PhD."

***

It's an hour before the movers come. Paul and I are sitting in silence at opposite sides of the table. I look into the living room, at the cardboard boxes piled almost to the ceiling, at the naked walls. Anna, Paul, and I came here on January 1, 2000. She left first. Tomorrow Paul will make his second trip to Mexico, and, if all works out as planned, will return with Carlos.

I go in search of a notebook, return, sit at the table, and write, crossing words out and replacing them with other words. *Our lives here, what have they been? What exactly have they been? I should ask Paul. No, it's too soon. When he's my age perhaps. Somewhere, I heard or read that the magic in promised lands ends once they've been reached, that promised lands should never be reached. For then tents won't do, and there are fields to till, shrines to erect, heresies to root out, wounds to inflict and heal ... And honey and milk come from bees, cows, and camels that must be cared for. The real deal. And the dwellers come to see that they'd been gulled. While in St. Vincent, Ma saw Canada as a promised land; and, in Grama's eyes, Canada was a promised land for Paul and me. And in the opinion of those who decide which are the best countries to live in, Canada is as close to the promised land as we'll ever get to on earth. Jonathan probably does not know it, but it's what he seeks in wanting to wed his life to mine. In the end Ma upgraded to an after-death one, and sang about getting there:*

> *To shady green pastures so rich and so sweet,*
> *God leads his dear children along;*
> *Where the cool flow of water bathes the weary ones' feet,*
> *God leads his dear children along.*

> *Some through the water and some through the flood;*
> *Some through the fire but all through the blood;*
> *Some through great sorrow, but God gives a song*
> *In the night season and all the day long.*

Who would want to sully such belief? She had "a home in that rock. / Don't you see?"

And so it has come to this: adulthood, every child's promised land. One phase of life dies to clear space for another; one crop ploughed under to produce another. We wean ourselves from tutelage so adult life can flower. Does adult life flower? (In our more despondent moods we think we're mere flotsam and jetsam in time's sea; now I'm less sure of Paul's labyrinth.) The agency we gain from leaving our parents' and teachers' leashes is quickly lost as employers, spouses, and children leash us anew. I never knew why I found Wordsworth's "Immortality Ode" deeply moving when I first read it in CEGEP. " ... Full soon thy soul shall have her earthly freight, / And custom lie upon thee like a weight, / Heavy as frost, and deep almost as life: ... shades of the prison house." (Not that my childhood resembled Wordsworth's.)

Some of the friendships we've made live on in memory, some in occasional contacts: in person, by e-mail, by phone, social media; but the bonds that hold them get brittle, and the activities that nurture them wither—like petals ceding to seed, children to parents, students to workers, social activists to corporate directors. And quickly our faces show the hieroglyphs of life's turmoil; our shoulders stoop and our backs bend under the burden of responsibility—for ourselves, our spouses, our children, and society's misfits. For a while we may cling to the detritus of tutelage, remain perilously poised in a neither nor; but we give in—must give in. For it is expensive to preserve what's already dead; and those who do so do so alone; and in the end they too give in, from wisdom or from weariness. Perhaps this is what Wordsworth meant by "the sad still music of humanity"; or Thoreau: "most men lead lives of quiet desperation."

Of course, we mourn all deaths, much like we cry upon meeting the cold when we fall from our mothers' wombs. And mourn we must, for death of whatever sort discords, dishevels, dismembers. And as for the new life this death clears the way for—we fear even the most exciting of beginnings—and in the new life that's adulthood, we've already read in our parents' lives what's waiting.

Now I begin to see why Treadwell forsook humanity for the company of the grizzlies, why Gulliver found solace among the horses in his stable after sojourning in the land of the Houyhnhnms: the one real, the other invented. But to be human is to live with the belief that tomorrow will be better than today; and to bear the burdens of our species, even when alone with grizzlies in the wilds of Alaska; and to know that alone, we're prey for grizzlies. Jay, brace your back. Begin.

Acknowledgements

I offer my thanks to the members of Ilona Martonfi's writing group for the valuable critiques they offered, to Michael Mirolla for a rigorous editing of the manuscript, and to David Moratto for his evocative cover design.

About The Author

H[ubert] Nigel Thomas was born in St. Vincent and the Grenadines and has been living in Canada since 1968. He was a mental health worker, a high school teacher and finally a professor of US literature at Université Laval. He is the author of several essays in literary criticism as well as three novels: *Return to Arcadia* (2007), *Behind the Face of Winter* (2001 — to appear in a French translation in autumn 2015), *Spirits in the Dark* (1993); three collections of short fiction: *When the Bottom Falls Out and Other Stories* (2014), *Lives: Whole and Otherwise* (2010 — translated as *Des vies cassées*, 2013); *How Loud Can the Village Cock Crow and Other Stories* (1995); a collection of poems: *Moving through Darkness* (2000); and two scholarly texts: *Why We Write: Conversations with African Canadian Poets and Novelists* (2006), and *From Folklore to Fiction: A Study of Folk Heroes and Rituals in the Black American Novel* (1988). In 1994 he was shortlisted for the Hugh MacLennan Fiction Award; in 2000 he received the Montreal Association of Business Persons and Professionals' Jackie Robinson Award for Professional of the Year; and in 2013 was awarded Université Laval's *Hommage aux créateurs*.

Printed in July 2015
by Gauvin Press,
Gatineau, Québec